Honor and Valor

Charles E. Frye

FIRST EDITION

Copyright © 2020 Charles E. Frye

All rights reserved.

Published by Charles E. Frye, Redlands, CA

Library of Congress Control Number: 2020901997

E259 .F78 2020

ISBN: 1652893981
ISBN-13: 978-1652893981

DEDICATION

To Isaac and Elizabeth's descendants; there are nearly two thousand of us now.

To U.S. military veterans, soldiers, and their families.

CONTENTS

	Acknowledgments	i
	Preface	iii
	Maps	v
1	Goodbyes	1
2	Recruiting	13
3	Preparing for the Enemy	27
4	Flight	53
5	Trials	75
6	40 Man Scout	97
7	On the Edge	111
8	Victory	139
9	Breaking Point	173
10	White Marsh	187
11	Winter Quarters	203

12	The Marquis	225
13	Fever	243
14	Northward	251
	Sources	263
	Appendix A	303
	Appendix B	307
	Appendix C	311
	About the Book Covers	313
	About the Author	315

ACKNOWLEDGMENTS

My wife, Amanda, for her continued support and advice.

Christina Kelly, the town historian of Schaghticoke, NY, provided the essential timeline for the Van Veghten narrative in Chapter 5. Given the disparate threads I had come across and the assumption of just one story, she managed to produce the basis for the much richer story portrayed here.

Eric Schnitzer, an interpretive park ranger at Saratoga National Historical Park, with whom I have corresponded several times over the years of researching what became Chapter 6. His encouragement to keep digging paid off as I spent hours transcribing the September 1777 and January 1778 company-level rolls from Enoch Poor's brigade. I found the forty men, and that was undoubtedly the most satisfying piece of research that went into this book.

The Sons and Daughters of the American Revolution, whose membership boasts many authors, historians, and genealogists, have encouraged me for many years. Chiefly, the Sons of the American Revolution has a mission to educate present and future generations about how the United States of America became a country. As I began learning about Isaac Frye, I realized his story was so much more than just family history. I especially wish to thank the members of the Redlands Chapter, of which I am a member. Their encouragement throughout my years of research and writing continues to be much appreciated.

Libraries and Librarians. In the writing of this book, I am

particularly grateful for the online and remote services offered by many libraries. In particular, the New York Historical Society Library and the William L. Clement Library at the University of Michigan provided scans of several documents that proved invaluable for filling in the little gaps in the narrative.

To The Written By Veterans Writers Group at California State University, San Bernardino, Veterans Success Center; in such company, there is no way to fail.

Charles E. Frye

PREFACE

Honor and Valor is the second of four books in the Duty in the Cause of Liberty series. The books trace the path of my great-great-great-great-grandfather, Isaac Frye, through the American Revolutionary War. For fifteen years, I have researched Isaac Frye's service in the Continental Army and his life in Wilton, New Hampshire in the 1770s and 1780s, and I still find it amazing I can account for his location most days, sometimes down to the hour and minute.

This book is fictional, though all the names of people, the events, and the dates and times they occurred are factual. The dialog, with a very few exceptions, is fictional, a product of my imagination. I styled the dialog to favor a little of an 18th century way of speaking. I sprinkled in a few 18th-century words for flavor. That said, I had no intention of mimicking the speech and idioms used by people at that time. My purpose is to tell Isaac Frye's story to a contemporary audience, allowing them to appreciate what duty, sacrifice, and American ideas about liberty might have meant to him, his family, and people he knew.

In The War has Begun, I included some information about the Frye Family's recollections of Isaac Frye's contributions, how I used maps and GIS to organize the research for these books, and some about my intentions in writing Isaac Frye's story. The War has Begun portrayed over fifty people in large and small roles as they crossed paths with Isaac Frye. In this book, that figure more than doubles, and I hope I

Honor and Valor

included your ancestors when they crossed paths with Isaac.

Honor and Valor is a continuation of The War has Begun, which you will need to read to learn how Isaac and his family become caught up in the war for American Independence, and what happens to Isaac as the Army takes him from Boston to New York and Canada.

Charles E. Frye

MAPS

Map of the Part of Wilton Isaac Frye Lived

I compiled this map using Wilton's lot and range map and Abiel Abbot Livermore's History of the Town of Wilton, Hillsborough County, New Hampshire with a Genealogical Register. In the genealogical register, Livermore included the locations of many of the inhabitants' farms, the names of the original proprietors, and the names of those who lived there during the Revolution. This made it possible to roughly locate Isaac's neighbors. Isaac's farm is highlighted and indicates the lots as described on the land records.

The roads are my best conservative estimate based on an 1805 survey by Daniel Searle, an 1858 railroad map of Wilton, which included family names, and the USGS 1:62,500 scale 1900 Peterborough quadrangle and 1906 Milford quadrangle topographic maps. I suspect the path that is today Gage Road was likely present before Isaac bought the property, and may have been laid by Henry Parker as early as 1760 when he built the bridge over the Souhegan River.

The grid on this map represents the proprietors' lot and range system used to first describe the land in Wilton. Range numbers run north and south, i.e., range 4 is a north-south column; and lots are numbered from 20 in the north, to 1 in the south.

Regional Maps of Colonial America

    I compiled these maps working from primary-source manuscript map documents or high-resolution scans of these maps. No map newer than a publishing date of 1785 was used. I had the good fortune to visit numerous libraries in the United States and explore their map collections. In my spare time, over several years, I used over one hundred maps to compile a 1:500,000 scale map of northeastern North America extending from the southern boundary of Virginia in the south, to Quebec in the north, and west into Ohio.

    I chose to depict only the towns, roads, landmarks, etc., appearing on the colonial maps, using the spellings shown on those maps. I used modern geographic information systems (GIS) data for terrain and bodies of water, though this required removing dams and replacing corresponding lakes with the original stream courses. The coastline around Boston was also adjusted to reflect my approximation of the 1775 coastline.

    These maps are all excerpted from one GIS database I created using ArcGIS software beginning in 2003, with the bulk of the work being done by 2008, though minor edits have been ongoing. Initially I intended to use this map as a research aid, helping to organize the locations and events in which there are records of Isaac Frye's participation. Early on, it became evident that I could use the GIS map as a basis to trace Isaac Frye's path through the Revolutionary War, both geographically and through time. I hope these excerpts work to help you do the same.

    The GIS map also acted as a proving ground for the various histories, journals, and records I was reading, at times disproving statements born of poor memories, license, and perhaps revisionism.

Charles E. Frye

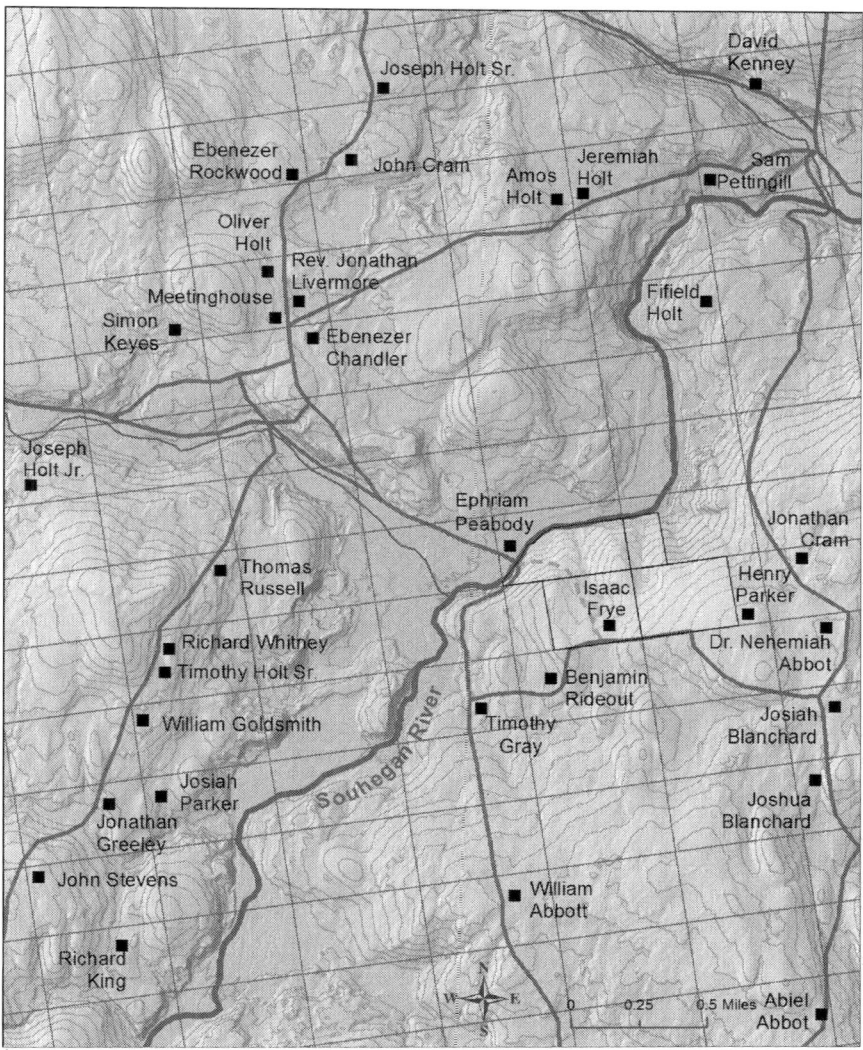

Map 1. The locale Isaac Frye's land occupies within Wilton, and his neighbors in 1775.

Note: Sources exist to locate only about one third of Wilton's inhabitants. Most who have not been located lived to the north and west of Isaac Frye's Farm. The empty lots to the south of Isaac's farm were not built on until later.

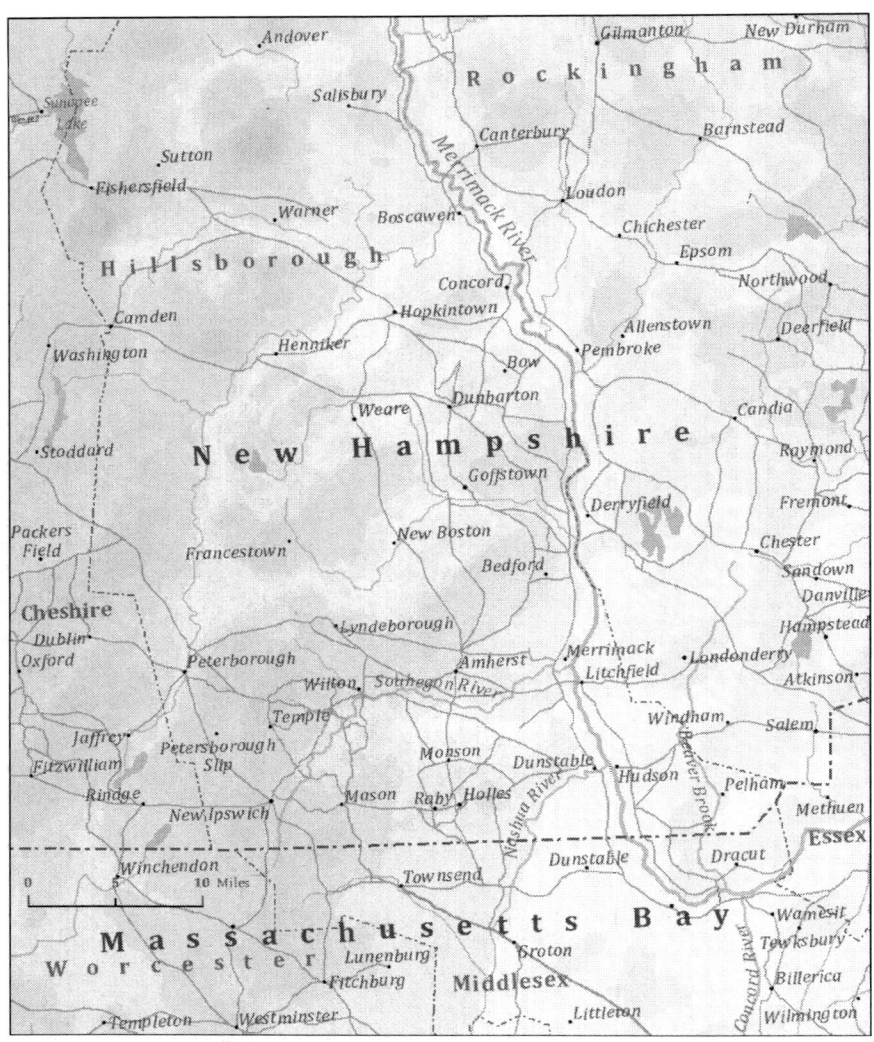

Map 2. Shows Hillsborough County, New Hampshire, including the towns where the men in Captain Isaac Frye's company lived.

Charles E. Frye

Map 3. Shows the territory where the American army traveled during the week after evacuating Fort Ticonderoga in July 1777.

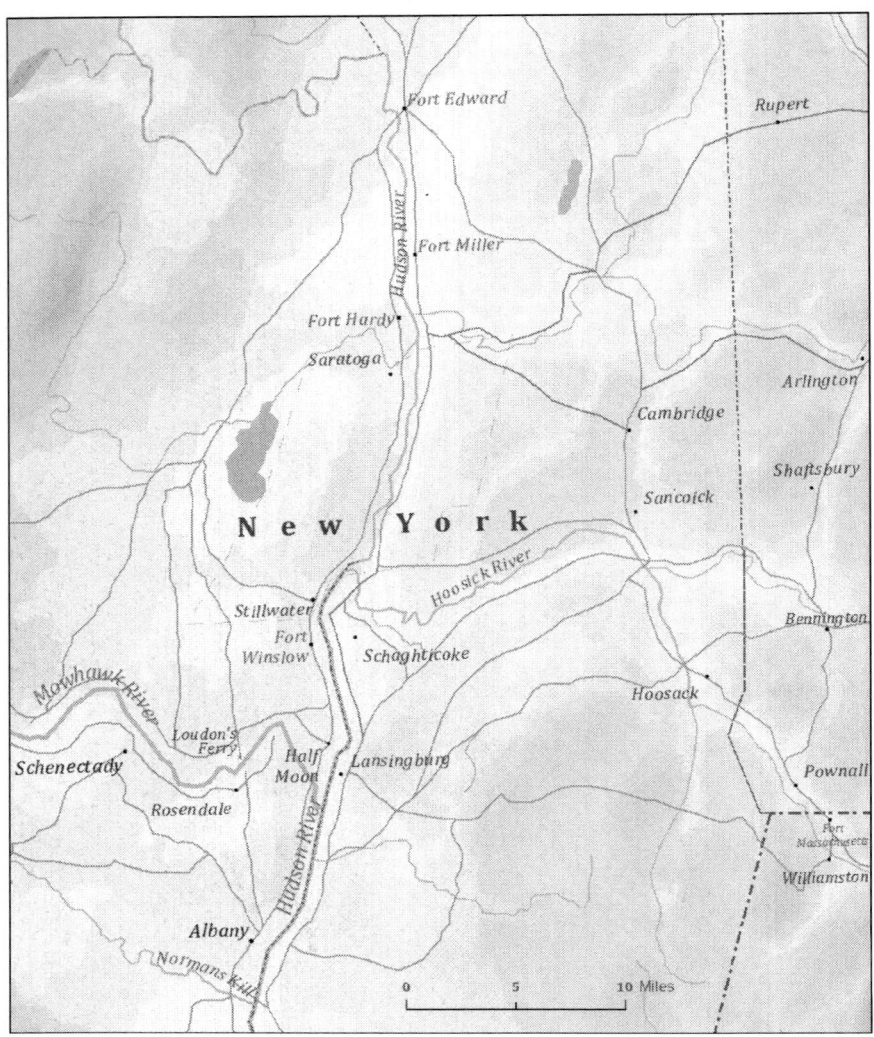

Map 4. Showing the territory around Saratoga, New York which includes the locations where the 3rd New Hampshire Regiment was encamped during the Saratoga Campaign.

Charles E. Frye

Map 5. Showing the area General Poor refers to in directing Isaac's 40-man scout. Source: Montrésor, J., Andrews, P. & Dury, A. 1777 "A map of the Province of New York, with part of Pensilvania, and New England." A. Drury, London.

Honor and Valor

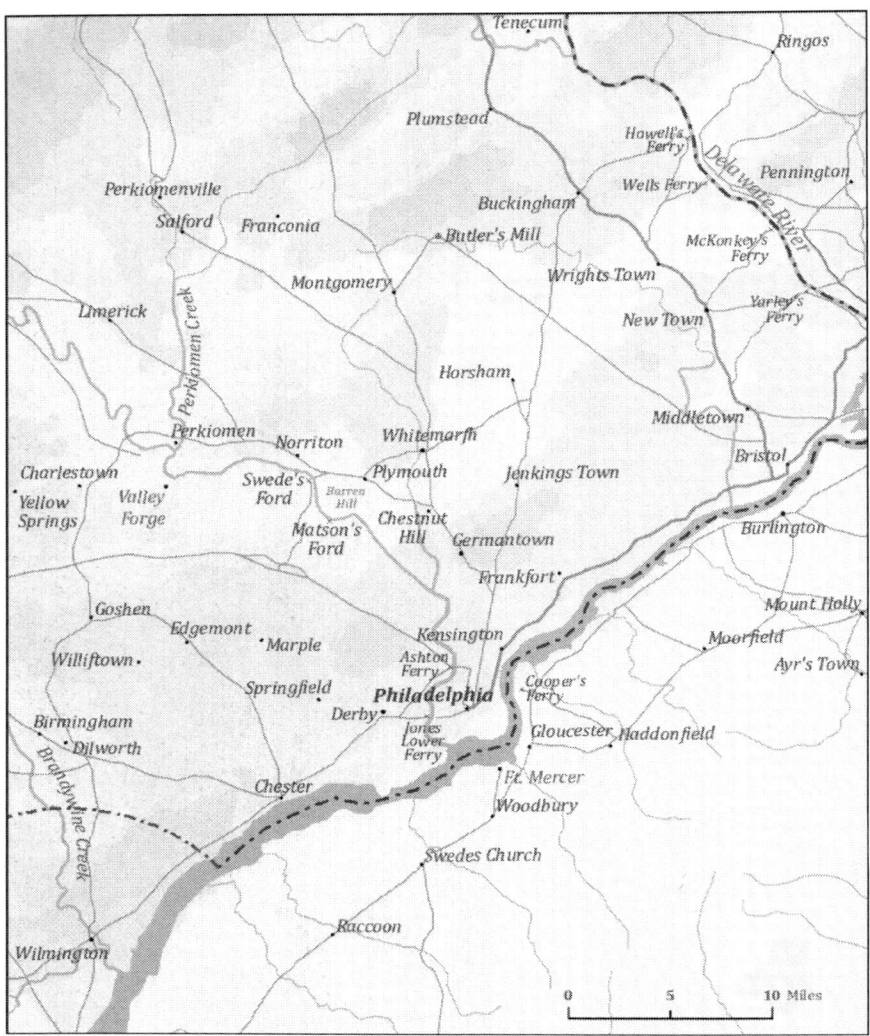

Map 6. The area north of Philadelphia, including Whitemarsh, Valley Forge and Barren Hill. The Poor's brigade camped near the "rsh" of the Marsh in Whitemarsh. In the Battle of Barren Hill, the small road led from the B in the Barren Hill label to Swede's Ford.

Charles E. Frye

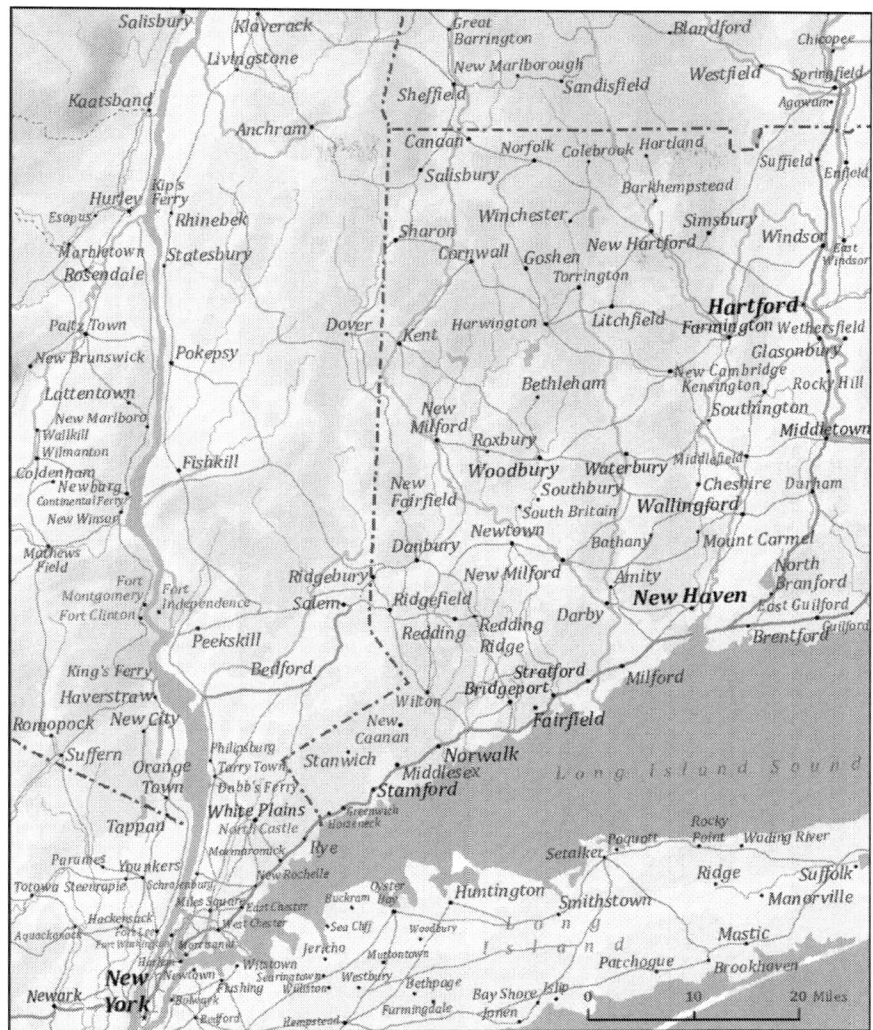

Map 7. New York, White Plains, Fishkill, Danbury, and western Connecticut.

Honor and Valor

Charles E. Frye

1 GOODBYES

"To Isaac Frye, Esquire : Greeting: We, Reposing especial trust and confidence in your Patriotism, Valour, Conduct and Fidelity, Do, by these presents, constitute and appoint you to be a Captain in the Third New Hampshire Regiment, in the Army of the United States, to take rank as such from the 1st day of January, A.D.1777."

From Introductory words from Isaac Frye's commission
to rank as a captain in the Continental Army
Signed by John Jay, President of Congress
June 16, 1779 (two and a half years after the appointment)

Isaac and Elizabeth stand in Wilton's burying ground before two graves early in January. He and Elizabeth are in their late twenties. Isaac wears his tattered and patched dark blue Continental Army coat, and his light brown hair is tied back beneath a felted tricorn hat. Elizabeth wears a charcoal gray cape over a nut-brown dress, and a lock of black hair strays from beneath her bonnet.

Standing half a dozen paces back beside the wagon and oxen is Elizabeth's father, Timothy Holt. In his fifty-sixth year, Holt's hair is gray well past his temples, and he stands several inches shorter than Isaac, who is finger's breadth under six feet.

The afternoon is warm, with the sun melting much of the snow within the graveyard. The dark spongy earth and matted brown grass stretch away into the woods where clumps of snow endure in the shady bases of large trees.

Isaac moves to the side of the graves, lost in his thoughts. Elizabeth walks to the wagon and retrieves a blanket and pouch with half a dozen crocus bulbs. She plants them around her mother's headstone. "I cannot believe nearly a year has passed. I hope these make this spring more beautiful than last."

Holt smiles wistfully. "I hope so too. Your mother enjoyed crocuses."

"They were little Timothy's favorite. He helped Sarah split these bulbs the fall before last."

They are all quiet for a few moments longer, then Isaac looks to Elizabeth and her father, "Our family has changed so much in only a year." He gazes at the earth in front of the headstones of his son and mother-in-law and swallows hard. Then he turns and walks to their wagon. Elizabeth and her father linger a few moments longer, then follow Isaac.

Elizabeth sits between Isaac and her father as they ride past the meetinghouse ten minutes later. The pale yellow paint on the clapboards contrasts with the large mullioned windows. No one has spoken since leaving the cemetery. Isaac shudders as he gazes to the second story. He, with two dozen men, had fallen in an accident from the upper beam during the building's construction three years earlier. "The memory of falling never goes away."

Holt looks to the high roof. "It was a terrible price we paid."

They ride in silence down the hill to the Souhegan River. Holt clears his throat. "Isaac, have you got a sense for how long you'll be home?"

Brows knit thoughtfully, Isaac collects his thoughts in the space of two breaths. "No, I think it wholly depends on my commission being approved. When the congress next meets in Exeter, I expect they will so, and then I'll be summoned and given orders to recruit a company."

Holt reaches around and claps Isaac on the shoulder. "Then you'll need to make the most of the next few weeks."

"I will, sir. Elizabeth already has a list of things to mend and build."

Holt looks to Elizabeth and winks. "I am sure she has, and I'm afraid I added a few items as well."

Isaac grins. "All well and good, I'll get as much done as I can."

They ride in silence for a minute. Isaac looks to his father-in-law, "I had a lot on my mind when we picked you up this morning. I forgot to give you my thanks for helping get our harvest and hay last fall. Twas a lot of work, and I'm afraid I've only got gratitude to pay you with for now."

Elizabeth lays her hand on her father's forearm. "Father also helped with Richard's land too, and some of the Greeles lent a hand as well."

Holt nods to Isaac. "Everyone in town helped on the farms of those were at Fort Ti. I am happy the good Lord has kept me fit to do a full day's work."

Isaac smiles warmly. "That makes two of us, and I'm doubly pleased to learn Hannah and Richard named their son after you."

"That was an honor, and I pray Richard will come home safe from Fort Ti this spring to meet his new son."

"Aye, though I'm not sure when General Washington will send troops north for the season."

Isaac waits a few seconds before changing subjects. "Elizabeth tells me you have the details of General Washington's victory at Trenton? The news hadn't yet traveled to the places we stayed on the way home from Fort George."

"There wasn't much. Just that the General had his army cross the Delaware River at midnight. They caught the Prussians sleeping in the early morning. It seems they were taking winter quarters for granted. Still, it was the only good news since May when it seems everything started slipping."

"Did you hear whether our men fought?"

"No, but I didn't hear that they didn't. I'm sure you'll get more news when you get to Amherst next."

"Aye," Isaac nods, "I'll need to go later this week."

They stop at Richard and Hannah Whitney's home. Hannah is

Elizabeth's younger sister. With Richard gone with the militia to guard Fort Ticonderoga, Holt has been staying with his daughter. Holt climbs out of the wagon then turns to Isaac and Elizabeth. "We will see you at the meetinghouse tomorrow. I expect many will attend. Twill be the first chance in almost a year to speak with you and the others who returned with you."

Isaac tips his hat to Holt. "Aye, sir, and it will be good to see everyone. It has been far too long."

•••

Isaac and Elizabeth sit in their pew with the boys between them. From the middle of the meetinghouse, the whispering and low voices belie tension from every part of the crowded meetinghouse. A few minutes past noon on a mid-January Sunday, the temperature outside warms to just above freezing, making the windowpanes as bright as Isaac can recall seeing them. The floorboards of the upper-level flex with the shifting of the weight of a quarter of Wilton's populace.

Reverend Livermore remains in the pulpit, his hands grip the sides of the lectern. His sermon, a thanksgiving homily, had followed the news of General Washington's victory at Princeton. Livermore had stood, staring at his notes for fully half a minute. Isaac figures the tension to be due to this being the first Sunday since the Reverend's return from defending himself in Exeter against the charge of being an enemy to liberty.

As the murmuring and movements increase, the Reverend looks up and raises his hands, palms outward, to the level of his shoulders. "My sincerest apologies. My thoughts refused to organize themselves just now. Let us bow our heads in prayer."

After the Reverend finishes the benediction, he releases the congregants who rise, grateful to be on their feet after sitting for nearly two hours.

Abiel Abbot, a tall, robust man in his late thirties, with active piercing eyes beneath a broad forehead, catches Isaac's attention with a wave.

Abbot's talent is engaging people with his wit and charisma. He motions for Isaac to join him. Isaac nods and begins making his way through the crowded meetinghouse. He and William Adrian Hawkins reach Abbot's pew at the same time. Hawkins wears his usual wide grin as he greets Isaac. Hawkins is six years Isaac's senior, and his eyes are framed by deep laugh lines. He carries himself with youthful and enthusiastic energy and clasps and shakes Isaac's hand and then Major Abbot's, as does Isaac.

Major Abbot begins, "Gentlemen, I am pleased to see Wilton's Continental officers returned home and in good health. You may already know I've been appointed as a major in the Sixth Regiment under Colonel Nichols. I serve as the regiment's muster master, and as such, I'm to aid with the recruiting of the Third New Hampshire Continental Regiment."

Isaac and Hawkins congratulate Abbot then Isaac relates the offer of their commissions in the Third Regiment. He explains the commissions need the approval of the Committee of Safety when they next meet in Exeter.

Major Abbot congratulates both men and raises a thoughtful, but puzzled eyebrow. "It was my understanding Captain Scott would be recruiting in this area. He's from Peterborough, and the state wished the captains to recruit from the areas they know best. Where will you be recruiting?"

"Well, I suppose we'll need the committee to decide that."

"Indeed. I hope you'll be assigned to recruit from nearby."

Isaac smiles. "Me too, and that reminds me to mention the Third Regiment needs musicians. I was thinking of Tom Powell from Amherst. He was Captain Crosby's drummer in Boston."

"I'm glad to know that, and I'll make an extra effort, starting with Tom at the next muster."

Off to the side of the conversation between the officers, Uriah Ballard and Will Burton meet between a pair of the meetinghouse's large windows. Will is fourteen with sandy hair. Uriah is a thin smallish eighteen-year-old with dark hair and a quiet, sometimes surly disposition. With a nudge, Will steers the pair closer to the officers, and they hear the last part of the conversation about needing musicians.

Will gives Uriah a couple of conspiratorial taps on his elbow with the back of his hand. "See, that's our in. My uncle says the army needs drummers and fifers. We've been practicing with the militia, and I bet we're good enough now. The Continentals pay better, and they're giving bonuses to sign on for three years. The war won't last that long, but you keep the bonus."

Ballard purses his lips, and his eyes narrow as he thinks a moment. "I only believe it because I heard them say it. We better keep practicing. It's no sure thing they'll take us. Besides, it's the year of the hangman now, you really want to join the army?"

"I don't believe in that. But, you might be right about needing more practice. Maybe later you could ask Major Abbot what we need to know for sure. I don't think my ma would be too pleased if she caught me asking. I bet you can catch him on his way out today. I'll come by your place tomorrow to practice."

Ballard nods slowly. "I'll try."

Twenty minutes later, as they leave the meetinghouse, Isaac, Elizabeth, her father, and her sisters Sarah and Hannah gather around Reverend Livermore and his wife, Elizabeth. First, Isaac thanks the Reverend for his sermon. "I served the past couple of years with a man I suspect is a cousin of yours. His name's Daniel Livermore. He's a carpenter from Concord. Do you know him?"

Reverend Livermore purses his lips as he thinks. "I believe so. If he is the same Daniel Livermore, his father is my father's cousin, David. Though I believe David died some twenty years ago. They were from Watertown, where my father grew up. Please convey my regards when you next see him."

"I will. Though I'll likely not see him until the spring when we muster. I expect to be here in Wilton for the winter."

Reverend Livermore nods and smiles at Elizabeth. "Madam Frye will be glad to finally have you at home. Though I thought you expected to be done with your service with the Continentals?"

"Aye, I did. Though as such matters seem to go, I agreed to an offer of a captain's commission in my last week at Fort George."

"Well, congratulations, Captain Frye." Livermore smiles warmly. "I pray your promotion brings us peace soon."

"I do too. The good news you shared about our victory at Princeton shows there's hope we will have a total victory this year."

"Indeed, I hope so as well." Reverend Livermore shakes hands with everyone in Isaac's family before they leave the meetinghouse.

•••

Having arrived early, Isaac and his family sit in their pew five Sundays later. They watch as an anxious crowd fills the meetinghouse. As Reverend Livermore begins his walk toward the pulpit, Elizabeth holds a hand to Isaac's ear and whispers, "I've never seen so many here."

The voices and whispers stop, leaving the sound of floorboards and pews creaking. As the Reverend looks out on the congregation, his usual smile is gone, replaced with a weary look of resignation.

"Friends, I stand before you this twenty-fourth day of February in the year of our Lord seventeen hundred and seventy-seven. Friends, I stand before you this one final time."

Throughout the room, sharp intakes of breath express shock at his words.

"I am no longer to be the minister or teacher here. We have agreed to a dismissal. Though my name has been cleared, it is plain that the confidence you need in a clergyman cannot be restored." He goes on to express gratitude to his neighbors and to the friends he and his wife, Elizabeth, have gained in Wilton. He also states they expect to continue to live in Wilton.

While he speaks, a few people in the back leave quietly. Isaac notes the leaving takings, but returns his attention to the Reverend, as he leads them for a final time in prayer. The meeting adjourns earlier than usual.

Elizabeth leads a trio with her sister Hannah and her neighbor Sarah Rideout to approach Elizabeth Livermore, who stands off to the side of the pulpit. "Madam Livermore, I am sorry this has come to pass."

"I am as well, though I must believe it tis for the best."

"I hope so as well. Isaac and I would be honored to host you and the Reverend for dinner one evening this week. I know this is very little notice. Isaac may not be here long, as he expects his orders to come soon."

"We would enjoy that, I'll consult, Jonathan and we will let you know which evening."

"Do you know whether the Reverend is willing to provide instruction during the rest of the winter school session? I very much would like Isaac Jr. to continue learning to write—he has made much progress in the last two weeks."

"I am certain Jonathan has something in mind until the town hires a new teacher."

"That would be a relief. It's difficult to get young boys to settle down long enough in winter to practice writing."

Meanwhile, Isaac and Hawkins speak with Major Abbot. After some small talk about the Reverend dismissal, Isaac changes the topic. "Abiel, was there any news from the Committee of Safety this past week?"

"I'm afraid nothing concerning your commission came up. We've not had any word from General Sullivan or the other captains who signed up in New York. I am of the mind no news is good news, and doubly so as it gives you a few more days to enjoy with your family. I'll be in Exeter on Wednesday, and if I learn anything, I'll stop by your farm when I return."

Isaac's shoulders relax a bit, and he thanks Major Abbot.

Hawkins asks, "Major Abbot, thank you for getting word to me of my appointment under Captain Scott, though I must say it wasn't what I expected." Hawkins gives Isaac a side glance. "Do you think it strange there is no word from Captain Scott or of any money for recruiting as yet?"

Major Abbot shakes his head. "Not especially. Until Captain Scott returns from New York there's little else that can be done. He and the other captains will bring the enlistment bounty money with them. I don't think there's much point to getting an early start on recruiting. Most of the men I've spoken to are waiting for the best deal on bounties that can be had. Once the men have heard the money from Congress has arrived, I expect the last few companies in the regiment will fill up quickly."

•••

Isaac steps down the ladder from the newly repaired barn roof the following Thursday afternoon. The sun had melted the last of the snow and ice on the roof, making it possible to work. As he turns from the ladder, he sees a rider coming from the west, passing Benjamin Rideout's farm. Speculating it to be Major Abbot, Isaac hurries to put the ladder in the barn and strides around to the front of the house.

After seeing Major Abbot approach from the window, Elizabeth steps down the step from the front door as Isaac rounds the corner.

Isaac walks with her as they come to the rail fence by the road, then steps forward. "Good afternoon, Major Abbot. Have you been to Exeter?"

Major Abbot dismounts. "Captain Frye," then nods to Elizabeth, "Madam Frye." He turns to his saddlebag and retrieves a sheaf of documents. He thumbs through them and pulls out a half sheet and hands it to Isaac. "Indeed, I have just come from Exeter. The committee has appointed you as a captain in the Third New Hampshire Regiment. Those orders you're holding indicate you are to report to the committee in Exeter on Tuesday. They wish for you to sign for the bounty monies to use in recruiting your company. You're to see Meshech Weare or Nicholas Gilman, either one can sign the money over to you."

Isaac shakes Major Abbot's hand. "Thank you. Do you know who will command the Third Regiment?"

"I do. It will be Colonel Scammell. Do you know him?"

"Yes, I met him when the Army was in Montreal last summer. I suspected he would be commanding a regiment within a year. He's as active and dedicated an officer as you could imagine."

"That's good. We need such men in command."

"Will you be traveling to Exeter on Monday as well?"

Major Abbot gives a slight shake of his head. "No, I am ordered to be there every Wednesday. That reminds me, take Lieutenant Hawkins with you. He will, as you expected, be the lieutenant for your company. When Captain Scott arrived last week from New York, he declined the appointment in Scammell's Regiment in favor of serving in the First Regiment. That apparently left the opening for you."

Issac nods once, "I see. I'll let Hawkins know tonight."

"Very good. Now, if you'll excuse my hurry, I've had a long ride, and wish to seek the comfort of my own home."

"Certainly." Isaac moves beside Elizabeth. "We will see you on Sunday. Have a pleasant evening."

Major Abbot returns the sheaf of papers to his saddlebags and mounts his horse. "Yes, on Sunday, and a pleasant evening to you both as well."

While Major Abbot turns his horse and rides back the way he came, Isaac rereads the orders then turns to Elizabeth. "I've got the barn roof done. I've time enough to ride to William Adrian's place and be back before it gets dark."

•••

Isaac and Hawkins stand beside one another in front of a long table the following Tuesday morning inside the Exeter Meetinghouse. Seated at the table are members of the state's Committee of Safety. Meshech Weare, who is a robust figure, despite being in his early sixties, presides with an air of stern authority.

Isaac wears the uniform coat he got over a year ago. Elizabeth had done what she could to patch it. Hawkins' uniform looks better for him being a tailor by profession. The members of the committee are all dressed in more elegant clothes. Self-conscious, Isaac waits in silence.

Less than a minute passes before Weare fixes Isaac with a look that says he means the most serious of business. "Captain Frye, we have appointed you to command a company of men in the Third New Hampshire Regiment. And you Lieutenant Hawkins are appointed to be second in command of this company. We, the New Hampshire Committee of Safety, do hereby order you to recruit said company from the towns in southern Hillsborough County. Major Abbot has the list of those towns. See Mr. Gilman at the end of the table to sign for three-hundred Pounds of treasury notes you will use as bounties for recruiting these men. You will account for every pound of it. Are the committee's orders clear to you both?"

Isaac and Hawkins answer with clear affirmatives.

Weare continues, "Plan to have your company rendezvous at Number Four on the first of May. We expect the enemy will begin moving south by that time." Isaac and Hawkins state their understanding. Weare thanks them dismisses them from the attention of the committee.

Nicholas Gilman, the state's treasurer, in his mid-forties, sits at one end of the table. Gilman's large eyes and calm demeanor give the impression of superior wisdom and prudence. Beside him at the very end of the table rests a black iron chest, which holds the state's treasury. He rotates a small receipt toward Isaac, then pushes a pile of treasury notes toward him. "Count these first, then sign the receipt."

Isaac counts the three-hundred Pounds of notes then signs.

Isaac is about to speak, for he had something to ask of Mr. Gilman, but the treasurer speaks first. "If you and Lieutenant Hawkins have a moment, I would speak to you both privately."

Isaac's eyes narrow in askance, "Certainly."

Gilman dries his quill and sets it in his writing box. "We can speak outside, so as not to interrupt the committee's discussion. It won't take long."

Gilman excuses himself from the committee. Isaac notes that Weare knew this was coming. Once outside, Gilman leads them to the side of the meetinghouse shielded from the wind. "Gentlemen, I am afraid I have ill tidings to convey."

Isaac frowns and mentally braces himself for Gilman's news. "Go on."

"You both served with Colonel Israel Gilman, and thus it is my sad duty to convey he passed away last Friday. I was told an illness was the cause."

The news comes as a blow to Isaac, who had spent a good deal of time with Lieutenant Colonel Gilman over the previous year.

Hawkins sees Isaac's. "You and your family have my deepest condolences. Colonel Gilman was as fine a man as I've known, and the army has lost a skilled commander, for that is what he was to us last year."

Isaac had gone pale and recovers somewhat while Hawkins speaks. "You have my condolences as well. I owe my commission to his efforts on my behalf. I was hoping to convey my thanks to him through you. I am afraid I am quite shocked by your news." Isaac looks Nicholas Gilman in the eyes. "Were you close to Colonel Gilman?"

"I am afraid I did not know him well. His was a different branch of the family. They moved north more than a generation ago."

Isaac is silent for a moment, then nods to himself, "Thank you, sir, for telling us privately. I came to know Colonel Gilman quite well last year, and will miss him."

"You're welcome." Gilman takes a deep breath and looks around. "I need to get back to the meeting, and I expect you've got a long ride ahead of you. Thank you for coming as quickly as you did, and I wish you good fortune in recruiting your company."

2 RECRUITING

"We the Subscribers are Ingage'd in the Continental Service Under Captain Isaac Frye of Wilton have received of the State Bounty by the Hand of Abiel Abbot of Wilton, Muster Master, the Sum of Twenty Pounds Each (viz) one Treasurers Note for Ten Pounds and Two Treasurers Notes of Five Pounds Each."

Receipt showing the signatures of the men recruited
Signed on April 1, 1777

Hawkins and Isaac slow their horses to a walk on the road from Temple to Wilton. It is the middle of the afternoon on a cold day. The horses are warm after galloping for well over a mile. Their exhalations expel dual streams of warm breath into the chilly air. Both men are clad in their Continental uniforms with scarves wrapping their heads and faces beneath their tricorn hats. The exercise of the hard ride now has their blood flowing.

Hawkins unwraps his scarf from around his nose and mouth. "Somewhat disappointing that only two signed up, don't you think?"

Isaac pulls his scarf down. "Aye. Though better than none at all. It being such a cold day didn't help."

"It's the coldest since we got back from Exeter."

Isaac purses his lips, and his eyes narrow, showing thought and determination. "Twill grow warmer soon, and we'll have to do better. I expect Major Abbot will be at the meetinghouse this afternoon. I want to see him before going home tonight."

"Sounds wise. You mentioning the meetinghouse reminds me Abby is worried our girls will fall behind in their lessons. She wanted to know if your wife had any luck engaging our former Reverend to teach a winter session?"

Isaac sighs with exasperation. "He hasn't agreed to anything formal. He took that infernal summons to Exeter hard. Too hard. His confidence is shaken. You knew him when you both lived in Northborough, did you not? Was he easily rattled when he was young?"

"I didn't know him well. He is twelve years my senior, and his father's home was in a different part of town than mine. He left to come to Wilton shortly after my apprenticeship ended and before Abby and I married. Abby's mother's a Livermore, but from Shrewsbury. Anyhow, we stayed in Northborough for almost eight years after the Reverend removed to Wilton."

"Aye. I s'pose Elizabeth'll have to keep working on him. I expect there's a dozen families or more who wish him to continue teaching."

Hawkins thinks a moment, then chuckles. "At least. A shame so many were set against him continuing in the pulpit."

"Aye, I wish we knew who started that business. I've got some ideas, but no proof."

"Abby has tried with exceeding discretion to learn the answer. Nothing came of it."

"Why is it you've always gone by William Adrian?"

Hawkins grins, "That was my mother's idea. From an early age, she told me I'd meet many Williams, Wills, and Bills in this world. So she said to me, you will be the only William Adrian, and whatever business you go into, people will know who they're dealing with."

"Clever. Your mother is a wise woman."

"That, and I think she was tired of trying to keep all the William Hawkinses in the family separate. My father and grandfather first among them."

"Aye, I'll wager she might have been." Isaac laughs, and then gives his scarf a couple of shakes to dislodge the accumulation of frost. "Let's pick up the pace so we don't miss Major Abbot." Both men wrap their scarves about their faces and urge their horses to a canter, making good time on the frozen road.

•••

The sound of horses arriving outside causes Major Abbot to look up from where he sits at the table near the stove in the rear of the meetinghouse. The papers with lists of men from the muster rolls of the various towns near Wilton cover the table. Through the mullioned windows, he catches of sight of Isaac and Hawkins walking to the meetinghouse steps. Immediately he moves paperweights onto the unprotected stacks and places his hands on the two remaining piles. The door opens, letting in the wind, Isaac, and Hawkins.

After Hawkins closes the door, Major Abbot smiles and takes his hands off the papers. "I am glad I saw you coming. When Colonel Nichols left an hour ago, I wasn't prepared, and most of this paper ended up scattered over half the floor." The men shake hands and take seats around the table. Isaac and Hawkins moving their chairs to the end of the table nearest the stove to warm up.

Isaac begins, "We're pleased to find you here. We've just come from Temple. Ebenezer Drury and Josiah Stone were the only two to volunteer." Some frustration is evident in Isaac's tone. "We expected as many as ten. This makes me think merely posting handbills with the dates we'll be in town is going to be of little effect. I pray you've got more expeditious ideas."

Major Abbot guides his index finger, pointing at one and then another of the sheets of paper on the table. Once he finds the correct sheet, he rests the tip of his finger on the paper. "This is the muster roll for Amherst. In five days we will muster them again. You both should be there with me. You can make your appeal to their honor and devotion to liberty. There will be several dozen men, and they'll be in a military state of mind. I cannot think of a better time to recruit."

Hawkins chuckles, "You'll have a good supply of rum on hand as well?"

Major Abbot cocks an eyebrow toward Hawkins. "You're right Lieutenant, rum would make it easier to recruit," he grins back at Hawkins, "and it has a way of making men forget they've enlisted."

Hawkins mimes tipping his hat. "Touché Major."

Isaac begins looking at the other muster rolls on the table. "I like this idea of attending the musters. We can post handbills ahead of time to advertise the bounties. Can you give me the dates for the rest of this month's musters?"

"They're right here." Major Abbot pushes a small piece of paper with a list of dates and town names toward Isaac.

"I would like to copy these," Isaac looks to the inkwell on the table, "if I may?"

"Go ahead, here's some paper." Major Abbot pushes a half sheet toward Isaac.

While Isaac copies, Major Abbot continues, "Many men, I expect, will need to hear this message more than once. It would be prudent, I am thinking, to offer the day they agree to serve as their enlistment date."

Hawkins grins with approval. "It's a shame, but it seems we need to provide as many incentives as we can. Perhaps we set a different date for the men to sign for their bounties. That way, word will get around, and I wager we'll attract even more volunteers on that day."

Major Abbot smiles and nods once. "April first in Wilton and April thirtieth at Number Four. I'll sign up any who come along after. Sound good?"

Isaac and Hawkins agree.

Within five minutes, Isaac has the list copied and turns to Hawkins. "We should get on our way—the horses are getting cold." He rises and shakes Major Abbot's hand. "Thank you, sir. We will see you here on Sunday, and then in Amherst on Monday."

"Very well. I should be heading to my own home as well." Within a few minutes, the three men leave the meetinghouse and taking their separate ways home.

Isaac and Hawkins wait on the first of the steps leading to the main door of the Amherst meetinghouse. A hundred militiamen stand at attention in the field twenty yards away. The damp morning feels more winter than spring. Half an hour earlier, the men and their horses churned the three inches of wet snow in front of the meetinghouse into cold choppy mud.

Major Abbot holds a hand at his brow to shield his eyes from the heavy mist blowing on cold gusts of wind. "Before I take the roll, Take notice of the men on the steps. Captain Frye and Lieutenant Hawkins of the Third New Hampshire Continental Regiment are here to recruit. They're authorized to grant twenty-pound bounties to all those who sign on for three years. It's a good offer. Think on it while I take the roll."

The men do not react.

Each calls out, "Here" or "Aye" as Major Abbot bellows their last, followed by their first names. When the Major is not looking their direction, a few steal glances at their horses.

As the Major nears the end of the roll, Hawkins leans in and whispers to Isaac, "Don't blink after he dismisses them. They may vanish."

"Aye, true. They'd rather be elsewhere. Standing in ranks up to their ankles in cold mud with this wind doesn't give our asking for volunteers much sway. I hope the Major reminds them to see us before he dismisses them."

"I expect he will. A shame more men don't just come to your farm like Joseph Lewis did yesterday."

Isaac gives Hawkins a flat wry grin. "I expect it'll come to us going to their farms."

They turn their attention to the Major, who finishes taking the roll. He calls out, "Any of you men who can see fit to sign up for Continental service come see Captain Frye, Lieutenant Hawkins or myself. Terms are three years, or for the war, whichever you believe will be shortest. There's thirty pounds more in bounties from the county to any who sign."

Major Abbot scans the faces of men to see who is looking up or down. After waiting ten seconds, he dismisses them, then approaches Isaac and Hawkins.

Many of the men immediately make their way toward their horses or walk directions other than the meetinghouse. Four men approach Isaac and Hawkins.

Leading them is a bluff Scotsman in his twenties, with curly dark red hair, and a big crooked grin. He is half an inch shorter than Isaac with a build that attests to years of hard heavy work. As he reaches Isaac, he extends his hand, "Cap'n Frye, I'm Sergeant Richard Hughes. I'd be pleased to serve. I'll sign on for three years if I can keep my rank to start."

Isaac shakes Hughes's hand. His firm grip and a slight nod from Major Abbot make the decision easy. "I think we can make that arrangement work, Sergeant Hughes."

The next man is several inches shorter, stocky in his late thirties, blond-brown hair, and a thick beard. "Captain Frye, I'm Richard Goodman. I've got the rank of Corporal. May I have the same arrangement and keep my rank if I join the Continentals?"

Isaac gets the same signal from Major Abbot, as he reaches for Corporal Goodman's hand. "You may."

Corporal Goodman motions with a jerk of his thumb back at one of the other men from Amherst. "Elijah Mansfield there is a good man."

"Glad to hear it."

Isaac shakes Mansfield's hand. Mansfield, the shortest of the volunteers, is about the same age as Isaac. He has straight dark brown hair, a wiry build, and excellent posture to make the most of his height.

"Good to meet you, Captain. I'll sign on for three years as well."

Isaac thanks Mansfield, and turns to the fourth man, the youngest, by far. "Thomas Powell, I was hoping you'd volunteer."

Powell, who is seventeen with dark brown hair and piercing blue eyes, shakes Isaac's hand. "I got word you were looking for musicians and perhaps a drum sergeant major for the new regiment. I'll sign on for the three years if you think there's a good chance of my getting that position."

"Given you were Captain Crosby's drummer when we marched into Charlestown, I believe you'll be at the top of the list of candidates. Do you know of any other fifers or drummers we could recruit?"

"Well, I expect you know I've been helping Uriah Ballard and Will Burton from Wilton maybe once a week?"

"No, I hadn't. How're they doing?"

"Burton has a fife and has learnt a lot pretty fast. Ballard's making good progress on the drum. They haven't drilled with a company, so a lot to learn yet. There's also John Drury from Temple, who I've heard is good with a fife."

Isaac thanks Powell for the information before introducing Hawkins to the volunteers. Then he looks to Major Abbot. "Have I forgotten anything?"

Major Abbott tells the new volunteers the company will muster in Wilton at nine o'clock on the morning of April first. They will pay the bounties to those signed up before then. The plan is they will march to and muster at Number Four on April thirtieth before continuing on to Fort Ticonderoga. He finishes with, "If you know of others who would serve, tell them to come to Wilton's meetinghouse on the first.

•••

Isaac checks the cinch on the saddle while his horse, a four-year-old bay gelding, stands patiently. The morning sky to the east is clear and the air chilly. His oldest son, Isaac Jr., now seven steps out from the back door of the house. He wears a coat, scarf, and a coonskin cap. Elizabeth follows, wrapped a blanket holding John. She pulls a fold of the blanket to cover John's head as gusts of wind from the west mark a change to the past few days of pleasant weather.

Isaac mounts and pulls Isaac Jr. up to sit in front of him. Over the wind, he calls out to Elizabeth, "I expect to be back about noon."

Elizabeth waves as they begin riding toward the road, "Good luck to you, I hope a full company signs up today."

Isaac smiles and calls back, "My wish as well!"

He looks to Isaac Jr., ensuring he is holding on. "Are you ready to ride?"

Isaac Jr. nods. Isaac gives the horse a light kick, and they trot out onto the road, around the hill, and over the bridge.

They arrive at the meetinghouse a few minutes later, where there are already several horses tied outside. After dismounting, Isaac catches his son's arm and turns him so he can look him in the eye. "After we go in, you go upstairs, Watch. Do not make any noise. Understand?"

Isaac Jr. gives an exaggerated nod to show he will comply.

They climb the steps, with Isaac Jr. moving ahead. Isaac admonishes, "Remember, no running inside the meetinghouse." The words and tone have the desired effect, checking his son's enthusiasm.

As they enter, Isaac Jr. moves off to the left and quietly climbs the stairs to the second floor, where he takes in the scene below. Lieutenant Hawkins and Major Abbot have set up a table in front of the pews, and seven other men rise as his father approaches.

Below, he sees his father shake hands with Ebenezer Carlton, James Hutchinson, Joseph Gray, Joseph Lewis, Asa Pierce, and Amos Fuller, all from Wilton. Isaac greets each of them with warmth and gratitude.

Isaac Jr. does not know the seventh, a dark-skinned man who carries himself with confidence as he steps up and shakes Isaac's hand. "Captain Frye."

"Mister Oliver, you must have gotten an early start this morning."

"I did, sir. I am pleased the Continental Army will accept my service."

Isaac turns toward the table and greets Hawkins and Major Abbot as he reaches the table. Hawkins is writing out a sheet for the men to sign.

Major Abbot pats a small strongbox. "We've got enough to pay twenty men today, and I'll sign for more notes tomorrow in Exeter."

Over the next hour, five men from Amherst arrive. They include the four who signed up earlier and Sergeant Robert Wilkins, who decided to volunteer three days ago. Privates Josiah Stone, Ebenezer

Drury, and his cousin John Drury arrive with Second Lieutenant Ezekiel Goodale from Temple. Goodale introduces the Ebenezer Drury as his brother-in-law. From Hollis, Ensign Samuel Leeman and Private Stephen Richardson round out the men from outside Wilton.

Seven more men from Wilton arrive during the next hour. The group makes it clear they are not ready to sign today. Nonetheless, they make the total twenty-one plus four officers. Major Abbot pounds a gavel on the table to quiet the room and explains the men will receive their bounties once they sign.

While the Major oversees the men signing, Isaac meets with his officers. Leeman is a quiet determined-looking man about the same age as Isaac, and Goodale is ten years older with a gruff demeanor. Both agree to help with recruiting. Isaac challenges them to more than double the number of men by the time they muster on April thirtieth.

After the last of the men sign, Isaac addresses them, "Gentlemen, it is my honor to serve as your captain and commanding officer. Before I dismiss you, I'll administer the Continental Army's oath of service."

Isaac directs the men to come to their feet and raise their right hands. Out of the corner of his eye, he spies Isaac Jr. standing solemnly at the balustrade with his hand raised. Isaac winks to his son, then administers the oath to the men before him.

Major Abbot announces, paying particular attention to the seven from Wilton, he will be here in a week's time to enlist any men who did not sign today.

A few minutes later, only Isaac, Hawkins, and Major Abbot remain on the main floor of the meetinghouse. The Major tells Isaac he will ask the committee for additional bounty money when he is in Exeter in two days and will stop at Isaac's farm when he returns to let him know the committee's expectations.

Isaac reaches for his coat and motions for Isaac Jr. to come downstairs. The two walk outside together. On the top step, Isaac puts a hand on his son's shoulder to halt him for a moment. "I saw you take the oath. Once I am gone, my orders for you are to do as your mother says. Help with the farm, and look after your brothers, your aunts and grandfather." Isaac makes a show of coming to attention and waits for Isaac Jr. to do the same. Isaac Jr. recognizes what his father expects, stands straight, and salutes. Isaac returns the salute.

...

A rapid knock on Isaac's front door on late in the afternoon of April third signals Major Abbot's arrival. Isaac invites the Major in and offers him a seat at the kitchen table where an oil lamp is lit against the fading daylight. Elizabeth, who already had some rum mulling for the evening, sets out three cups.

As soon as they all sit, Major Abbot takes a sip then sighs. "Well Captain Frye, I've got good news and some news for which I'd rather not be the bearer."

Elizabeth clears her throat before Isaac can reply. "Please forgive me, but I have some news you should know as well, Major Abbot."

The Major nods at the steaming cup warming his hands and then looks to Elizabeth. "Thank you, Madam Frye, please, I would hear your news first."

"You're welcome. Phebe Parker had a fine healthy son yesterday. She and her baby are well. My sisters and Sarah Stevens are taking turns helping at her house."

Major Abbot offers a warm smile. "That's wonderful. I will let my Dorrie know when I get home. Does Pheobe have any immediate needs?"

"No, and though she has not said as much, I expect she worries about her prospects. Everyone's kind words and support raised her spirits last fall. I expect she needs to hear more of the same as she sees to the needs of a new baby."

Major Abbot nods and holds up a hand to placate Elizabeth. "The town will see that Phebe and her children are cared for. She should have no fear of dispossession or want for food."

Elizabeth nods several times as the Major finishes speaking, satisfied she has made her point.

Everyone takes a drink, and Isaac fixes Major Abbot with an inquiring look. "Let's have the good news first."

"Very well. The committee gave me enough notes for twenty

additional men. But, they expect to run short on funds soon. Their plan is to ask prominent men in each town to sponsor bounties. I'll get word out to the men who've waited for higher bounties so they'll know none will be better than what we've got now."

Isaac smiles. "Good." Keeping his expression neutral. "What's the not so good news?"

"Yesterday, the committee ordered all companies and parts of companies that are fully equipped to march to Fort Ti."

Elizabeth sets her cup on the table. "That sounds like they expect Isaac and what men he has to march as soon as they can."

Major Abbot closes his eyes, not meeting her gaze, and slowly nods. "Yes, we need every man who can to march to Fort Ti. From the Third Regiment, Captains Beal, Stone, and Weare are preparing to march within the week. Captain Frye, you're ordered to march as soon as you can, with all haste, to Number Four, and then to Ticonderoga. The committee authorized sending a wagon from Number Four onward to carry what supplies your company needs."

Isaac is silent for a few seconds. "I see. Well, I suppose the season is upon us. I'll get word to the men who have signed, and we'll march the day after tomorrow. Hawkins and Goodale will march the rest of the men later this month."

Major Abbot finishes his rum and pushes back from the table. "It seems General Burgoyne has decided winter will end a little earlier than we planned. I'll do my utmost to get your company filled up and send them along to Number Four by April thirtieth."

The Major rises, and Isaac and Elizabeth thank him as he leaves for his home.

Only a minute passes before Isaac gets his coat and turns to Elizabeth. "I need to ride to see William Adrian and let him know to ride to Temple and New Ipswich tomorrow. I'll go to Amherst. That's about all we can do on short notice."

Elizabeth nods and hands Isaac his hat. "You will be home after that?"

"Yes, an hour, maybe a little more."

•••

Honor and Valor

Isaac steps out through his back door onto the stone step. He shoulders a pack and takes up his firelock from just inside the door. He turns to check on Isaac Jr., who leads his horse from the barn. The low gray clouds block the sun, making it seem earlier. Elizabeth comes to the doorway holding their youngest son, Timothy. Isaac kisses her as Abiel, now age five squeezes by Elizabeth and gives Isaac a hug.

Isaac steps away and hands his firelock to Isaac Jr., then mounts. He takes back the firelock and slips his arm through the shoulder strap and snugs it in against his pack then pulls Isaac Jr. up to sit in front of him.

Elizabeth remains in the doorway, tight-lipped, and can only nod. The image of her oldest son looking as though he is riding off to war strikes a deep negative chord.

Isaac Jr. had begged to go with his father to the meetinghouse to see the men off. He had been riding for nearly a year and was also worried his father would take their horse with him.

Isaac had mostly allayed those fears, telling his son he had no intention of donating his horse to the army, and he would be given a horse if he needed one. Isaac offered the solution of allowing Isaac Jr. to ride the horse home once he and his men began their march to Number Four.

Isaac turns to Elizabeth, taking in the sight of her holding Timothy standing, framed by the door. "I'll write as soon as we reach Fort Ti, or before if plans change."

Elizabeth gives Isaac a slight nod, then blows him a kiss. "Come home safe husband, and as soon as you are able."

Once they leave the farmyard, Isaac urges the horse to a trot. After crossing the bridge, he speaks for the first time. "Your mother told me you did well when I was gone last year. I expect you'll do so again."

"Yessir. Like you ordered."

"Look out for the welfare of your brothers, and do not fight with Abiel. Help grandfather and your aunts if they should need it. My being gone will put a burden upon you, and it cannot be helped." Isaac pauses, letting his words sink in. "You're strong enough and big enough to do some of the work of the farm. It would please me to have your mother write telling me how much help you are this season. Am I clear?"

"Yes sir. I will do what mother says." Isaac Jr. trembles a little, working up the courage to ask, "When will you come back?"

"In truth, know not when. I told your mother it would be after this season. Twill depend on a victory against the enemy coming from Canada, and General Washington taking back New York. We prayed both come to pass this summer."

Isaac is the first to the meetinghouse. Major Abbot arrives a few minutes later. Within the next hour, Ensign Leeman, Sergeant Hughes, Corporal Goodman, and privates Carlton, Powell, Stone, Oliver, and Mansfield arrive.

Isaac orders the men to form a single rank, then turns the command of the formation over to Leeman. Isaac takes in their motley appearance. No two dressed the same. Yet, their militia training shows through as the rank is straight and the interval between each man and the next is correct. On Leeman's order, they shoulder their firelocks in a military and consistent fashion.

Isaac turns and shakes hands with Major Abbot, then walks to Isaac Jr., who is already astride their horse. Isaac Jr. offers a salute. Isaac returns it. "After we march, you go straight home and tell your mother we got on our way in good order."

Isaac walks back toward Leeman. "Let us be going. Give the order to march."

Seven men step off marching on Leeman's order. Thomas Powell strikes the rim of his drum every fourth step. Isaac calls out, "Step it up a few paces." Powell quickens the cadence, and the men's pace accelerates.

Isaac hastens to the front of the formation beside Sergeant Hughes. "Sergeant, take the Peterborough road. Once we get there, we'll rest and have a meal. Then we march for Keene, where we'll spend the night."

Honor and Valor

3 PREPARING FOR THE ENEMY

"Keen, May, 9th 1777.
Gentlemen - The backwardness of the men to engage in this Quarter & the fewness of men in Captain Ellis's Company render it necessary that a full complement of Officers should be immediately employ'd in filling it. Many of the towns in the vicinity of this place have rais'd but very few men. ..."

Letter to the Keene Committee of Saftey
Signed Alex'r Scammell

The men under Isaac march through the gap between Pack Monadnock and Temple Mountains. They gaze into eastern Peterborough, where farms occupy less of the land than in Wilton. From the height of the pass, they see several clusters of farms. Three well-established farms surround a large pond at the front of the valley to their right.

Isaac jogs up beside Leeman, "Call for a halt beside the last of those farms, and we'll give the men time to eat a midday meal."

"Yessir."

After the men halt, Isaac removes his pack and digs through it to find a loaf of raisin bread and pulls off a quarter of it. He squats next to Leeman sits, leaning against the rail of a fence. "Let's you and I

Honor and Valor

finish quickly and put Sergeant Hughes in charge of the men. Then we'll pay a visit to one of these farms and see what we can learn about the state of recruitment here. We need to add a few men to those who will march at the end of this month."

Isaac and Leeman stride along the worn path leading to the front of the nearest farm. When they are about fifty feet from the house, the front door opens, and a stout Scotsman with brilliant red hair and a wiry beard steps out. He leans a firelock against the side of the door and crosses his arms. "That's far enaw. State yer business."

"I'm Captain Isaac Frye of the Third New Hampshire Continental Regiment. This here," Isaac hooks a thumb towards Leeman, "is Sam Leeman, the ensign of my company."

"Aye, nae th' enemy, tis good." The Scotsman motions Isaac and Leeman forward. "My nam is Randall McAlister."

As McAlister speaks, Isaac sees a large gap of missing teeth on the right side of his mouth. An angry scar on his right cheek mars his beard.

McAlister's reaches out to shake Isaac's hand. "Ah dornt spick so weel on account of takin' a bulleh in mah gob at Bunkah's Hill."

While Leeman shakes McAlister's hand, Isaac nods as his memory offers up information. "You were in Stark's regiment?"

"Aye."

"I heard about you. I'm relieved to see you looking fit."

"Thank ye."

"I'm marching those men by the road to Fort Ti. We got orders to march early. I'm not done recruiting, and I was hopeful of finding a few more recruits in Peterborough. What do you think of that?"

"Looks loch yoo've barely started. I hink ye will hae no luck. Cappin Scott has awready taken the lot of 'em frae aroond haur'"

Isaac purses his lips and takes a deep breath. "Can you still shoot?"

McAlister snorts impudently, then asks, "Dae ye see onie squirrels?"

Isaac and Leeman laugh as they can see no squirrels anywhere about the farm.

"Tae answer yer question, ah got a month o' wark tae dae oan mah farm, an' ah'm awready in Nichol's regiment."

Isaac smiles. "I understand. If you don't mind, next time you're at the meetinghouse, let the men know Captain Frye needs more men to fill up his company. They can see Major Abbot at the Wilton meetinghouse, or I expect they can go to Number Four at the end of this month."

"Ah will dae sae. Ah bid ye an' yer men a safe march an' good fortune this season."

"Thank you Mister McAlister. We will be on our way shortly."

"Ye and yer men want a side ay bacon? Me an' mah neighbors jist butchahed a hog."

"That'd be welcome."

"Ah will gie it fur ye." McAlister disappears into his house for a full minute and reappears with a package wrapped in waxed linen. He hands it to Isaac who produces a few coins.

McAlister holds up his hand to reject Isaac's offer. "Nae, nae, it is fur th' cause."

"Very well, we thank you kindly, Mister McAlister. A good day to you".

"An' a good day tae ye an' yer men Cappin Frye.'

Halfway back to where the men rest Leeman asks, "You said you heard of Mr. McAlister's wound?"

"Aye. An enemy's ball went straight into the right side of his open mouth, busted his jaw and split the ball. Half sheared off and went out his cheek. The other half went straight through and came out the back of his neck. One of the Peterborough men carried him off the field. I can only attribute his survival to divine providence."

"I should say so. That's as bad as losing a leg. It's good to see him doing well enough to be back with the militia."

Isaac murmurs his agreement, then changes the subject. "Have sergeant Hughes march the men this afternoon. I want to see how he handles them. While we march, I want to go over your duties and what I expect for drilling the men. That duty will fall mostly to you until Lieutenants Hawkins and Goodale bring in the rest."

•••

The sun is low on the horizon, and the chilly air begins to feel sharply colder as the men approach Keene. Their breath now easily visible proves the exertion of marching rapidly for much of the afternoon. Isaac calls for Sergeant Hughes to bring the men to a halt.

After they have a drink of water, Isaac asks, "Anyone know Captain Gregg from Keene, and more particularly, where his farm is within the town?"

Ebenezer Carlton, a strong twenty-three-year-old with sandy blond hair and smooth cheeks that show no signs of having had the pox raises a hand. "I do. My father does some business with him."

"Good, tell us how to get there, and then run ahead and let him know we're coming, and that we'd be grateful to stay the night on his farm."

Carlton describes the route, about three miles in all. Isaac looks at the setting sun to gauge the time. "Tell him we will arrive shortly after sunset. You best be on your way."

Isaac gives the rest of the men a few more minutes to rest, then orders Sergeant Hughes to continue the march.

Carlton meets them three-quarters of an hour later and points out a pinpoint of light ahead as being a lantern marking the last turn to John Gregg's farm. He continues, "I would have met you sooner, but Captain Gregg is ill. His wife says we are welcome to stay in their barn. She sent me to get Lieutenant Ellis, who will meet with us there in an hour."

For the next hour, Isaac orders his men to clean up the barn by the light a pair of lanterns. It was apparent Captain Gregg, or more likely his wife had no time to spare for such a mundane task. Once the barn was in proper order, the men set about making pallets to sleep on. Leeman nudges Isaac with an elbow and nods toward the barn door.

It slowly opens to permit a man of slight build to squeeze through and pull the door shut. He turns and takes in the scene within the barn at a glance. "Which one of you is Captain Frye?"

Isaac steps forward. "I am, are you Lieutenant Ellis?"

"Yes, though you can call me Will if you like. I don't much care for keeping military custom when I'm not at drill."

"Well enough," Isaac motions to Leeman, "This is Ensign Sam

Leeman."

After the men shake hands, Isaac asks, "You don't look familiar. Did you serve in Stark's or Poor's regiments?"

"At the time, I needed to stay close to home. So I've been drilling with the militia the past two seasons. Captain Gregg was a lieutenant with Bedel's regiment last year. He convinced me I'm better off serving as a Continental."

Isaac laughs appreciatively. "Good for him, and for us."

"I hope so."

Isaac changes the subject. "This is part of the first group of men in my company. How's Captain Gregg faring with filling up his company?"

"Looks like you've got four more than we do. Captain Gregg signed a few in February and one more a few weeks back. That's it. He's been sick for a couple weeks now. Says it's the worst sickness he's ever had."

Isaac sighs and shakes his head. "That won't do. Make sure word gets out the next time the militia musters. Be less than gentle when you remind them that when it comes to fighting the redcoats, we'd rather do so at Fort Ti than here."

"Aye, though I expect such an appeal will hold little weight. The men are determined to get their crops in. Especially those who were at Fort Ti last season.

"When is the next muster?"

"We muster on Friday afternoons nowadays."

"Tell the men they have no more than two weeks to get their farms in order. We need them at Number Four by the end of the month. They'll need training once they get there."

"I'll do my utmost, but you know the men out here, they're as independent-minded as they come, and don't take to being pushed when they know they know better. So, what's your plan?"

"We'll march to Number Four tomorrow, and then on to Fort Ti."

"You got more men coming?"

"The balance of the company will rendezvous at Number Four at the end of the month."

Ellis offers his hand, "You and your men should get some sleep.

You'll be off early, I expect?"

"We will, and tell those men who know better, the enemy's already moving south. That's why our orders to march were changed."

They shake hands and Ellis departs. Isaac turns to Leeman. "He's right. We'll make an early morning of it, so let's get some sleep while we can."

•••

Sergeant Hughes gives the order to march as the soft blue-gray sky to the east silhouettes the forested hills. They take a late morning meal at a farm in Walpole, where they look out on the Connecticut River. Isaac has them set a quick pace, though they frequently slow to make their way around muddy stretches of the rutted, overused road.

Isaac and Leeman bring up the rear, marching in silence as the sun reaches its zenith for the day. To pass the time, Isaac asks, "I've not heard much of your story, you were at Bunker's Hill?"

"I was. Enlisted as a private in Reuben Dow's company in Prescott's Regiment."

"So you were in the redoubt?"

"From the start til the end."

"I was in Charlestown and helped cover the retreat. Do you have a farm in Hollis?"

"I did, but I sold it a few years ago. Twas to be married, but my intended died of a sudden illness. Caused me to lose interest in the farm."

Isaac looks over to Leeman before responding. "Can't say as I blame you."

They stride along for several minutes before Leeman asks, "What about you, have you had your farm long?"

"I bought my land in Wilton eight years ago. It took some time to get the house in shape and fields re-cleared. My wife didn't come for over a year. She wished to be with her family in Andover when our first son came. It's taken some time to get everything in working order, orchards planted, and so forth. Then I got hurt when a beam burst during the raising of our meetinghouse. That nearly did us in, with my not being able to work all winter."

"I remember hearing about your meetinghouse. What was it, five men killed in the fall?"

"It was three that day and two more not long after. It put the whole town in a bad way."

Leeman shakes his head. "Now we have this war to compound the interest of our misfortunes."

"I pray last year was the worst of it, and this year is the last of it."

"I take your point, these last few years haven't given me much to hope for."

Isaac claps Leeman on the back. "That should make it easy to figure on this year being better."

By mid-afternoon, Isaac and his men reach Number Four, a fort and depot for supplying New Hampshire's troops at Fort Ticonderoga. The guards tell Isaac to report to Mr. Grout, the Commissary Officer, and they point the way to the building with his office.

Inside, Isaac finds Elisha Grout seated at one of several desks. Each holds stacks of paper and folios of what Isaac guesses to be account ledgers. Grout is short, with a reedy build, and half bald with stringy dark hair. He rises and offers his hand to Isaac as he introduces himself. Isaac explains that he and his men are on their way to Fort Ticonderoga per the Committee of Safety's new orders.

"Very well, Captain Frye, you're the first. In fact, I just got the orders yesterday." Grout looks about the desk where he was sitting. He locates and thumbs through a stack of papers before finding the list he needs. You and your men can take three tents immediately. You'll need them tonight. The Committee of Safety instructs that your men are to receive a quarter pound of powder, half of lead, and two flints each. You'll sign for all that. You'll cross the river tomorrow by ferry. You'll also sign for a packhorse to carry the tools your men'll need to repair to the road. It's suffered somewhat from the winter weather. We expect to be sending wagons regularly very soon, so the road must be fixed wherever you deem a wagon cannot pass. Other men will come within days after you, so don't spend more than a day fixing any part, and no more than three for the whole of the trip. Set guards while your men work. The enemy's scouts are expected

Honor and Valor

throughout the whole of the countryside from here to Fort Ti."

For a moment, Isaac is silent, absorbing everything Grout listed off. "Aye, where should I sign?"

Grout chuckles. "I'll make a list and send one of my men who will take you to where everything is stored. He'll have you sign for each of the items as you go."

•••

Isaac and his men trudge cold, drenched, and dispirited through the southern gate of Camp Independence. Much of their dismal state due to marching the past two days in heavy rain. The officer on duty, a Continental captain from Bradford's Massachusetts regiment, directs them to continue through the camp to Fort Ticonderoga. There, he instructs Isaac to see the duty officer and learn where his men will encamp. The captain adds, "No need for batteaux, we've got a bridge from the northern tip of camp straight across the narrow part of the lake. You and your men can march the whole way. You know how to get there?"

Isaac points with movements in the correct directions. "I do. I was here last summer and fall."

The sun drops behind the steep hills to the west an hour later as Isaac and his men arrive at the fort. The gate to the interior is a tunnel about a dozen paces in length. Isaac leaves his men there, out of the weather, and continues to the headquarters building. As he enters, the warmth from a fireplace to his right greets him. He does not recognize the tall burly man, in his sixties, seated at the desk before him. Isaac removes his hat, gloves, and coat, and hangs them on pegs near the fireplace before turning back to the officer at the desk. "Sir, I am Captain Frye of Scammell's regiment. I've just arrived with some of my men. Can you direct me to where Colonel Scammell's regiment is to encamp?"

The officer at the desk rises and extends a meaty hand to Isaac. "Good evening, Captain Frye, I'm Hercules Mooney, Lieutenant Colonel of Pierce Long's regiment." After shaking hands with Isaac, "I believe you're the first of Scammell's men to arrive. How many are with you?"

"Just eight. We got orders to march with those who signed on so far. My lieutenants are still at home recruiting, and they'll march in less than two weeks."

"Damn. Only eight?"

"Yessir. Eight. I got the order on the same evening it was given in Exeter, and we marched three mornings later."

Mooney shakes his head in disbelief. "I s'pose I'll need to check with General Wayne as to where you're to encamp. Tonight you and your men can sleep in the fort. The storerooms are near enough to empty, so there's extra room. Come back in the morning to find out where General Wayne wishes you to encamp."

The next morning Isaac and Leeman find Mooney in the same office. "Captain Frye, I have two items for you," begins the older man. "First, I expect I'll be sending one Benjamin Smith. He enlisted with Colonel Long's regiment, but several weeks ago, he volunteered to serve for the rest of the war as a Continental. He's most recently from Temple, which I understand is your territory for recruiting?"

"It is."

"Then it makes sense to add him to your company. I will send him to you later today. Second, your men will be garrisoned inside the fort until enough men arrive to safely occupy and guard the French Lines."

Isaac nods, though Ensign Leeman looks less than confident of what he's heard. Mooney notices and asks, "What is it, Ensign?"

"The French Lines, sir?"

Isaac supplies, "It's a set of earthworks running west and north of the fort, protecting it from attack by land. About half a mile long."

Mooney fixes one eye on Isaac and nods, looking impressed. "Good you've been here before. General Poor has command of the New Hampshire Brigade now. They began marching north from the Jerseys not long ago. Poor's Brigade will have responsibility for the French Lines. In the meantime, your men'll be improving the works by day. He points to a map showing the Fort and the coast immediately around it. "Start here in the north and work your way west. Colonel Baldwin will be around in the next few days to inspect the work."

Honor and Valor

•••

Isaac paces a few hundred yards west of the fort, overseeing his men as they begin refurbishing a second of the old earthworks. They spent three days on the first berm and abatis. As he turns, he sees four men approach from the direction of the fort. One is Mooney. Isaac does not recognize the other three. Mooney motions for Isaac and Ensign Leeman to join them.

Mooney introduces Captains Benjamin Stone, Richard Weare, and Zachariah Beal. Stone, who is tallest at six feet, is a large-framed man with blond hair and ruddy cheeks. He shakes Isaac's hand with an iron grip. Weare is almost as tall as Isaac with thick dark hair and a quick charismatic smile. Beal is shorter with broad shoulders and a bristling black beard to go with the hairiest hands Isaac can recall seeing.

Once the men finish their introductions, Mooney continues, "Captains, the northern part of the French Lines are vulnerable to enemy scouts. General Wayne has ordered your companies to encamp over there," he points northward. "You're also to set up two twenty-man picquets. One to patrol the whole length of the lines and the other to range out to the north, half a mile to discourage scouts. Any questions?"

Captain Stone responds first, "That sounds excellent, sir." Then he turns to his fellow captains, "Let's get encamped while the sun's still up. After that let's meet at my tent to organize the picquets. Captain Frye, you and your men are welcome to encamp with mine."

Mooney responds, "I bid you fine gentlemen, a good afternoon." He turns and begins striding back to the fort.

That evening Isaac has dinner with the newly arrived Captains. They sit inside Stone's tent. Isaac volunteers that he served as the quartermaster in Reed's regiment, and learns that Beal and Weare were in Poor's Second New Hampshire Regiment. They were also in Canada, though instead of in Montreal, they were with General Sullivan at Sorel.

Captain Beal asks Isaac, "Reed's regiment was at Bunker's Hill, were you in the battle?"

"Aye, the Adjutant and I were assigned to Crosby's company. We got sent into Charlestown. We covered the retreat as well."

Weare clears his throat. "I hear that was hot business. People said they could see the smoke from New Hampshire."

Isaac replies, "Aye, it was. How about you, Benjamin?"

Stone replies, "Call me Ben. It's what my friends call me. That or Stoney. I was there as well, a sergeant in Captain Dow's company under Colonel Prescott. Last year I was a lieutenant in Colonel Waldron's militia regiment. He put a good word in for me with the committee last fall, and here I am."

"So, you know my ensign, Sam Leeman, from Dow's company."

"I do. Shared a tent with him for far too long."

Beal laughs. "I'm pleased to know we're all experienced officers. I did hear in Exeter that we are to have new firelocks for this campaign. A ship from France carried them into Portsmouth last month. Captain McClary's and Gray's men have the duty of transporting them." Looking at Isaac, "I don't know either of them, do you?"

"James Gray, yes. He was the sergeant major for Reed's Regiment. A fine and well-spoken gentleman. McClary, I've not met."

The others shake their heads, indicating none of them know McClary. Stone asks, "That leaves Livermore and Gregg?"

Isaac fills them in. "Livermore was a First Lieutenant with Reed. Gregg, I've not met, though we stayed in his barn when we marched here. We met Will Ellis, his lieutenant that night. Gregg's been sick and hadn't recruited but a few men."

Weare sounding tired, "I suppose we'll meet them all soon enough. Colonel Mooney offered to me that we should also send some hunting parties out. Keep them well to the south. Provisions are low at the fort, and that's not likely to change until June. I suggest sending at least six to a party. I get the feeling from Mooney the enemy's Indian scouts are expected in large numbers."

Stone asks, "Isaac, your men want to hunt tomorrow?"

"I expect they'll be happy to."

"If they bring back a couple of deer, we'll all be happy," quips Beal. They all laugh.

Honor and Valor

The routine of Isaac's men hunting, guarding, and working on the defenses make the next three weeks pass quickly. One afternoon in early May, Isaac and the other captains meet with Colonel Baldwin, who directs the engineering of the army's fortifications. Baldwin shows them plans for a new redoubt they will construct in the coming days. As he finishes, they hear a man call out, "Captain Frye!" They all turn to see a group of about thirty soldiers marching towards them from the fort.

As the soldiers approach, Isaac recognizes Hawkins striding out front, and waves for him to come to their location. After introductions, Isaac excuses himself and directs his men to the area where they will encamp.

...

Ten days earlier. Will Burton checks the front window for the third time in five minutes, hoping to see his friend Uriah Ballard. Will arranged for Uriah to stop by on his way to the meetinghouse. Over the space of two weeks, Will convinced his mother to allow him to enlist in the Continental Army. He recently turned fourteen and through persistence, had worn down her resistance to the idea of her oldest son joining the army. Will had even written to his uncle Jonathan in the militia at Fort Ticonderoga, who confirmed there were others his age already serving.

Will's mother had spoken firmly with Uriah and Chris Martin at the meetinghouse two days ago. She extracted promises they would look out for Will's safety. Lieutenant Hawkins had recognized Martin's abilities to lead and enlisted him as a corporal. Will's mother had been especially firm with Martin.

With Will's attention focused out the window, his brothers David and John quietly extract the fife from his pack on the floor. David produces a shrill upper register blast the moment Will sees Uriah come into view. Before Will can muster a shout at his brother, his father whisks the fife out of David's grasp.

John Burton, a Deacon in Wilton, sees Uriah through the window as steps by his younger sons and hands the fife to Will. "Looks like

Uriah is here." He continues, "Be safe. Will, there's far more to life than armies and war. I would have you see it for yourself."

Will's eagerness dissolves to solemnity. "I know, sir. I promise to do my best not to be in any real danger."

John Burton gives a grim smile in return, then opens the door for Uriah.

Will moves to retrieve his backpack. Before he can pick it up, Rebecca Burton, his mother, pulls him into a fierce hug. "Do as Captain Frye and the officers tell you, and let the men do the fighting. Use your fife to help them. Always remember that I love you. You can come home if you don't like it."

After a few seconds, Will pulls out of the hug and nods, very nearly on the edge of tears as he tries to smile for his mother. He looks away, then grabs and shoulders his pack. Before turning to the door, he tousles the hair of David and John.

His older sister, Rebecca, has been uncharacteristically quiet all morning, finally steps forward and takes him by the arm. "Be smart and safe, brother. Write to me."

To Will surprise, her features show worry and sadness. He nods to her and surprises himself with a sincere tone, "I will."

Uriah waits on the step while Will's family say their goodbyes. As Will turns to the door, he asks, "You ready? We're due before long."

Will's mother catches Uriah's attention, pointing her index finger at his chest. "You watch over him and yourself, Uriah Ballard, you hear me?"

"Yes, Ma'am."

Will's father offers his hand to Uriah. While shaking hands, he asks, "You told Major Abbott you wanted to be a drummer?"

"I did, sir."

"That means you and Will have to look out for each other."

"We will, sir."

With that, Will and Uriah turn and set out for the meetinghouse.

They arrive fifteen minutes later to find ten others waiting. Lieutenant Hawkins is in conversation with Corporal Martin. Amos Fuller, who is in his late twenties, stands by himself off to the side. Joseph Gray is sixteen and is already the best in a fight amongst them.

His abilities developed from having strong opinions and the need to back them up. Amos Holt, a lanky, quiet seventeen-year-old and his cousin Nehemiah Holt age twenty-one, stand together. Off to their side is Will Pettingill, who is eighteen and Joseph Lewis, who is twenty-one. Pettingill has sandy brown hair and penchant for issuing dares to his friends. James Hutchinson is eighteen and quiet, and Jacob Blanchard, a sturdy hard-working nineteen-year-old round out the group.

As Will and Uriah approach, Will notes all the others all have firelocks, marking them as privates and not musicians.

Hawkins turns toward all of them. "Fall into a straight line formation." He waits a few seconds for the men to comply. Martin remains at Hawkins' side as he continues, "As of this moment, you are soldiers in the Continental Army. You will follow Corporal Martin's orders as if they are my own. Your friendships and your past relations are subordinate to the orders of the officers lawfully appointed over you. We have two days to reach Number Four. Corporal Martin, take charge of the formation. Set a quick pace, so we make good time."

For two hours, Martin's pace along the road to Peterborough has them all breathing heavily. Amos Fuller, who leads, points ahead to the side of the road where he sees three men waiting by the roadside. They step forward as the group from Wilton approaches."

Hawkins calls for Martin to halt the formation as they draw alongside the men. One of them is much younger, about sixteen, while the other two are in their mid-thirties. Though the older pair could not be more different, one gaunt and withdrawn, and the other robust and quick in his movements.

The latter man's blond hair is tied back, accentuating his prominent jawline. He steps toward Hawkins with his hand extended. "Good morning, Lieutenant Hawkins."

Hawkins shakes his hand. "How do you do Zeke," he clears his throat, "I mean Lieutenant Goodale, I hope we didn't keep you waiting long."

"Not at all."

Hawkins turns to the men from Wilton. "This our company's second lieutenant, Zeke Goodale. With him are Eben and John Drury.

They're from Temple."

Goodale and the elder Drury have firelocks with them, and the younger Drury only has a pack and blanket. The Drurys look somber and hungry compared to Goodale, who appears ready to jump into action at a moment's notice.

Hawkins instructs the Drurys to fall into line with the Wilton men and orders Corporal Martin to resume the march."

They reach Number Four late in the afternoon the following day. Will, breathing hard from the last three hours of the march, done in one stint with no rest, looks to the other men. Only Hawkins, Goodale, and Joseph Gray seem unaffected. The rest are like Will, sweating, and tipping their canteens skyward.

The fort is quiet. Only four guards are on duty at the gate. Hawkins looks around and then to Martin. "Corporal, keep the men here while I see whoever's in charge."

Fifteen minutes later, Hawkins returns with five men. "Gentlemen, this is Sergeant Wilkins from Amherst." Wilkins, well proportioned, in his early twenties, tips his hat to the men. Hawkins continues, "From Hollis, we have Corporal Godfrey, Stephen Richardson, and brothers Tom and John Youngman."

All but Richardson are in their teens. Godfrey is stout and as tall as Goodale. Richardson is in his late twenties, thin, and wears a critical look as he purses his lips, inspecting the other men.

Wilkins wastes no time, "Form two ranks on Corporals Martin and Godfrey." As soon as the men are in place, Hawkins addresses them. "Tomorrow, we will start for Fort Ticonderoga with six wagons. One with our company's tents, and five with provisions." He turns to Sergeant Wilkins, "Sergeant, take the men to where we will sleep tonight. Musicians come with me."

Hawkins leads Will, Uriah, and John Drury to the same building he went into earlier. Before entering, he asks, "Do both of you have a fife?"

Will responds with an affirmative, and Hawkins asks to see it.

Will reaches into his pack, removes the fife, and hands it to Hawkins, who examines it for a few moments and then begins playing a series of short passages and trills in both registers. He hands it back.

Honor and Valor

"This will do."

Hawkins looks to Drury, who shakes his head, then instructs all three to wait as he enters the building. In less than a minute, Hawkins returns carrying a drum and a fife. He hands the fife to Drury. The drum, which includes a leather carrying harness and sticks in a case tied to the side, he gives to Uriah. "Starting tonight after supper, I'll review your abilities as military musicians." He points to where Sergeant Wilkins led the men, "We'll be sleeping in that building tonight. Find me there at eight o'clock."

While the men eat dinner outside the building assigned to them, Hawkins brings six more men from Mason into their midst. He introduces Sergeant Hall, who is even taller than Corporal Godfrey and powerfully muscled. Next is Reuben Hosmer, a short man in his late thirties who is almost entirely bald. Thomas Blood and Jonathan Foster are tough-looking eighteen-year-olds. Foster's intense, serious expression makes him look years older. Nathaniel Smith has an open, friendly face and is in his early twenties. Ebenezer Abbot, who at only fifteen, is almost as large as Sergeant Hall, though his manner is by comparison innocent.

Hawkins addresses them for a few minutes, laying out that Sergeants Hall and Wilkins will divide the men into groups of four. They will assign a group to each of the six wagons tomorrow.

That evening Will learns the months of practicing with Thomas Powell put him good deal further along with the fife than John Drury. Hawkins assigns Drury to learn from Will while they march. Uriah demonstrates he knows the basics of drumming while marching. Hawkins surprises him with dozens of commands he had never heard of and instructs him to master three per day until he masters them all.

The next day proves cold and rainy. Hawkins begins by swearing them in as soldiers in the Continental Army. The formality of the oath causes Will's stomach to become light. Hawkins' deadly serious tone makes a strong impact. Repeating the oath's words infuses a weighty and unexpected responsibility.

Next, Wilkins reads the assignments for the wagons. He assigns Will, John Drury, and Amos Fuller to Martin. Martin designates Fuller to drive since he has the most experience. Their wagon also holds half a dozen long hardwood beams to use as a bridge over soft or sunken places in the road. Mr. Grout, the commissary officer, instructs them to make all haste in getting the provisions to the fort because the supplies there are low. It takes all morning to get the wagons across the Connecticut River on the ferry. Then they make a few miles progress in the afternoon. The rain abates by the time they reach a clearing where Hawkins calls for them to halt and encamp.

The men opt not to pitch tents and instead sleep beneath the wagons. They cut and layer pine boughs to put between themselves and the hard wet ground. Hawkins assigns eight men to guard the camp in two shifts of four. Will calculates he will have guard duty every third night.

Waking early the next morning, Will needing to relieve himself, rolls out from under the wagon, and seeks the privacy of the woods. Martin, hearing Will's departure, wakes and pulls on his boots as Will disappears into the trees. Once out from under the wagon, Martin looks about for Sergeant Hall, who has command of the guards, and finds him on the other side of the wagon ahead. As he approaches the sergeant, "Did you see Burton leave?"

Hall shakes his head. "No. Did you see where?"

"Yes." Martin points at the spot where Burton entered the woods. "There. I'll go after him."

Hall considers as Martin turns. "Half a minute, no longer, I'll get some men ready."

Martin enters the woods at the same spot, though now cannot see Will and moves slowly among the trees before stopping by a large pine tree not far from a gully. For several seconds he looks about before turning to head back to camp. Just before leaving the woods, he hears something moving quickly well back in the woods. He turns and scans the trees, but sees nothing.

Hall calls out, "What's going on, Corporal Martin?"

"Couldn't find him."

Hall turns to the men he had just woken. "Blanchard, Hosmer, Gray, Ballard, Lewis, get your firelocks and follow me. Martin, report this to Lieutenant Hawkins."

Honor and Valor

Hall leads the men to the edge of the clearing. "Fan out slowly. Look for tracks or other signs of Burton. No more than twenty paces apart, go no further in than fifty paces."

Lewis reaches the gully first and finds fresh evidence at the bottom of Will having been there.

Hosmer finds Will's tracks moving uphill through the gully. "Looks like he got spooked. He started running. One set of tracks."

Once on the far side of the gully, Lewis adds, "No tracks over here."

Hall asks, "You who know him, what would he do?"

Uriah answers, "Likely circle back to the road. He's fast in the woods. The best at circling around to flush deer when we hunt."

Hall thinks a moment then sighs. "Let's figure that's what he's doing. Go back to camp. We better not need to wait long."

In the camp, Hawkins instructs the rest of the men. "Nobody goes out of camp alone or without telling the commander of the guards. Use groups of three or more, and at least two with firelocks. Each wagon crew takes care of its own. Nobody is to go out more than twenty yards."

A few minutes later, Hawkins spots Will jogging on the road into the clearing. "Burton! Get over here!"

As Will approaches, Martin joins Hawkins. Instead of speaking to Will, Hawkins turns to Martin, "Corporal, you will see to the instruction of this man. His actions wasted a quarter-hour and risked others by exposing us to the enemy for having to roam around these woods searching for him.

As Will looks to Hawkins and Martin, he realizes Hawkins had already berated Martin and hangs his head with embarrassment.

Martin leads Will back to their wagon, his voice terse as he recites the new rules, emphasizing the part about no one going off by themselves. He adds, "You're lucky you showed up when you did, or I expect some would have figured you for a deserter."

"I'm sorry Chris-"

Martin cuts him off harshly, "It's Corporal Martin. You're a soldier in the Continental Army now. You swore to follow orders. You're a private. That means asking if you don't know the orders. Your newest order is that you'll be scrubbing everyone's dishes, pots, and pans every night for the rest of the march."

"Yes, Corporal Martin. I understand."

They average eleven miles a day for the next seven days. A two-hour downpour on the fifth day slows their progress. They arrive at Camp Independence late in the morning on the ninth day of May.

Will gazes at the lake stretching away to the north. He turns to Joseph Gray and, in a low voice, "It's much bigger than I ever thought."

Gray, whose eyes are also wide for seeing the lake for the first time, responds absently, "Yup."

They take the wagons as far as the northern tip of the camp, where they find a crane for lowering heavy items down to the lake. They unload and carry their tents, marching single-file down the narrow trail and over the wooden bridge to the west side of the lake. They arrive at the shore below the fort. From the level of the lake, the fort looks unassailable. Its stone buttresses and walls rising another twenty feet above the outcrop. After a short wait inside the fort, they learn the rest of their company is camped north of the fort, and begin marching in that direction.

•••

Ebenezer Carlton leads Hawkins to Isaac's tent through the darkness of the cloudy evening. After Isaac calls for him to enter, Hawkins turns to Carlton. "Thanks, I'd have disturbed half the tents here if I had to find my way on my own."

Isaac offers a seat on a canvas folding stool along with a small cup of rum. Isaac's tent has two poles on either end and enough space for a desk, a cot, and three small folding stools. "Good evening. I am glad to have you and the men here in camp."

"Me too, though I didn't expect to have to bring half a dozen wagons of provisions. I should've learned from last spring."

"We've been sending hunting parties out, but I don't know how long that will last. Once the enemy gets closer, we'll be back to whatever they can send from Number Four and Albany."

"They won't be able to get much this way from Number Four for another month. The road isn't good. Too much rain this spring."

Isaac sighs. "So we have three sergeants, three corporals, and twenty-six privates. That's a little better than half a company."

"Major Abbott promised to continue sending men. John Moss failed to muster, and we listed him as a deserter. Jonas Perry's been sick, so he didn't muster. The major says he'll send any others later this week."

"We'll likely lose Thomas Powell to the Colonel's company as he's clearly the most competent musician."

Hawkins, mid-sip, holds up a finger. "On that front, at least we are in good shape. Burton is adequate on the fife and Ballard is gaining confidence on the drum. John Drury is catching up to Burton on the fife."

"Good." Isaac raises his cup, "Here's to Major Abbott and his success in sending us more men."

•••

A week later, Sergeant Asa Wilkins, the younger brother of Sergeant Robert Wilkins, arrives at Isaac's tent leading seven men. Asa carries himself with confidence and determination, much like his older brother. He introduces the new men to Isaac. From Hollis, Joel and Andrew Bailey, who are brothers in their mid-twenties. Stephen Powers, who is even younger than Will Burton.

From Wilton is Ichabod Perry, the fifteen-year-old son of Wilton's town clerk. He raises a hand with a sealed letter toward Isaac. "A letter from your wife, Captain Frye, sir."

Isaac takes the letter and gives Perry a nod and thanks to him.

Wilkins hands Isaac another letter. "Sir, from Major Abbot," Then he introduces the remaining men as Abijah Allen and Nathan Fish from Mason. Allen looks to about the same age as Isaac, and Fish is well into his forties."

Isaac points toward the partially finished redoubt about fifty yards off where several dozen men work. "Sergeant Wilkins is- I mean your brother is over there. I'm going to have to call you Sergeant Asa to keep the two of you straight in my head. Find your brother. He'll show you where to set up the tents, and he's in charge of assigning messes."

Perry speaks out before realizing he should have waited, "What are messes?"

Sergeant Asa looks to Isaac, who nods very slightly, giving him permission to respond. "Messes are the men with whom you cook, eat, and share a tent."

The new men march to the redoubt, leaving Isaac with a moment to himself. He unseals and reads the letter from Elizabeth.

"Wilton, April 18, 1777

Dearest Husband,

I have yet to receive any lines from you, though I hope and expect we are both writing at this moment. Unhappily there is more ill news than good to share. I will Begin with the good, as it Happened first. Two days after you left Sarah Rideout's baby came. A beautiful baby girl. I am also quite certain I am Again with Child. I pray daily for its good health.

In spite of that news, we are in a melancholy state. Two days ago Phebe Parker's baby died, then yesterday Sarah Rideout's youngest son John died. I cannot recall two such years in a row as we have had.

I pray you are safe and dry, as it has been very rainy here. The boys are fine, and Father and sisters send their love and affection.

Your Loving Wife

Elizabeth

Isaac takes a moment and re-reads Elizabeth's letter twice more, letting the news sink in. Then he unseals the letter from Major Abbott.

Honor and Valor

"Wilton, May 5, 1777

Capt. Frye,

I send this letter with Sergeant Asa Wilkins, younger brother of Sergeant Robert Wilkins who is already in your company. Our efforts to fill your company have grown more difficult. The province now lacks the funds for bounties and we depend upon the towns and prominent citizens to sponsor soldiers. As such they deemed it better than naught to enlist men for the term of eight months. Pvts Powers and the Bailey Brothers are enlisted under these terms. The Baileys are known to be superior woods men and hunters. Ichabod Perry comes in place of his uncle Jonas, who is severely ill. Ezra Fuller is similarly ill and will be sent along as soon as can be arranged. Pvts Allen and Fish are 3-years men, as is Sergeant Wilkins.

Your most Humble and Obedient Servant,

Major Abiel Abbot

Isaac walks with Captain Beal three days later along the western shore of Lake Champlain. They stop a hundred yards north of the outermost of the fortifications of the French Lines. Beal adds to a map he is drawing of the locations the enemy might disembark troops and where they might find cover. Beal notices a pair of batteaux beginning the journey across the lake towards them. He takes out a small telescope and brings it into focus. "Looks to be Captain Stone's scouting party." He pauses, his effort to make out details through the imperfect device intensifies. "Ha! They've got a couple of prisoners."

Isaac squints, but cannot discern the figures in the batteaux. "Redcoats?"

"No, look more like woodsmen or trappers. Let's finish quickly, I want to hear what this is about."

Almost an hour later, Beal and Isaac intercept Captain Stone, who comes their way from the fort. "Was that your scout just returned with a pair of prisoners?"

Stone grins in return, "You don't mince words, do you, Zach? Yup, those were my men. They took a couple of woodsmen claiming to be living north of here in the Grants. One says he was recently up in Quebec and told of the enemy's building ships at St. Johns. I hope you two made good work of mapping the shoreline."

Isaac responds, "Aye, we did. Did you see any reason to trust these men?"

"No, not really. But that's the new general's problem now, isn't it." Stone juts his jaw out, offering a sarcastic grin.

Beal cocks an eyebrow at Stone's mention of the new general, "You met General St. Clair?"

Stone nods once, "I was in the room, though he spent his time questioning my sergeant. The general did a fine job of it, though I'm still not inclined to worship any general from Pennsylvania."

Beal slaps Stone on the shoulder. "Ha, that's no religion for me either."

Isaac adds, "Nor me. Their men turned out to be a bunch of quarrelsome rascals last fall."

Stone raises his hands to signal he needs to move along. "I've got to see to my men. I'll let you know if I learn anything more."

•••

Corporal Martin arrives at Isaac's tent in the early afternoon two days later. "Captain Frye?"

Isaac sits inside, sewing a button onto a waistcoat, sees the corporal through the open flap. "What is it, Corporal Martin?"

"A runner arrived not a minute ago from the fort. Colonel Scammell's in the fort now, reporting to General St. Clair. We've got orders to parade immediately."

"Very well. Inform the sergeants and pass the word to the officers."

"Yessir." Martin dashes off, and within half a minute, Hawkins pokes his head in. "You heard the news?"

"Only that Colonel Scammell arrived. Was there more?"

"Looks like he has a company of men with him, but no details. They're already marching from the fort."

Within five minutes, most of the men from the five companies

Honor and Valor

already encamped have formed their ranks. Scammell and three other officers are mounted and continue to the head of the formation. Captain Daniel Livermore orders his company to a halt joining the other companies.

Scammell dismounts and calls for all the officers to attend him. As Isaac strides up, he gets a closer look at Captain Livermore, who is two inches shorter with a broad open face, dark mousy brown hair, and a calm, almost detached demeanor. Isaac recalls him as being one of the lieutenants in Colonel Reed's regiment but did not know him well.

As soon as all the officers reach Scammell, he addresses them. "Gentlemen, it is my honor to introduce to you Lieutenant Colonel Andrew Colburn, Major Henry Dearborn, and Adjutant Nicholas Gilman." As he speaks, he motions to a wiry man in his forties with smooth, hard-looking leathery skin as being Colburn. Then a much younger man in his mid-twenties who is slightly taller than Isaac and who wears a confident smile as Dearborn. Gilman is younger still, and his large eyes are familiar. Isaac realizes him to be the son of New Hampshire's treasurer. Scammell introduces each of the captains in turn and asks them to present their company's lieutenants and ensigns.

After the introductions, Scammell explains, "I'll inspect the men next. An hour after that, the captains are to meet at my tent." Scammell orders the captains and junior officers back to their companies and spends the next hour inspecting the men.

Isaac waits outside Scammell's marquee tent with Stone and Weare. Beal arrives next. "Gentlemen, it seems today is a day of new arrivals. I just heard Colonel-, I mean General Poor arrived with the first and second regiments."

Weare gives a little snort, and in a wry tone, "I hope they brought something to eat."

Livermore jogs up to the group. "I hope I'm not late."

Weare shakes his head. "We're waiting for the Colonel to call us in. He's going over the notes from the inspection with the adjutant."

On cue, Gilman emerges from the tent. "Gentlemen, Colonel Scammell is ready."

Charles E. Frye

The captains file in. Scammell, who sits at a field desk already involved with several sheaves of paper, nods appraisingly. He rises and steps around to the front of the field desk. Even Captain Stone is several inches shorter than Scammell who towers over Livermore, the shortest of the five.

"Gentlemen, we haven't much time. General Poor has arrived and I expect to be called to meet him shortly. However, my first order of business is to convey that it is my honor to be served by such able and dedicated men as yourselves. I expect we will be tested in the coming months, and I'll do my utmost to deserve the honor of this command. My remaining order of business is to redouble recruiting efforts. The state has given out the last of its bounty monies. We will also need to find those men willing to furnish bounties and prevail on their devotion to our cause."

Scammell pauses and takes up one of the sheets of paper. "Captain Frye, your company is incomplete by eleven men. You will repair immediately to Amherst, Hollis, and the other towns in your quarter and do your utmost to recruit and fill up your company. Use your gravitas as a captain as you remind every man of his patriotic obligations. When we stopped in Keene, I was able to secure the enlistments of twenty-six men to add to Captain Gregg's company."

Scammell pauses and takes a deep breath, expelling it slowly before he continues. "Tis, however, my duty to inform you that Captain Gregg resigned due to his poor health. His lieutenant, William Ellis, is to be the captain of that company. Captains Weare, Stone, and Livermore, you are to send one of your officers back to New Hampshire as well. Their goal is ten men each by the fifteenth of June. That would give us upwards of forty men we sorely need."

Scammell sets the paper with the recruiting needs down and smiles. "I do have some good news. Within a week, we will have new firelocks. The French have sent us enough to outfit all three regiments from our state. Captains Gray and McClary are bringing them in with their companies. Captain Ellis and his men will join them when they reach Keene, which should have been," he raises his eyes as he calculates, "yesterday."

Stone clears his throat, and Scammell looks his way. "Yes, Captain

Stone?"

"Any chance we'll have uniforms for the men, sir?"

Scammell grimaces and shakes his head. "I am afraid not any time soon. Therefore, you must ensure the men keep what clothes they have in good repair."

Seeing no further questions, Scammell continues, "Those leaving to recruit are to depart at first light tomorrow. I'll arrange for you to have horses."

4 FLIGHT

July 5, 1777

"The Enemy appeared on the Mount above on the S.W. opening a Battery, a large ship came up. a high wind at N. the Enemy made a disposition of an attack but were prevented by the high wind or from some other motive, but now appeared to be in readiness to open there Batteries. About 10 o clock at night. A Speedy retreat was ordered and the main body of the army got off from Ty & Mount Independence a little before Sun rise followed by the Enemy but did but little damage."

Journal entry of Colonel Jeduthan Baldwin

In the west, the twilight sky holds the last of glow of daylight as Isaac ducks into his tent. The pair of candles on his field desk give enough light to see as he settles onto his cot and pulls off his boots. Before he can finish a long sigh, the sound of Hawkins clearing his throat too noisily intrudes. "William Adrian, come in."

Hawkins enters the tent with a sheepish grin. Isaac motions to a folding stool, and Hawkins flips it open and sits.

"My apologies for disturbing your evening. I'm glad you've rejoined us. You missed near the whole of June."

"Yes, though Colonel Scammell wasn't particularly pleased when he learned I brought just three new men given all that time."

Hawkins quirks a skeptical grin at Isaac. "I expect he knew captains and lieutenants, even Continentals, wouldn't have the same influence he did in Keene last month. Captain Ellis told how he cajoled more than a dozen men into signing at one meeting."

"Aye. At least I had some luck in Wilton. But, before I get to that, I have a letter for you from your wife." Isaac hands Hawkins the letter. "She says all is well."

"Thank you."

"Elizabeth and Abby, along with the Rideouts and Stevens, came to an agreement with the Reverend Livermore. He'll provide lessons every other week. They'll take Phebe Parker's older children too."

"Good. The Reverend's a natural teacher. I still say it was foolish business him being dismissed."

"Aye, it was. How has it been here?"

"More drilling. That began a few days after you left. Scammell has his mind set upon our being the best-drilled regiment in the whole army. He's convinced we've got an advantage for looking like militia for our lack of uniforms. We need more men and not just our regiment. There's fewer than half of what was here last summer and fall. That's not enough to hold these lines and Camp Independence. There's a rumor Burgoyne is only feinting in our direction and will march by here on his south to overwhelm General Washington. It's nonsense. They'd need supplies, and we'd cut him off."

Isaac's eyebrows rise involuntarily, though he lowers his voice. "Who carried such a ridiculous rumor?"

"General Poor after you left. Though the bearer is incidental. Apparently, Congress is certain of this idea."

Isaac closes his eyes and bows his head turning back and forth in disbelief. "Is he playing politics?"

Hawkins shrugs. "No way for us to know. You mentioned having some luck in Wilton?"

"Aye, but nowhere else. Beyond the three men I brought, three others will come later."

Hawkins raises an optimistic eyebrow. "Who are the three new men?"

"You likely know Humphrey Cram. Then there's Peter Chandler

and David Heseltine, who came this past year to live in Wilton. Both from Massachusetts. Chandler, I know from Andover."

"Good, we can definitely use them. What of the other three?"

"Asa Pierce from Wilton, Matthew Worthington from Mason, and John Ball from Hollis. They will join us next winter or spring, depending on where we are. Those three got bounties for only eight months. Too short a term if you ask me."

Hawkins drops his eye to the earth at his feet and shakes his head with deliberate slowness. "It was disappointing to hear there weren't enough bounties to fill the regiment."

"I did succeed in engaging a deacon from Mason to provide Fuller's bounty. Most of the men who signed in the past month only did so when such was the case. Of us that Scammell sent, we got twenty-four new men. I believe that justified him sending us."

"Far better than not."

"Any other news here?"

"What you expected. Thomas Powell is the drum sergeant major now and moved to the colonel's company. The rest are here, a few have been sick, nothing serious. The hunting trips ended a few weeks ago. The enemy's scouts are now all around us to the west. The fortifications are in good repair, and I think we could hold them off if Burgoyne comes at us. Our scouts say Burgoyne's got more than double our number. We all worry about being spread too thin to hold these lines. We all expect Burgoyne will attack soon. In a few days or a week at most. Depends on how soon the generals tire of sending threats and insults back and forth."

Isaac nods once. "You think the men are ready?"

"Their drill has improved. Ballard is now competent as a drummer. We tried both Drury and Burton at fife. Burton finally got up the gumption to do it well. He was too timid at first. He's young. I had the sergeants and corporals ride all the young ones into line, and Burton took the longest. Yesterday, he finally showed he could do it well."

"Good. I needed some good news to write home about. Elizabeth's been getting an earful at services from Holt's, Gray's, and Burton's mothers."

"How about Elizabeth? Is she getting help?"

"Sarah is staying at the farm again. Elizabeth can run much of the farm herself with Sarah minding the boys. Oh, and she's with child."

Hawkins cocks an eyebrow and grins at Isaac, who cannot help himself and returns the grin twofold. "She says this one's a girl for sure."

"Your four boys seem a strong precedent. I'd bet on another son. Though I got my son on the fourth try, so I suppose Abby's been giving Elizabeth hope."

Isaac winks and adds, "Of course she would. Sarah and Elizabeth bought five goslings from Timothy Gray, Joseph's father. Those will be good for the boys to raise this year. I hope there's a hen or two so they get some eggs once they're grown."

Hawkins rises. "Good for them. We should get some sleep. We've been rising at first light. It gives us a few hours to drill before breakfast. Thank you for bringing the letter."

"You're welcome and good night."

Throughout the camp on the afternoon of June thirtieth, the drummers begin beating the rolling burr signaling alarm and to arms. The men scramble from the places where they are digging and building to the bell of arms, a small protective tents for their muskets. Within three minutes, two thousand men, now ready, gaze outward from the fortifications.

Moving to the north, Isaac catches sight of and angles toward Hawkins, who directs Will and Uriah to stay behind him but not far from his position. The terrain is flat, and from where they stand, it is impossible to see over the fortifications and learn the location of the enemy. Isaac looks to the fort's walls for the colonels and generals to see the direction of their spyglasses.

Turning to Hawkins, Isaac points north to where his men lean, ready to rise, on the sloped banks of piled and packed earth that hold the parapet in place. "Make sure the men keep low, and nobody rises til ordered to fire."

Isaac turns again to check the activity in the fort. A new red and white striped flag with thirteen white stars arrayed on a blue field in the upper corner has been hoisted. Below the flag, a group of officers direct their attention to the west. A moment later, from that direction, the report of a single musket firing from within the fortifications echoes off the hillsides.

The shot causes Isaac to whip around in time to see every man rise, nearly in unison, and fire outward, including some officers. The concussion of so many muskets firing at one time rocks Isaac back a half step as the cannons from the fort fire. The men on the parapet reload and fire again before Isaac can make out the orders to hold fire being shouted from the direction of the fort. The men get off another volley before Isaac and the other captains can gain their men's attention and call them back to order.

A gentle wind sends the billowing mass of musket smoke northward. Less than two minutes pass before Ensign Leeman runs in from the west. "The enemy's hightailing it into the woods. That first shot dropped one who'd gotten too close." Leeman stops for a moment to catch his breath, then chuckles half to himself, and exclaims with some dismay, "Jesus! We just wasted a ton of lead and powder."

The drummers pick up the signal conveying the alarm is over. Isaac feeling relief more than anything else sighs deeply. "Thank you, Ensign. Go collect our men and direct them back to their work."

A few minutes later, Captain Beal saunters over to Isaac, who is inspecting his men's spacing of the sharpened logs of the abatis. "Would you believe we didn't kill anyone at all?"

Isaac looks up, his expression verging on exasperation. "You're jesting, right?"

"Not at all. Not even a little bit. Wilkinson sent a corporal and some men to fetch the poor soul we killed on that first shot and bury him. The rascal jumped up and started spewing nonsense. The ball stunned him good, but otherwise, he's fine. So they made a prisoner out of him."

Isaac shakes his head. "Looks like we all played an act in a theater of idiots."

Beal laughs and claps Isaac on the shoulder." Well, I saw it as the men let loose a good bit of fight we'd bottled up for too long."

"That as well, but still, every man on the walls fired without orders."

Honor and Valor

"It was a good show, but that's all it was. I expect the militia General St. Clair requested to reinforce us are going to be rather late. We'll have to see if they can break a siege instead of eating our food." Beal turns toward his company's part of camp, and after a few steps, looks back and grins. "You're supposed to laugh at that Captain Frye."

•••

Isaac sits at the desk inside his tent. The candles burn low beside the notes and diagrams of the command sequences for maneuvering his company in battle. From outside, rapid footsteps approach and an unfamiliar voice barks, "Captain Frye. Colonel Scammell orders the captains to attend him immediately at his tent."

"I'll be there in an instant." Imagining an imminent attack, Isaac re-buttons his waistcoat as fast as he can and grabs his hat as he rushes out of the tent.

He arrives at Scammell's tent, several privates are already half done with the job of taking it down. Five of the captains are already present. Colburn and Dearborn flank Scammell. Captains Ellis and Stone arrive within half a minute.

Scammell wears a grim but determined expression. "Gentlemen, not ten minutes ago, we received orders to evacuate this position and the fort. The enemy has or is very close to placing a cannon atop Mount Defiance." He points up in the direction of the nearest mountain top. "This place is very much within range."

Scammell pauses to let his words sink in. "Most of us will be under General St. Clair and march for Castleton. A small detachment will take our cannon and the bulk of the army's baggage on batteaux south by way of Skenesborough. Colonel Francis will have charge of a rearguard to protect wagons carrying the invalids and provisions and will follow the main body. The entire Second New Hampshire Regiment will be with the rearguard, though we need to assign an officer and guards to accompany our regiment's sick and injured."

Scammell pauses and scans the assembled captains. He settles on Isaac. "They will come from your company Captain Frye. Who do you assign? One officer and two guards."

Isaac thinks for a few seconds and makes his decision. "Ensign Leeman and privates Oliver and Foster."

Scammell nods once, then adds, "As soon as we finish, send Leeman to Colonel Hale to learn where to muster our sick and injured men. The two privates will have charge of the wagons to carry those who cannot march."

"Yessir."

Scammell releases Isaac from his gaze. "As I said, most of our baggage will go down lake to Skenesborough. We must get the batteaux loaded by midnight. Captains Gray and Weare, your companies are assigned to guard and assist with the baggage. The rest of us march at midnight with the main body. That leaves two hours to break camp, load, and assemble to march. Any questions?"

The gathering of officers waits motionless, shocked. Scammell, seeing no reason to wait, dismisses them.

Isaac hurries back toward his tent. As he enters the area of his company's tents, he barks orders for the men to assemble immediately. Within ten minutes, the men are scrambling, taking down tents, packing, and staging the baggage.

Hawkins finds Isaac where his tent stood a few minutes earlier, pulling the cover of his full haversack to meet the buttons. "I've just sent Leeman, Foster, and Oliver to Colonel Hale."

"Thank you. Isaac sighs with an air of disgust. "Retreating, after all we did to invest and fortify this place."

Hawkins hands Isaac a letter. "Leeman wrote a few lines to his mother once he learned of his assignment. He has a firm grasp of the dire nature of his duties."

"I picked him because he's level headed, proven, and a bit of a loner. You and Goodale have wives and children. Foster and Oliver, they're loners too."

"I wasn't challenging. Just conveying the letter to you."

"I know. I know. I needed to say it." Isaac brings a hand to his forehead, massaging his temples with a thumb and index finger. "I just needed to say it."

"I think it was rightly done. Nothing to regret."

"I pray no ill comes of it. Have the men begun to move the baggage to the landing?"

"Not yet. Perhaps in five, not more than ten minutes."

"Hurry them along. Send Sergeant Hall with the first group. His height makes him easy for the rest to find. Once the baggage is moved, assemble the men to march. It's good there's a bridge now since there are nowhere near enough batteaux to convey the baggage and the army."

•••

Will and Uriah wait at the rear of the company. A few steps ahead, the other members of the company form rows flanked by a sergeant on the right and corporal on the left. They stand at rest in anticipation of the orders to face to the right and begin marching. Several minutes after midnight, the barest sliver of a new moon sheds little useful light. Will nudges Uriah with an elbow, and whispers, "Do you know why we're marching tonight?"

Uriah shakes his head once then freezes as Hawkins approaches and addresses them.

"Listen close," Hawkins begins in a low voice, "There will be no music when we march. Ballard, once we reach the fort atop Mount Independence, start a light tap on the rim every fourth step. If we're attacked, both of you find Captain Frye quick as you can, or failing that find me."

Will's eyes go wide, and before he can stop himself, he asks, mimicking Hawkins' low voice, "What's going on?"

Hawkins studies Will for a moment, then leans in. "The enemy has brought cannon atop Mount Defiance. We're well within range and must quit this place. We'll march south through Camp Independence, and that's all anyone knows. Now keep quiet. We'll march shortly."

Standing, as one minute stretches into the next, Will strains his eyes and leans in the direction of Mount Defiance. The weak moonlight silhouettes the hill's profile. A poke of Uriah's drumstick and Uriah pantomiming two deep breaths breaks through Will's near panic. A deep breath makes him aware of his rapid heartbeat. It takes a few more such breaths and a long sigh to break his mind away from the intensity brought on by Hawkins' words.

A minute later, they hear the orders to march called out a few companies ahead. They arrive at the narrow bridge, which forces them to split into columns of twos to cross the lake. As they cross, they pass a few posted sergeants who and who in low voices caution them to keep quiet. Will feels the energy and excitement from earlier ebb, soothed away by the cool air on the lake. By the time they climb the mile to the main fort within Camp Independence, he finds himself shaking his head to keep his eyes open. A hand on his shoulder jolts him awake.

Lieutenant Goodale had somehow got behind him. He gives Will a firm pat on the shoulder. "Steady, we've got a long way to go tonight."

Will can only nod. Awake with the odd sensation of Goodale's hand on his shoulder, even as he sees Goodale striding ahead. Twice he sees Goodale bring other men back into focus.

It takes more than an hour of marching and waiting at intervals to cross Camp Independence. They pass through the southern guardpost of the camp and again hear orders to halt. This time Will is grateful to hear word come back, directing them to take a small drink of water.

The halt lasts over an hour. Several officers ride back and then forward along the column before the march resumes. Colonel Joseph Cilley's First New Hampshire Regiment leads, and Scammell's regiment is next. Within the regiment, they march by company number, putting Isaac's Seventh Company next to last.

Uriah's steady soft tap ... ... tap ... ... tap on the rim of his drum is matched by boots and shoes, meeting the ground in the same rhythm. Will looks into the trees alongside the road. He can see only a few feet and then only the darkest blackness. Several times he hears the soft hooting of an owl.

Keeping his voice low, to himself as much as Uriah, Will wonders, "I'm amazed anyone can find their way on a night like this."

Uriah mumbles, "I'm sure the General has got someone knowing the way to guide us."

Hearing Uriah's words, Corporal Martin drops back and motions with a shake of his head and a finger to his lips for them to be quiet.

Will does not perceive the sunrise. He had grown used Lake Champlain providing a broad eastern horizon and seeing the skies change hue before allowing the rim of the sun to emerge. Within the dense tree cover, daylight seeps in slow stages into the ribbon of space created by the road.

General Poor rides back along the column. He exhorts the men in a soft voice to continue the brisk pace. An hour later, he rides back again, and the daylight allows Will to finally get a close look at the man leading the New Hampshire regiments. Short in stature, and by Will's reckoning, in his fifties. A round face sporting a strong chin and nose. His look is kind and pleasant, but when he notices something, not to his liking, his mouth gets small, and his eyes narrow, giving him a fierce visage.

In the daylight, the pace of the march increases for the ease of seeing where to step. Will and Uriah exchange glances as they pass several men who sit exhausted beside the road. As the sun nears its height for the day, the heat becomes oppressive when they pass through clearings. Will's shirt, soaked back and front, sticks to his skin. Not at like all like a few months ago, marching in the chilly spring air. Today, humidity and heat lay as wool blankets on the land, stewing each man in his clothes.

Ahead, Josiah Stone stumbles and goes to one knee. Corporal Goodman pulls him to the side where they both lean against trees. Will turns as he passes and sees Stone's chest heaving from exertion.

Every five or ten minutes, Will sees men, especially older and heavier men in the same state, exhausted from the pace and the heat. Will adjusts his pack, filled with three days of food, a blanket and a change of clothes. Twenty pounds of extra ammunition make his as heavy as any other man's pack.

They come into a large area of cleared fields where a pair of farms occupy a gentle slope. Ahead of Will, someone asks if this is Hubbardton or Castleton, with emphasis on the latter. The answer is Hubbardton, and Castleton is another six miles.

Orders to halt ripple back along the column. They wait in the hot sun. Lack of sleep and twenty miles of soreness in his feet give Will a powerful urge to lie down in the shade of the trees fifty yards away.

Isaac calls Martin out of the ranks and sends him ahead to learn the reason for the halt.

Martin returns shortly with the news they will stop here and rest, allowing the rear guard and stragglers to catch up. Hawkins gives the men brief instructions to find their rest in the shady woods at the edge of the field. Sergeant Hughes and Privates Carleton and Gray will have guard duty for the first hour.

Two hours later, the aroma of roasting meat triggers Will's empty stomach, and he awakens. Several of the men are awake, including Martin, who sees Will's eyes scanning about for the fires where the meat is cooking. "It's not for us, Burton. We drew three days of provisions. Eat a bit of that if you're hungry. Not all the regiments got provisions, so those men have to eat what can be butchered and cooked while we rest."

After eating a little, Will rises and stretches. Looking about, he sees Josiah Parker and Corporal Goodman rejoined the company while he slept.

Martin doesn't miss the opportunity, "Since you're up Burton, take my firelock and relieve Lewis. We had to double the guards on account of an enemy raiding party being in the area. Keep a sharp eye out. Loyalist rangers and Indian scouts. Not likely redcoats." Martin motions to his firelock and then points into the woods. "Lewis is that way about thirty paces."

The woods are still, and Will can see no sign of any movement. With an army about, the birds are quiet, making the woods seem too still. An hour later, the order comes to form ranks and resume the march.

About an hour into the march toward Castleton, orders ripple back along the companies to halt and ware the woods for enemy scouts. The company scrambles to form two lines on either side of the road. Within a few minutes, the sporadic reports of musket fire sound from up ahead. They stare intently into the woods for signs of movement. Some of the men lie on their bellies while others kneel and use trees for cover. Will and Uriah wait in the middle of the road with Isaac and Hawkins, ready to relay their commands on their instruments.

In the distance ahead, they hear a brisk firing of muskets and then

Honor and Valor

silence. Word comes back that the lead elements of the column encountered the enemy raiding party and took some as prisoners.

The march resumes, and two hours later, they reach Castleton and make camp such as they can without tents or baggage. Much like Hubbardton, it is a place of a few farms on the north side of a large creek. Within fifteen minutes, Will finds himself positioned on the east side of camp at the rear of the picquet, a line of guards assigned at the perimeter of the encampment. Will's instructions from Hawkins were brief, "Keep yourself hidden and if any guard signals, falls, or goes out of sight, sound the alarm." Will's chooses a fallen log near a large chestnut tree a few dozen yards to the north of the road to Rutland. He can see the sentries on the road and those arrayed in the trees in front of him.

Only half an hour passes before a commotion inside the camp gives Will a brief moment of conflict before hazarding a glance backward.

The day is still light enough he can make out two regiments of militia forming ranks. Many of the men vent frustration about their enlistments being expired. Their anger rises, and they shout their intentions to march home. Turning back to his duty, Will hears someone give their orders to march. Within a minute, the lead elements of the militia stride past the confused sentries who were not expecting this exodus.

As the last elements from the first regiment pass the sentries, General Poor rides at a furious pace to cut off the leading company. Poor's visage is florid as he shouts at the commanding officer. "What's the meaning of this, you cowards?"

More horses race up alongside the militia as General Poor continues berating the militia's commanders. "If you don't turn around at once, I swear I'll send my men to fire on you."

General St. Clair and his aides arrive. St. Clair cuts Poor off with a motion of his hand and begins speaking in a tone low enough Will cannot hear. The militia commanders continue in their obstinate poses as General St. Clair speaks. Within a few minutes St. Clair's speech includes what the militia commanders need to hear, and they relax and order their men to reverse course.

Well past dusk Will hears someone approaching his position from inside the camp. Another of the regiment's fifers motions that he is here to relieve him.

After a few minutes of searching, Will locates his company and his mess, which was now the company's corporals. Will's hopes the corporals had cooked something for dinner was in vain, as they were already preparing to get a few hours of sleep. Martin motions to a place on the ground for Will to sleep.

Will asks, "Any news?"

"The enemy captured our baggage at Skenesborough, so we won't go there tomorrow. We are to be up early, and when the rearguard arrives, we'll march, though none of us knows where."

Will, feeling unsettled, asks, "You ever hear of anything like our situation before?"

Martin shakes his head, "Never."

Corporal Smith chimes in, "Even gettin' run outta Canada last summer didn't match the pace of today's march."

Corporal Godfrey perks up at that. "You were in Canada too?"

"Aye, with Reed's regiment. In Towne's company."

Godfrey nods. "I was with Stark." He turns to Corporal Goodman. "What about you, Goody?"

Goodman already lying down, rolls and props his head on his elbow. "I didn't sign on last year. I was in Boston from the first alarm with Spaulding's company in Reed's regiment. I was at the rail fence with that lot. Like Martin says, we never marched anything like today. Christ, I thought I was gonna hafta carry Parker the last few miles. Once I got some water into him, he recovered a bit."

Goodman, also the eldest of the company's corporals by ten years, lies back down. "Get a bite to eat Burton, then sleep. I can tell morning's gonna come too early for sure."

After what feels like only a minute, Will wakes from a deep sleep. He hears the groans and complaints of men waking up sooner than they wished. The faint lightening of the sky tells him sunrise is still several minutes off. He rolls his blanket and pushes it into his pack. Looking around, he notices he was among the last to wake and cannot figure how he did not hear the rest of the men moving.

At that moment, Sergeant Hughes walks into their midst. "Listen up lads. Until we get word from the rearguard, we stay put. Eat then get some water for the march."

For two hours, nothing happens. The men rest, make cartridges, and talk in small groups. Then, like a wave flooding through the camp, men hold up hands and turn their ears to the north. The barely audible reports of distant musket fire drift in. In seconds cries to form ranks break the quiet.

The men wait in formation for thirty minutes. Several officers ride into the camp from the north. Following them are the two militia regiments Will saw trying to leave the evening before. A minute later, the orders to march east toward Rutland arrive.

The pace of the march is almost as quick as the previous day, and the heat as oppressive. Shortly after noon, they come to Rutland and turn south. Feeling lightheaded at least twice, Will wonders at the wisdom their rapid course. Even more men than yesterday struggle and drop from the ranks throughout the afternoon. They march another six miles south along Otter Creek then encamp for the night. The area is clear of the trees used to build part of the road. Will recognizes the place as being the junction to the road leading to Number Four. They had passed this way on the way to Fort Ticonderoga.

The men wait in ranks while the officers decide where to place the regiments and set picquets. Isaac returns to his company and addresses them. "Our rearguard was attacked this morning at Hubbardton." His voice becomes monotone. "They were driven from the field. The militia that marched in this morning defied orders to go to their defense. General St. Clair dismissed them just now." He scans the company's ranks, looking at the men's faces. "Those on picquets tonight, keep watch for our men who were in this morning's battle coming in through the woods. Double the usual number on picquet duty to ensure the enemy don't surprise us."

•••

After addressing the company, Isaac turns to find Hawkins and Goodale waiting. "Any luck finding shelter for tonight?"

Both shake their heads. Hawkins adds, "Just generals and colonels with a proper roof tonight. We can cut some saplings for a lean-to."

"Then let's get the piquets set and find some higher ground to spend the night on. Set Sergeant Asa Wilkins in charge of the piquet, and send the older Sergeant Wilkins and Carlton to wait on Colonel Scammell. That'll leave Hughes and Hall with the rest of the company. Once the Colonel's heard from General Poor, I expect I'll be called to plan tomorrow's march."

Hawkins bobs head once in agreement. "I'll find the Wilkins."

Goodale squints, his habit when in thought. "I'll check with the other lieutenants. There's got to be a barn or someplace more comfortable for us to spend the night."

An hour later, Ebenezer Carlton finds Isaac waiting with Captain Livermore. Both men clad in only shirts and trousers. Like most of the men, they had hung their sweat-soaked coats and waistcoats to dry. Carlton salutes them and offers, "Sirs, Colonel Scammell's callin' for the captains. He says to meet in the road about 100 yards south of the junction to Number Four."

Isaac thanks Carlton and dismisses him. Turning to Captain Livermore, "Let's be on our way."

"Yes, I've learned the Colonel doesn't like to be kept waiting."

Already walking, Isaac grins. "You're right, waiting is what he despises most."

They find Scammell already surrounded by the other captains, Dearborn and Colburn. Unlike the six captains, who all look as though they'd done more than a hard day's work. The higher-ranking officers, who had ridden horses for the past two days, still wear their waistcoats. Though their trousers and boots carry a good bit more spattered mud than usual.

As soon as Isaac and Livermore join the group, Scammell begins. "Gentlemen, as you have likely surmised, there'll be little rest for us on this march. General St. Clair received intelligence of the enemy taking our baggage at Skenesborough. Our guards now make for Fort Anne. Thus, tomorrow we will march to Manchester. Twill be a long march on a poor road. Make sure your men know their utmost efforts will be required. We've also learned the enemy sent only a quarter of

Honor and Valor

their forces to pursue. We are now a full day ahead of them. I want the men to know that General Poor and I are pleased with their effort in reaching this place today. They have borne up well. Do what you can to keep their spirits high."

Scammell pauses and studies the expressions of the six captains to judge whether his words are having the intended impact. "Starting tonight, we will rotate the guard duty, starting with Captains Beal and McClary's men for tonight. Captain Livermore and Stone, your men are to get their rest tonight. Captains Frye and Ellis, you will each pick ten of your most capable men and a sergeant. They are to go halfway back to Rutland and collect the stragglers and get them here in good order. No wagons. Take four horses to carry any who can no longer walk. Once they return, report to me the number of men they collect. Any questions?" Scammell gives them a moment to respond before dismissing them.

Twilight envelopes the wooded roadside an hour later. Isaac, Hawkins, and Goodale sit twenty yards upslope of the road with their backs to a pair of large oak trees. Between the trees, a frame of saplings with leafy branches rests awaiting any rain that may come. The camp is quiet. No fires. A light breeze pulls strands of pipe smoke through the air.

Hawkins stretches and resettles himself. "Looks like you finally got to meet Captain Livermore. What's your impression?"

Isaac responds, "Aye. As even-tempered a fellow as I can remember meeting. He seems to know what he's about."

Hawkins chuckles. "All business, and damn good at it from what I can see. Everyone says the same. Captain Gray got it right when he said, the man's got the most infectious confidence of any he'd ever met"

Goodale, in a drowsy voice, adds, "Our Captain Gray, he does have a way with words. The Colonel's the only one I've met who's better."

"Aye," starts Isaac, "the Colonel's a natural orator. I'm fairly certain he makes it all up as he's speaking. His wit is sharp. Major Dearborn seems to be the only one who can follow it all."

Hawkins adds, "The Major's a determined one if there ever was."

For a moment, no one responds, then Goodale begins lightly

snoring.

Later, Sergeant Robert Wilkins climbs up most of the way up from the road, making enough noise to bring Isaac out of his dozing state. "Sirs-"

Isaac holds up a hand to cut Wilkins off and motions that they should go back down to the road together. Once on the road, Wilkins reports his detachment found and returned with forty-five men. Major Dearborn intercepted them as they returned and has the report.

Isaac instructs him to get his men settled and sleeping.

In the dim pre-dawn light, Isaac waits beside his company already formed up and ready to march. The air carries a promise of rain. Isaac works a knot in his lower back, a favor from the oak tree.

Hawkins joins him. "It seems everyone is surly and not themselves this morning."

"Aye, True. Though I suspect today's march will take their minds off the night's accommodations."

Hawkins murmurs his agreement. From ahead, the orders to march begin to get louder. "Here we go."

Within minutes, the road narrows and is in poor repair, forcing the men to go two abreast. All morning they climb gently southward along the east side of Otter Creek. Rain begins to fall at noon, becoming steady and heavy within thirty minutes. Scammell and General Poor pass back along the column, admonishing the men to keep their powder and cartridges dry. They soon return with orders for men to go back to help the several wagons through the mud.

Late in the afternoon, orders to halt trickle back slowly along the distended column. Dearborn rides back again, stopping to address Isaac and Captain Ellis. "We're at Dorset. Move your men up past the clearing with the farms and find someplace to sleep. Stone's and Livermore's companies have the guard tonight and will set the picquet beyond you."

After acknowledging Dearborn's instructions, Isaac asks, "Dorset? How far is Manchester?"

Dearborn, responds as he turns his horse, "Another six miles. The rain and mud slowed us. Tell the men not to eat all their provisions.

The earliest we will see any stores will be at Manchester."

Isaac and his men make their way ahead and find Dorset to be another clearing with a group of a few farms, similar to Hubbardton and Castleton. They move uphill into the woods but discover all the trees to be soaked, offering no refuge from the rain. They try to sleep with their backs to trees, some lean, others squat to rest their legs. From the tree across from Isaac, Goodale mutters, "Would've been better to be on the picquet tonight. Infernal rain's keeping me from any sleep at all."

At dawn, Isaac hears calls to form ranks coming from below. Still wet, but no longer soaked, he notes the rain has stopped and pushes himself up from the squatting pose he'd spent the night in. "Wake up all ye fine Yankee gents, it's time to go."

Too little movement and a good deal of complaining greet Isaac's command. Isaac adds volume and annoyance to his tone, "If you don't believe I would personally give each of you twenty lashes for indolence, then you're damned fools. Now get moving."

Before Isaac can get the last words out, every man is up and gathering his pack or wringing out wet clothes. Within three minutes, they form ranks ready to march to the road. Dearborn strides toward the formation. "Captain Frye, seeing as your men are ready, send them to that barn on the other side of the road. Have them load the provisions General St. Clair purchased last night into our wagons. As soon as they're loaded, we begin marching for Fort Edward."

Goodale signals Isaac to indicate he will take the men to the barn Dearborn pointed out. Isaac catches the major's attention. "Is there any other news? I've heard nothing about Ensign Leeman, who was at Hubbardton."

Dearborn shakes his head slightly, then his look softens to show he shares Isaac's concerns. "Nothing from that quarter. We got news of a battle at Fort Anne yesterday, but no specifics beyond what we already heard. Our baggage lost, and most of our men got away."

Isaac thanks Dearborn and moves on to follow his men.

By midmorning, the clouds break up, and by noon the day turns steamy beneath a hot summer sun as they pass through Manchester. By mid-afternoon, the roads dry enough for the wagons to pass with little assistance. Late in the afternoon, they halt at Arlington, a village of a dozen or so farms.

Isaac pulls Hawkins aside. "We'll split tonight's piquet duty into two shifts. Take half the men and get an hour of sleep now. You and those men will have the first shift until midnight. This way, the men get at least half a night of sleep." Hawkins gives Isaac a weak grin. "You'll get no argument from me on being first to get an hour of sleep."

Early the next morning, just as the light begins to add color to the day, Isaac walks in amongst his men who are still asleep. He can tell it will be much hotter today. The muggy night retained much of the previous day's heat, making it unpleasant to sleep. He notices Sergeant Hall is awake and squats beside him. "Sergeant, I think the men would be best served to get up now and go down to the creek we've been following and make sure we carry plenty of water. Twill be a hot march today."

"Hall sits up. "Yessir." Then to the men who are beginning to stir. "You heard the captain. Let's get going."

An hour into the day's march, still heading southwest on the road along Batten Kill, Isaac realizes his intuition to have enough water was on target. It is already hotter than the previous day had been at noon. Early in the afternoon, men begin dropping out of the march. Weakness from the meager rations garnered a day earlier, and the day's broiling heat put even the younger men at the point of exhaustion. They continue to march at a grueling pace until late in the afternoon. They halt near Hebron, another small place of only a few farms.

Later in the evening, John Drury finds Isaac speaking with Lieutenants Goodale and Hawkins. Their waistcoats removed to take advantage of a breeze that had begun in the past hour. "Captain Frye, Sir." Drury offers a salute, which Isaac returns. "Sir, Colonel Scammell is calling for the captains to meet to meet with him." Isaac reluctantly retrieves his waistcoat and asks Drury to lead the way.

Scammell waits with Livermore, Colburn, Dearborn, and Adjutant Gilman. They gather in the shade of a barn the generals and colonels put to use as their headquarters.

Scammell paces, his eyes on the ground, as they wait for Ellis, McClary, Beal, and Stone, who arrive within minutes.

"Gentlemen, we've received some news." Scammell's countenance is grim, and his words forced. "As you know, we learned a battle was fought at Fort Anne three days ago. We got news today that our Captain Weare was grievously wounded, and Sergeant Davis from Gray's company was killed in that action. Captain Gray commanded our men during the battle. They came close to defeating the enemy until their reinforcements arrived."

Scammell pauses for a few seconds, taking a deep breath. The set of his jaw relaxes as he takes in the faces of the officers assembled. "General Poor ordered an accounting of our men, particularly in light of rumors of men deserting. As I call you, list off the number and ranks of the men in your company you cannot account for. Captain Stone?"

"Sergeant Knight, my Fifer, and three privates were among the sick at Hubbardton. No Deserters."

"Captain Beal?"

"Two corporals and seven privates among the sick at Hubbardton. No deserters."

"Captain McClary"

"Sergeant Batchelder fell out at some point during the march on the sixth. I presume he has deserted."

"Captain Livermore?"

"One private, sick, at Hubbardton. I heard talk that two men died of exhaustion during today's march?"

Scammell replies, "Yes, the report of two men dying today is accurate. Make sure your men carry enough water. Captain Frye?"

"Ensign Leeman and two privates at Hubbardton. No deserters"

"Captain Ellis?"

"Three privates deserted, I presume, during the march on the sixth."

As they report, Gilman records the tallies. Scammell's jaw once again set, and his tone turns tight and a little angry. "Remind your men that deserters will be found and hanged. Give descriptions of the deserters to Adjutant Gilman, who will send them back to the muster masters."

Scammell pauses and looks to the ground in front of his boots for a moment. When he looks up, his eyes show a fierceness and drive that almost takes Isaac aback. "We've only had a few skirmishes and now five days of hard duty. In the coming weeks, our duty will surely be harsher than these past five days."

Scammell's eyes lock with each of them before continuing, "This is our crucible, and we must use it to bond these men. Tomorrow we march to Fort Edward, where we'll organize to face our enemy. As of tomorrow, the men need to know we are no longer retreating. We will most definitely turn the tables on General Burgoyne. Tell your men we have invaders in our lands, and it is our duty to confound and expel them. At Fort Edward, we begin that work. Get what rest you can. Tomorrow's march will be almost as long as today's."

By noon the following day, Isaac notices a breeze carrying cooler air. As they march into the next break in the trees, Hawkins points to the west, where clouds are building. "Looks like more rain's going to find us before we get to Fort Edward."

Isaac grins. "A month ago, if someone had offered you the choice of a long march on a broiling day or a long march in mud and heavy rain, what you have taken?"

Hawkins barks a short laugh. "I'd have asked for another option."

"Well, today it looks like we get both. No options."

Within fifteen minutes, the clouds complete their approach, and shortly large drops begin to fall. Isaac calls out to his men, "Check your powder. Keep it dry."

Soon the pace of the march slows. They reach the North River, opposite Saratoga, with an hour of daylight remaining.

Honor and Valor

5 TRIALS

> *"... our whole force was Collected at a place called Moses creek about five miles below Fort Edward, where we remaind a number of days & then retreeted to Saratogea, had several scurmishes with Enimies advanc'd parties, consisting most of Indians & their more savage brothers, the tories ..."*
>
> Journal entry of Major Henry Dearborn
> Describing the events from July 5 through August 2, 1777

"How is it this army is so much better at making mud than any other army in the history of armies?" Hawkins stands rooted, ankle-deep in mud, a dozen paces in front of the company. Dense morning fog makes it feel as though they are by themselves instead of in a camp of two thousand soldiers. Hawkins rolls his eyes, keeping them wide to emphasize the rhetorical nature of his question. The men only offer a few weak chuckles in response.

An unexpected response comes from the rear of the company, "We damn well better be the best at making mud, for that's what the generals have ordered us to do."

Hawkins missed Isaac's approach in the fog. As Isaac slogs around to the front of the company Hawkins steps aside. "General Schuyler's got axes and shovels for us. There's food at Fort Edward, and we'll pass through there on the way north. We're assigned the duty of felling trees, ruining bridges, and especially damming creeks. We are to make as much untraversable mud and swamp between Fort Anne and Fort Edward as possible. We'll pick up a day's worth of provisions on the way through Fort Edward and go as far north as we dare."

Knowing what the next two days would bring did not have the hoped-for effect on the men. Instead, they continue to look tired and defeated. A few men sniffle and two sneeze. Isaac raises his voice, "Look here, we spent last night getting rained on, again. If we don't keep busy marching, working, or whatever it is armies do when no enemy's in sight, we will surely get sick. I am sure this is the last place any of you would wish to be sick. If we're out working, that'll be the best thing for us. Now buck up and start acting like the irritating rascals I know the enemy will name us to be once they try to march to meet us."

The men straighten their backs and stand taller as they put their best effort into ignoring the mud, wet clothing, soaked boots, and chilly fog. "Sergeant Hall," Isaac calls out, "march the company up to the road leading north, then halt and wait for Captain Ellis's company. They'll be coming with us."

Isaac turns to Hawkins. "This afternoon, we'll need to find some high ground for a camp. We'll send Corporal Martin out with Eb Carlton, the Youngman brothers, and Tom Blood to scout for signs of the enemy. Then we'll send Sergeant Hughes with Mansfield, Richardson, Hosmer, and the Bailey brothers to get the lay of the land. They're the woodsmen who know how to find the low lying places. After that, we'll get some rest so we can get an early start on the work in the morning. Have Sergeant Wilkins, both of them, and their squads sleep tonight. We'll need them to be fresh tomorrow for picquet duty. Am I missing anything."

"Food. We're all hungry."

"Good point. The sooner we get to Fort Edward, the sooner we eat."

That evening on the west side of a wooded ridge five miles north of Fort Edward Isaac speaks with Hawkins and Goodale. "Tomorrow, we'll need four men for an advanced picquet. Who do you recommend? They need to know to keep off the tops of ridges and keep still once in position."

Goodale responds first. "Joel Bailey and Elijah Mansfield for sure. Bailey's one of the best hunters in the whole province."

Hawkins adds, "Carlton and Lewis. Lewis is almost as quiet as Bailey. Carlton is good and quick at judging difficult situations."

"Very well, put Sergeant Wilkins in charge of them and send them out first. Instruct them to rotate one coming to report to us every hour or so. Robert Wilkins, I mean. Have his brother Asa handle the rest of the men on the picquet."

Late the next morning, Isaac shifts his attention from the men who lever a small bounder into a creekbed to Elijah Mansfield, who trots into their midst. He approaches Isaac. "Cap'n Frye, sir, no sign of the enemy again this past hour. Bailey says he's sure there's no one out here but us and Cap'n Ellis's men."

"Have you seen any of our scouts or rangers? I expect they sent some from Fort Edward to keep an eye on Fort Anne and Skenesborough."

"No, though I expect they're further out than us."

Isaac raises his eyebrows at their good fortune. "Tell Sergeant Wilkins three more hours, then we'll make our way back to Fort Edward."

As Mansfield moves away, Hawkins strides up to Isaac. "Any change?"

"None. Three hours and then back to Fort Edward."

"Good, it's about time fortune smiled on us."

Four afternoons later, Isaac and his company make their way into the New Hampshire part of the Army's camp opposite the small island in the Hudson River that is home to Fort Edward. For shelter, they had built several wigwams and lean-tos. Scammell, Colburn, and Dearborn share a large lean-to. Dearborn rises from beneath as Isaac's company halts and calls out to Isaac. "Capt Frye, come see me once you've dismissed your men."

Dearborn waits for Isaac outside the lean-to. "What progress have your men made these past two days?"

"Five more creeks dammed, and we left over seventy large trees stacked, wedged, and blocking the way. No sign of the enemy."

Honor and Valor

"Excellent. Though I cannot help but wonder what our enemy is doing."

"They'll need to make a new road to reach us. It may be that we've been far more effective in our work than we could have planned for."

"That may be true. Either way, the generals decided to move the majority of our men downriver to the other side of Moses Creek. We will have easier access to supplies, and won't be tempted to move to the Fort where we could be pinned down on that island while Burgoyne and his men take control of the river."

Isaac nods in agreement. "When do we leave?"

"First light tomorrow. Have your men draw two days of provisions tonight."

"Have we got any paper and ink yet?"

"No, and I haven't been able to write reports, much less my family. We've sent messengers home telling that most of us are safe and well."

"Thank you, sir."

•••

Isaac follows his company as they march single-file over the bridge of wagons to cross Moses Creek and continue into camp, half an hour ahead of sunset. In the week since making this camp, muddy trails had branched off the river road into the wooded hillsides where wigwams occupy every piece of ground flat enough for a man to sleep on.

After Sergeant Hall calls for the men to halt, Isaac takes a good look at them. Several have torn shirts or trousers. All wear the dirt of two weeks of cutting or digging in the woods in heat and in heavy rain. As Isaac is about to dismiss them to eat and rest before taking a shift of picquet duty, a familiar voice calls out, "Captain Frye, hold your men there a moment."

Major Abbot approaches, and Isaac offers him a salute. "How do you do Major, tis good to see you."

Abbot stops before Isaac and waves a bundle of papers above his head. To the men, "I've got some letters from home." His expression changes to a small regretful frown. "I wish I'd known of your need for paper and ink. I'd have brought some."

"I understand. I'm sure some will arrive soon."

Abbot calls the names of over half the men, including Isaac and his lieutenants. Isaac dismisses the men. Hunger and fatigue forgotten, the men with letters stand absorbed reading in the waning light.

"Wilton, July 16, 1777
To my Dearest Husband, I pray these lines find you well and with time to write. We got the news of Fort Ticonderoga falling into the hands of the enemy. Our prayers for your safety are constant.

The news came from one of your men, a Mister Foster. He came into town five days after the battle he was in to find Major Abbot. He told Major Abbot he was with the rear guard helping the sick men make their way on the march and once the enemy had run our men off the field, they all had to make their own way. He knew not what became of the men he was with. At No 4 he volunteered to take another wounded man to his home. Major Abbott sent him to his home owing to Mister Foster being very sick himself.

The Major says he will carry these lines and others from Wilton to No 4 tomorrow. We are all safe and well. Isaac Jr. tends the new geese, they are adept at keeping weeds out of the garden. With all the rain we have a fine crop of vegetables. I miss and worry terribly for your safety and for all the men with you.

Your Loving Wife,

Elizabeth Frye

Major Abbot waits for Isaac to finish. "We got the news Captain Weare was wounded. Do you know how he fairs? I got to know him over the winter on my trips to Exeter."

"Mister Hovey, he's our surgeon, says he's not doing well. A bad wound. He's in a hospital at Albany, a little better than half a day from here by batteaux. If you have time, I expect it would raise his spirits to have a friend visit."

"I'll do my best, though I was not expecting to go that far. I need to get back and report on the state of things here."

"At this instant, I am overcome with a fear that it is vital you should go visit Captain Weare. As you mentioned needing to report, I realized that meant in Exeter and to his father."

Abbot considers Isaac's words for a long moment. "I see. Very well, I will undertake a visit to Albany. Have you any word of Ensign Leeman?"

"None yet. It's been long enough that he is either a prisoner or worse. Thank you for asking. I have a letter for his mother. He wrote it the night we left Fort Ti. Can you take it to her?" Issac plucks the letter, folded into a small square from inside a pouch of papers, and offers it to Abbot.

"Oh." Abbot pauses, taken aback. "Yes, yes. I suppose I was not prepared for this sad duty."

"I am sorry." Isaac averts his eyes, looking to the ground as he sighs. "I worry this will be a much harder season for this sort of news. When I have positive confirmation of Ensign Leeman's disposition, I will write to you."

"Thank you, though I'm afraid I am inclined to agree with your worry." He takes the letter from Isaac. "Have you got a message for your wife?"

"Only that I love her and think of her and the boys often. Tell her we are doing our best so that we may come home soon."

"I will. I expect I'll see Madam Frye when I return. For now, I need to get back to General Poor. It was good to see you, Captain Frye."

"Thank you, and likewise."

•••

Will and Uriah sit on the ground in the ebbing daylight beneath the shade of a large oak tree the next Sunday evening. Beside them, Sergeant Hughes, Corporal Martin, Joseph Gray, and Amos Holt play whist. Jacob Blanchard approaches and stacks his musket with the others against the trunk before joining the group.

Martin turns to Blanchard. "Where were you?"

"Duty with General Poor."

"You overhear anything interesting?"

Blanchard sits down in the group. "I did. Turns out Burgoyne's sent savages ahead of any of his troops to take scalps and run all the sutlers and weak-hearted folk off. They butchered a family a few miles east of here a couple days ago. Today they killed and scalped a real pretty girl. She was a Tory too. I heard them say she was engaged to a lieutenant in Burgoyne's army. The general thinks Burgoyne can't control his savages, and they've begun to run wild killing and scalping."

Martin mops his brow and shakes his head in disbelief. "Damn, Jake. That's some unwelcome news. They're not going east, are they?"

"No, not east. Colonel Cilley said they were sent to hem our scouts in close. One of our scouting parties, militia from New York, got attacked. A lieutenant and four men got scalped and hacked up real bad. The men who escaped said the savages were painted up like nothing they'd ever seen. Definitely not Iroquois."

Hughes, with a stern and solemn tone, "I heard a man got scalped not twenty paces from the picquet at Fort Miller. So, don't go out past the picquets."

Blanchard's news catches Reuben Hosmer's attention. He'd been dozing behind Sergeant Hughes and rolls over and up onto a knee to see the group. In his late thirties, Hosmer's dirt-streaked bald head and round eyes give him an ominous appearance. He focuses on Will and Uriah sitting wide-eyed on the far side of the group. "You best heed the Sergeant. I don't see that any of ya would know what to do if ya crossed the path of one of them savages when they've got their blood up and tomahawk drawn back." Hosmer's grin goes wide as Will flinches at the thought.

Sensing a bluff, Hughes cuts in. "As if you wouldn't fill your drawers on the very spot Reuben."

Hosmer's grin disappears, and his voice drops to the tone fathers use to lecture sons, "I most definitely wouldn't. I'd charge him with everything I got. Right from the first instant. Fight like my every breath depended on it. If you don't, you're gonna get scalped and die knowin' you got scalped." Looking Will and then Uriah in the eye, Hosmer goes on, "Don't play dead either. They'll take a scalp from anyone lying on the ground. If you squeal, they'll take it with their teeth. Your screamin'll add to their frenzy."

After a few moments of stunned silence, Hughes breaks the mood, "Lord's sake Reuben, where'd you hear such things?"

"Friends of mine in the last war. They told far worse stories about the savages. Chilled my blood cold as ice" Hosmer feigns an involuntary shiver. "Not just scalps. They take hands and feet too. Proof to their chiefs, there's one less enemy."

Hughes turns to Blanchard, "Any other news?"

"Nothing much. A few more desertions. Though it seems stupid to leave now. Like as not, they'd come across those savages within a few miles for sure."

"Not if they go south," Hosmer offers. "Most of 'em have run out of tobac and lost their interest in fighting now that a few men are getting killed. Those same friends of mine shamed me a good bit for not fightin' in the last war. But they told me at least I wasn't a deserter. I decided I wasn't going to get shamed again, so I'm here now. But I'm old and need my sleep." Hosmer winks and rolls back onto his blanket and settles his hat over his eyes."

A few minutes later, Will notices Isaac and Hawkins striding their way. "Get ready, Captain's coming."

Before the men can grumble, Hawkins calls out for the company to assemble. Within a minute, thirty-eight men form four ranks, each flanked by a sergeant and a corporal.

Isaac stands before them. "Gentlemen, not an hour ago, Colonel Scammell in a state of dire seriousness instructed us to tell you the hour of our country's need is soon to come upon us. The scouts say Burgoyne's army has begun moving south. It falls to us to make them pay dearly for every inch. We'll take turns on the advanced picquet starting tomorrow. We must convince the enemy to cross to the west side of the river above Fort Miller. Once we're certain they've done so, we'll fall back to Saratoga. That's where they took the artillery last week. The Colonel also had the news that three regiments our state's militia will join with Colonel Warner at Manchester. They're to check the enemy should they try to move east. Brigadier General Stark has got command of our militia." Isaac pauses a moment to see if the men catch on to Stark's promotion and only sees a few eyebrows raise. "You heard me right, John Stark is now General of New Hampshire's militia and woe to Burgoyne should he try to move east."

Sergeant Hall, who served as a private under Stark at Bunker Hill, seizes the on Isaac's intent and speaks out of turn. His words slow, and his tone ominous, "About damned time they made him a general. No man'll turn the tables on Johnny Burgoyne faster than he will."

•••

Isaac sits with Hawkins and Goodale inside the wide doorway of a barn the company occupies as its quarters. The barn and farm are on the edge of Stillwater on the west side of the North River. Unsplit logs taken from a nearby woodpile serve as stools. The late morning sun roasts anything not shaded. The three officers drink from their canteens, their shirts soaked with sweat, adding to the yellowed stains of the past few weeks. A hundred yards off, beside a field recently cut for hay, a group of soldiers unloads a line of wagons, carrying the contents into the neighboring barn.

The two lieutenants stare at the ground listening to Isaac. "I cannot believe Captain Weare is dead."

Hawkins clears his throat. "I was growing used to telling myself he was recovering. His was a bad wound, I know, but after three weeks, I had convinced myself we'd hear better news."

Goodale takes a drink from his canteen. "Sam's still missing too. His name wasn't on the lists for exchanges when we got word of Aaron Oliver being a prisoner. Sam could've made it to Number Four within a few days. He had nothing to go back to, not that I think he would' ve-"

Isaac cuts in, "General Poor told us what Colonel Warner reported. It was a pitched battle for the better part of an hour, and dozens were killed, including Colonel Francis."

"I know. Though that doesn't keep me from thinking Sam's out

Honor and Valor

there making his way to us or to Number Four, or take away a powerful urge to return the favor." Goodale grimaces. His jaw clenching with bitterness. "Instead, we retreat another ten miles."

"We'll meet Burgoyne's army soon enough. Every day that goes by runs down their supplies, and stretches their lines thinner. I bet they can't even get provisions from Fort Ti now. Remember our duty last summer William Adrian?"

Hawkins nods once and grins. "I doubt they have enough men to do that work, even if they did build a road from Fort George to Fort Edward."

Goodale changes the subject, fixing Isaac with a cocked eyebrow to encourage a response. "What do you make of the New York regiments they assigned under General Poor? I heard half their men deserted in the past few days."

"I heard a couple companies lost most of their men. It wasn't half the regiment. To their credit, I didn't hear of any officers leaving."

Hawkins adds, "I don't blame their men. If we'd heard Burgoyne sent hundreds of blood-thirsty savages into howling into New Hampshire, our men'd be deserting in droves too."

Amos Holt jogs up to the barn and offers a salute. Goodale scoots his stool back and motions for Holt to come into the shade. "Get yourself out of the heat, Holt. What do you need?"

Holt enters and looks to Isaac. "Colonel Colburn's asking for you and Captain Ellis. I think they're going to send us to guard a village on the other side of the river so its people can evacuate to Albany."

Isaac shrugs. "Looks like we may not be digging fortifications until dark." He rises and reaches for his waistcoat and hat. "Give me a moment, Holt."

With his waistcoat buttoned and hat on, Isaac looks to Holt. "Let's go."

As they walk, Isaac notes a bank of clouds to the west with mixed feelings. "Looks like rain later today."

"Yessir. It's good we have the barn to keep ourselves dry tonight. I've thanked the Lord dozens of times for not giving me the ague or phlegm since we left Fort Ti."

"I count myself lucky as well. Have you written your family now that we've gotten some paper and ink?"

"Yessir."

"Good. Tell your father I send my regards, though I expect he's already been called up with the militia. I heard Nichols' Regiment is with General Stark now. They're at Manchester."

"Yessir. Two days past, Ichabod Perry got a few lines from his father. He's in Packersfield's militia. They're with General Stark as well. My father and most from Wilton are in Captain Putnam's company."

"I expect my brother-in-law, Richard is with them too."

They reach the small house Colburn shares with Scammell and Dearborn. Ellis, already inside, breaks off the conversation with Colburn and two other gentlemen as Isaac enters.

Colburn nods to Isaac. "Captain Frye, this is Major Derrick Van Veghten and Mr. Solomon Acker. They're from the 14th New York militia." Then turning to Van Veghten and Acker, "Captain Isaac Frye of Wilton New Hampshire."

Van Veghten, in his late thirties, is tall, whipcord thin, and offers a bright, enthusiastic smile. Acker is short with a paunch and keeps back a step from Van Veghten, marking him as an aide or waiter.

They exchange pleasantries and shake hands before Colburn continues. "These gentlemen are from a town a little over a mile away on the east side of the river called Schaghticoke. Some of the townfolk already evacuated to Albany, and the remainder now wish to go. They've requested a guard. General Poor ordered us to supply two companies to ensure the Tories and savages keep their distance." He motions to the pair of New Yorkers. "Major Van Veghten and Mr. Acker will accompany you. You're to leave this afternoon and use the ferry just above camp. Your men will guard and assist them in getting their possessions staged at the meetinghouse and the ferry landing. Guard the ferry landing and meetinghouse tonight. Then tomorrow guard the ferry while they cross."

Looking pleased, Van Veghten asks, his Dutch accent emerging, "How soon can you march?"

Isaac looks to Ellis, who does not appear concerned, then responds, "An hour, or maybe a bit sooner. We can meet you on the road just

Honor and Valor

there." Isaac points to the road about forty yards away. Van Veghten smiles with approval. "Excellent. We will see you there shortly."

Two hours later, after crossing the North River at the ferry, the companies form ranks. The column is short, sixty men in all, owing to nearly two dozen being sick. Four farms occupy the fertile swath of land that surrounds the ferry and lies at the bottom of a broad hill. As they march southeast away from the river, Isaac and Ellis walk beside Van Veghten, who leads the way. Acker follows a few paces behind them.

Isaac looks around as they begin climbing the hill, then turns to Van Veghten. "As you and your men are in camp on the other side of the river, I assume your family is already in Albany?"

"They are. It's been a difficult year. My wife, Alida, insisted on removing to Albany after she heard the news of the first attack by Fort Edward. One of my cousins was the commander of our scouting party. I take it you know their fate?"

Isaac looks Van Veghten in the eyes. "Your cousin and four others."

"Yes. So, I don't blame my wife for wishing to seek a safer situation. It's been a difficult year for us. She gave birth to twins early this spring, a son and daughter. Sadly, they weren't strong, and their passing put our house in a melancholy state."

Isaac and Ellis express their condolences to the major. They walk in silence for a minute before Ellis asks, "Has your family lived here long?"

"My grandfather bought the land here when he was a young man. He was one of the original settlers of the town."

Isaac continues with the change of subject. "How's the farming here? Good soil?"

"I've not had cause to complain about my land. You'll be able to see it for yourself soon. Most of it is on the rise we are heading for."

"My farm in New Hampshire is up on a hillside, though the Souhegan River, running below it, is a trickle compared to the North River."

"How long have you owned it?"

"Eight years. It's on a pair of lots that sold early in Wilton, though I suspect it was timber the first owner was after. The soil's fair, so I put in apple trees. They'll be small for a few more years, but I hope they prove to be a wise investment."

"Sounds like a good plan. What about you, Captain Ellis, been in Keene long?"

"No, I haven't," starts Ellis, who is several years older than Isaac, "I moved there recently. A distant cousin," Ellis points back toward Lieutenant Benjamin Ellis, "Ben, his father's one of Keene's first settlers. I had heard from them that decent land was available in Keene. We've been there for a few years, but I hadn't done much but clear a large field when the war broke out. Most of us in the militia who didn't join the army around Boston pitched in and worked our neighbor's fields. That system worked to give us enough food during the past two winters."

As they reach the top of the hill, they can see a broad expanse, clear of trees with several farms. Acker points ahead and to the left. "There's the meetinghouse up ahead."

"My farm is just beyond." Van Veghten points to the right of the meetinghouse. "It's a good defensible spot. One can see for a mile in most every direction."

They march the few hundred yards to the meetinghouse. As they approach, Isaac judges the building to be a bit larger than Wilton's, though the main difference is the Dutch-style mansard roof. A dozen men and women emerge from around the corner of the building. Van Veghten strides over to greet them. Isaac and Captain Ellis follow. Behind the meetinghouse are five wagons already loaded with household goods.

After some discussion, the nervous assemblage of Schaghticoke's remaining citizens agrees to work in two groups. The first will move the wagons already at the meetinghouse down to the ferry so they can begin moving them across the river at first light. The second group will go to the farms in turn and bring the possessions of nine other families to the meetinghouse.

Isaac and Ellis split their men into three detachments. Isaac takes charge of the men who will move the goods already at the meetinghouse. Captain Ellis will lead the families to their farms, and

Lieutenants Ellis and Hawkins have charge of a smaller group to guard the meetinghouse. Van Veghton and Acker take their leave, stating they must rejoin their regiment on to the west side of the river before sundown.

By late evening the goods of the outlying families rest beside the meetinghouse where the residents agree to spend the night. After learning one of the houses beside the ferry is Tory-owned and abandoned, Isaac decides to make use it for the night. Before sundown, Isaac and Hawkins meet Captain Ellis at the farmhouse nearest the meetinghouse, where he chose to stay the night. They agree to set up one picquet surrounding the meetinghouse, and a second at the ferry landing—the latter extending to the crest of the hill to be within shouting distance.

Once they return to the house by the ferry, Hawkins issues the orders for the night's guard duty, and the men draw lots for two shifts. Half move off to set the picquet and the others to a barn to get their sleep.

Inside the farmhouse, Goodale lights a fire in the stove. Turning to Hawkins and Isaac, "In such a short time a stove to cook on and a roof has become a luxury, hasn't it?"

"Aye, true. Thanks for volunteering to cook."

"I thought I volunteered to eat."

Hawkins grins as he replies, "We all did."

Isaac takes a seat at the small dusty table. "The residents of this town are in a nervous way. Did either of you see or hear anything we need to act on or a reason to add more men to the picquet?"

Both lieutenants shake their heads. Hawkins adds, "We can't know whether the Tories or the savages have something planned here tonight or if it's for another town or another night."

Isaac offers Hawkins a knowing smile. "Aye, William Adrian, true."

Goodale finishes cutting the last potato for the pot. "Speaking of Burgoyne's savages, I heard Major Dearborn say it was the Tories as being the more savage brothers of the Indians Burgoyne sent to harass us."

Isaac chuckles briefly without smiling. "The major can certainly turn a phrase. Both him and the colonel."

Hawkins adds, "I wonder which one of them came up with that. It's quite good."

Goodale turns away from the stew. "It's revolting how the King, Burgoyne, and the damned Tories have set aside their honor."

"Aye," begins Isaac, "My uncle Joseph once told me honor and civility are fine friends until you're fighting for your life. It makes me think the King and Burgoyne have become desperate."

Well after midnight, after drifting in and out of a light sleep, Isaac lays with his eyes shut, thinking the roof was not the luxury he had presumed. The solid walls of the farmhouse worked well to keep the warm, humid air inside despite their propping the door open. The sounds of camp and the outdoors had become comfortable over the past few weeks. The quiet left his mind open to distracting thoughts. The report of a distant musket cuts through the thick air and into the room, ending the thoughts and jolting Isaac's eyes open.

Goodale's snoring stops. "Was that?"

Isaac already on his feet, "It was. Get Sergeant Wilkins and ten men." He looks back as he moves out of the room. "I'll find Sergeant Hall and see what that was about."

Taking his hat and musket, Isaac hurries out into the night with Hawkins a few seconds behind.

Even with his night vision fully intact, Isaac finds he can barely see in the darkness. The sliver of a moon is little help with the unfamiliar terrain. After taking a few deliberate steps, he stops at the sound of a pair of boots running toward him and waits.

Corporal Martin materializes from the dark side of a barn. Captain Frye, Sir."

"Martin, where did the shot come from?"

"Our picquet, up on the hill where we posted Joseph Gray. Sergeant Hall is already there. He sent me to bring you."

"Good," turning to Hawkins, "Find Goodale and Wilkins and tell them no lights or lanterns. Then bring them up."

A few minutes later, Isaac and Martin reach Sergeant Hall and Gray, who wait on the road to the meetinghouse. They peer northeast into the darkness.

Hall turns at their approach. "Captain Frye?"

"Yes, what's this about?"

"Gray says he thought he saw something move toward him from the woods on the far side of this field."

Gray picks up his story, "For worry, it might have been one of our men, I gave the challenge. It kept moving, so I fired. By the time the smoke from my musket cleared, I couldn't see it anymore."

"Good," Isaac responds. "Either of you hear or see anything since?"

Hall responds, "No, Sir, nothing."

"Sergeant Wilkins is coming with ten men. I'll stay here with Martin until they arrive. You and Gray go to the meetinghouse and tell Captain Ellis what's happened. As soon as it's light enough, send men to investigate."

"Yessir."

Three hours later, Isaac and Hawkins watch the first load of possessions depart the landing, heading to the west side of the North River.

Martin, having jogged down the road from the top of the hill, approaches, clearing his throat to catch the officers' attention. "Begging your pardon sirs-"

Hawkins cuts him off, "What is it, Corporal?"

"Thank you, sir. It seems Gray did see something. We found a skinny white bull at the edge of the woods."

"That's a relief. Have Captain Ellis's men begun moving the other residents' possessions?"

"Not when I left. His men were finishing their meal. I expect they will start soon."

"Good. Return and tell Captain Ellis we will be ready for their wagons in less than an hour."

Fifteen minutes pass. Martin rushes back to the landing where Isaac, Hawkins, and Goodale oversee the loading of the ferry. "Captain Frye! Captain Ellis says to send for reinforcements. There was a skirmish down in the valley. Lieutenant Belding said some of it came from the fusee muskets the French traded to Indians."

Isaac orders Goodale to send the next ferry immediately back with Private Blanchard and just the one wagon already on the ferry.

"Blanchard is to go directly to General Poor's headquarters and request reinforcements. Another company should be sufficient."

Then to Hawkins, "Send Sergeants Hall and Wilkins with twenty men up to the meetinghouse. Send one man back to me immediately with news of the situation."

Forty-five minutes pass. Isaac turns to see Joseph Lewis running down the hill from the meetinghouse, passing ahead of a pair of wagons. Isaac and Hawkins intercept Lewis, who offers a salute as he catches his breath. "Sir, there were two men who took it upon themselves to go out early and get some things from one of the farms about a mile from the meetinghouse. As they crossed a creek, Indians attacked and killed one of the men. The other escaped and rode back, calling for help. Captain Ellis went with twenty of his men, and they got the man's body."

Two comings and goings of the ferry see the last of the five wagons to the west side, and Captain Stone and his men to the east side of the North River. Major Van Veghton, Mr. Acker, and their horses come with the second group. While Captain Stone's men fall into formation and ready themselves to march to the meetinghouse, Isaac meets with Van Veghton and Acker to tell them of the attack.

As Isaac finishes, a black boy, about ten years old, approaches them. He addresses Van Veghton. "Sir, may I ask a question?"

Isaac looks to Van Veghton, who nods. "This is Tom. He's Colonel Knickerbocker's negro. The colonel commands our regiment and lives to the northeast on the far side of the hill."

Van Veghton looks to Tom, "Go ahead, ask."

"Sir, the Colonel wishes to know how long before his goods will cross the river?"

Van Veghton looks to Isaac, who responds, "Tell the colonel it will take three hours."

Van Veghton thanks Isaac, then to Tom, "You can ride with Mr. Acker to the meetinghouse. When we get there, find the colonel's goods and we will move them next."

After Van Veghton and Acker ride toward the hill, Captain Stone approaches and greets Isaac with a warm handshake. "Good morning Captain Frye, I heard you say three more hours here. Colonel Poor

Honor and Valor

decided we should not tarry here given the attack. He suggested my company act as a rearguard and those wagons and families at the meetinghouse go south to Lansingburgh. It's about four miles, and they can cross the river there."

"Aye, that's a sound plan. I'll keep my picquet in place until these three wagons are across. Then we'll join you at the meetinghouse."

Stone looks around, then asks, "Where're your men? I only see half a dozen here."

"Hawkins has twenty up at the meetinghouse already. They can return here to help with these wagons, once your men get to the meetinghouse. Then we'll join you at the meetinghouse."

Stone nods his agreement. "Anything else I should know?"

Isaac shakes his head.

A little over an hour later, thirty minutes longer than Isaac expected, he sees Hawkins leading the detachment from the meetinghouse. Trailing them is a disturbing sight, three horses, two with bodies draped over the saddles.

As the formation nears the landing, Isaac moves toward Hawkins, who had gone to the rear of the group, joining Acker and the horses. Before Isaac can reach them, he recognizes one of the bodies as Major Van Veghton, bloodied from a wound to the abdomen and scalped.

Isaac's voice fails him as he points to the major. The question of what happened showed on Isaac's face.

After the column comes to a halt, Hawkins takes Isaac aside. "You saw the major last when he and Mr. Acker rode to the meetinghouse. They stopped there for a minute. The major said he wanted to check on his property, so they continued to his farm. I suppose he was worried the local Tories were helping the savages or the savages were sacking the abandoned houses. A few minutes later, we heard the exchange of fusees and the major's pistols. From the sound of it, he and Mr. Acker put up a warm defense. That's when Mr. Acker says the major took the wound to his belly. Mr. Acker says the major told him to save himself and get back to the meetinghouse. We were retrieving his body when Captain Stone arrived."

Isaac looks to the major's body, then shakes his head. "A damn shame. He has a young family." Isaac lowers his eyes, thinking of his own young family."

After a few moments, Isaac comes back to himself and the business at hand. "I'll send Mr. Acker and the bodies over on the next trip. We'll all march to the meetinghouse once they're away."

•••

A week later, in Wilton, Henry Parker pulls gently on the reins to slow the pair of oxen pulling his wagon as they come alongside Isaac's farmhouse. One of the younger boys is out in the front yard shooing the geese towards the rear of the house. The geese honk and squawk as soon as they see Henry step down from the wagon. He has to call out loudly, "Good day. Is Madame Frye about?"

Abiel turns at the sound of Henry's voice, but the geese drown out the words. He waves and turns back to shooing the geese past the gate and behind the house before returning to the front gate.

As Abiel returns Henry, repeats his question, this time with neighborly friendliness.

"Good day to you, Mister Parker. She's in the barn."

"I've got a letter for her."

Elizabeth comes around the side of the house. "Good afternoon Henry. I heard the geese. I had to finish what I was doing before I could come to see who they were so excited to greet."

"Good afternoon to you too, Madame Frye. Those geese are true to their species." Henry chuckles. "Never know whether they're inviting me to stay or to leave."

Elizabeth smiles warmly. "I'm sure it was to stay. How are you and Sarah getting along?"

"We're well. I've got a letter for you. I expect it's from Captain Frye. The old man's militia, for that's what we are: a dozen old men with muskets, were drilling over at the meetinghouse when Lieutenant Butterfield rode in. He had a packet of letters, so now we're out delivering the mail." Henry hands Elizabeth the letter, a folded and sealed two-inch square of paper.

"Thank you, Henry."

"Your father sends his regards as well. He and your sister received letters from Richard. He says the militia is in Manchester and Bennington. They're confident that between them and the Continentals, Burgoyne will have no hope of pushing eastward, and thus, we are safe."

"I suppose such news should come as a relief."

"Aye, I take your meaning. Well, I've got get up to Cram's and Abbot's places with these other letters."

"Thank you again, Henry. I will stop by to visit Sarah one of the next evenings. Otherwise, I fear I won't see her until we get the hay in."

Henry climbs up to the wagon seat. "That would be nice, I'll let her know to expect you."

As Henry continues, Elizabeth breaks the seal on the letter and begins reading.

"Camp at Stillwater, August 5, 1777

Dearest Elizabeth, I am well, though dirty and tired. I Keep you and the boys constantly in my thoughts. We at last have a new supply of paper and ink. Ours was lost With our baggage taken by the enemy last month at Skeensburough. Two companies of our regiment fought a sharp engagement then. Mesesch Weare's son Richard was mortally wounded and died a few days past. He was a fine captain and we miss him sorely.

Yesterday we Garded off the citizens of a town call Shaticoke so they could evacuate to Albany. Mr. Burgoyne has sent a Hord of savages to demoralize us. It has not worked as I think he Intended. Everyone in these parts are mad as hornets. We have done our best to make the enemy's progress a hellish trek by felling trees and making dams to form new swamps and clouds of noseeums that come with such wet terrain. May they all rot with irritation and disease.

Our men have faired as well as one could expect given one set of cloths and no tents. Some are sick with phlegm and ague, tho very few with anything worse. We hear the militia under General Stark have blocked they way east, so I am confident you are safe.

I sorely miss all of you. Give my love and affection to your sisters and father.

With Love and affection,

Your husband Isaac

Elizabeth carefully folds the letter. A tug at her skirt reminds her that Abiel is still at her side.

"Did Papa have a battle?"

"No. He is well and sends his love. He misses us all."

"Did he say when he can come home?"

Elizabeth sighs. "He didn't. They're doing their best to stop the redcoats, but it will take more time."

The last words catch uncertainly in her throat. Pushing the dire thoughts to the side, Elizabeth points into the garden. "Let's get some cucumbers and onions and take them to Sarah to cut for dinner."

Honor and Valor

Charles E. Frye

6 40 MAN SCOUT

> " ... *General Burgoyne acknowledges that he allowed the Indians to take the scalps of the dead. It must be painful for the impartial historian to record, and it will require the strongest faith of the reader in future ages to credit, the disgraceful story, that Britons, who pride themselves on their civility, and humanity, employed the wild savages of the wilderness in a war against a people united to them by the ties of consanguinity. ...*"
>
> Excerpt from the Journal of Dr. James Thacher
> September 2, 1777

Will Burton sits cross-legged, outside leaning against the back tent pole of the tent he shares with the company's corporals. Their tent is within a group of several dozen for the regiment arrayed in eight rows. Three other groups of tents for General Poor's brigade fill the clearing a minute's walk south of the Mohawk River. Small cooking fires burn around the edges of the groups of tents. Men gather in twos, threes, and fours throughout the encampment talking and drinking.

Will holds a flat wooden board in his lap. On it a new sheet of paper. A ceramic jar of ink and a lantern sit at his side. He leans a little toward the light as he writes.

Honor and Valor

Camp at Lowden's Ferry, August 28, 1777
Dear Mother and Father,

I am in good Health. For my part there is little New to tell about since I wrote last. We Moved our camp a day later to our Present location on the south side of the Mohawk River. The recent victory at Bennington came with the bitter cost of Mr. Perry. Ichabod continues in his duty in our company tho he is Saddened and at times angry.

Our fortunes improved considerably a little over a week ago when we got tents and earlier this week some of the men, who needed them badly, got new clothes and Shoes. The men are pleased to have General Gates in command as well. We have eaten well this past week for being provisioned with Chickins and Beef. The men who were sick from our being obliged to sleep work in the Open in all weather are now getting well

Our duty is changing from retreating to readying to advance as it is now widely held that we now have the advantage of numbers given our recent reinforcements and the enemy's losses.

Give my affection to my brothers and sisters. I often think of you.

Your most humble and obedient son,

William Burton

•••

As Will finishes the letter, he overhears the conversation inside the tent between Corporals Goodman and Martin.

Goodman begins, "Looks like we will be without Hawkins and the captain a bit longer."

Martin responds, "Could be a long while. I don't expect the light infantry companies General Gates formed will get disbanded any time soon. They've been drilling separate from us for over a week now, and I figure they'll send them out on scouting duty soon."

"Only four from our company got picked. All of them young."

"I know. Cram, Holt, and Pettingill are hunters and good shots. I don't know Heseltine well, but I figure the same for him.

Goodman coughs and clears his throat. "Think they can hunt Indians without gettin' hunted themselves?"

"Maybe if those Oneidas on our side guide 'em."

"They're lucky then. As for me, I'm gettin' damned tired of sittin' on my hands. We do all that work and nothing but orders to retreat. No logical reason for it."

"No argument from me. Now that we're getting supplied, I can't think of any reason not to be moving back north again."

Will replaces the cork on the ink jar and wipes his quill in the grass before getting to his feet and collecting the lantern. He walks to the front of the tent and pokes his head in beneath the flaps. "I haven't got duty tonight, so I'll take the back?"

Martin looks up. "Sure. Take a piss now, so you don't go wakin' us up in the middle of the night."

•••

Isaac arrives at General Poor's tent late in the afternoon four days later. He finds a lieutenant he recognizes as belonging to the first regiment already waiting. The lieutenant is a few inches shorter than Isaac with sandy blond hair tied back with a leather thong. Before Isaac can greet the lieutenant, Colonel Scammell steps out and beckons the two of them inside and then towards General Poor's desk.

Isaac offers a salute. "Captain Frye, reporting as ordered."

"Lieutenant McCalley, reporting as ordered."

The man appeared unremarkable a few moments earlier when standing still. Isaac notes the transformation as McCalley's eyes and features animated as he spoke, shifting to bright and self-aware.

General Poor returns their salutes. "Please sit." Pointing to a pair of chairs now just behind them. Colonel Scammell sits in a chair beside the general's desk.

Once Isaac and McCalley sit, Poor begins. "Captain Frye, tomorrow you will command a scouting party to the north and west of here. Lieutenant McCalley here will be second in command. Forty men, including yourselves. Your purpose, should anyone in camp ask, is to learn how far General Burgoyne's scouts have come in our direction. We also wish to know the intent of the Mohawks. We got word today the Fort Hunter Mohawks and their Tory friends are preparing to evacuate their homes. We don't want them scouting us."

Poor unrolls a map and places weights on the corners. "Here, come see where you'll need to go." As soon as they gather around, Poor continues. "We are here, just below Loudon's Ferry. To the west, here's Fort Hunter. If the Mohawks are moving directly to join Burgoyne, they will take this road and travel above Saratoga Lake. We wish to be certain they've done so, and are not lingering in the territory just to the north of the Mohawk River. Thus, you will first go to Alplaus Creek, here, and follow it up to the road. If those Mohawks are truly leaving, they should precede you to that point, leaving evidence of their passing. Your route, according to the Oneida's in General Gates' camp, is also the easiest route for those Mohawks to send scouts. Keep a wide presence as you move up the valley. Intercept and capture their scouts. Once you reach the road, turn back to the east and search for any signs of Burgoyne's scouts. Your return should be on the east side of Long Lake here. You will leave tomorrow morning, an hour before sunrise, and return, I expect late the following day." To Isaac, "Do you have questions?"

"Yes, sir, a few. May we pick the men?"

"No. Colonel Scammell here and Major Dearborn will pick them from the New Hampshire regiments. Major Fish will pick men from the Second and Fourth New York. They will muster with you before dusk and draw provisions for two days."

"Are we to engage the Mohawks?"

"No. Only their scouts and any of Burgoyne's scouts. They'll have their elders, women, and children. I think you cannot afford a pitched battle, as their warriors will outnumber you by two, perhaps three to one. They'll be protecting their families. Bidding them good riddance without a fight serves our purpose well enough."

"May I study that map for a few minutes to get the distances and other landmarks fixed in my mind?"

"Certainly, come back here after six o'clock and bring ink and paper so you can copy what you need. Now, before we adjourn, are there one or two men either of you would request?"

Isaac thinks a moment. "There's a private in Captain Ellis's company. Day is his name. He carries a Pennsylvania Rifle."

Poor nods and turns to Scammell as if to say, take care of that. "How about you, lieutenant?"

"Sergeant Kemp from my company."

Poor's gaze rises a tiny bit as he eyes McCalley with a look of skepticism. "He's your friend?"

"No, sir. He's the one all the men respect, and one of the few men I'd want at my back when dealing with savages."

Poor nods. "Sounds like he'll do fine. I'll leave the map out so both of you can return study it." Poor looks to Scammell. "Anything to add?"

Scammell responds, "I'm certain you've seen the way the light companies have been drilling. There's some rivalry between the regiment and states. We need to put that in the past. The men need to know one another as being in the same unit. Their first thoughts should be to come to the aid of their fellow soldiers."

"Well said." Poor pushes back from his desk, signaling an end to the meeting. "I wish you gentlemen good fortune."

Well before dawn, a guard wakes Isaac, as he had requested. He dresses rapidly in the dark, his things laid out before going to sleep. On his way out of the tent, he shoulders his musket and pack.

He met the men chosen by Scammell and Major Fish the previous evening as they drew provisions and forty cartridges each. As they assemble on the side of camp nearest the Mohawk River, Isaac takes in their ragged, almost unmilitary appearance. No regimental coats. Most look to be backwoodsmen and dirty as at the end of a two-week hunt. Isaac checks each to ensure they carry everything needed for their duty. Most have new muskets, and all possess an array of tomahawks and hunting knives.

Isaac addresses the men, "Once we're across the river, we'll move fast. Stay on the road for about five miles until just before the big bend, where it turns to meet Alplaus Creek. Once we get a few miles up the creek, we'll slow and begin the work of scouting for the enemy. After we leave the road, no noise. Use the hand signals we chose last night."

Two hours later, they arrive at the bend ahead of Alplaus Creek. They cut straight across and angle northwest for the creek. On the map, a small line symbolized Alplaus Creek. That line turned out to be twice the width of the Souhegan River near Isaac's farm, leaving no choice but to continue along the east side. Dry ground and sparse undergrowth allow them to move in near silence.

By noon, five miles up Alplaus Creek, they cross at a rocky stretch, then Isaac calls a halt. Now within a distance where they might encounter the Mohawk scouts, Isaac alters their formation. Before sending four men fifty yards out to each side of the creek with twenty yards spacing between each of them, he admonishes them in a low voice. "Do not get so far from the creek that you can not see one another."

The bulk of the men form two columns along either side of the creek. Isaac puts the New Hampshire men on the left side of the creek, and the New Yorkers on the right. Each man affixes his bayonet and wraps its connection to the musket with thin strips of cloth to muffle the metal on metal rattling. They began moving forward with deliberate caution.

Sergeant Kemp, who is not the grizzled veteran Isaac imagined, leads the outer scouts on the left. Kemp is in his mid-twenties, stocky, and strong as an ox. Isaac now sees Kemp as a man who leads by doing. Dan Day carrying his Pennsylvania rifle, follows Kemp.

McCalley leads the column near the left side of the creek. Dan Cook, a private from the Second New Hampshire Regiment, follows him, six steps behind. Both swivel their gazes from Kemp on the left to Sergeant John McEvers, leading the outer scouts higher up on the right. McEvers, a calm, confident man, creeps ahead while scanning the upper part of the slope for movement. Sergeant Archie Burges leads the column of New York men on the right side of the creek while Isaac brings up the rear of the left column.

Over the next three hours, they negotiate the valley's terrain for nearly four miles. In the last mile, they begin moving northwest and reach the end of Alplaus Creek. They crest a low ridge and find another creek flowing to the northwest. They follow it, and before long, the ground to the right becomes swampy, forcing Isaac to merge the center columns into one. The boggy ground forces them to keep well to the left of the main channel.

Half a mile later, a steep ridge forces the creek to bend to the northeast. They continue for half a mile before nearing the end of the ridge. McCalley slows as he watches Kemp start to move past the nose of the ridge. The sergeant stops, freezing in place for several seconds, looking about before taking three cautious steps. He turns to Day and points back up the ridge.

Seeing the Kemp point, Isaac uses a low voice, "Griff," catching the attention of Corporal Samuel Griffith from the second New York Regiment. "Take," Isaac points to Asa Boutwell, Noah Russell, Ben Taylor, James Thompson, James Wooster, John Hilton, and Job Jenness, all of New Hampshire. "Go back around the backside of the ridge and see what's to the rear of where Kemp pointed." Griffith and his command melt back, running in a low crouch along the creek.

Kemp takes a few cautious steps, as does McCalley with the central column. Isaac signals to McEvers, pointing to Kemp. As McEvers' gaze finds Kemp, he whips up his musket and shouts, "Ambush."

Isaac hears what sounds like a dozen shots from the left before McEver's musket discharges. The force of a ball striking Kemp propels him down the hillside. At the same time, the lower part of the ridge explodes with Mohawk warriors. They rush out of the musket smoke, howling bone-chilling war cries. The clacks, thuds, and thunks of tomahawks, war clubs, and muskets meeting one another in a brisk melee mixes in with the war cries.

Isaac shouts, after realizing the men immediately in front of him have frozen. "Bayonets forward. Drive them back up the hill." As those men react to the command, several of the men behind McCalley and Cook get swept into the creek and swampy ground beyond by a second wave of Mohawks. The men in the middle column surge forward, blunting the Mohawk's charge, felling two of them. A volley

Honor and Valor

from the Mohawk reserves up on the ridge breaks the progress of Isaac's men.

Looking ahead, Isaac cannot see McCalley in the fray ahead. Instead, he sees two of his men fall. Isaac remembers Poor's warning about the Mohawk's numbers. "Retreat!"

Sergeant McEvers with the three scouts on the right fire a volley into the front line of Mohawk's. Their muskets drown out Isaac's order but create an opportunity to break off from the melee.

"Retreat!"

McEvers and his group begin angling toward Isaac's position. The sergeant shouts, "Keep firing. There's more in the draw behind the ridge."

As they back away from the site of the ambush, Isaac orders, "Fire in fours, no more. Keep the gaps between volleys short."

Near the base of the ridge, Isaac sees Kemp. On his belly, bleeding from his arm, leg, and a wound to his back, Kemp crawls, pulling with his uninjured arm and pushing with his good leg toward the creek.

McEvers points to the first four men who have reloaded, signaling them to fire.

After two volleys and at least half a dozen shots returned from the ridge, Isaac turns to where Kemp was, and cannot locate the sergeant.

"Dammit! Keep falling back. Anyone see Kemp?"

As he finishes, a much larger volley of musket fire erupts from a few yards higher up on the ridge. Andrew Newell from Stone's company, only a dozen paces from Isaac falls, struck in the head.

Isaac orders, "One more volley, then get back quick. Out of range."

As they backtrack along their earlier route, Isaac calls out, "How many are we missing? I sent Corporal Griffiths back with seven men to come around the other side of the ridge."

McEvers checks with Burges. "The lieutenant and Kemp are missing. All but Griffiths from New York are here."

Noah Russell from Cilley's regiment speaks up, "Corporal Lovekin, Leeland, and Page fell when they charged us. Lieutenant McCalley, Cook, and Day are missing."

Isaac turns back and scans the faces of the other New Hampshire men. "Anyone see them fall?"

They shake their heads.

Ahead, in the distance where Griffiths led his men, a volley of musket fire echoes. "Hurry, if Griffiths' men get pinned down, they won't last long."

They break into long loping strides, running with their muskets held ready to swing up and fire. They hear whoops and war cries well behind them. Sporadic musket fire in the distance ahead and behind continues as they run. After a minute, the firing stops. Isaac and his group reach the toe of the ridge and turn northwest toward the source, Isaac figures, of the musket fire. Within twenty strides, with Isaac in the lead, they stop, seeing Griffiths and his men running in their direction.

Griffiths points ahead, indicating they should continue retreating. Isaac orders, "Back to Alplaus Creek."

As they jog back the way they came, Isaac asks Griffiths, "What happened?"

"We found the rear of their column of wagons on the road. We had heard the firing from their ambush, so I figured firing a couple volleys at them would draw off their warriors. We wounded one of their rear-guards, but we were too far off to do much harm. We did get their attention. What happened at the front of our column?"

Isaac relates the story of the ambush as they forge ahead at a jog. After a mile, they slow as they climb the rise separating the two creeks. Once they reach Alplaus Creek, Isaac brings them to a halt. "We go east from here. We need to go a couple more miles before we make camp for the night. We need to stay sharp and keep an eye out for Burgoyne's scouts, and any those Mohawks may send."

They spend the night anxious and exhausted about ten miles west of the southern end of Saratoga Lake. In the morning, they begin at dawn, trekking eastward through a broad wooded valley. By noon they reach Saratoga lake, and for not seeing any sign of the enemy, Isaac decides to veer southeast to meet the road leading to Loudon's Ferry.

Early in the evening, they cross the Mohawk River and make their way back into General Poor's camp. Isaac dismisses all but McEvers and Griffiths with orders not to talk about the last two days.

Honor and Valor

By the time Isaac, McEvers, and Griffiths reach General Poor's tent, Isaac's stomach knots itself with guilt and dread. Four men dead for sure. Kemp with bad wounds and three men missing.

Inside the tent, Isaac finds Captain Scott of the first regiment to be the sole occupant. "Evening Bill. I need to see the General."

"Isaac, good to see you're back and on schedule. I'll get the General."

Isaac holds up a hand. "You'll need to get all the Colonels. We got ambushed."

"Oh." Captain Scott pauses a moment. "I only have two guards."

"That's fine, I'll get Colonel Scammell."

Isaac finds Scammell in his tent, reading a book. "Sir, I've returned, and you and the other colonels should hear my report to General Poor firsthand."

"That bad?"

"We got ambushed."

"I'll be there in an instant."

Shortly, Colonels Cilley, Adams, Scammell with the New Yorkers Cortlandt, and Livingston gather in Poor's tent. Isaac describes the encounter with the Mohawks and the outcome. The mood inside the tent is grim, though professional. They question Isaac, McEvers, and Griffiths with a focus on evaluating the sequence of events and then the performance of the men. Despite the circumstances of the ambush, they are generally positive. They all recognize the ambush could have turned out much worse.

Near the end, Poor acknowledges, "In hindsight, I should have pressed to acquire Oneida guides to send along. Tis obvious, they would've been of some benefit." He adds, "The whole affair took place in territory the Mohawks have long claimed dominion over, so I suppose it's moot."

Much of the meeting repeats half an hour later, this time including the captains whose companies to which the slain and missing men belonged. Afterward, Isaac returns to his tent in the company of Scammell and Dearborn.

As they walk, Scammell offers, "Sometimes surviving the battle is more important than winning, and thus, survival is victory."

"I am afraid, sir, such sentiments seem difficult for my mind at this moment."

"After the battle at Princeton, I felt much the same, very raw. And that, even though I commanded no men." As they come to Scammell's tent, he stops and holds up his index finger. "I have an idea. The book I've been reading, Memoirs of Fredrick III, describes his memorable battles. More importantly, it discusses the differences between the intended gains and the actual gains. I will lend it to you, as I believe it will offer some perspective."

Scammell ducks into his tent and returns with a substantial book, about two hundred pages, and hands it to Isaac. "I expect you're exhausted, and we will march to Albany early tomorrow with the light companies. Bring it with you so we can discuss it as we march, and during the evening."

Dearborn chuckles, and Scammell raises an eyebrow in his direction. "Yes, Major?"

"Ever the schoolmaster, sir."

Scammell grins. "I suppose I am." To Isaac, "I taught school for a number of years after receiving my education. The major occasionally reminds me that I am an opportunistic instructor."

Isaac takes the book. "It seems the opportunity is mine, sir. Thank you."

Dearborn smiles to both men, "Well said, Captain Frye."

"Thank you, sir. Please excuse me, the Colonel is correct, I should seek my tent and get some rest."

•••

Elizabeth sits on one of a pair of quilts spread beneath a large birch tree on the west bank of the Souhegan River. The river valley remains brilliant green for the nights not yet having become too cold. Her father and sister sit nearby, forming a triangle to keep John from roaming away. John, already a year old, can walk a few steps at a time but makes faster progress crawling. Isaac Jr. and Abiel have fishing poles in hand doing their best to add a few more brook trout to the day's catch. The mid-September afternoon feels pleasant and untroubled compared to the oppressive, muggy heat of summer.

In the distance, the sound of rapid clopping of horseshoes on the road emerges and becomes distinct. Everyone turns to see Major Abbot riding to the bridge then catching sight of the party downriver, he turns about and rides in their direction.

After tying his horse to a nearby tree, he approaches. "Good afternoon Mister Holt, Madame Frye, and Miss Holt. I am glad I glanced upstream. I almost took a wasted a trip up the hill."

Timothy rises, smiles, and shakes the major's hand. "Good afternoon Major, I'd have worried if you hadn't looked. What brings you over this way?"

"I've got a letter for Madame Frye, from New York. We got a packet today. With the militia spread from the Connecticut River west into New York, we get the mail a bit faster from Albany."

Elizabeth beckons for Sarah to help her rise. Now seven months along, she offers a grateful smile for the hand in getting to her feet with some grace. "Major, it's a pleasure to see you-"

Sarah shrieks, interrupting everything, as she dashes to the water's edge to pluck John from the river. The opportunity to join his brothers while the adults conversed proved easy. He slid off a rock and into the shallow water for a second before Sarah could reach him. For two seconds, nobody says anything as Sarah holds John. He breaks into tears from the surprise of his unexpected soaking, and Sarah firmly snatching him from the water.

Smiling, Major Abbot hands Elizabeth the letter. "I'll be on my way." Instead of going immediately to his horse, he turns to the older boys, "Isaac, Abiel, how many have you caught?"

Isaac Jr. turns, "Six, sir. The cooler weather is bringing them out of their hiding places."

"I wager it is. I hope I'll have some time to put a line in soon."

After the major departs, Elizabeth breaks the dark red seal and unfolds the letter.

Camp at Lowden's Ferry, September 7, 1777
My Dear Wife, Please give my love and affection to father and to your sisters and the boys. I continue to keep in good Health as does

much of our army now. A few weeks with tents and other comforts and hot food has revived us. I continue to serve as the commander for the regiment's light infantry company.

Elizabeth asks her father what this means.
"They're scouts and generally the best soldiers in a regiment. They do irregular duties. By that, I mean they go out in small groups or even alone. Isaac must be regarded as a capable officer."

My duty causes me to think often of you and the boys. I had command of a scouting party this week. We got ambushed by some Mohawks and were forced away from the route they traveled. I was unharmed and thanked the Lord for my continued Preservation. I am saddened and deeply Mortified for three of my men were killed. These were men picked from other companies of the NH and NY regiments. We thought it was worse, as two Men and a lieutenant got Separated from us during the fight. I was extremely Glad to learn of their safe arrival in camp yesterday.

Our men have done their Duties well and such gives me Confidence we will Prevail in the coming weeks. Our Army has Grown while Burgoynes has shrunk and this has raised our spirits. I do not know whether there will be a battle, if there should be, I believe we shall win.

We prepare to move North soon and I expect we will have hard duty investing wherever we encamp as many of us Presume we will Defend that ground. I have not seen brother Richard, tho I frequently hear News of the Militia and expect he is safe.

Your loving husband,

Isaac Frye

Elizabeth conveys the rest of the letter to Sarah and her father, then asks her father, "If there's a battle and we win, do you think

Isaac will be free to come home?"

"I suppose there is some small chance he could, though, to my thinking, tis unlikely."

"How so?"

"Isaac's with the northern part of the army. The southern part under Washington would also need to defeat Generals Howe and Cornwallis, and I would guess that less likely."

"Well, that's not going to stop me from hoping for a decisive end to this war."

7 ON THE EDGE

" ... I believe it was the severest Battle ever fought in America ..."

Alexander Scammell
In a letter to his brother, September 21, 1777

Well after sundown, by the light of a pair of dwindling candles, Isaac writes at his desk. Beside the candle are a half-eaten loaf of bread and a slab of mutton on a small plate. He munches on them between paragraphs. His tent flaps are tied shut against the evening chill.

Camp upon Bemis Heights September 17, 1777
Dear Brother Simon, My love and affection to you, Hannah and Uncle Joseph. It has been too long since I have written and far too long since we have Seen on Another. I am in good Health spirits and understand Elizabeth and my sons to be so as well.

I write to you on this occasion, with the Knowledge that tomorrow or one of the next Days we will meet our Enemy on the Field of battle. I therefore Request that should I Fall, you should take what steps as you can to See to my family's future and well Being.

Have you any news on where our brother Abiel lives now? I would write to him if I knew.

I am now in the left wing of our army under Command of General Arnold. Our camp is possibly the largest army I have ever seen, certainly on one patch of earth. The camps about Boston for being in a large arc about the city did not give quite so grand of an impression.

General Arnold seems most Agitated to get to the Fighting and winning of the war than any Officer with the possible Exception of our Col. Scammell. Our colonel is not so agitated as driven by some inner fire to do more than anyone else. He and Major Dearborn are ever plotting tactics and strategies and have drilled us for the past weeks with No mercy. He has had all the Captains read Memoirs of Frederich III. The effect of such has made us strong. The men respond to commands instantly and now take pride in their soldierly skills. We all know what we face, yet we are somehow boyant.

My duty tomorrow is with the light company from our regiment. We are ordered out for three days to watch the Enemy's camp for signs of an attack.

I must write to Elizabeth next. I do not Wish to Alarm her altho she must know our situation cannot be resolved by any means other than violence. It pains me doubly as we yet have rec'd no pay this year. Try as I do to honor my promises to her and my duties as an officer, I have managed to come upon the meaning of something I recall Uncle Joseph having said. A man's honor can be spread too thin.

With humble respect and deep affection, Your Brother

Isaac Frye

Isaac finishes his meal while the ink dries, then folds and seals the letter. Next, he writes to Elizabeth.

>Camp upon Bemis Heights September 17, 1777
>
>*To my Loving Wife Elizabeth, My love and affection to you and the boys. Tell them each I recall my memory of their faces to mind and that it gives me strength. I am well, though the time is coming soon that a resolution to the current circumstance will be upon us. Tonight that prospect keeps me awake, though I have put my affairs in order and have asked Simon to do what he can on your behalf should I fall. Though for the life of me, I cannot imagine such a fate coming to me. There is much talk in camp of Divine Providence having a hand in our cause. I am inclined to agree.*
>
>*Know that when it comes to it, I fight for you father our sons Sarah and even our farm and our right to determine our future. I know that you would fight to your last breath and would be disappointed if I should not do as much. I regret my My lines are less Straight tonight than usual.*
>
>*I will be on duty for a few days before I can write next. I will write as frequently as I circumstances allow.*
>
>*Your Loving Husband, till Death do us part,*
>
>*Isaac Frye*
>
>*P.S. Please give my love and affection to your father and sisters.*

Isaac sits early two mornings later with Colburn, who pours a third cup of coffee to stave off a severe case of the phlegm. They sit inside a cabin with Captain Amos Emerson of the First Regiment and Captain William Rowell from the Second. The cabin abandoned weeks earlier, is on the east side of the North River. It serves as headquarters for their reconnoitering of the enemy's camp a mile to the north. This morning a small fire burns in the stove for the coffee and to warm the room. They agreed the thick morning fog would mask the smoke for another hour should the enemy look their way.

Hawkins lets himself in, along with a cold draft causing an involuntary clench of Isaac's teeth. The heavy coat of frost that bends the grass outside the door is hardly visible against the fog. "Colonel Colburn, you better come have a look, they're parading and carrying packs."

Colburn sets his empty cup down and wraps a damp white handkerchief about his head. He ties it off, then he closes his eyes and exhales with an air of banishing his ailment. "Are you gentlemen certain none of you clubbed me on my skull with the butt of a musket while I slept?"

Emerson clears his throat then grins with mischief. "We swore a pact of secrecy on that topic, sir."

Colburn comes to his feet with exaggerated effort, tall, wiry and energetic, despite his current ailment. He nods to the captains. "Very well, Emerson, I won't pursue questioning your nocturnal activities. But, please do me the favor of sending Lieutenant Moore to General Gates. I expect the General will wish to send an aide to observe. Also, send a sergeant to General Poor, a man he knows, to apprise him of what Hawkins observed."

Rowell, a sturdy man of similar size and age with Isaac, responds first. "I'll send Sergeant George."

A few minutes later, riding rapidly north with Hawkins in the lead, Isaac notes the chilly morning's fog is thinning into patches along the river. They ride to the top of a wooded rise, with a view to the northwest. The enemy camp on the far side of the river comes into view through the trees as they arrive. They dismount and move to a place where Colburn can use his spyglass. "They're definitely up to something more than usual. The main part of their camp is empty. Several regiments and the followers have assembled on the river road. Captain Frye, go intercept whoever Gates sends and bring them here."

Isaac rides seven miles back past the cabin and down toward the bridge of rafts spanning the North River. As the bridge comes into view, he sees a rider pelting across. Isaac hails him with a wave, and within a few moments, he sees it is Lieutenant Colonel James

Wilkinson. Wilkinson, whose ambitions have taken him from General Arnold's service to General Gates' staff, fixes Isaac with a proud look. "Captain Frye, lead on."

The fog, even on the river, is gone when they reach the hill where Colburn and now only Captain Emerson wait. Wilkinson spends a full two minutes panning the spyglass back and forth over Burgoyne's camp. "You and your men should return to their regiments. God grant us strength, for today, it looks as though we may have the chance to gain a measure of satisfaction."

•••

Will and Uriah face north, peering out over the fortifications to the woods beyond. The orders to prepare for battle had come an hour earlier. Most of the regiment's men line the walls or gather outside their tents, all facing north.

Uriah points over the trees to a curl of smoke. The moment Will's eyes find the plume, the report of a cannon reaches his ears, causing him to jump, even though logically he knew the sound would reach him quickly.

Behind them, Goodale gives voice to his thoughts. "What's that about? Dearborn and Morgan can't be there yet. Even if they double-timed the whole way."

Goodman, who had been in the battle at Bunker's Hill, supplies an answer. "I expect they're finding their range, Sir."

Martin jogs in beside Goodale. "Captain's inbound."

Not far behind, Isaac and Hawkins stop at the edge of the section of tents his company occupies. Hawkins barks, "Gather around." The men of his company come together anxious for an update.

Isaac looks from face to face, seeing looks ranging from sober calmness to intense focus. A few of the younger faces show open fear. Isaac blows out a forceful exhalation before speaking. "Unless Major Dearborn and Colonel Morgan manage to drive off six thousand redcoats, the order to march will come very soon. Check your flints, get your hands on every cartridge you can carry, and top off your canteens. Make your peace with the Almighty now. Bring to mind who and what you fight for. When the order comes, jump to your place. Our lives will depend on it."

The men disperse to gather their muskets, cartridge boxes, hats, tomahawks, and canteens. They also secure the little things each keeps close to provide comfort, strength, or connections to home and family.

Minutes later, the concussive reports of volleys from rifles and muskets drift into the camp from over the trees. On the road leading north out of camp, Colonels Scammell and Cilley, stand ready next to their horses. They mount and as one shout for their regiments to fall in, on the double.

Will feels every hair on his head, neck, and arms stand on end. The energy of the men running into position is the most he's ever felt. Their backs straight, stomachs in, and shoulders back. Months of drills had long since displaced the stigma of being the regiment without uniforms. The precision and speed of their maneuvers erased any doubts that the Third New Hampshire's men were Continentals. Though Will knew the Connecticut militia regiments now assigned to Poor's Brigade had taken up the challenge to erase what separated them as militiamen from Continental soldiers.

The Third Regiment's pride swells as Scammell rises up in his stirrups. "With our arms, we carry our duty, our honor, and our valor into battle today. We fight for more than a King's sixpence. We fight for Liberty!"

Sergeant Major Adino Goodenough barks, "Hip Hip," and the regiment thunders "Huzzah!" in response.

A hundred yards away, Cilley's regiment roars their own "Huzzah!"

Scammell shouts, "We fight for Independence!"

Goodenough follows with a deep, "Hip Hip," and the regiment's, "Huzzah!" exceeds the previous.

The First Regiment's rejoinder does not come. Isaac turns to see General Arnold, who had galloped in a moment earlier, issuing instructions with voice and body to Cilley. Cilley turns and orders his regiment to march while Arnold urges his horse toward Scammell, who rides to meet him. They confer for only a few seconds, with

Arnold moving on up the hill toward General Gates' headquarters. Scammell thunders the orders for the regiment to march.

Their column marches three abreast through the gate. Scammell rides back along the column to confer with his captains a pair at a time. Ellis joins Isaac when Scammell reaches them. "Colonel Cilley will keep to the road and bear to the right before reaching the farm on the far side of the ravine. General Arnold orders us to go straight through the woods and look for Colonel Morgan or Major Dearborn to learn where we are most needed." Not waiting for confirmation, Scammell urges his horse forward toward the front of the regiment.

As the regiment bears off the road, the lead elements slow to negotiate the irregular terrain leading into a ravine. Isaac turns to Will and Uriah, "You two stay with me, keep me between yourselves and any action. The men need to hear you, so play your loudest.

They come to the bottom of the ravine that is several hundred yards wide. The dense tree canopy rearranges the sounds and echoes of the intermittent exchanges of musket fire. Though the battle is ahead of them, it sounds as though it is being fought all around them.

After crossing the brook at the ravine's center, they pick their way up the slope toward the fields a few hundred yards to the north. Well ahead, a booming volley of musket fire washes through the ravine followed by the battle cries of men charging. Another immense volley of musket fire responds, accompanied by cannon and the screams of wounded and dying men.

At the front of the column, Scammell urges Second Lieutenant Adna Penniman to make speed toward the sounds of battle. Penniman, age twenty-four, is the youngest of Scammell's company commanders. He found himself in command after Captain Gray obtained a furlough for sickness, and Lieutenant Huntoon went to recruit.

After a few minutes of difficult progress, the column halts. Isaac cannot see the reason. Colburn jogs back to Stone's company, which is immediately in front of Isaac's men. Isaac and Ellis rush to join Stone and Colburn.

"We just intercepted Cilley's men. The enemy drove them and our picquets off the field. They're now in the woods ahead of us." He points to the northwest. "We'll form a line with them on our left and come at them from the cover of the woods. Have your men load and fix bayonets.

The column resumes its progress northward, and Isaac sees Colburn ahead, directing them to turn right to form their battle line. After turning, they move one hundred yards further before General Arnold rides in from the left. Riding to Colburn, he points back in the direction they came, and shouts, "They've left a gap. We can flank them with your regiment and drive a wedge between their divisions. Counter march this line and have them follow me."

The orders ripple through the regiment to countermarch by company. Isaac and Ellis follow suit, and within seconds are trailing General Arnold, who guides them.

Arnold admonishes, "Keep low. There's a clearing just ahead to our right. The enemy's men are in the midst of the clearing. Cilley's men will front them, and we'll flank them."

Colburn catches up to Isaac and calls for Ellis to join them. "Once we enter the field, Ellis, you and Frye will be in the lead. Do not let them flank you and ware the woods on the far left of the road, enemy's troops may be within those trees."

They emerge from the woods, and Arnold leads Ellis's men at a jog into the field. Cleared of trees, but not stumps, each column weaves through the obstacles. Isaac looks about and takes in a trio of enemy regiments to their right. Woods and a road to their left, as Colburn described. The leftmost of the enemy regiments wear red coats with white facings and black tricorn hats. They epitomize the king's unwanted presence in America. Arnold wheels his horse and starts back along their line as Scammell gallops up past Isaac. As Arnold passes, he slows and shouts to Scammell, "Flank that regiment, don't give them a chance to turn. Cook's regiment is coming behind you. You have charge of them."

Scammell shouts to Isaac and Ellis, "Keep moving ahead."

The captains and musicians keep pace on the left of each of their company's columns. Scammell rides beside Isaac then wheels to check the progress of the regiment and that of the enemy regiment to their right. "Halt." Scammell's order stops them almost three quarters through the field.

In a booming voice, Scammell calls, "To the right, face! We approach, fire a volley, and charge."

"Forward ... march."

"Regiment ... halt." Isaac estimates they are sixty yards from the enemy regiment that is already pivoting companies to face them.

"First rank ... kneel."

"Second and third ranks ... close ranks."

"Poise firelocks."

"Make Ready."

"Cock firelocks."

"Take aim."

"Fire!"

The volley of lead balls rips into the redcoat's line throwing and spinning well over a dozen soldiers to the ground. The smoke from the volley obscures their view. Isaac orders his men to reform their ranks and to reload. The smoke clears while most of the men are ramming their cartridges home, and a problem becomes apparent. The redcoats had marched efficiently, avoiding Arnold's attempt to flank them. Isaac watches as a large division, twice their number, marches to front them.

Scammell, seeing the same, orders his regiment to fire by platoons while retreating. They began the sequence, but the redcoats, aware of their advantage, press forward with their bayonets fixed."

At that moment, Will grabs Isaac's arm and points to their rear. Several companies of grenadiers form a line, having just emerged from the woods to the west behind them. The grenadiers begin marching and cross the road, angling to Isaac's right. Their intention clear, cut off the majority of Scammell's regiment and their means to retreat.

Isaac sends Will running toward Scammell, pointing to the grenadiers. Meanwhile, to the east, the redcoats finish wheeling a company to flank Scammell's original firing line. They march, rapidly closing the distance on Ellis's company.

Behind him, Isaac hears the grenadiers and the companies at the other end of Scammell's line exchange volleys.

With Scammell's attention focused on the grenadiers, Ellis wheels his men to face the redcoats who flanked the line. Isaac orders his men to wheel about so they can cover Ellis's men who will soon need to retreat.

With the redcoats marching into range, Ellis's orders his men to fire. Two companies of redcoats return the volley, ripping into Ellis's company. Several men fall. Isaac feels a ball plunk into the ground next to his left boot. Somehow it had passed with no harm through six ranks of men in front of him.

Scammell directs Stone and Lieutenant Wedgewood, who commands Weare's company, to wheel their men to cover the Isaac's and Ellis's companies. Then he orders Isaac and Ellis to get their men back.

After retreating about thirty yards, Isaac's company begins moving in alongside Stone's men to their right, facing the enemy to the east. One of the enemy companies charges and begins to clash with the men at the front of Ellis's company. Glancing left, Isaac sees one of the grenadier companies peel off and charge toward his and Ellis's men. Isaac calls out, "Ware the left."

Scammell responds by ordering Livermore's men in that direction. They cannot respond fast enough. They fire a hurried volley, checking a quarter of the grenadiers. The grenadiers reach Isaac's and Ellis's men.

The men in front of Isaac's company have no choice but to join in the melee. Ellis's men all fight, several swing their muskets like clubs. The big men in Isaac's company, Sergeant Hall, Ebenezer Abbott, William Pettingill, and Ebenezer Carlton, rush forward. Hall and Abbott, who is only fifteen, form the center of the counter thrust. Carlton moves faster than any man near him. He tosses his musket to Joseph Gray, who had fired his own a moment earlier, and shouts, "Cover me," then dives in low with a tomahawk in hand. His first slice is deep into the back of the calf of one grenadier. He rolls right, and rises, cutting wickedly upward into the face of a second grenadier. Turning toward Ellis's men, he rushes to join their line. His ferocity spreads to them as they drive back a dozen redcoats and grenadiers, wounding half of them.

At the rear of his company, Isaac, worries at the number and sheer size of the grenadiers. They are shock troops with the largest of enemy's men. He turns to look for Scammell, whose situation is similar. Another company of grenadiers closes in on his part of the line. Those grenadiers force Scammell to raise and fire one of his pistols to help the men from Wedgewood's company frantically fight off the assault.

Ahead, in Isaac's company, Josiah Stone, a man of not quite average size, had not once in his forty-eight years faced a grenadier, much less the two now pressing him. He feints a jab with his bayonet at one. Not waiting to see if it drives the grenadier back, he pivots and swipes the butt of his musket into the knee of the other. The first grenadier held his ground, dodging Josiah's feint. He thrusts, taking Josiah in the ribs, instantly killing him.

Ebenezer Drury, Josiah's neighbor howls with rage at the sight of his friend's mortal wounding and charges with fury at the grenadier. He passes too close to another grenadier who heaves the butt of his musket into Drury's belly, knocking the air from his lungs, sending him to his knees.

Before anyone can reach him, a grenadier sergeant steps through the line and by main force drags the gasping Drury by his collar back into their lines. Goodale roars, "No!" as he snaps his musket up and fires at the sergeant. The shot strikes the next grenadier in the shoulder and serves to incense the sergeant, who delivers a vicious punch to Drury's head with the hilt of his hanger while glaring at Goodale. Drury slumps to the ground, unconscious. The sergeant directs another grenadier to drag Drury away and raises his musket. Sergeant Robert Wilkins is faster, having finished reloading his musket as Goodale fired. He fires at the sergeant, the ball, despite the short distance, veers off-center, piercing the right side of the sergeant's hip, causing him to twist away. The wound is serious enough to cause the grenadiers to pull their sergeant back. Then with no apparent explanation, the grenadier line begins a general retreat.

A moment later, the reason for the retreat becomes evident as a regimental sized blast of musket fire sounds from behind Isaac. Turning, but not able to see that regiment's flag through the great cloud of smoke, he sees their impact. At the far end of the grenadier line, they begin a rapid retreat back toward the woods to the west. The grenadier's departure opens the path for Scammell's men to make their way back to the safety of the wooded ravine.

Wasting no time, Isaac orders his men to reform their ranks and join the line formed by Penniman's and Livermore's companies. With practiced speed, they move into place and march to the end of Livermore's company. Ellis's men follow close behind to join the rest of Scammell's men in an orderly retreat.

Isaac recognizes Colonel Thaddeus Cook at the head of a regiment of Connecticut militia who had come to their aid. Isaac doffs his hat to the colonel. Dozens of other men do the same.

Once they reach the woods, they continue until reaching the small stream at the center of the ravine. After crossing, Colburn orders the column to turn right, upstream. They halt a minute later. Isaac addresses his company, "You fought well." He scans the men noting John Drury bent over his musket, which supports much of his weight. "Anyone wounded so bad you cannot fight?"

Drury doesn't move, but Hawkins, also having noticed his posture, steps to have a closer look. "Drury, your shoulder's a mess." Then pitching his voice toward Isaac, "He's been hit in the shoulder. No way he can shoot. His wound needs cleaning and binding."

Isaac looks to James Hutchinson, "Hutchinson, get him back to camp, then get back to us as quick as you can." Then to Hawkins, "Get his cartridges. We'll need them."

A soldier arrives at a run and stops before Isaac, offering a salute. Isaac returns it. "Cap'n Frye, sir, Colonel Scammell wants his commanders to assemble and report immediately."

The leaders of Scammell's companies arrive, holding heads high and with jaws set with simmering anger. Their eyes dart and scan the woods around them, searching for threats in all directions. Scammell begins, his tone is distracted and neutral, belying anxiousness to be in the fight instead of waiting for it to find him, "Report your company's losses."

Isaac keeps track as his fellow captains provide the toll from the engagement. Eight who are likely dead, seventeen wounded, and

Ebenezer Drury captured.

Scammell scowls for several seconds after Ellis gives the last report. "When we take the field, each of you must exercise more prudence not to give up our blood so freely. I'm going to find General Arnold and Colonel Cilley and get the plan for our counter-attack. Be ready to march when I return."

Isaac returns to find his men resting on the south side of the creek, then scans the area around them to find Hawkins with Goodale, who is in a state of agitation. He alternates between both hands on his hips and one pounding the trunk of a tree.

As Isaac approaches, he hears Hawkins working to calm Goodale. "We'll get him back, Zeke."

"What's this?" Isaac asks.

Hawkins turns and responds. "Eb Drury is his brother-in-law. He doesn't fancy breaking that news to his sister."

Isaac takes a deep breath then fixes his eye on Goodale. "The day's not over by half. It's my responsibility to break that news if that's what it comes to."

Goodale, grinds his teeth and growls, "That may be, but it's not right if I say nothing."

At that instant, the sound of not so distant cannon interrupts them. A ball plugs into the soft dirt on the far side of the creek about two hundred feet away, throwing clumps of mud into the air.

"Let's, move back a bit—no sense in one of those things adding to the day's toll. Colonel Scammell is with General Arnold now. When the colonel returns, he'll call again for the commanders. Then keep an eye out for my return and have the men ready to march, the instant I do."

Ten minutes and a dozen encroaching cannon shots pass before the arrival of a runner with orders for Isaac to attend Scammell. Scammell's demeanor fills with belligerence and determination, and his features animate as he addressed the captains. "General Poor arrived with the Second Regiment, and we are to form in a battle line with Colonel Adams on our right. The Connecticut militia will be on the far end, past Cilley. Some of Morgan's men will be on our left to cover the woods past the road. Dearborn and the rest of them are to

Honor and Valor

engage the grenadiers and keep them pinned down. Our line is to advance while firing and capture those field pieces before they find their range and push us further back. We outnumber them now. As we march, our object is the same, turn or flank the regiment on their right. Beal, Penniman, McClary, and Stone keep half your men in reserve should the grenadiers come through the woods like earlier. We will approach in a measured way, overwhelming them with our fire. Fire by ranks once your company is within one hundred yards range. Do your best to keep up enough smoke so the enemy cannot see where you march. If you come within range of the enemy, tell your men to use the fallen trees and stumps for cover. Keep your musicians back far enough so they can see me. Now get your men into the battle line and have them load. We fight to take back our land and country. Make sure your men know that."

After taking their place in the battle line, Isaac glances down the line, and even in the dappled dark green shade of the woods, he sees over a thousand men in the line stretching down the ravine. To his company, "Look down the line. We have numbers on our side. Do your duty and show those arrogant jackanapes we fight for far more than they do. Show them how many of theirs Josiah Stone's life was worth."

The orders come to make their way forward through the woods. As they move, Goodale remarks grimly, "I like these odds better. General Arnold's eyeballs are bigger than the stomachs of only two regiments."

Well before Isaac's company reaches the field, firing erupts far to their right. Isaac calls out, "Get ready. They're waiting for-"

The thunderous booms of cannon cut off his warning. Well down the line, the screams of men echo in the ravine. "Step lively men. Those guns are begging the honor of our company."

At the edge of the woods, the company reforms its ranks. Isaac sees the same regiment of redcoats they attempted to flank earlier still on the left two hundred yards distant. The enemy's line now extends diagonally with two regiments in the field. A third regiment extends into the trees to the right, explaining why Cilley's and Cook's men had already begun fighting. Hearing Scammell's order to march,

Isaac, orders his men forward.

One by one, Scammell's companies halt and begin firing by ranks. The first rank drops to a knee and fires, and then they start reloading; the second rank waits for a ten-count before firing. The third rank moves forward ten paces, drops to a knee and fires. As they advance, several of the men stepping to the front falter, balking at kneeling on corpses.

Each company times their firing to keep up a near-constant barrage of lead and smoke between themselves and the enemy. After hearing the enemy return a volley, Isaac catches a glimpse of them falling back in an orderly retreat to the far edge of the field.

Over halfway across the field, Isaac's gorge rises as he steps around a fallen redcoat soldier. A wide-eyed boy with the side of his head freshly blown apart. Isaac's eyes lock onto the carnage, fresh blood pooling in the grass. He keeps looking as he tries to comprehend this one tragedy.

"Steady, keep moving forward." Scammell's firm commanding tone issuing between volleys pulls Isaac's attention back to his men.

Once out of range, the redcoats began a counter-attack, also firing by ranks. In response, Isaac orders, "Front ranks take cover. The men fall to the bellies and move behind stumps. Third rank, fire, then fall back." The men in the third rank fall back about twenty yards after firing and begin reloading. Instead of ordering the front ranks to fire, Isaac waits, ordering the third rank to take cover after they reload. The redcoats advance within their range. Before they can raise their muskets, Isaac shouts, "Fire!"

The volley from the front ranks, along with similar volleys from Ellis' and Stone's companies, punches devastating holes in the line of redcoats. The enemy's line holds and returns the volley, but to little effect due to Isaac's men taking cover. The enemy officers shout orders to retreat. In response, Isaac orders his men to reform their ranks and continue forward.

As they march, Isaac looks to the right along their line and sees the entire line pushing the redcoats into the woods. Cilley's men begin celebrating the capture of the cannon. The euphoria of their success in driving the redcoats off the field erodes only a few seconds later. The wails of agony from wounded and dying men and anguished screams of doomed horses still hitched mercilessly to the cannon, outlast the cheering.

In the background, musket and cannon fire rages angrily behind the screen of trees to the west. The woods to the east begin emitting a rolling staccato of musket fire, signaling the start of the enemy's counter-attack against the Connecticut militia. Over that din, Isaac hears Scammell order the riflemen to keep firing upon the enemy in the woods. The men from Cilley's regiment heave and struggle to turn the cannon to face the redcoats, but without the horses, the heavy carriages prove immovable.

Will comes forward. Before he reaches Isaac, he trips on the outstretched arm of a fallen redcoat soldier. Isaac turns to see Will gag and throw up. The sun, still high overhead, and the strong smells of blood, excrement, and urine mixed with gunpowder and smoke make the field cruel and unpleasant. Over a hundred bodies strewn in grisly poses fill the middle of the field. "Buck up, Burton. This is the Hell that makes everything else in life sweet."

Recovering, Will wipes his mouth and nose on his sleeve. "Yessir."

Martin and Hall use the interlude to reload their muskets. Martin glances at the woods and pulls on the front of his shirt. "I bet they're wondering what the hell kind of militia we are with no fine uniforms."

Squinting into the woods, Hall mutters, "I'm pretty sure they're done underestimating us. Get ready."

As if Hall had given the order, the redcoats at this end of the line launch their counter-attack. Over a hundred of their light infantry sprint from the trees. Isaac turns to Will and Uriah, "Get back, look for the Colonel.

Isaac turns to face the attack. "Form the battle line. Form battle line!"

His men scramble into position, as do the men from several other companies. A second line of redcoats emerges from the woods. Out of range, but well-organized, they march with a vengeful posture. The first redcoats launch themselves onto their bellies as they come within musket range and prepare to fire from that position.

Isaac swears and orders his men back to his position. As they march, the redcoats fire their first volley. David Heseltine, a Wilton man, gives a pained shout, then falls to his right knee, his left leg not working. He rises and hops after the line then falls, calling for help. Amos Holt and Rueben Hosmer dash out, each hooking an armpit, lift Heseltine and lug him, in a lumbering run to catch up and pass through their line.

Will and Uriah find Colburn a moment after the redcoats fire their first volley. "Get back over there," he points to a spot halfway to the woods behind them, "then beat retreat."

Isaac orders a halt, faces his men toward the enemy, and orders them to fire by ranks. Their volleys prove premature as the redcoats remain out of range. Just before the smoke of their volleys obscures the field, Isaac catches sight of the redcoats marching to concentrate their numbers and fire toward the center of Scammell's men. Isaac's, Ellis's, and most of Stone's men reload. As they do, their peril of the remainder of Scammell's becomes apparent as the smoke clears.

Four companies of redcoat light troops had issued from the woods to the north. On the double, they close in on the far side of Scammell's line. They stop to fire a volley, then move forward again, forcing Penniman's, Beal's, and McClary's men to retreat. The redcoats change their angle march, driving a wedge between Scammell's men and the Second Regiment. They push forward, isolating Scammell's men on the field.

Will and Uriah keep their position forty yards back. Uriah furiously beats retreat, while Will puts everything his lungs can muster into his fife. Ahead, Hawkins is the first to recognize the call for retreat.

Isaac, in frustration, turns to his right, to see half of Scammell's regiment turned and driven to back toward Will and Uriah. The redcoats cut off the route to the woods and support from the Second Regiment as he watches.

Isaac orders his men to wheel march back towards Will and Uriah, with his men facing the enemy when they complete their ninety-degree pivot.

Over half of Scammell's line, in less than two minutes, has

Honor and Valor

collapsed on itself. The concentration of redcoats on their right, who have cut them off from the woods, advances. Scammell orders the left side of his regiment, which is now all but Isaac's and Ellis's men, to fire by ranks while retreating westward. He orders Isaac and Ellis forward, angling in toward the redcoat's flank.

Isaac's men begin firing by ranks. They fire two volleys, then Scammell orders Stone's company to break off and follow suit. The enemy responds. They focus their fire on Livermore's company, behind which Colburn, Scammell, and Sergeant Major Goodenough command.

In the space of a few seconds, the noise of musket and rifle fire increases, causing the smoke-filled air to quiver with a life of its own. Isaac's senses expand, attempting to accommodate the fury of the moment. He hears the zzst ... zsst zsst as three balls pass within a few feet of his head.

Glancing in Scammell's direction for any changes in orders, Isaac sees Colburn. He still wears the white handkerchief on his head, making him conspicuous even in the smoke, twist and fall from sight. At first, it doesn't make sense as Colburn should be out of range of the redcoats. Turning to the west, Isaac sees a dozen puffs of smoke at the wood's edge.

"Ware the rifles," Isaac shouts at Scammell, pointing back to the west. Scammell turns, as Goodenough falls, his back arching and legs giving out. Scammell jerks and lets go of his musket, as it spins out of his left hand.

A second later, a great volley of musket fire erupts from the woods to the south, cutting into the flank of the redcoats pressing Scammell's men. Scammell retrieves his musket, bleeding from the forearm where the ball ricocheted. Ignoring the blood, he orders his men to advance and calls for two men to assist Goodenough.

The redcoats fall back, firing in retreat, pulling back toward the middle of the field. Within a few minutes, Colonel Morgan's riflemen drive the enemy's riflemen out of the western woods. Scammell's men wheel and re-establish their line before the trees to the south. Behind Scammell's line, Isaac catches sight of Captain Emerson marching his men away to the east, back to Colonel Cilley's part of the battle line.

Not content, the redcoats begin advancing. Their numbers are double Scammell's. Their second volley forces Scammell to order his men to retreat into the woods.

At first, they make their way back into the woods in good order, though once past the initial steep slope, the men move at a full run down to the creek. Scammell's foresight to keep some men in reserve proves sage. They provide enough firing to check the charge of the redcoats entering the woods, as the rest of Scammell's men pass through their ranks.

Isaac's men, along with several riflemen, who shimmied down from their perches in the trees, continue for two hundred yards. They take cover behind standing and fallen trees as the redcoats begin to pour into the ravine.

Scammell roams behind his regiment exhorting any near enough to hear. "Take cover, make ready to give those the redcoats a warm New Hampshire welcome."

For several minutes the New Hampshire regiments avail themselves to the cover of the trees and fire at will at the redcoats who manage to stay out of range. Scammell, still ranging behind his regiment's ragged line orders, "Fire by platoons. Advance one while the others cover."

Livermore sees Scammell's forearm bright and bloody to the elbow. "Sir, your arm, the wound needs binding."

Scammell, as if noticing the wound for the first time, grimaces. "I'll return in an instant." He moves further back, searching for anyone with a cloth to bind the wound.

Isaac calls, "Martin, Sergeant Asa, Youngmans, Gray, Holt, Richardson, Blood, Abbott, and Lewis," the names of the front-most of his men. "Fire on Lieutenant Goodale's command, then move forward. Hall, Wilkins, Goodman, Carlton, Fuller, Blanchard, Smith, Perry, Powers, and the Baileys, fire on Lieutenant Hawkins' command. Cover them, then move up. The rest you will fire on my command and cover Hawkins' men."

Ellis and Stone order similar arrangements to organize their companies. Isaac calls out, "Lieutenants, have your men load and ready to fire."

After his men load, Goodale peers out from behind the oak tree he had found for cover. He searches for an exposed redcoat up the slope. One of Stone's platoons fires a volley, causing several redcoats to shift position and into view. Goodale calls to his men, "Now … Take Aim, "he gives them two long seconds to find their targets. "Fire." Goodale squeezes his trigger, and feels the jiggle of the flint striking the frizzen, then the delay and jolt as his musket discharges.

The smoke from their volley masks any view of whether the shots find their marks, but allows them time to rush forward. "Move. Stay low."

Immediately, Hawkins men fire a volley. Goodale spots a decent sized tree half a dozen steps ahead and alters his path to put it between him and the redcoats. He peeks out both sides to verify his men have found good cover as well. Isaac orders his men to fire, covering the movement of Hawkins' men.

They reload and repeat four times before forcing the redcoats to retreat out of the woods, back into the field. Morgan's riflemen waste no time, rushing through the line of the Continentals and up to the edge of the trees, to fire their deadly volley.

General Arnold emerges from the center of the ravine, riding from the direction of their camp. He urges them to reform their battle lines. "Take it to them while they are on the run. Retake the field!"

Isaac and his platoon follow Goodale's and Hawkins' platoons into the field. Goodale points across to the far side at a figure astride a horse. "There's Burgoyne himself." In less than a minute, the rest of Scammell's men emerge from the woods, to form their battle line and begin marching toward the redcoats on the far side.

Over the next two and a half hours, the sequence of taking the field and having the recoats force them to give it back repeats itself three times. Each time, less effort is needed to push the redcoats out of the wooded ravine and back across the field. On their third advance, the redcoats do not even attempt to enter the woods. They fire one volley before the New Hampshire regiments force them back to the middle of the field.

Scammell had returned in less than twenty minutes with his wound bound. All afternoon, his presence is as energetic as at the beginning of the battle. "Push 'em back one more time, boys and the field is ours. There's not enough of them left to stop us."

As they form the battle lines at the edge of the field, Isaac appeals to his men, "We keep the field this time. Be ready to turn them and charge with bayonets."

Andrew Bailey gripes, "I'm out of cartridges." Half a dozen men admit to the same. Before Isaac can say anything, Goodale barks, "When you pass one of our fallen, take his cartridge pouch. If you need a musket and must take the enemy's, take their lead too. Theirs is too large for these French muskets."

With the sun nearing the horizon to their left, the enemy's crimson coats glow brilliantly red, making them easy see. Isaac senses victory is close at hand. As they close within firing distance, Goodale and Hawkins order volleys in close succession then charge. Isaac orders his men to move forward and fire a covering volley, and then they join the charge. The ablest of the redcoat soldiers put up enough resistance to allow the others to retreat, before backing away themselves. Then, to their right, in the glow of the ebbing daylight, Isaac hears as much musketry as when they marched out from the woods early in the afternoon. Soon, shouting and drumbeats calling for retreat sound from the direction of Cilley's regiment.

Turning to his men, Isaac catches sight of Amos Holt and James Hutchinson, each with an arm supporting Elijah Mansfield. The Amherst man hops on one leg, the other bleeding profusely from a wound just below his hip in the meaty part of the thigh. Hutchinson grunts, "Bayonet."

The rest of his men stand warily, but uncontested, on the field. The same is true for Ellis's, Stone's, and Livermore's companies. The redcoats facing the right side of Scammell's regiment form ranks well out of musket range at the north edge of the woods. From behind, Scammell calls, "Retreat!"

Isaac, in angry disbelief, shouts orders for his men to form their ranks. Once the line forms, Scammell calls out for them to face to the right, putting Ellis's men in front. They march, angling toward the road back to camp as the sun lowers into the trees to the west. As they turn toward the road, Isaac finally sees the reason for the retreat. Two fresh regiments of Brunswickers emerge from the woods at the far right of the field. Distinguished by their tall headgear, they march in, taking possession of the field.

Only the sounds of buckles knocking against musket stocks and barrels and the tramping of feet accompany Scammell's men as they march through the ravine. Dusk fades to darkness as they push up the hill, and pass, exhausted, through the gate in the outer wall protecting their encampment. The light of a near-full moon bathes the hundreds of tents within.

Scammell calls out as they reach their tents. "Captains, get the state of your companies before dismissing them. Choose six men for guard duty—only your best most fit for duty as tonight may be the most important night this Army will face. See to your wounded, get some food, then meet at my tent in one hour."

As before, when the company commanders give their reports, Isaac keeps a mental tally. Ten killed and twenty-eight wounded. The light of Scammell's lanterns highlights the wild streaks of gunpowder and sweat on the commander's faces. Penniman's, McClary's, and Livermore's clothes bear stains of blood from minor wounds. They wait in silence for half a minute before Beal asks, "How's your wound, sir?"

"It's of no moment. Part of the bullet grazed the underside of my forearm. Mr. Hovey wisely sent his mate forward with dressings for such wounds. I met him within a few minutes of leaving the lines. I didn't take much notice of it afterward."

Beal continues, "Pleased to hear that, Colonel." Then in a solemn tone, "Have you got any rum?"

Scammell looks to Beal, whose visage is weary, then offers a small smile. "Yes. Yes, we should drink a toast to our fallen brothers. As Scammell retrieves a bottle and cups, he continues, "General Poor is meeting with Gates and Arnold. The worry is Burgoyne, despite his losses today, will attack early tomorrow. If that happens, we've got worse problems." He begins handing out the cups, pouring a generous measure for each captain. "We used most of our powder and lead today. They've sent an urgent request to Albany. If it comes to it, we will do like Stark ordered at Bunker's Hill and have only the best shots fire, and the rest of the men load and be ready with bayonets."

Dearborn enters the tent and takes in the sight of the captains on their feet with cups in hand. "Gentlemen, should I have brought a cup?"

Scammell responds, "I've got plenty Henry," and hands him the one he had filled for himself and turns to fill another.

Scammell holds his cup out. "To Lieutenant Colonel," his voice shakes, "Andrew Colburn, a most noble ... and brave officer-"

Dearborn raises his cup, "To Colonel Colburn." The captains solemnly echo the toast and drink.

Captain Stone raises his cup. "To Second Lieutenant Joseph Thomas, a young man of rare conviction and courage. I shall sorely miss him."

In unison, "To Lieutenant Thomas."

Scammell, having recovered his composure, "Gentlemen, if you're able, get some sleep. Tomorrow may be longer than today."

At three o'clock the next morning, Scammell's prediction comes true. The alarm comes with orders to strike their tents should the need to evacuate arise. The men work in tired silence amid dense fog. Isaac walks through his company's men as they dismantle, fold, and roll their tents.

As they begin loading their wagon, Livermore approaches. "Any idea what we face today?"

"None."

The pair stand in silence, observing their men. Scammell approaches from behind and joins them. "When they've finished loading, have them take up their arms and go to the walls."

Ten minutes later, the men lean against the fortifications, a few peering out into the fog. The chill, fog, and quiet feel surreal in contrast to the previous afternoon. Scammell, who remained with Isaac and Livermore, fidgets with irritation and looks to Livermore. "Send a dozen of your men to draw what ammunition they can. I did not think to send anyone last night."

To Isaac, "The more I think on it, the more I know we were cheated of a victory yesterday. General Gates could have sent just two more regiments in the middle of the afternoon. We would have swept

Burgoyne from the field and back to his camp. It was a singular opportunity."

"Aye. When you put it that way, the truth of it is undeniable. We had them beat at the end, and suffered more losses for the lack of those extra men."

"By my count, there were three of theirs on the ground for every one of ours." Scammell's tone turns to disgust. "Now, we sit here like hens in a house waiting for the fox Burgoyne to bring the fight to us on his terms."

"Begging your pardon, Sir, I'm no damned hen. Burgoyne learned as much yesterday. Perhaps Generals Arnold and Poor will make a case for taking the fight back onto the field where our numbers will have full advantage."

"I'll not hold my breath waiting for that. Though those generals both must know how close we came to a victory yesterday."

A long hour later, the fog showing no signs of lifting, Isaac turns toward a commotion by the gate to their left. Dearborn leads an enemy soldier toward the center of the camp. Wilkinson meets him and takes charge of the prisoner.

For two tense hours, the fog keeps those peering over the fortifications from seeing anything. The certainty of an attack keeps the men anxious and quiet. As the sun comes overhead, the fog dissipates, revealing no sign of the enemy.

Orders arrive to send out picquets and to assign men to burial crews. Goodale and Corporal Benjamin Smith volunteer to lead the latter. Of the six men in Isaac's company from Temple, they are the only two still fit for duty. The older men in the company, the Bailey brothers, Stephen Richardson, and Nathaniel Smith, also volunteer.

Late in the afternoon, Goodale finds Isaac in his tent, finishing a letter to Elizabeth. Isaac offers him a seat on his cot before asking, "Did you find Josiah?"

Goodale nods twice and lets go of a long sigh. "We did." Goodale hands Isaac a small bundle of papers. "These were still on him. Everything else was already gone, even his shoe buckles. Their savages took every scalp they could while the fog lay on the field. Our men caught some of Burgoyne's camp followers looting bodies. Some had already taken Colonel Colburn's watch and buckles. On the whole, they stole the uniforms and boots off most of the dead and left many naked. We marked the looters and caught one in the woods. He didn't have any of what we were hoping to find. We clubbed him hard anyway."

Goodale looks around the tent. Everything but Isaac's blanket remains packed. "Looks as though we should expect another early morning?"

"Aye. Thank you for bringing these." Isaac holds the papers up. "A grim task."

"It needed doing, and for Abby's sake - that's his wife, I thought it better if someone who knew him laid him to his final rest."

"Any sign of Drury?"

"No. It's a good bet he's a prisoner."

"I'll make sure the Adjutant knows. Anything else?"

Goodale shakes his head. "No."

From beneath his coat, Isaac produces a pint-sized bottle of rum and offers it to Goodale. "For you and your detachment. Compliments of the Colonel. Then get some rest."

Goodale sets his jaw, not quite able to grin, rises, and takes the bottle. "Much appreciated."

The next morning begins the same way, though at four o'clock, and by the time the sun burns away the fog, there, again, is no sign of the enemy advancing. Late in the afternoon, the officers meet in Scammell's tent. He begins, "Our picquets report the enemy is content to fortify their position." Scammell shows his consternation and disbelief as he rubs his chin while shaking his head. "General Gates seems willing to keep us in the routine of the past two days. If tomorrow should go like today, then plan, if you have not done so, to get some letters written. Write to the wives, fathers, or mothers of the men who fell. Tis the cruelest and most melancholy of your duties. I urge you to write with tenderness and to the nobility of our cause. None of our men died in vain." Scammell pauses, gathering his thoughts. "Write to your own families afterward. Send your lieutenants and ensigns to the wounded to offer to write for them and then for those who cannot write."

•••

In Wilton two days later, Elizabeth steps down from the back door of the farmhouse. She yawns as she places a hand on Sarah's shoulder and steps with care around her sister, who scrubs laundry over the washboard. The afternoon is warm though the sun is already more to the west than overhead.

Moving to the side, Sarah asks, "Did you enjoy your nap?"

Elizabeth's hand moves over her belly, giving her unborn child a gentle jostle. "Only a little. This one seems set on kicking every time I lay down. The only place I can get any rest is in the rocking chair." To emphasize her point, she straightens and rubs her lower back.

Sarah smiles with sympathy, then glances past Elizabeth. "Madame Rideout is walking this way."

"I may walk out to meet her. A short walk will feel good."

Elizabeth makes it past the corner of the garden before greeting Sarah Rideout, who carries her newest daughter. At five months, she is full of cheerful curiosity. Sarah begins, "Good afternoon. I'm pleased you saw me and came out where we can speak without little ears nearby."

With a look of sharp concern, "Is there anything the matter?"

"Ben just returned from taking a load of firewood up to the meetinghouse. He said a rider from the Army came in from New York and dropped off a packet for Major Abbott. The rider is already on his way to Exeter carrying news of a large battle fought four days ago."

For several long moments Elizabeth holds onto the breath she had taken in upon hearing of a battle. Not knowing what to say or ask next she looks everywhere but at Sarah's face. She slowly lets out her breath and gathers her wits. "Did he have news of any of the men?"

"No, Ben said the rider left before the battle ended. He confirmed all of General Poor's men had marched, and-"

Elizabeth interrupts, "that means Isaac fought." Thinking of Hannah's husband Richard, "Did he say anything of the militia?"

"He said most were not in General Gates' camp, so it seems unlikely they fought."

They stand in silence for a few moments. In a crisp tone,

Elizabeth's thoughts escape, "Now we must ignore this news or surely go mad with exceeding anxiousness."

With a kind look, Sarah makes an effort to keep her chin high, "No news is good news."

Sarah reaches and clasps Elizabeth's shoulder, then pats it before parting company. Elizabeth walks back to Sarah, who has finished with the washing.

Four tense evenings later, Elizabeth sits in the rocking chair, stitching a patch into one of the boy's shirts. At the table, Sarah cuts into a squash.

Isaac Jr. bursts in the front door, banging it against the wall. "Mama! Mister Parker's here."

Elizabeth resists the urge to scold Isaac Jr., and looks to Sarah, "Could you invite him in?"

Sarah follows Isaac Jr. out the front door, and returns a few seconds later without Henry Parker, but holding a letter. "Mister Parker begged not to impose. He said letters from the Army arrived at the meetinghouse today."

Sarah swaps the letter for the sewing, and Elizabeth sags with relief for seeing Isaac's handwriting on the outside. More to herself than Sarah, "My husband lives."

Camp Now or Never September 20, 1777
To my Dearest Elizabeth, I am pleased and grateful to the Hand of Heaven for Preserving my life yesterday so I may this Evening write these lines to You. My Love and affection for you are Greater than ever. This inst. I receive your lines. Tell my sons that I Wish I could see Them and hold each of them today more than any Day since I have been gone. Send my love and Affection to your Sisters, Brother and Father.

My regiment was yesterday called early into a general battle. We Fought with courage and valor for the Entire afternoon directly against Burgoyne himself. Some say he was wounded. In Truth we came close to winning the Field and the Day. We now expect any day to meet the enemy again. We saw two or three times as many redcoats dead or wounded than our own men. We now have three times more men than Burgoyne and his supply lines and means to escape are now sever'd.

Our men from Wilton fought with bravery and the ferocity of lions. I am grateful to Heaven that none were lost and only David Heseltine Wounded. It is not a severe wound tho it will take weeks or months to heal. Alas I can not say the same for the brave men from Temple. Josiah Stone was slain in the Early Part of the battle. I next have the sorry duty to write those difficult lines to his widow Abigail. Some of our men went out yesterday and buried him. Eb Drury was taken prisoner in the same part of the battle. His cousin John, a boy of 16 was sorely wounded in his shoulder. Just one other of my company was wounded. It is remarkable for the battle lasted many hours and we expended at least twenty rounds per man. Colonel Scammell says this was the largest and most violent battle to have ever occurred on this continent. Many of us are now convinced Divine Providence is guiding us to victory.

We are kept busy today with the constant expectation of the enemy attacking, and tomorrow will be more of the same. I believe they are much fatigued. We are fatigued as well, tho our morale has turned for the better for having turned back and worn down the finest troops King George could buy or send against us. This, above all, lightens our hearts and steps.

I shall write again soon with answers for your questions. My time is short today and I wished to get these lines to you as quick I can.

Your Loving Husband,

Captain Isaac Frye

8 VICTORY

> " ... *General Arnol says to General Gates it is Late in the day but Let me have men & we will have some Fun with them Before Sun Set upon which the Briggades Began to march at the Lower Lines three quarters of a mile from us But in Plain Site of us & soon a Very heavy fire Began Both with Cannon & Small Armes, such a seen my ears never were greeted with Before the Sun was about an hour & half high you can not conceive. ...*"
>
> Nathan Bachellor
> In a letter to his wife, October 9, 1777

Will sits cross-legged on his blanket in the rear of the tent he shares with the company's corporals. The corporals play a game of cards around the light of a pair of candles while Will, head down, practices fingerings on his fife.

As the corporals finish their hand, Goodman turns to Will. "Burton, you should join us. We're only playing for these pebbles and pride."

Will shakes his head, and his fingers continue moving over the fife.

Martin looks to Goodman, who nods once. "You've not said ten words to any of us since the battle."

Will's fingers stop as he fixes one eye on Martin, his expression a mixture of sullen defiance.

Honor and Valor

After several seconds, Martin tries again. "You don't have to talk about it, but if you think you can keep all inside and to yourself, your thoughts will eat your mind from the inside out. You got to do other things. Now get over here and remind us how easy twill be for us to take your pay when it finally comes."

Will's expression doesn't change. "Fine." He scoots over as Godfrey and Martin make room. As Goodman deals, Will mutters, "I got plans for your pay too."

Goodman chuckles. "That's more like it. Though my wife don't want you wastin' no money on sweets."

Smith harumphs, "You still haven't wrote to her about the pay chest bein' taken by the enemy three months ago, have you?"

"Nope, didn't want to risk the enemy intercepting such a letter and learning the pay chest held only worthless paper."

Godfrey wins the hand and the deal. As he deals, "You see those boys from the second regiment?"

Martin grunts his confusion.

"The ones that were prisoners at Fort Ti. From the looks of them, they had it worse than we did."

Goodman murmurs in agreement. "All except Colonel Hale. Burgoyne sent him home on parole. Tis what I heard. Seems mighty odd he didn't go to Number Four, then turn right around and join with some militia and march to rejoin us."

Martin shows his winning hand. "They say Colonel Hale takes himself quite serious. Got a strong sense of honor and not the sort to go back on his word, no matter who he gives it to."

Smith rolls his eyes and shrugs. "We're in a war. I don't care if he is a colonel. Putting his honor above our cause is not right."

Godfrey flips his cards to Martin. "Aye, neither was Gates' replacing General Arnold with General Lincoln."

Martin doles the cards out. "Gates has to prove he's in charge. He don't like how so many are saying Arnold's the reason we fought so well."

Will, with a hint of anger in his tone, "Arnold about got us all killed."

Goodman adds, "That's right. It was General Poor and our colonels who kept us in the fight."

Will shows his winning hand.

Smith sighs with disgust. "At least these pebbles ain't worth more than a Continental. Deal me some better cards, Burton."

As Will deals, "Maybe Burgoyne will surrender now that we got Fort Ti back."

Godfrey shakes his head. "The king would put his head on a pike. You're right though, Gentleman Johnny's lost his supply lines, and we've got him caught between here and Fort Edward. There'll be another battle. Two if he's stubborn."

Goodman glares at his cards. "They're low on food and quite a few deserters coming in over the past few days."

Martin wins again and grins. "Our fortunes are definitely on the rise. One more hand?"

About forty paces away, Isaac joins the other company commanders in Scammell's tent. Scammell's mood is lighter than in the previous days. "Gentlemen, our prospects get better with each day. The more I've thought upon this, the more I know tis true. If General Gates had sent enough men, we would have swept the enemy from the field and won the day. But now, I have it positively that General Gates knows this for certain, and we will not be short of men the next time we take the field."

Scammell meets the eyes of the gathered men. The lanterns hanging from the poles of his tent provide enough light to see their faces. No eyes on the ground, though their posture is hardly energetic given two weeks of early morning alarms. "Our men need to know this. Our recent battle was of great moment in our cause. Even with the news of General Washington's defeat at Brandywine, what we did offset that. Our men stood eye to eye with the enemy and didn't flinch or shirk their duty. They withstood blow after blow and hit back harder every time. One of the next days will bring an alarm, and the Generals will call on our men again. Drill them hard tomorrow. Forbid them false confidences and remind them of what we fight for. Do any of you have questions?"

William Ellis clears his throat. "About General Arnold. Are we to follow his orders?"

Scammell does not hesitate. "Yes. He is a general officer appointed by the Congress. You will respect him as such. Even though General Lincoln commands our division now, General Arnold remains under General Gates' command. You are to presume any order he gives as coming directly from General Gates. Is that clear?"

"Yessir. I assumed you know why I asked."

"I did, and the politicking between the Generals' aides must not become a distraction. Most of you know Colonel Wilkinson, and his canny ability to place himself at the center of things. I met that conniving rascal in Montreal when he was currying General Arnold's favor. His latest gambit is cultivating sleights of honor and playing their owners off of one another to ends only he and Heaven knows. Be prudent and do not spread rumors, or speak ill of, or backbite any of your fellow officers. Am I perfectly clear on this subject?"

...

Isaac and Goodale stand off to the side as the regiment practices their drill four days later in the warm early afternoon sun. Hawkins takes his turn in command of the company as they work on perfecting the timing of oblique marches. Their goal is to stack two or three companies on one end of the regiment's line of march. First Ellis's company angles back, then before the last man steps clear of the lead man in Isaac's company, Hawkins gives the order for Isaac's company to turn, precisely on time. The result is a hammerhead on the left side of the regiment, capable of tripling the firepower on a single enemy company. At the rear of the regiment, Scammell, not displeased, orders the men to hurry back to their original line so they can repeat the drill.

As the men fall into place, the drummers on guard duty begin the ominous drum roll to call the men to arms and then to their posts to defend the camp. Isaac looks to Goodale, "It's been, what, three days since we last heard that?"

"Four, I think. Before that, at least twice a day for ten days running. So, I bet," he raises his eyebrows, "this one's real."

On cue, a rider pelts at full gallop into the camp through the northern gate below their tents. Hawkins joins them as the rider passes. "That's one of Dearborn's men."

Scammell shouts orders for the men to retrieve their arms, then to immediately form ranks to march before he turns and strides in the direction of General Poor's tent. His course takes him not far from Isaac. "Pass the word. Inspect your men. Have them retrieve what they need to take the field. I sense our waiting is over."

As Isaac completes the inspection, General Arnold gallops by, heading out the gate. Half a minute later, General Lincoln follows. As Isaac dismisses half a dozen men to retrieve their missing equipment, Colonel Wilkinson rides past.

Livermore and Ellis converge on Isaac. Livermore deadpans, "The enemy must be marching. No other reason to send two generals and a colonel out to reconnoiter."

"Aye true." Isaac grins in response. "General Gates himself might ride out next."

Ellis, looking up toward the sun, "A fine day to finish this business with Burgoyne. Those scouts won't return for at least ten minutes, so we best let the men get some water."

Isaac looks out to the north. "Good idea, no excuse for not being ready on a warm day like this."

Not long after buckets of water and ladles begin circulating, Wilkinson enters the camp at a gallop, riding toward General Gates' headquarters. Hawkins moves beside Isaac and Goodale. "He gave no sign to stand down."

Goodale murmurs his agreement, the barks to the men, "Move that water faster."

Two minutes later, two long columns of Colonel Daniel Morgan's riflemen stride by with their usual mix of swagger and steely attitude. Fifty yards behind them General Poor approaches, flanked by Colonels Cilley and Scammell. The latter breaks off, motioning for his officers to meet him.

"The enemy has sent out a rather large foraging party to one of the rye fields to the west of the farm where we fought the last time. They've got several field pieces and posted guards in the woods to the south. Morgan will assist Dearborn's men in driving them out of the woods. The grenadiers are on their left, our right. We'll post ourselves in the ravine below the closest corner of the rye field opposing the grenadiers. Colonel Cilley will have the center of our line, and our men on the right and the rest on Cilley's left. Keep the men quiet as we march. The less they know of our numbers, the better. We'll have the lead. When we reach the creek bed, we'll cover the rest of the column as they pass on their way west. Learned's Brigade will follow ours and go to the western end of the field, giving us superior numbers. Prepare your men to march. We leave within the minute."

Once past the gate and marching northward through the early autumn foliage, the reports of musket and rifle fire to the west and north grow in frequency. As they cross the ravine, the skirmishing ahead dissipates and ends entirely within a minute. Hawkins surmises, "Sounds like Morgan's men have run off the skirmishers."

Isaac returns Hawkins' look with grim optimism. "Aye, We'll be able to get to our work directly."

A few minutes later, they make way down into a smaller ravine below the rye field. Isaac catches glimpses of the redcoat's battle lines forming in the field above and teams of horses pulling their cannon into place. A few yards to the left, he sees a fallen redcoat light infantryman, who lies still, bloody and crumpled. Orders come back along the line of march to fix bayonets and load once they halt. As they come to the creek, they cross, then Scammell splits his men, sending all but Isaac's and Ellis' companies to the right.

As Cilley's men begin marching by them, the first cannonball hurtles overhead, preceding its report by only a short interval. It severs branches and produces a wake of spinning twigs and leaves. As another ball passes overhead, Livermore calls out, "Keep marching. It's no different than when Colonel Stark marched us to Bunker's Hill."

More regiments pass by as the redcoats keep up the barrage of cannon fire. The trees and the ground on the far side of the ravine take the brunt of the damage.

As Cilley's men pack into place, Cilley and Scammell confer for half a minute behind Isaac's company. Scammell directs Ellis and Isaac to condense their men into six ranks with their largest men in front.

Once the men adjust their formation, Scammell adds, "General Poor's orders: wait for the order to fire. Twill not come until after the enemy fires their first volley. We'll give hand signals to move forward." Scammell moves down the line repeating the orders.

Goodale approaches Isaac, his eyes narrow and his jaw set. His tone grim and determined, "Mind if I have the honor of leading our men up the hill?"

Judging Goodale's intensity as being sincere and born of long considered intention to settle a score with the grenadiers, Isaac nods once. "Not that any of us could stop you. Keep your wits and our men about you, as I don't fancy writing a letter to your wife tonight."

"Aye." Goodale's eyes narrow with purpose. "I expect the rest the men will be on our heels."

Isaac clasps Goodale's arm, "They will."

Goodale moves off with Sergeant Hall. Their rank includes Carlton, Abbott, Pettingill, and Goodman.

Scammell returns a few minutes later. "We'll move forward shortly. Keep your men silent and low, and do not return fire until ordered. If we can get close enough, we'll charge."

A few minutes pass before Cilley's men begin moving, and Scammell signals his men forward. Isaac signals to Goodale, pointing to his eyes with two fingers and then rapidly back and forth between himself and Goodale. Then Isaac motions his men forward and to keep low. They move with cautious attention to keeping quiet.

About thirty yards later, through the trees, Isaac sees the grenadiers' line already a dozen paces into the woods marching two ranks deep. Scammell and Cilley, in voices barely above a whisper, order their regiments to halt. They wait between ten and fifteen feet below the level of the advancing grenadiers, who stop about forty yards away. Their commander orders, "Take aim.", Isaac waits a moment longer then fights to keep from shouting as he commands, "Get down."

Isaac ducks into a low crouch then motions to Will and Uriah to get behind him and to stay down. As they drop to their knees, the grenadiers' fire their volley. Most of their lead flies overhead. A few men yelp and grunt with pain. Ahead of Isaac, Amos Fuller, from

Wilton, doubles over clutching his upper arm. After moving close to Fuller, Isaac asks, "Can you make it back to camp? Fuller sets his jaw against the pain gives a pair of quick nods. Isaac lifts the strap of Fuller's cartridge box over his head and nods to Fuller, who slides, making his way back down the slope toward the creek. Isaac hands the cartridge box to Martin and returns to his place in front of Will and Uriah.

From above, Isaac hears the grenadier commander issue orders. His tone is a mix of frustration and arrogance. "Fix bayonets and charge those damned rebels."

Cilley, unable to let the insulting tone and words go without rebuke, shouts with defiance, "Two can play that game. Go ahead and charge."

Needing nothing more than Cilley's last word, the several hundred men in the front ranks of his and Scammell's regiments roar and surge forward. Isaac shouts to the remaining men. "Steady ... Move forward. Cover the front rank."

The grenadiers move back in good order, offering the points of their bayonets for resistance. The men leading the charge begin firing as they close within a few yards. At such close range, they break the grenadier's discipline, sending many of them running for the rye field. A few small groups attempt to hold their ground. The New Hampshire soldiers swarm them in a fury, stabbing and clubbing with their muskets. In less than ten seconds, the grenadier's line erodes and disappears. Dozens lay dead and wounded. The others regroup in the field beyond the trees.

Scammell shouts for his men to reform their ranks. Isaac sends Hawkins and Sergeant Wilkins forward to call the men from the front rank back and for Sergeant Asa to have the remaining men reload.

As Scammell's and Cilley's men reform the front rank, the commander of the Grenadiers shouts with furious anger at his men to reload and advance. Still coming up the slope, well within the woods, Scammell and Cilley order their second and third ranks forward. Scammell orders a halt and for the men to prepare to fire from one knee and take cover behind the trees. The grenadiers fire an ineffective volley. Scammell orders the second and third ranks to fire.

Isaac, on a knee with the third rank fires, but the great cloud of smoke that results obscures everything.

Scammell orders the second and third rank to reload, while the first rank marches through. Isaac peers ahead, the smoke is still too thick to see anything. Scammell orders the men all the men forward a dozen paces. They wait there, listening for the grenadier commander's orders.

As the smoke finally thins, a line of one hundred fifty grenadiers stands ready to fire. Forty yards in front of them are three ranks totaling a thousand New Hampshire Continentals with their barrels leveled. The commands to fire are simultaneous. The result is another great cloud of smoke. Scammell and Cilley immediately order their men to reload. Isaac feels his heart pounding like never before. As the clanking of the men returning their ramrods ends, they all listen but hear nothing from the grenadiers. Scammell and Cilley press their advantage and order their men to advance.

As Isaac and his men emerge from the cover of the trees and smoke, they see the grenadiers more than a hundred yards ahead in the rye field. Cilley directs his men to the left toward capturing the enemy's cannon. Scammell splits his men, the left half, including Isaac's men, to move forward with orders to counter anything the grenadiers do. The others turn to the north, facing another detachment of redcoats. Isaac recognizes their uniforms as belonging to the regiments they fought two weeks earlier. That enemy detachment turns and marches to join the grenadiers, forming a group about a company larger than Scammell's regiment. They begin advancing and collecting the redcoats who had been with the cannon.

Scammell and Cilley order their men back into the woods to form their lines anew. Once reformed, Scammell orders his men forward. As they enter the rye field, the redcoats are waiting. Scammell orders them to fire by platoons. The range is too far, and the first two ranks fire with little effect. As the third rank moves forward, the first rank of redcoats fires and the next ranks charge, leading with their bayonets. Scammell and Cilley immediately call for a retreat back to the woods, and for the third rank to fire as needed to cover the retreat.

As they reform their ranks, Cilley shouts to Scammell, "We've got numbers. Advance. Make them fire first. Then fire and charge."

The simple plan works. As they advance, the redcoats fire, and to Isaac's amazement, none from his company fall. After ten paces, the first and second ranks fire, and then charge. As they come roaring through their smoke, the sight of the backs of most of the redcoats greets them. The beaten redcoats run headlong for the center of the large field.

To his right, Isaac sees Wilkinson ride into the field and take stock of the circumstances. Looking left down the line, Isaac sees the rest of Poor's Brigade push through. They overwhelm the left half of Burgoyne's line, who abandon their field pieces to seek the safety of the center of the rye field.

Closer, just a hundred yards to Isaac's left, Cilley sits astride one of the captured twelve-pound cannon having a good laugh and taunting the redcoats. His men begin to reform their ranks a few dozen yards further into the field.

Isaac turns back to see Wilkinson ride fifty yards out into the field where one of Scammell's men is poised to bayonet a wounded redcoat officer, whose legs are wounded, rendering him unable to move. Some smoke clears, and to Isaac, it appears the officer is the commander of the grenadiers. Wilkinson calls off the over-zealous private and dismounts. After a few words with the commander, he lifts and carries him to his horse, then drapes him over the saddle. He leads his horse toward the woods and camp.

Scammell shouts for his men to hurry as they reform their ranks. Isaac seeing the enemy now advancing, joins Scammell in urging the men to speed. Once the men are in their ranks, Scammell yells, "Let's remind these misbegotten rascals that this is our ground. Advance and fire by platoons. Drive them off the field."

The distance between the opposing forces shrinks. General Poor's men outnumber the redcoats by two to one. The redcoats halt first. Scammell, Cilley, and the rest of General Poor's brigade continue a few more steps. Isaac estimates the distance to be a little over sixty yards. A moment later, Scammell orders the first rank to fire. The line of redcoats fires a few seconds later. Along Scammell's line, six men fall. Stone orders his second and third ranks forward men forward, and Isaac echoes the order. After ten paces, they halt, and Hawkins orders the second rank to fire. Isaac orders the third rank forward and fires with them. He hears Goodale ordering the first rank ahead into the thick cloak of musket smoke. As they pass by, Scammell orders, "Fall back fifty paces out of the smoke, they've retreated."

Once out of the smoke, Isaac counts his men. Three are missing. Remembering Amos Fuller was on his way back to camp, he scans the men again. Nathan Fish and Thomas Blood. To the company, "Where are Fish and Blood?"

Hall responds, "Fish took a bad wound in his leg. Blood's his nephew and took him to camp."

Isaac sees Adjutant Gilman jog from the south where General Poor commands, toward Scammell. Catching Stone's and Ellis's attention, he leads three captains as they converge on Scammell.

They arrive to hear Gilman relay Poor's orders, "The general directs us to march immediately north along the east edge of the field to cut off their retreat, then flank them and box them in. We have a chance to capture Burgoyne and this part of his army."

A look from Scammell sends the captains back in the direction of their companies as he orders regiment to face to the right, then to march on the double. A large cloud of musket smoke blows between them and their goal, and as they emerge from it, Isaac sees they are too late. Two hundred yards ahead, the remaining grenadiers cover the last detachment of Burgoyne's men as they march straight into the woods to the right.

Most of the regiment hears Scammell's clipped tone and deep frustration, "Infernal smoke. Regiment, by companies, countermarch!" As they begin the maneuver, Scammell jogs toward Isaac. "Send runners to General Poor to get orders. Give me three men."

Isaac doesn't hesitate, "Sergeant Wilkins, Carlton, and Gray, get over here."

The three arrive, and Scammell sends them running again before they can come to a full stop.

The regiment begins retracing its path. Halfway back along the field's edge, Wilkins, Carlton, and Gray emerge at a run from the thinning smoke. Scammell jogs forward to meet them.

Wilkins reports, "General Poor orders us to turn east through the woods. General Arnold has already got Paterson's and Glover's brigades moving to attack their fortifications in the field on the other side."

Scammell surmises, "Likely where those who retreated have gone." Looking to Wilkins. "Anything else?"

"He's sending Cilley and Reid too. Their men are spread out and will arrive as they can. Cook's militia will come behind cover the woods for us."

Scammell's grin is fierce as he looks to the company commanders who had joined the group while Wilkins reported. "The sun's getting lower and will be at our backs. Let's move fast and see who we can surprise."

Scammell orders the regiment to face to the left and make their way east into the woods. Unlike in the ravines to the south, the ground within these trees slopes gently downward. Almost immediately, they hear the sounds of a heated battle commencing ahead and to the right. Less than halfway through the quarter-mile trek, Isaac begins catching glimpses of the conflict ahead. The enemy's redoubt is a long rambling earthen wall ten to a dozen feet high and stretches several hundred yards across the field. As they approach, the sound of musket fire and the enemy's cannon becomes more tumultuous, and all concentrated to their right.

Within a few minutes, a flash ahead and to his right alerts Isaac to the location of the enemy's cannon. Between the trees, the sharpened ends of thousands of branches forming the abatis come into view. To their right, six Massachusetts regiments pull back from the fortification. Their attempt to storm the right third of the fortification repulsed. They fire at will, taking advantage of having enough numbers to provide constant covering fire. A dozen paths torn through the abatis at that end of the redoubt give testament to their bravery.

As Scammell's men come within twenty yards of the edge of the trees, a lieutenant from one of the Massachusetts regiments

Charles E. Frye

approaches. He shouts to Ellis and points left, "Keep to the edge of the woods, you'll be out of their range. They've got men in a small redoubt to your left."

Turning in that direction, Isaac sees an outer work intended to create a no man's land between the woods and the massive redoubt. Isaac passes the information to Stone on his left.

After surveying the situation, Scammell calls his commanders together. Speaking rapidly, he lays out the plan, "Companies one through four will keep well within the trees and move further left. The other companies move just a little left of this spot. Choose a position that puts the redoubt between you and the enemy cannon. Companies two, three, six, and seven will charge while the others cover. Shout at the tops of your lungs as you charge. Scare them into firing early, and they won't have time to reload. I'll go with the group on the left and fire a shot," he pats hilt of his left side pistol, "to signal the charge." Looking at Captain Stone and Isaac, "The sun is getting low, so watch for the flare of my shot."

Within minutes they are in position only a few yards within the trees. Stone and Isaac move out ahead of their men and keep their eyes on the trees a hundred yards to their left. An orange flare and a puff of smoke precede the sharp report of Scammell's pistol. Isaac nods at Stone and turns to his men, arrayed in three ranks behind him, and shouts, "Charge!"

Isaac and his company begin sprinting toward the redoubt, roaring at the tops of their lungs. The men in the redoubt fire immediately, no more than ten shots.

In the rank ahead of Isaac, Ezra Fuller, a young black man, cries out twists and crumples to the ground, struck in the shoulder. He had been sick in the spring and joined the company in the past week.

As they close within twenty yards of the redoubt, the last of the redcoats exits the far side, sprinting for the main fortification. Out in front of the men, Goodale points toward the fleeing redcoats and shouts, "Fire on them!" Stopping, Isaac takes aim and fires. Barely a moment intervenes between a cannon's report, to his right, and the sizzling blur of a cannonball passing a foot beyond the tip of his musket. The force rags the barrel of his musket to the left, and it pulls hard on his coat.

The shock makes Isaac's next breath require a conscious effort. A few of his men fire, others stop, transfixed by the sight of the ball passing so close. Not wasting time, Isaac points to the redoubt and shouts, "Charge," and begins running again. A few of the fastest men in Isaac's and Stone's companies arrive first and race around to the back of the fortification. They enter and report it to be empty.

Isaac stops along the side of the small redoubt. Captain Stone arrives a moment later and asks, "How close?"

Isaac spreads his hands about four feet wide. "Just past the end of my musket. Stone's eyes go wide, then a big grin splits his ruddy cheeks. "So close enough to get a good shave?"

Isaac cannot help himself and chuckles softly. "No."

Hawkins joins them. "Our charge, despite the interruption, was quite impressive, yes?"

Isaac thinks a moment before responding, "Apparently. They must have been pouring out the back before our men had taken ten steps. Can't say as I blame them, outnumbered twenty to one." Looking about, Isaac greets Livermore and Beal, whose companies arrived twenty seconds after Isaac's. "Looks like we've got this well in hand. Any word from Colonel Scammell?"

Beal answers, "Aye. He wants us to reform in the woods. Cilley's and Reid's men have arrived. I expect we'll be charging the main works next." Isaac catches Hawkins' gaze, "Get the men back into the trees."

As they hurry back to the woods, Hall runs to catch up with Isaac. "Sir, I sent Ezra Fuller to camp with Ichabod Perry."

Isaac grimaces and shakes his head in frustration. "Thank you, sergeant. Anyone else hurt?"

"No, sir."

They reach the trees, and Isaac directs Hawkins and Goodale to get the men formed into a battle line. He strides north along the edge of the woods in search of Scammell. In half a minute, he finds the Colonel with most of his commanders already present. Scammell points out places along the enemy's fortification on which to focus. In a low voice, Livermore tells Isaac, "We're waiting for Lieutenant

McGregore to return with orders from General Poor."

The relative quiet becomes even more so as the firing far to the west on the other side of the woods drops off. Jubilant whoops and shouts began drifting in through the trees. Beal speaks first. "Sounds as though General Learned has had some success. I don't imagine Burgoyne's men would have any reason to celebrate."

Scammell nods with a positive look in his eyes. "Yes, it does sound as though that part of our army has succeeded."

McGregore arrives a minute later. Scammell motions for him to join the group. "What are General Poor's orders?"

"Sir," beings McGregore, "he would have us attack straight ahead. Cilley's and Reid's men will be on our right and Glover's and Paterson's brigades beyond them. The general believes we have enough men to overrun these works. He orders us to advance on Colonel Cilley's lead and to fire by platoons to soften them up. He says you are to ascertain where they have the fewest men. If conditions look favorable, he will give the order to charge such a place as you see fit. He says if they receive reinforcements from their main camp, we may retire."

"To your companies, gentlemen, our time is now."

No sooner than Isaac finishes briefing his company, they see Cilley's men step out into the field. As they advance, Isaac directs Will and Uriah to keep back about twenty yards and to give warnings of any changes to the direction of the enemy's cannon. The cannon on the right side of the redoubt fire, causing Isaac to look south. The smoke wafts toward the Massachusetts regiments advancing toward the far end of the redoubt. Some of Cilley's companies, now close enough, begin firing volleys. The enemy opposite them responds with light scattered fire.

Eighty yards, seventy yards. Isaac strains his eyes and ears for signs of activity atop the fortification. Twelve feet tall and no hint of movement. Sixty yards. Still no sign of the enemy. Fifty yards. In a low voice, Isaac calls, "Steady" to the first rank. Along the front rank, his men continue with their muskets raised. Three paces later, the top of the redoubt breaks its silence. At least a hundred muskets rise and drop outward toward the advancing line. Isaac, along with the commanders in Scammell's line, shout, "Fire!"

The first rank discharges their volley followed a split-second later by the enemy firing in return. Isaac orders the second rank to advance a few paces ahead of the first. Unable to see the walls through the smoke, Isaac waits for a ten count before ordering them to fire. After sending the third rank forward, he waits until the smoke thins. It reveals a great smoldering porcupine with muskets for quills arrayed before them. Scammell shouts, "Fire!".

Their ragged volley mixes with the enemy's firing at the same time. Peter Chandler, who moved into Wilton shortly after Isaac left for Fort Ticonderoga in April, jerks hard to his left and falls. His musket strikes Joseph Gray as he goes down.

Scammell orders them to stay in place and fire. They fire three volleys with no response. With each volley, Isaac feels the tension rise as the order to charge does not come. Instead, the drummers beat retreat. Isaac orders, "Ranks two and three, to the rear, face. Forward March. Get our wounded as you go."

As they pass through the first rank, Isaac orders them and Goodale to back away and to fire at first sight of the enemy muskets. They arrive and take safe positions within the edge of the line of trees opposite the redoubt. Word comes down the line of the enemy getting reinforcements from their main camp located down the hill behind the fortification.

The smoke lingers on the field. The enemy cannon continue to fire for several minutes. Their flashes alert the men from Massachusetts and New Hampshire to get down or take cover behind trees. As they wait, the deep shadows cast by the last light of the day drain into darkness and smoke. With the moon hidden by thick clouds, the night is dark.

The occasional musket firings from the top of the southern end of the redoubt cease as do the cannon. Standing just out front of the trees with Hawkins, Isaac peers into the darkness. "I see no evidence of reinforcements. If anything, it's become quieter by the minute."

"Aye. By my reckoning, it's dark, and here we stand with unfinished business."

Scammell walks down the line, passing Isaac and Hawkins. Every few steps, he repeats, "Quiet." Scammell's admonition trickles through to Cilley's men and on down the line.

In half a minute, the woods are as silent as the redoubt.

Scammell and Cilley confer, and then each sends a few men in dark coats toward the redoubt. The men begin returning five minutes later, and all report redoubt is empty. Scammell again walks down the line, telling his men they are awaiting orders and keep quiet and remain in readiness to attack. A long chilly half-hour later, orders come to return to camp.

•••

Isaac twists the excess water from his soaked coat and clothes then hangs them from hooks on the ridge pole of his tent. As midnight approaches, the rain that had begun an hour earlier continues. It turned into a downpour as he had walked from Scammell's tent, sufficient to soak through everything he had been wearing.

From outside, "Captain Frye?"

Recognizing Will's voice, Isaac answers, "Bring them in."

Will ducks into the tent carrying a wire basket with three steaming hot stones.

"Put them under the cot where I've made some space. Has the rain let up any?"

"Yes sir, somewhat." Will kneels beside the cot and turns the basket to roll the stones into the space beneath.

"Good, have Lieutenants Goodale and Hawkins returned?"

"Yes, their stones are in the fire now."

"Tell them I'd like to see them tonight."

"Yessir, anything else."

"No, that's it."

"Will rises and moves out of the tent, "Good evening, sir."

After wishing Will a good evening, Isaac wraps himself against the cold damp air with two blankets. He sits on the small folding stool, and from his haversack, takes a sheet of paper from a folio, a quill, and his inkwell. Setting these before the pair of new candles, he yawns. The heat from the stones begins warming the inside of the tent. Setting the quill down, he shakes his head and rubs his eyes. Shivering, he looks from the blank page to the bottle of rum he carried from Scammell's tent. He pours a generous portion into his cup and takes a drink, swallowing slowly, letting the heat of the alcohol warm his throat and chest.

From outside, Hawkins calls, "Cap'n, you there?"

"Aye. Come in."

Hawkins followed by Goodale, both dripping wet, though not soaked, crouch and shuffle in. Isaac motions them to sit on the folding stools leaning against the end of his cot. "How are they?"

Hawkins answers, "They'll all live. None will be fit for duty for months."

"That first part is a relief." Isaac reaches for the rum bottle, "Cups?"

The lieutenants each reach into their coats and produce a cup. Isaac fills them, then raises his own.

"Thank you. You led our men with bravery today. That we lost none is testament to you both."

Goodale takes a drink then raises his cup back to Isaac. "Thanks should be to you. Our discipline would have left us many times if not for you."

They all drink. Hawkins downs the contents of his cup and holds it out for Isaac, who fills it again.

"What news from the Colonel?"

"The wounded are to go to Albany tomorrow. The rest of us go back to the field. They've abandoned their outer works and moved all their men to the main camp down by the river. We're to guard the artillerymen while they set up their cannon and begin the bombardment."

Goodale downs his cup and holds it out for Isaac to refill. "After today, I'm going to need a little sleep if we've got to do as much again tomorrow."

Isaac sets the bottle back on the desk and raises his cup to toast Goodale and Hawkins. "You've both more than earned a few hours of rest."

They drain their cups, and Isaac tips his head toward the tent flaps. "Go on. The morning will come far too soon."

After his lieutenants depart, Isaac looks at the blank piece of paper on his desk and mutters, "No rest for the weary."

> *Camp upon Bemis Heights October 7, 1777*
> *To my Dear and Loving Wife, It is with gratitude and relief that I write to offer my my love and affection to You and our Sons. This afternoon we fought another great battle. We chased the enemy from the field and they have abandoned their outer works.*
> *I have not rec'd any lines from you in over a week. I pray daily your health is good and I look forward to news of our next child. I trust father and sister are close at hand.*
>
> *I am grateful to the Devine power that none from my company lost their life today. Amos Fuller and Peter Chandler who recently came to Wilton were wounded and will be sent with the others to Albany tomorrow to recover. Two others from my company were wounded too. Mr. Ezra Fuller a colored man from New Ipswich and Nathan Fish from Mason. The regiment fared less well. Eleven were kill'd including Lt. Webster of Capt. Stone's company.*

Isaac sags on his folding stool, the weight of the day's events sapping his energy. Yawning, he replaces the cork in his inkwell, lays the quill beside the page, pinches out the candles, then rolls into his cot.

The burring rattle of drum rolls grows louder as drummers throughout the camp wake and take up their sticks to call the men of their companies to arms. Isaac sits upright in his cot. A short distance outside Uriah takes up his drum and adds to the din.

In the darkness, Isaac reaches up and finds his shirt. Cold, hard to the point he cannot feel the dampness. Coat and trousers the same. Taking a deep breath, he throws off his blankets. The familiar routine of placing his clothes, boots, and musket in the same place each night makes the effort of dressing minimal. He ducks out of the tent, musket in hand in half a minute.

Well after dark that evening Isaac returns, tired and wet, though not so wet as the previous night.

>   *Oct 8*
> *Early today we marched to close the noose around what remains of General Burgoyne and his army.Our progress was blocked by their artillery which was already in place. A great ravine separates us from their main camp. There was som skurmishing and General Lincoln who commands our wing of the army took a wound to his leg. He passed too close at the front of our lines. The enemy cannot win and must know it. They behave with anger for seeing their situation will not improve.*
> *The weather has ben very rainy of late. It is night now and a steady heavy rain has already begun as I write. I am grateful we are encamped now with tents and up on some high ground.*
>
> *Your Obed't and Loving Husband,*
>
> *Isaac Frye*
>
>   *Oct 9*
> *P.S. The rain continued so heavily that today that we have orders to stay in camp and rest.*

Isaac, with Hawkins and Goodale, pick their way through a thick fog that hugs the ground and trees. They move through the soggy gray woods to the west of where General Burgoyne's main camp had been a day earlier. A few yards ahead a shape splits away from a large tree trunk. The three officers pause as Hall, whose size doesn't help them to recognize him in the fog until he is ten feet away, and gives the countersign in a hushed voice.

A few minutes earlier, Isaac sent his men out in groups of two and three with instructions to move fifty paces ahead. They wait, listening for signs of enemy patrols. Isaac and his lieutenants lower their muskets as Hall steps toward them.

Isaac holds his hand over his mouth to keep his voice from

carrying, "Anything?"

"No sir, nobody out here. We crossed paths with a group of Captain Ellis's men and some from Colonel Cilley's regiment. No fresh tracks, either."

"Good. Keep the men in place until we have orders to the contrary."

Isaac motions for Hawkins to stay with Hall. Isaac and Goodale retrace their steps back to the crossroad where Scammell waits with Adjutant Gilman. The latter had arrived in their absence. Within a minute, the other officers arrive.

Scammell in quick succession points to each commander. None reports any signs of the enemy. "Good. Captain Gilman has brought new orders. We are to break camp and move north immediately. Dearborn's men have reconnoitered the enemy have made a new camp on the north side of Fish Creek. Have your men draw provisions for two days before breaking down the tents. Call your men back here. We'll form ranks and march back to camp."

•••

Will and Uriah march beside one another at the rear of the company. The men march in two columns alongside the river road on the west side of the North River. The recent traffic of two armies had churned and muddied long sections of the road. They pass crews working to repair those by converting them to corduroy with fresh-hewn logs so the wagons can pass.

Immediately in front of them, Nehemiah Holt and Jacob Blanchard march. Blanchard is the younger of the pair by two years, though four years older than Will. "I bet we'll finally get our pay if we can take back the pay chest in this siege."

"A better bet is the money's long gone or burnt if it was Continentals." Holt laughs harshly. "Maybe they sent it to Tories to spend. Either way, they got no reason to keep it."

Blanchard glares at Holt, narrowing his eyes for a moment. "Then how're we gonna get paid."

"Cap'n said the Colonel's got to go to General Gates. I don't believe he's done so yet."

Blanchard turns around, marching backward as he faces Uriah, "What do you think Uriah, we gonna get our pay?"

"Not soon. Even if we take some money from Burgoyne, it'll be weeks before the likes of us see ours. Besides, I need new shoes more than I need paper money."

Holt turns at that, "Me too. Can't even get shoe leather to cut in. Got birch bark in the bottom of this one." He kicks his trailing foot high enough for Uriah and Will to see a hole large enough for Will to put his fife through.

Uriah whacks at Holt's heel with his drumstick and misses. "Be fine with me if they sent us home for the winter after we finish this business in front of us."

Blanchard turns back to marching forward. "Maybe, but with all the militia already turned out, I doubt Exeter will want to pay even more for them to guard against General Clinton coming north. That'll be us for sure."

"Look at this." Blanchard and raises his right arm, and shows a long rip in his coat from the armpit to the waist. "Caught it on a big splinter on our tent pole this morning. The cloth has got thin and weak."

Holt laughs, "Twill make tomorrow morning's piquet duty cold. I hope you've got a pin or two."

"I'll trade you," Will offers.

"Trade me what? For my coat?"

"I got a needle and thread. I'll sew it for you if you carry the heated stones to all the tents tonight for me. The stones and the fire will keep you warm while I sew."

"Deal."

As they march by the ruins of a wagon abandoned by the redcoats, the stench of a dead animal carries on a sudden breeze. The stench assaults both columns. On the far side of the wagon, the remains of a horse, bloating yet clearly undernourished, is the cause. Once clear of the stench, Holt, his mouth narrowed with a look of sour disapproval offers, "That's what, the seventh or eighth dead horse? What a senseless thing. Burgoyne leaving his sick and wounded for us to care for and the waste of good horses so they can have what? The pride of surrendering on a different patch of ground?"

After a few steps, Will mutters, "It's disgusting."

•••

Isaac is among the two dozen New Hampshire officers gathering atop a long hill running parallel to the North River. The sun is high in the sky and holds a few small white clouds. The officers include General Poor, Colonels Cilley, Scammell, and Reid, and the commanders of all the companies. Several recently felled trees lay before the group making their location ideal to see in all directions.

Dearborn, promoted to lieutenant colonel a few days earlier, steps to the fore and addresses the assembled officers. He points south to the next hill, about the same height, "There is General Burgoyne's main camp. Half his army is within its perimeter. That includes their remaining riflemen and some smaller field pieces." Turning to his left, stopping his hand at the base of the same hill. "Colonel Nixon's men are moving onto the ground by old Fort Hardy. Last night Burgoyne's men burned buildings down there, including General Schuyler's home." Several officers swear at the audacity. Dearborn moves his hand to a point a bit north of Fort Hardy, but well inland. "Burgoyne's put his light troops, grenadiers, and Canadians there. His artillery park is beyond that. To the north of them, immediately between us and the river, are the Germans. Their works are not strong for their having only yesterday to be at that task."

General Poor thanks Dearborn. "We've got two tasks, gentlemen. First is to throw up some works from which we can mount our field pieces and bring them to bear on the enemy below us." He indicates the Germans and the others not within Burgoyne's main camp. "Second is to block any attempts to forage or retreat. This business ends here. Patterson's got his brigade to the west of Burgoyne's main camp, and Colonels Morgan and Dearborn have blocked everything to the north. On the far side of the river, Colonel Fellows has three thousand militia. General Gates believes that once our field pieces begin playing on them, Burgoyne will sue for terms. I cannot imagine

Honor and Valor

that taking more than a day or two, as I suspect they are rather miserable for want of food, forage, and the loss of so many of their men."

Turning to the assembled captains and lieutenants, "Do this work well, gentleman. Your vigilance and duties will soon deliver a victory."

The next afternoon Isaac and Livermore peer downhill over the top of the earthwork at the edge of General Poor's encampment. Livermore's men had extended the works during the morning and now hand their axes and shovels over to Isaac's men.

Looking at Livermore's face with a week of stubble, streaks of dirt, and still gaunt from the trials of the summer, Isaac realizes his own must look the same. Isaac asks, "Anything interesting this morning?"

"Just three Germans. They crawled on their bellies until they were out of range of their fellows, then came running waving white cloths. Some of Dearborn's men took them."

From a little behind, and fifty yards to their right, a pair of cannon boom, firing simultaneously. One ball flies a little high arcing over Burgoyne's artillery park by the river. The second ball throws up a plume of dirt and mud, scattering a mortar crew for half a minute. Isaac exhales a hard sigh. "That one was close."

"Not close enough. Our crews need to get about finding their range."

Further to their left, the artillerymen fire a second pair of cannons. The balls sizzle through the air then blast through portions of the earthen wall protecting the German light infantry.

Livermore smacks his fist into his palm. "We need more of that. A dozen more like that, and those Jaegers'll have to fall back."

Isaac nods in agreement as Livermore continues, "I can't figure why they're still putting up a fight. They've got no chance."

One of the British cannon below fires. As the ball arcs toward the cannon to their right, a man shouts a warning to take cover. Isaac and Livermore crouch behind their earthen wall. They hear the ball whoosh and thud, well short, plugging into the hillside in front of them.

Livermore's sets his jaw in annoyance. "I'm not ready to pity them just yet. They deserve a good pounding, and I'm happy to oblige."

•••

Isaac, with Hawkins and Goodale, lead their men through drills two mornings later in a field atop a ridge west of General Poor's encampment. They practice charging and firing downhill in anticipation of forcing an end to the siege.

As the men advance and Sergeants Hall and Wilkins give the orders to Make Ready and Aim. Isaac calls out and interrupts the drill, "Aim lower. Aim at their knees, so you're sure not to send your lead over top of their pointy hats." His tone turns from exasperation to lecturing, "We learned our drill on flat ground, but most of our fights have been on hills. A level aim will not help you when moving down a hill like this. A week ago, those grenadiers aimed too high and gave us the opening to charge them." Turning to the sergeants, "Start again."

As he turns back to Hawkins and Goodale, Isaac catches sight of Ensign Jonathan Cass from Lieutenant Penniman's company jogging towards them. On the far side of camp, the cannon fire again. Cass, like most of the officers, is taller, though he is several years younger than Isaac.

"Captain Frye, Lieutenants," he greets them and offers a salute.

Isaac returns the salute, "What's the news?"

"The colonel requests the presence of all the officers to meet at his tent this instant."

Isaac turns to his men, "Sergeants, drill them another half an hour. Pay special care to the angle of their aim. Then march back to our tents and take your noon meal."

Isaac and the trio officers with him are among the last to arrive at Scammell's tent. Scammell begins speaking a minute later. "Gentlemen, news of great moment has arrived. General Burgoyne has called for a cessation of arms. It appears this is in anticipation of negotiating the terms of his surrender."

One of the officers shouts, "Hip-Hi-"

Scammell cuts him off, "No!" His glare is fierce, eyes wide, and mouth narrowed for a moment before regaining a measure of control.

"No. We must not celebrate yet. The next few hours or days are when things are most likely to go wrong. Our vigilance must not waver." His voice drops in pitch and volume, "We've fought too hard."

Scammell looks around, taking in the faces of his officers, "No more taking in deserters. There will either be terms or a battle."

Isaac walks with Hawkins and Goodale, returning to their tents. Hawkins rubs his hands together to warm them. "I bet when General Stark showed up yesterday on the hill north of the Germans with a thousand militia, they told Burgoyne they'd had enough."

Goodale looks up as he calculates. "We outnumber them five to one now."

Isaac finds himself smiling for the first time in weeks. "Even a few weeks ago, before the first battle, we couldn't have predicted we'd be here at this moment."

"Aye," Hawkins claps Isaac and Goodale on their shoulders, "this feels good."

•••

The drummers in General Poor's camp begin beating the wake up call early three mornings later, well before sunrise. Isaac sits up and feels around for, finds, and pulls on his boots. He reaches for his coat draped over the chest he packed the previous night after learning of the agreement on the terms of Burgoyne's surrender.

Isaac stands an hour later in a parade formation with his company near the bottom of the hillside field they drilled in a few days earlier. Dawn is still two hours away. Numerous lanterns cast extra light, though the full moon provides enough to see General Poor. The three New Hampshire regiments form the shape of a horseshoe, and their general stands in the middle to enable them to hear his words. Poor holds a sheaf of papers, and an ensign from Cilley's regiment leans pole with a lantern over the General's shoulder.

"Article one. The troops under Lieutenant-general Burgoyne, to march out of their camp with honors of war," Shock and invectives spread through the ranks and cause Poor to pause.

He looks around at the men, then holds up the sheaf of papers and shakes them three times. "Gentlemen of New Hampshire, attend these words with patience."

Poor turns his focus back to the papers. "They will march with the artillery of the entrenchments to the verge of the river where the old fort stood, where the arms and artillery are to be left; the arms piled by word of command of their own officers."

"Article two. A free passage to be granted to the army under Lieutenant General Burgoyne to Great Britain, on condition of not serving again in North America during the present contest; and the port of Boston is assigned for the entry of transports to receive the troops, whenever General Howe shall so order."

General Poor goes on to read all twelve articles and ends with the news they are to be signed at nine o'clock this morning.

"We will decamp and march to the south side of Fish Creek and down the River Road a short way where we will encamp then break our fast. Afterward, we are to line the road to honor General Burgoyne's troops. As those soldiers march by, you will give them your utmost respect. There is to be no speaking or unnecessary movement. When they look our way, they will see not just men, but soldiers. Soldiers who have earned victory these past weeks. Soldiers who have earned the right to view the first British army ever to surrender."

An hour after sunrise Isaac sits on a folding stool outside his tent with Hawkins. The tent and the surrounding encampment are almost a mile south of Fish Creek on a gentle rise above the river, several hundred yards to the west. The morning is bright, with a few white clouds drifting eastward. Goodale arrives carrying breakfast, a basket of biscuits, a small crockery jug with honey, and a pot of coffee. He sets all but the pot on Isaac's field desk beside a trio of apples and Isaac's small wooden box filled with raisins. A wagon arrived the previous day from Wilton, carrying four bushels of apples compliments of Major Abbot, and the raisins from Elizabeth.

Hawkins takes an apple and turns it around, inspecting it. "If we should winter here, at least we'll be well supplied."

Isaac takes his coffee. "Thanks, Zeke. I need this drink more every morning. Maybe we'll finally get a full night of sleep tonight."

Honor and Valor

"I think we will." Goodale sets the pot down and takes an apple. "First time in far too long that we've not had an immediate duty waiting for us. It seems strange to have the time to idle and eat a meal."

Isaac dollops some honey onto an open biscuit and adds a few raisins before replacing the top. "You had a letter from home. How's Elly and your children?"

"As good as can be expected. Not happy about our lack of pay. Needs to have a few things fixed and needs fabric to make some new breeches for little Zeke. How's your family? Your wife give you another son yet?"

"Not yet. Twill be a little less than a month is what she wrote. It makes me more than a little nervous not to be there. Her sister Sarah is there, and our neighbor Sarah Parker will come too."

Hawkins chuckles. "Not likely they were gonna ask you to help."

"Aye, true enough."

Hawkins points down toward the river road. "Things must be getting started. The militia is marching to Fish Creek. They're to form up on the road to the south of the creek."

Goodale points back towards the hill where Burgoyne's encampment sits. "So, they're gonna march out, ground their arms, march here on that road, and then what, keep marching to Boston?"

"I expect so." Isaac grins. "There's nothing else for them to do. Dearborn's and Morgan's men will take possession of their camp once the last of them are out, so there'll be no place for them to go back to."

Hawkins quirks an eyebrow up with a sudden question coming to mind. "What about their Canadians and Loyalists?"

With no humor in his voice, Goodale asserts, "Wouldn't want to be them, but I expect they'll have to go to Boston first, then a ship to Nova Scotia or Quebec."

Isaac turns back to finish the last of his biscuit and a swig of coffee. "Zeke, Parade the men. Make sure they're as presentable as they can be."

Goodale nods, "Aye," and takes his honey and coffee pot back to his tent.

Hawkins rises and stretches his arms overhead. "It was a piece of good timing that Major Abbot arrived with his wagon yesterday. Quite a few of the men needed coats, stockings, and leather and fabric to patch their clothes."

"Aye. It's a shame we couldn't get more boots and shoes. If we have to march any distance, some of the men are in a poor state of affairs."

"Indeed."

The two put the desk and stools in Isaac's tent before walking to the open part of the field where the men begin forming ranks.

Twenty minutes later, Isaac dismisses his men. He turns toward his tent and catches sight of Livermore walking his direction with a bounce in his step. Livermore calls out, "Burgoyne's signed."

Isaac stops as if struck, feeling a colossal unseen weight lift from his neck and shoulders.

Livermore, unsure what to make of Isaac standing stock-still, repeats the news, holding out his hand as he reaches Isaac.

Isaac shakes his hand. "That's tremendous. How do you know?"

"Word came like a wave through Nixon's men." Livermore points to the north. "Not from one place but everywhere. They say Burgoyne is riding to meet Gates. Let's go see him ride by."

Isaac motions Hawkins and Goodale to follow as he sets off with Livermore down the hill toward the river road.

When they are within fifty paces of the road, Hawkins stops and points northward. "There they are."

Colonel Wilkinson astride an elegant white horse rides at the side of a man wearing the finest uniform Isaac can recall seeing. Behind them, half a dozen of Burgoyne's aides and generals follow.

Under his breath, Hawkins exclaims, "They're emaciated."

Confused, Livermore turns, "Huh?"

"The horses. They're doing all they can to carry those men."

"Mmm. They've had no fodder for a week and some."

"It takes me aback a bit. After all, we've only seen the hot ends of their muskets and field pieces. To see them passing by with no more concern for us than farmers in a field is quite unexpected."

Isaac turns to Hawkins. "It is strange to see them in such an ordinary way."

Livermore exhales, betraying equal parts amazement and amusement. "It certainly is, and on this extraordinary occasion, it does boggle my mind somewhat."

"Almost as much as seeing Wilkinson in a place of such honor." Isaac continues, "Last spring, all he seemed to be was the cause of strife for Colonel Reed with his refusing a captain's commission."

Livermore nods once. "Aye, I remember. It seems Grover got the worst of it, and Wilkinson has benefited at every turn since."

"I have to keep telling myself I don't know the man very well. He's well-educated and been of some value to Generals Arnold and Gates, but I cannot keep myself from doubting his character."

Livermore nods and twists his mouth into a skeptical smile that does not reach his eyes. "He seems a most loyal hound if you ask me."

"Aye, a hound. At least he's fetched a good bone for his master today." The others in the group laugh in agreement as Burgoyne, his officers, and their escort pass from view.

Isaac turns back toward camp and finds the hill dotted with more than a hundred men. All had come to witness the procession, individuals, and small groups such as theirs.

Well into the afternoon, Isaac stands at the head of his company. They line the west side of the river road looking across to Captain Ellis's men and the North River beyond them. Isaac takes one step and leans into the road, peering in both directions. The American soldiers line the way for as far as he can see in both directions. Scammell approaches from the south where the other companies in the regiment wait.

Captains Stone and Livermore call their companies to attention as Scammell approaches. Isaac and Ellis follow suit.

Scammell stops opposite Isaac and Ellis and turns, taking in the men of the four companies. "Think on this gentlemen: the soldiers who are about march between our ranks faced you not once by but twice in battle. Was their valor any less than yours? They must've known they couldn't win that second time, yet they faced us and gave battle. These men are not their king or the king who hired them. They've earned our respect, and you'll give them their due as they pass. Keep your heads high and your eyes forward. Let them see this army from New Hampshire. Let them see the men who required no more than the clothes on their backs and the muskets in their hands to earn this victory. Make no mistake; this is not the time for pride. Tis the time to honor those soldiers who will march between these ranks. They must face each of you and the truth that they could not by a contest of arms take our God-given liberties or our independence. Think on these things as those soldiers pass by you."

Scammell turns to Isaac and steps forward, offering his hand. As Isaac takes it, Scammell offers, "It has been my honor to serve with you in this campaign Captain Frye."

"The honor is mine to have served with you, sir."

Scammell nods and turns to offer the same to Ellis before walking back to shake the hands of Livermore and Stone.

A few minutes later, captains down the line begin calling their companies to attention as Burgoyne's soldiers approach. Isaac waits for them to reach the company to the north of his before calling his men to attention.

Burgoyne's soldiers begin filing by. Their faces are a mix of jaws hard set against the pain of humiliation or blank gazes locked on the backs of the men in the rank ahead. Regiment after regiment of redcoats, some depleted, their men in hospitals or buried in the fields a few miles to the south. Hollow eyes and cheeks. Their pace is not quick, and many of their shoulders droop a little forward, showing them as men done with a long day, week, and campaign.

For over an hour, until the shadows of the hills and trees consume those of the men along the road, Burgoyne's defeated army plods by. Red coats, blue coats, and green. First British, then German. Breeches, shoes, and boots muddy from wading across the Fish Creek. Last come the camp followers, a gaggle in tow of their army. Lacking the discipline of soldiers, they gawk, mutter, and occasionally shoot defiant looks and make rude gestures.

Minutes afterward, the Third Regiment halts near their tents as daylight gives way to twilight. The order, "Dismissed", is met initially with silence. As the men move off, the conversations and cheers begin to dominate the camp as they start the familiar routines of cooking

Honor and Valor

the evening meals. Tonight, for the first time, a cheerful mood permeates the camp.

Well after dark and dinner, Isaac sits at his field desk, heating the end of a new goose feather after slicing it into the form of a quill. He startles at hearing a voice outside, "Captain Frye?".

Not immediately recognizing the voice, Isaac sets the new quill down and turns. "Yes, who's there."

"Corporal Duncan from Beal's company, sir. Colonel Scammell's requesting you."

"Thank you, I'll be on my way in an instant."

Isaac arrives at Scammell's tent. Livermore, Ellis, McClary, Stone, Gilman, and Beal are already present and form a circle with Lieutenants Wedgewood and Penniman around the Colonel. They make room for Isaac. Behind Scammell, a pile of fine pistols dominates his field desk.

Scammell steps into their midst. "Gentlemen, tonight, it is my honor to bestow a small token of my esteem upon each of you. I wish to honor the duties you performed these past months. We secured this collection of pistols earlier today from among those surrendered by the enemy. I have here a pair for each of you who led our men in the recent battles. I wish there was more for me to give."

Scammell takes pairs of matched pistols and hands them to each of the commanders. As he hands out the last pair, Captain Gilman produces two bottles and a set of cups and fills them near full.

Scammell takes a cup and invites the commanders to do the same. "It's not General Burgoyne's Madeira, but it will do, I think." He raises his cup and smiles with genuine warmth. "To our victory and to the United States of America."

Scammell's smile changes the mood from somewhat solemn to one of good cheer, and the men's voices as they repeat the toast take on an upbeat his tone.

After downing his rum in one pull, Scammell offers, "You're all welcome to stay and help finish these." He motions with his cup to the desk, where Gilman deposits four more bottles.

Captain Beal laughs. "That's the best order you've ever given. Let's fill our cups again. I've got a toast for our commander."

With cups again filled. "Colonel Scammell, sir, It is our good fortune to have you as commander. For in this Army, there is no more gallant an officer than yourself. In the field of battle, there is no better leader than yourself, and in the cause of freedom, no one has more fire in his belly than you. Raise your cups, my fellow captains and honor, for it is our honor, sir, to be in Scammell's Third New Hampshire Regiment."

Captain Stone leads an immediate chorus echoing Beal's toast.

Honor and Valor

9 BREAKING POINT

> "The pay Chest of my Reg't was unluckily taken by the enemy at Skenesborough after the Evacuating of Ticonderoga with the regimental papers & accounts except the Memorandum of what money was in it. Viz. two hundred & ninety two Pounds, nineteen Shillings, & Six Pence LM which belonged to my officers and men and had not been paid out by the Pay Master. ..."
>
> Alexander Scammell to General Gates
Livingston Manor, October 26, 1777

Pacing outside his tent, Isaac watches as the first hints of blue seep into the eastern sky. Awake early, whether from the residual euphoria of the previous day or intuition, becomes moot. A drummer in a distant part of camp takes up the call to arms. Isaac walks to the corporal's tent, where Uriah sleeps, pulls the flap open, and taps Uriah's back with his toe. "Let's go. The business of liberty is upon us again."

Uriah rolls backward out of the tent and to his feet. Still half asleep, he moves out of the way as Martin, the fastest of the corporals, rolls out next and begins running toward Scammell's tent to await the orders. Uriah wobbles while struggling to wake. Isaac puts a steadying hand on his shoulder then gives him a couple of hard pats to bring him fully awake. "They're playing To Arms."

Uriah shivers and reaches inside the other flap and retrieves his drum and sticks. Isaac moves off toward the other tents calling for his men to wake and form ranks.

Martin returns a few minutes later, stopping before Isaac, Hawkins, and Goodale to offer sharp a salute, which Isaac and the lieutenants return.

"What's the alarm for?"

"They say General Clinton is marching on Albany. We're to strike camp and march immediately. General Gates aims to be there tonight."

Goodale's brows come together, and his jaw juts forward with dismay and irritation. "That's well over thirty-"

Not waiting for him to finish, Isaac interjects, "Then let's be about it. If it's true, we'll get the chance to drub a second army before the season's out." Turning to the men. "Strike the camp and get the wagons loaded. We're marching to Albany."

The following afternoon atop a rise to the southwest, Isaac glances out over Albany and upriver before turning back to Hawkins, who stands with Hall and Wilkins. The sky had been clear for much of yesterday's march, though now a few high clouds begin to encroach. The sergeants requested the meeting to present the men's ideas on several issues "pertaining to the conditions of the army."

Isaac motions toward the open area set aside for the regiment to parade and take rolls. The four begin walking toward the middle of the clearing. "Speak freely, as I take this meeting to mean the men have complaints."

Hall nods to Wilkins, who by prearrangement speaks. "Sir, thank you. The men have many small complaints. Most relate to the season growing cold and the poor condition of their clothes, shoes, the want of blankets. For being here in Albany, we figure much of that will soon be put right. We, I mean the men, have one significant complaint. Namely that when we signed on we expected monthly pay as you and Major Abbot represent-"

Hall lays his large hand on Wilkins' shoulder, cutting him off. "The men want their pay. When we learned yesterday's march was for a false alarm, quite a few was angry enough to say some unwise words about which direction they'd march the next time we get orders like what we got yesterday."

Wilkins picks up the argument. "The last time we received anything to improve our fitness for duty was the morning of the second battle. Only five of the dozen who needed them got new shoes. That was it."

"I see." Keeping his face calm, Isaac grinds his fist into his palm as he considers a response. "Tell the men I agree. They should have their pay every month." He looks to Wilkins. "Properly clothed too, and not just owing to their sacrifices for our cause. But the truth is, the pay is out of my hands — I will tell the colonel. In the meantime, get a count and make lists of what clothes the men need. The quartermaster will need an exact quantity. It may take a few days. I expect going to the colonel means he will want counts from all the companies. Keep the men busy today with getting the camp set up. I expect the weather will turn in the next day or so. Encourage the men whose families can help to write home to tell of our need for extra coats, hats, gloves, and the like. I'll see if I can get some extra rum on account of our successful march."

Hall looks around, his jaw set with frustration, then his expression softens. "Sir, we appreciate your agreeing to inform the colonel. We'll do our part. I would hope the Colonel notices."

After the sergeants leave, Isaac turns to Hawkins, "I hate even suggesting this, but as you visit our men in the hospital, look for opportunities. Dead men don't need shoes."

"I will, but don't get your hopes up or tell the men. Most of the men who will die have friends watching, and they're all practical men."

"I know, but we need to make our own luck, and every pair we can get will help."

•••

Honor and Valor

Camp at Albany October 20, 1777

To my Loving Wife,

For the army Moving several times over the passed two weeks, I have not rec'd any lines from you. Give father and Sisters Hannah and Sarah my love and affection. My anxiousness for news from you grows daily and I pray daily for your health and the same for our sons.

Since my last lines I have Witnessed the Surrendur of General Burgoyne and all the soldiers of his Army. Our men lined the road along the river while Burgoyne and his men ground their muskets and gave us their cannon and then marched between us. It was a strange yet glorious sight. I rec'd from Colo. Scammell a matched pair of pistols from those the enemy grounded. He gave such a pair to those who commanded his companys during the battles.

The state of our being paid is not changed and the men have complained. It seems General Gates lacks coffers for paying the army. This afternoon I wrote Major Abbot to request he send shoes, clothes, gloves, hats and blankets. We enjoyed the apples other provisions he brought when he last visited. Our duty and the battles has wor out everything. I expect we will be camped here for a few days and I Hope there is time to get us these supplies.

I trust father moved the cows from the town lot and all is ready for winter. I sorely miss being there with you, particularly now that we have done our job of securing New England. We have no word where our winter quarters will be, yet I hope it will be close enough to allow me to come home for a week or even two.

Your Loving Husband,

Isaac Frye

After waiting a minute for the ink to dry, Isaac folds the letter, seals it, and sets it atop the letter to Major Abbot. Outside, a gust of wind whips the side of his tent, causing it to ripple and snap against the poles. Little drafts of cold air push inside and cause the flames of the two candles to shiver and dance.

Also outside, Hawkins approaches, "Captain Frye."

"Good evening. Come inside." Isaac shields the candles with his hand as Hawkins enters, permitting a burst of chilly air and a few snow flurries inside.

"Good evening to you as well. We got lucky." Hawkins pulls a pair or of shoes from inside his coat and deposits them on Isaac's cot. "Poor fellow, a militiaman. He died of an infection of his wounds. The surgeons said he had no one to give his belongings."

"See if they'll fit Ballard. We need our drummer."

"Aye, we do."

"How're the rest of our men?"

"They'll all live. Chandler, Heseltine, Blood, Mansfield and Ezra Fuller should recover in a couple months. Fish, Blood, Drury, and Amos Fuller will take longer and likely will be sent home to recover when they're able. Though, I think it best if you request a discharge for Fish. He'll keep his leg, which is good, but he won't be fit for the Army."

"I'll see what I can do. Thank you for getting the shoes."

"Well, they may have come at a cost."

"How so?"

The wounded, they needed tailoring done—patches and repairing tears and the like. Anyhow, General Gates came through and noticed my handiwork. He asked how I came to my skills.

"Aye, and no good deed goes unpunished?"

"I hope not."

"What do you expect'll come of it?"

"Not sure. Cobblers are far rarer and more valuable, so maybe nothing."

"Get some rest. Tomorrow will be here sooner than we'd like."

In the morning, the sounds of the encampment seem dull and quiet, though the wind that blew late into the night is mercifully gone. As Isaac puts his coat on, he brushes against the inside of the tent. The reason for the relative quiet becomes obvious. The canvas is heavy with snow.

The day passes with only light duties owing to the snow. In the late afternoon, Isaac crunches along the path worn into the foot of snow as he returns to his tent. Before he can enter, Martin calls out to him as he approaches from the direction of Scammell's tent. Martin conveys Scammell's orders for the commanders to convene immediately.

Once they are all present, Scammell gathers them into his gaze. "General Gates has ordered General Poor to march his brigade to the Fishkill Depot. It's three or four days south of here on the east side of the river. He designs to set a series of hard checks on the North River should General Clinton decide to leave New York and come to visit." Scammell smirks. "A warm reception is our task should we be obliged to entertain that General."

Scammell drops the humor from his tone. "Tomorrow and the following day, we need to be about obtaining shoes and clothing for the men. We'll march on the morning of the twenty-fourth. The evening prior, we are to draw food for five days."

Scammell, hands-on-hips, looks down, pausing to consider his next words. "I've made inquiries as to our state of our being unpaid since beginning this campaign." He Looks up again and meets the gazes of the assembled officers. "That, I assure you, is a subject no one wishes to entertain. Not even General Poor has received his pay, though I am quite aware that fact will be of little solace to any of our men. Use it anyway. If it keeps one complaint at bay and morale from slipping any lower, tis worth it. If there are no questions, all but Captain Frye are free to go."

As the others leave the tent, Scammell picks up a half sheet of paper. "I've received orders to place a lieutenant in command of the invalids after we've marched. General Poor strongly recommended Hawkins. His skill at tailoring was mentioned. I am afraid he'll be staying here in Albany. Let him know he is to report to General Gates on the twenty-fourth to receive his orders.

On the way back to his tent, Isaac chuckles under his breath, thinking Hawkins had likely known more the previous night than he had told.

•••

The sounds of wagons creaking and bumping along, hooves clopping, men coughing, and drumsticks clacking on rims melt into the thick cold fog blanketing the road south from Albany. Several inches of snow survives along the thawing road. "Winters here are very gray." Not getting a response, Will looks to Uriah to see if he heard. Uriah cocks his head and looks the other way to show he doesn't care. Will persists. "At least the roads freeze at night. Makes the going for the wagons easier."

"Another mile, and twill be a mess again. All the way to Fishkill is my bet." A fine mist begins and gains strength, adding to Uriah's gloominess.

As the mist turns to drizzle, Uriah removes a felt pad from inside his coat and lays it atop his drum, then adds an oilcloth cover. "We're the victors, and here we are marching further away from home in the cold and rain."

Joseph Gray, marching in front of Uriah, turns his head back. "It was two battles, not a war."

"Maybe, but it seems to me we're due some spoils, or at least our pay."

Martin fires back from two ranks ahead, "Knock off the grumbling Ballard. It could be a lot worse. Besides, you got new shoes a few days ago. Mine are apt to fall to pieces any step now."

Five afternoons later, rain falling for the third day in a row, Will, soaked to the bone and shivering, slogs through the thick sucking mud alongside the road. They turn to the southeast and begin a downhill grade into the village of Fishkill. Uriah smirks as he catches sight of the village. "Looks like we've arrived, Will. Even more gray, mud, and cold."

Looking up, Will sees the rain changing to snow, and his shoulders sag in resignation. His shoes, soaked and clumped with mud, squish and pop with each step. "I can hardly feel my feet."

They cross the Fish Kill over a new bridge. The Fish Kill is thirty feet wide and flows west toward the North River, reminding Will of the Souhegan.

Situated between two forested hills on the south side of the Fish Kill, the depot consists of dozen buildings in all. Poor's Brigade marches into their midst. Will begins shivering as they wait several minutes.

Isaac returns with orders to make their camp tonight at the foot of the taller hill to the southwest of the buildings.

Will's fingers, cold and almost numb, fumble the rope to secure to the tent poles on the stakes. Martin hands him a small shovel. "Here, dig the ditch around the tent. Make it deep enough so the snow won't clog it. That'll get your blood moving. Then go dig the ditch around the Lieutenants' and the Captain's tents."

Will begins digging. "Isn't there just one officer's tent now that Lieutenant Hawkins is in Albany?"

"Oh, right, the Captain and Lieutenant Goodale are sharing a wall tent now. Once you're done with theirs, you Ballard come with me down to the depot and see if they've got any food we can have. Most of us ran out last night."

•••

Camp at FishKill November 2, 1777

To my Dear Loving Wife and Family, My love and Affection to all of you and to Father and Sister Hannah. As you have No Doubt notised we have Marched south. A march of four days became Eight for Rain Snow and Mud we have encamped at a supply Depot for the Army. I pray there are Cloaths and shoes along with plentyful Food here. We arrived late Yesterday soaked by a Very cold Rain that turned to Snow as we began setting up Camp, and the Weather has got Worse by the Hour since. They men are of a Foul mind for this march was as Bad a time as I can remember. Wind, Sleat, even some small Hail buffet and soak the New tent I share with Zeke Goodale. William Adrian is to Winter in Albany in charge of the regiment's Wounded and Invalids.

Nothing of Note happened here today. We spent our time finishing our Encampment Then we drew some rations and Now All but the Guards have time to rest. Some of the New Yorkers in Our Brigade know some of the Local people and will see if we Can get some Items to Make our encampment more Comfortable. How we will Pay is a Mystery as we still Lack even One month of pay. This Burden no Longer Sits well with the men.

I pray You are All Warm and Dry. As you can see my paper is wet in Places. I will have to Hang it to Dry fully before I fold it. After the Summer I am grateful for A decent tent. We have heated stones Keeping the inside Tolerable warm and our cloaths are almost dry, though it is getting toward late afternoon. I am well, the exertions of the March have warded off the various sicknesses sum of the men of the Brigade suffer. Thus, I Expect our condition to improve daily.

Your Loving Husband,

Isaac Frye

Isaac lifts the letter by the corners and waves it back and forth in front of the nearest candle. Within their tent, Isaac and Goodale have their cots along the sides, leaving a center aisle. Each sits on the end of their cot, as they share Isaac's fold-able writing desk and the light of two candles.

Goodale looks up. "I see yours is as wet as mine. I wasn't watching, and my ink ran and made a blotch the size of my thumb."

"I've got half a dozen myself. There's no help for it. Looking on the bright side, tis a little drier in here than this morning."

Goodale yawns and then yawns again. "True, though I'm giving up on this until tomorrow. Keep the candles lit. I'm so tired, they won't bother me at all."

Isaac cannot avoid yawning himself. "You've got the right idea. I'm too tired to write any more tonight."

•••

Goodale returns to the tent late the next afternoon to find Isaac struggling to pull his wet boots off. Sitting on his cot, opposite Isaac, he motions Isaac to lift a boot. "How was your patrol?"

Issac puts new effort into wiggling his heel. "Wet, cold, and uneventful. No sign of the enemy." The first boot relents and allows Isaac's heel and ankle to slip free. "Nobody out today from here to the landing on the North River."

Goodale motions for Isaac to lift the other boot. "A young colonel come through today. Scammell clearly knew him." He affects a tone of easy light formality, "Colonel Scammell, tis a pleasant surprise to find you here. Colonel Hamilton, likewise. What brings you to this quarter?" Their greeting fairly well shouted some private joke between them." Goodale turns his attention to the other boot. "Damn, this one's stuck like you were born with it. Let me get a better grip. The colonels stayed close to where I was with Blanchard, who I was seeing about getting some blankets. This Colonel Hamilton says General Washington's sent him north to see Generals Putnam and Gates and order them to send the bulk of the army south. Scammell tells him where to find Putnam's headquarters, and Hamilton says, get your men ready to march, you're much needed by General Washington."

The boot finally stretches, and Isaac pulls his foot free. "Thank you." Isaac shifts over and places his feet on a pair of warm stones and sighs with relief. "Did he say where Washington's has made his camp?"

"Well, that's what our colonel asked next. Pennsylvania, near Philadelphia. Then Colonel Hamilton rode off toward Putnam's headquarters."

Isaac rolls his eyes in frustration. "Damn. Elizabeth is not going to like reading tonight's letter."

"That's not the worst of it. Blanchard, when he heard that, turns to me and says, fat chance we're marching anywhere. Commissary here won't give us any credit. Won't even set up the account, so the clothes, coats, and stockings we need continue to sit unused. Then he says he heard from the quartermaster of the Second who said their men are talking of going home if they don't get paid."

"Tis no good, not at all. Tomorrow, remind our men that we're well-fed, and Scammell expects to hear any day from General Gates about the funds to replace our lost pay chest."

"Aye, though they might be a might bit tired of hearing that."

"Tell them anyway. Ours are good men, and they'll do what's right."

The next morning Isaac and Goodale walk around to the front of the depot's headquarters with a group of officers from Poor's and Learned's brigades. They had just finished a meeting in the field to the rear of the building. General Poor had given the details for coordinating the day's march to the Fishkill Landing and crossing of the North River.

Goodale nudges Isaac. "They've got coffee inside. You want some?"

Isaac rubs his eyes, then searches inside his coat and finds his cup. "Sure."

Goodale returns with his and Isaac's cup filled. "You get much sleep?"

"No. Too anxious. Still no news from Elizabeth."

"I don't blame you. I'd be pacing around the camp all night if my Elly was so close to taking to bed."

As they approach the encampment, they see the tents still up with no sign of any effort to decamp or load the wagons. Here and there, angry shouts punctuate the normal din of the camp.

Goodale sighs, looking from one end of the encampment to the other. "What the devil is going on? They had orders to decamp."

Isaac snorts with disgust then spits. "Find Hall and Wilkins and send them to me. They'll need to answer for this."

A few minutes later, outside their tent, Hall and Wilkins wait contritely before Isaac and Goodale. Hall speaks first. "Sirs, the men have had enough of not bein' paid. We've not got proper supplies and clothes. That's made worse for us sittin' in the midst of a depot full of those things."

Wilkins adds, "We're not much good to General Washington in our current state, and we'll be much worse by the time we reach him. We didn't even draw provisions for today's march. How was that to go?"

Isaac scowls, fixing Wilkins then Hall with a glare. "This is an army and soldiers follow orders in an army. Not following orders is mutiny. You know that? Yes?"

Hall licks his lips and swallows to steady his nerves. "That may be true, Sir, but not paying soldiers has got to be a just as much of a crime."

With a trace of defiance in his tone, Wilkins adds, "It's a crime against the honor of those who promised to pay us. General Washington or the Congress needs to make this right-."

Before Wilkins can finish, a drummer begins beating assembly, and the other drummers quickly take up the call.

Isaac scowls, looking toward the sound of the drums and shakes his head. "We'll finish this later."

Once the men assemble, Scammell calls them out of their ranks so they can gather in close. His tone is even and deliberate, free of anger, endeavoring to appeal to them. "You gentlemen gave your solemn and sacred oaths when you joined this army. That oath included obeying the officers put over you. Our orders to march south came from General Washington himself."

A sergeant near the back catches the Scammell's eye with a motion. "Might be better, sir, if you give this fine speech to the Congress and make it about them neglecting to pay us." Murmurs and ayes come from several men throughout the regiment.

"That's a fair point. You deserve your pay, every penny of it. We all do."

Another voice adds, "We know you haven't seen any pay either, sir, though respectfully, it affects some of us more deeply."

"I've written once already to General Gates about replacing the pay chest and expect a response any day now. I-"

An older soldier interrupts Scammell, yet his voice is calm. "Beggin' yer pardon, sir, that chest, it wasn't enough to pay us for even one month. Many of us here is owed seven months. Now we're being sent on another long march. Too many of us haven't got shoes or proper clothes."

Another man calls out, "Blankets and hats too."

Scammell forces his expression to one of tight-lipped neutrality as he listens. "Are you men going to sully your honor by refusing to follow orders for want of a blanket?"

Some of the men take on more contrite postures. Another voice from the back calls out, "It's not just one blanket, sir. We need dozens. It's the same for shoes, trousers, coats, and shirts, and damn near all of us needs stockings."

Nearby, but not from a face Scammell can see, "You're mad if you think we're fit for duty without clothes!"

Another voice, "We've done our duty this season, and no pay means no duty."

"Tell that to General Washington!"

Scammell throws up his hands, palms facing the men. At his full height, he is nearly a head taller than any of the men. "Gentlemen! Enough!" The regiment goes quiet in an instant. "Remain here while I go consult with General Poor."

Several long minutes later, Scammell returns. "General Poor agrees. It may be that the order to send us south today is ill-conceived. But he has one condition. You all agree to break camp and form ranks to march. If we haven't secured provisions and the items you've listed by then, we will release you to set up camp again."

Very early the next morning, in the camp still beside the Fishkill Depot, a drummer beats alarm. Shouting accompanies the drum rolls. "Wake up and parade immediately."

The shouting repeats, and Isaac realizes it is Scammell's voice, and the time is closer to midnight than sunrise. Isaac pulls his boots on and grabs his coat. "Let's go. Something's wrong for Scammell himself to be out there."

Isaac emerges from his tent and notes the position of the moon and realizes it is not much past midnight. The men begin spilling out of their tents and moving towards the parade ground.

Scammell passes by Isaac, and with an uncharacteristically gruff tone, he orders, "Get them moving. It doesn't matter if they wear their blankets. Time is of the essence."

Like the day before, the men come to stand close around Scammell. He paces with irregular agitated steps in the small space before the men. He wears as severe a look on his face as Isaac can recall seeing.

"Commanders take your roll. If any is missing report immediately to me."

After confirming his men are present, Isaac takes in the larger scene. Not only is Poor's Brigade parading, but also Learned's. All are taking a roll. Livermore and Stone walk with a strong sense of purpose to Scammell's at the head of the regiment. Half a minute later, Lieutenant Dennet from Captain Beal's company joins them.

Scammell sends them back to their companies. He addresses the regiment, his voice stony and cold, as he suppresses a need to shout. "Gentlemen. Tonight I have the miserable duty to inform you that a group of men from our state deserted. Those black-hearted cowards marched from camp less than two hours past."

Isaac feels a cold drop of rain hit the back of his neck and glances up to see clouds cloak the moon, darkening everything by several degrees. Another drop hits his ear as Scammell continues.

"There was no honor in leaving that way. Their mutiny is worse still, for they stained their characters with the blackest treachery. The one who led them shot our Captain Beal." Scammell pauses and looks to his boots. He swallows, struggling with great effort to regain his composure. After two breaths, he lifts his gaze, locking eyes with several of the men in the first row. "Captain Beal, I fear, will not live to see to see the light of this day."

For a few moments, gasps, quiet invectives, and confusion wash through the gathered men. They gape wide-eyed at one another in the near darkness trying to make sense of Scammell's words.

Scammell's loud, angry tone quiets them. "Some of the filthy scoundrels fled. General Putnam has sent the light troops and dragoons to retrieve them. The rest are in the gaol. I cannot conceive of a way our lack of pay outweighs a good man's life. I pray you good men are now of that same mind."

Scammell's mouth opens as if intending to say more, whether grief, tiredness, or the rain is the cause, he stops. His eyes find the ground again. In a soft and exhausted tone, he dismisses the men to find their tents.

Charles E. Frye

10 WHITE MARSH

"... Gen'ls Poor and Peterson with their Brigades & Col. Baily with Larned's are now in camp. The last arrived on friday Evening; the other two in the Course of yesterday. I have not yet obtained particular Returns of their Strength; but from the accounts of the officers, they will amount in the whole to twenty three or twenty four hundred rank and file. But I find many of them are very deficient in the articles of Shoes, Stockings, Breeches, and Blankets. ..."

Journal entry of Colonel Jeduthan Baldwin

Colonel Scammell walks ahead of Captain Zachariah Beal's coffin. Lieutenant Nathan Gilman, now in command of Beal's company and Second Lieutenant John Dennet, guide Beal's coffin to the back of a wagon. Isaac and the other company commanders, who are the bearers, move the coffin completely into the wagon. Captains McClary and Gray follow. The late morning sun, though bright, makes little impact on the mood of the crisp fall morning. The snow and rain of the past weeks hastened the falling of leaves, and now the wintry gray of bare trees blankets the hillsides.

After passing through the assembled troops on the parade ground, the wagon arrives at the small cemetery south of the depot. Many of the officers, including all of the generals and regiment commanders, follow the wagon in a long procession.

After lowering the coffin into a newly-dug grave, Isaac notices a recently filled grave with no marker. Yesterday they learned Beal had run his killer through before the mortally-wounded man brought his musket up and fired into Beal.

Nathaniel Porter, the Third Regiment's Chaplain, speaks. He shares the stories of Captain Beal culled from the officers of the regiment during the previous day's rainstorm. Porter finishes the eulogy telling of Beal's bravery in the recent battles.

After the service, Isaac walks back to the encampment with Livermore. They say nothing for several minutes. Livermore sighs to break the silence. "I expect this day has done more to reconcile us to not seeing our homes or families soon."

"Aye, though I am of a split mind. I've still not heard from Elizabeth and worry every hour something has gone badly for her or the baby."

"You have a good wife and a fine young family. Yet I am strongly glad I do not just now. This war and what its led to is a burden no family should carry."

"Fate and timing are what they are. Eight years ago, we had no idea these would be our circumstances."

Livermore claps Isaac on the back. "Of course you're right, and one must have hopes for the future."

"Aye, true. I've learned to set my worries aside to do what must be done."

"Speaking of which, our New York regiments drew a month's pay, clothing, and sundries this morning, and I expect we shall do the same this afternoon."

"Well, that is good news."

They reach their part of the camp, and the smells of the meat cooking for the midday meal hasten their pace. Both men express surprise for how hungry they feel before parting ways.

•••

Heavy rain pelts the outside of Scammell's tent three afternoons later. Inside the oblong marquee, Scammell sits on his cot with his desk before him. Two lanterns hang from the center posts illuminating the interior against the deepening gray of the day. Isaac sits with the other company commanders on folding stools in the second of two semicircles around Scammell's desk. Their expressions betray a grim state. Some with eyes half shut, and others with jaws slack from fatigue. The previous month's optimism is gone.

The din of the rain on the tent forces Scammell to raise his voice. "We are still short shoes, trousers, and coats. At this rate, we won't be able to march for three more days."

The tent door slides aside, admitting Dearborn's soaking wet face. Scammell's jaw drops in surprise. "Henry! Come in and join us. Hang your coat and hat." He points to the pegs on one of the the center posts. "I take it you are once again an officer in this regiment."

"I am. Gates disbanded my command two days ago, after I spent a day at my desk, accounting for everything. Good fortune got me passage on a sloop, so my trip was fast as the weather allowed." Dearborn carries his pack to the foot of Scammell's cot and sits.

Scammell sighs, changing his tone. "Have you heard?"

Dearborn sets jaw with a solemn look and nods once. "The news arrived late the day before I left Albany. Have they caught the deserters?"

"All but a dozen, though I expect those who have been caught will be acquitted owing to the circumstances."

"Is that for the best?"

"I believe so. Tis been wrong not being paid. Punishing men who have worked hard, fought hard, and suffered would, years from now, be seen as the greater wrong. Speaking of pay, see Mr. Weeks, he's got a month's pay for you. We got ours yesterday."

"Still, I regret not being here." Dearborn pauses and digs into his pack and produces two bottles. "I pray this Madeira, courtesy of General Gates in appreciation for my former command, will in some small measure help. I wish to make a few toasts to Captain Beal. I had known him and his wife, Abby, for several years."

"Isaac," Scammell begins, "would you mind? The cups are in my trunk beside you."

They toast Captain Beal. Then Scammell leads belated toasts to Dearborn's promotion and his successful command of the light infantry.

Dearborn's eyes go wide. "Oh! I've nearly forgotten the most important thing I carried from Albany." Reaching back into his pack he retrieves a small stack of folded letters. "Mail arrived the day before I left." He passes one to Ellis and another to Penniman before handing two to Isaac. "One for you and one for Goodale. I hope it's good news. Hawkins pressed me to order you to write him with the news, so consider it so ordered."

As Dearborn passes the remaining letters out, Isaac, too anxious to wait, cracks the seal on his.

> Wilton October 29, 1777
>
> To my Dear Husband, After my Love to you our Sons send theirs. Father and sisters Hannah and Sarah send theirs as well. I pray you will forgive my indulgance to wait two days before Writing these lines with My Own hand. I wished you to Know Very certainly that I am well. On Monday a strong helthy New Son has joined our Family.

Isaac exhales with relief. "A boy. She's had a boy, and they're both well."

Scammell lets out a whoop of joy and leads the others in congratulating Isaac. "Let's have one more toast, this time to a happy occasion."

Later, back in his tent, Isaac finishes reading Elizabeth's letter.

> He came into the World quickly just before noon. Sarahs Parker and Rideout took care of me and our new son. The older Boys are staying with Hannah and Richard for another Week. They met their new Brother Today and Everyone is now much Relaxed. Sister Sarah is here now. I am most grateful for a little quiet.
>
> I rec'd yours telling of the Victory over Burgoin's and his Army two days before the Baby. We were all very relieved that none from

Wilton Perrished. I pray this means you will come home soon. We all miss and need you here.

Your Most Affectionate & Loving Wife,

Elizabeth Frye

Isaac folds the letter, tucks it into his pack, and sighs. Goodale sits reading his letter, then folds it half and presses it against his thigh, and shakes his head. "Sounds like we've got the same problem. Elly's not going to like the news we are joining General Washington down in Pennsylvania."

"Aye true. A month's pay isn't going to blunt the disappointment."

"No, it won't, and I regret having nothing more to offer."

Isaac pulls a blank sheet of paper, a quill, and ink from his knapsack beneath the desk. "Twill have to be enough. Besides I am too relieved and happy of the news of my new son. I cannot imagine a better time to write."

Goodale chuckles and rubs his chin. "I'd rather face General Howe and his army than Elly the moment after she reads my lines."

"Then General Howe's a fool for giving this tired army a reason to be angry."

•••

Scammell pulls aside the canvas flap that serves as the door for his tent and pokes his head outside. Martin and Gray, who flank the entryway, come to attention. Thick gray clouds blanket Washington's camp at Whitemarsh, Pennsylvania. Scammell's tent stands amid a cluster of larger tents around General Poor's headquarters. The brigade's camp is on the north side of a broad hill that runs east to west.

Scammell looks to Martin. "We're not to be interrupted unless Generals Sullivan or Washington themselves wish to enter." The vapor from Scammell's warm breath cascades into cold mid-morning air.

Martin turns and dips his head in a sharp nod. "Yessir, no one but the generals."

"Good, and keep anything you overhear to yourselves. A great deal depends on your discretion."

Both guards give their affirmatives before Scammell turns to the inside of his tent. He steps with care through the captains and lieutenants to reclaim his seat between Dearborn and Gilman. Isaac sits between Goodale and Livermore, opposite the door flap. He nudges Goodale, noting Scammell's intense demeanor. Different than his usual positive, energetic posture, he is wary as if expecting a fight.

Scammell's admonishment to Martin and Gray serves to bring the officers to order, though he remains quiet, alternating between pursing his lips and working his jaw back and forth as he considers how to begin.

Captain Stone's pragmatic nature takes over. "Has this got to do with the conversation you had with General Washington as we were marching into camp yesterday?"

Scammell looks to Stone, whose ruddy complexion makes it impossible to tell if he is self-conscious, chilled, or suffering a cold.

"No. Though since you've brought that up, His Excellency was, as you may have noticed, less than pleased with our state of readiness. Lack of shoes, coats, blankets. The only good he noted was every man carrying a musket. He said the men already here are no better off, and the enemy is much better off. He also admonished me to ensure every man knows the inhabitants of this area are displeased with the presence of the army. They've sought to take advantage of us and charge triple or more for ordinaries and liquor or simply refuse to have anything to do with the army. He was deadly serious in giving us orders not to molest, injure, or steal from these people. He mentioned it twice. We'll need their goodwill in the coming months, even if they're unwilling to show it now."

Gilman clears his throat. "It was fortunate he saw us come into the camp."

"It was," Scammell continues, "and he went on about how Congress has managed to ignore the condition of our men. He said he's finishing a report to them and would add some lines detailing the deficiencies our men endure."

Dearborn huffs with derision. "So there's nothing extra here. No public stores and not much food. Is that about right?"

"Correctly stated." Scammell puts his hand up to forestall more comments. "Like it or not, that is the state of this army's stores. Morale is wanting here. I met with General Sullivan late last evening as we're assigned to his division now. He says they've just finished courts marshaling himself, General Maxwell and General Wayne. They were all falsely accused. General Sullivan over his conduct during an attack on Staten Island a few weeks back. General Wayne for recklessness, and Maxwell for commanding while in a drunken state. Each was acquitted with full honor. It goes to show the pettiness of those wishing to use politics to gain power."

"And the accusers?" Dearborn's eyes widen with anticipation.

"Nothing."

"Are you serious?" Dearborn punches a fist into the palm of his other hand.

"My reaction matched yours. General Sullivan explained our Articles of War lack provisions for how to treat those who make false accusations."

"That's outrageous. Compared to this, the nastiness between Generals Arnold and Gates seems small."

"Yes, but we won." Looking to Dearborn, Scammell shakes his head once to forestall further comments. "All of what I just mentioned is old news in this camp. The general asked us to tell our men as much. We don't want the candle of discord lighting itself again through ignorance or indiscretion."

Scammell lowers his voice. "There's another candle we must not relight. The general believes several other generals have been politicking to replace Washington. He heard it was to be with General Gates, though he could not confirm whether Gates himself had anything to do with it." Scammell watches as eyebrows cock and eyes widen throughout the tent. "He says His Excellency successfully quashed this plot. I believe he mentioned this with a purpose. We'll be engaged often, I think, to tell of our victory over Burgoyne's army. Such talk is fine. Have care in the telling of it to avoid comparing the generals to one another. If such talk reaches one of those generals, there'll be hell to pay. They're all too sensitive by far and in no mind to suffer criticisms from junior officers. Is that clear?"

Scammell looks around the tent to be sure his point is understood. "We didn't know how lucky we were up north. The severity of the business at hand kept our generals busy. Some of the idle time that occurred here, it seems, got put to ill use." Scammell clears his throat and narrows his eyes slightly and intensifies his tone. "I don't recall any of you having met, or spending any time with General Washington. I have, and I can assure you he is the very embodiment of commitment to our cause. No other general, not Gates, not Schuyler, not even General Sullivan, whom I have known many years, can match His Excellency's honor. Thus, I cannot state this too strongly, do not get drawn into discussing the merits or faults of the generals."

Many of the men nod in agreement before Scammell changes topics. "General Washington is considering whether we should march on Philadelphia. Generals Howe and Cornwallis command divisions for the enemy. Both are out between here and the city. Thus, we must get ourselves into a high state of readiness. Make certain the men know we are evaluating the prospect of marching to retake the city. Our position here is strong, and we are equally well-served by inducing Howe and Cornwallis to give battle here. General Sullivan says we outnumber them in total, though the count of our men who are fit for duty is much lower. Thus, I believe we shall be defending this ground, so get to know it well. General Poor will order frequent patrols in the next days to afford us the chance to do so."

The next afternoon Goodale pulls the tent flap aside and enters, causing Isaac's candles to go out.

"Sorry about that. It's gotten windy since this morning."

Isaac reaches down, finds his tinderbox, and relights the candles. "It has. The tent's been flapping a bit. We need to tighten the ropes before it gets dark."

"Writing to your wife?"

"No, my brother Simon. He and my uncle like to get the details about the doings of the Army. I expect my uncle thinks we should be marching on Philadelphia rather than fortifying this camp. Simon's a prudent sort, so that will give them something to debate for a month. Did the abatis get built?"

"Eighty stakes worth. We were lucky up north, I s'pose. Burgoyne didn't have any cavalry. A lot of work to make those things and the men haven't had any meat since we got here. Tis wrong to expect much from them on half-full bellies."

"That reminds me, I was going to ask Simon to advocate for sending provisions to us. Pennsylvania, it seems, doesn't intend to feed us. But, I did hear some clothing and such will be coming in from New Jersey."

...

Uriah breaks the quiet of the Third Regiment's camp well before sunrise a week later, sending the long roll of the call to arms into the early morning darkness. Isaac wakes with a start. In the tightly packed camps at Saratoga, it was common to hear four or five drummers take up the call before the regiment's drummer on duty would begin. This camp, spread over several long hills, feels different, like several camps, each isolated from the sounds of their neighbors.

The duty sergeant bellows, "Strike the tents! Assemble on the south side by Washington's headquarters. General Howe marches our way."

Isaac rolls up and pulls on his boots. "Let's go. If there's one thing I never want to see, it's the look on the men's faces when I'm the last one to arrive."

Goodale coughs, dislodging phlegm deep in his throat and rises to rest on his elbows coughing again. His voice is ragged as he turns and sits up. "Fair point. Don't want to be seen that way."

They make their way, a minute later, through the cold morning air toward the crown of the wooded hill. The crescent moon provides enough light to see the path between the trees. Behind them, the men form into platoons and ready themselves to march. From ahead, Gray jogs toward them. Isaac catches his attention and asks, "Are we to form at our designated post?"

"No, Sir. Colonel Dearborn sent me with orders to light more campfires. General Washington wants our army to look huge, and cause General Howe to slow his advance."

Isaac nods his acknowledgment and turns to Goodale, "Once they've loaded the tents in the wagon, send the men out in groups of four to light those extra fires."

Isaac stands on the north side of the Sandy Run with Livermore two hours after sunrise. The army had spent the last week clearing the land along the creek. They removed trees and any other cover the enemy could use while building a three-mile-long line of fortifications. Isaac scans the trees a quarter-mile across the valley to the south. "Looks like the extra campfires succeeded. No sign of any redcoats."

Behind them, half the men wait in ranks a dozen yards in front of the fortifications, ready to march out and check the enemy should they attempt to cross the creek—the other half rest behind the earthen walls taking their breakfast. Isaac and Livermore hold cups of hot broth as they continue to survey the valley.

Livermore takes a sip. "Mm, tis hot, but my teeth and my belly need a bit more substance."

"Aye, true. I'm doing my best not to complain, lest the men overhear."

The distant sounds of musket fire to the southwest yank their attention away from the broth. The firing continues, and Isaac turns back to the men. "Sergeant Wilkins, get the men behind the walls formed up. If that action comes this way, we'll want to be ready."

The distant firing continues, sounding like a running skirmish as opposed to men organized and firing volleys by ranks. Livermore turns, so one ear is in line with the direction of the firing. "A couple miles away, at least."

"Could be three or four. Sound carries better along the valley now that we've cleared this stretch."

The firing comes no closer and lasts for twenty minutes, then stops. Stone and Ellis join Isaac and Livermore. Stone passes a small basket of biscuits around.

Isaac tries one, his mouth twists in disapproval.

Stone shrugs. "Sorry, they're a bit dry. Bacon grease and lard are in short supply."

"Nothing to worry on Ben," Livermore begins, "just one'll fill me up--already got two cups of broth waiting in my belly."

As they finish the biscuits, Dearborn approaches. "We're to stay in this position. That skirmishing earlier was a part of Howe's forces attempting to invest Chestnut Hill. Keep the men alert and warm. Drill them by companies and keep an eye to the south."

Early in the afternoon, a significantly larger volley of musket fire to the southwest starts another round of skirmishing. Isaac and Goodale, at the front of their company, jump at the sound. "I hope that was ours who fired."

"Me too."

From behind the men, Dearborn calls out, "Keep watch to the south. I swear I'll find some bacon for the first man who sees any sign of the enemy in the trees on that ridge."

The woods across the valley remain still. The reports of several smaller volleys and a good deal of scattered musket fire continues to travel upstream to reach them. After several minutes, Goodale, his voice betraying exasperation, "Show me an enemy. This standing about and waiting is infernal. Why are these redcoats in no hurry to enjoy our hospitality."

"Do you suppose it's because they found out all we've got are biscuits and broth?"

Goodale chuckles. "If they knew that, they'd have come with wagonloads of food to bait us."

"There's a good deal more firing this time."

"Tis already disorganized. I hope we've got them on the run."

As the sun begins to slide behind the hills to the southwest, Dearborn calls the company commanders together. "We've got orders for the night. We're to make a show of some extra campfires and make it appear we've changed our position since last night. Our part will be a hundred yards back of here. Any of you have questions?"

Captain Stone clears his throat and raises his eyebrows with curiosity. "Any word about the skirmishing today?"

"The enemy's advanced corps took Chestnut Hill. Some militia from this state skirmished with them first. General Washington sent out two more militia regiments and a Continental regiment from Connecticut at noon. The enemy drove them back, and the commander of one of the militia regiments, a General Irving or maybe it's Irvine, was wounded and captured."

Isaac joins Livermore and Ellis two days later. Ellis points toward the woods across the valley where several redcoat soldiers, almost hidden in the trees, dig fortifications. "I could hear 'em for the past ten minutes. Just took me a bit to find them."

Livermore catches sight of them. "There've got to be others then."

Every hour the sounds of sporadic skirmishing on the same ridge far to their left also reaches them. Ellis shakes his head in frustration. "They're right there, digging themselves in more and more every hour, and we've tried nothing beyond a small party to draw them out."

Livermore, with his hands on his hips in thought, nods. "I'm certain if Colonel Scammell was out here with us, instead of doing His Excellency's desk work, we'd have attacked yesterday. What do you think of that?"

Ellis cocks a skeptical eyebrow at Livermore. "No disrespect to Colonel Scammell, but if the enemy showed any sign of interest in us, I'm sure Colonel Dearborn would've had us marching on the double to meet them."

"You're right. I meant no sleight. It's just that I'm now appreciating how active and committed our colonels and General Arnold was up north. No desire for anything resembling a general action here."

Isaac blows in his hands to warm them. "We've been digging in here for weeks. Our position is perhaps too well-defended. Perhaps Howe doesn't have the numbers to overrun our works. Neither side, I think, can afford to lose."

Livermore raises his eyes, looking to the left where Dearborn strides towards them. "Captain Ellis, send runners to the other commanders and have them join us."

Once the other commanders arrive, Dearborn wastes no time. "We're to go out as soon as the sun's down. Our objective is to draw their dragoons out from their camp on the right end of the ridge. Have the men light their fires just like they did last night. Some men from the Second Regiment will move in and keep them lit. Pick a company from all our men who are the swiftest. Penniman will have command of those men." Dearborn points to their right. "They'll move down the road in front of General Greene's men. Before they do, the rest of us will go out and keep hidden a couple hundred yards further right, then crawl to within range of the road. If the men on the road fail to draw out the dragoons, they're to take up a position a hundred yards out from the enemy and fire into their works. If that fails, we'll send in one or two more companies to do the same."

Captain Stone asks, "Anyone else coming with us, Sir?"

"No. Too many men and they'll send out foot troops in larger numbers. This needs to look to be an easy job for their dragoons." Dearborn scans the faces of the commanders, then adds, "I expect we may be out all night, make sure the men do as well."

Two hours before dawn, Isaac and Goodale arrive back at their hastily constructed wigwam. It sits among the dozens the men had produced two nights earlier. After crawling inside, they find the low fire gives little warmth. Reaching outside, Goodale pulls in a few small pieces of cut branches. "It's going to smoke, but I'd rather warm up."

Isaac lies on his side, propping his head with an elbow. "Aye, no choice."

Goodale puts the smallest of branches on first. "That was a wasted night. They had dug in too well and showed good discipline for staying within their works."

"I don't think they were there. I couldn't see enough horses, and they only returned a little of the fire we gave."

"Maybe. Either way, I'm chilled to the bone for lying on the cold ground. At least this fire has dried out much of the ground in here."

"Yes, definitely better than last night. Let's get some sleep before they start beating another alarm."

•••

The wind outside ruffles the broad side of their tent every few seconds. Isaac sits at the end of his cot furthest from the tied-off tent flaps. He hunches over the desk writing. Goodale lays curled in two blankets, facing the side of the tent, coughing. His cough is dry, tight, and with a wheezing tail. Goodale's hair, wet from feverish sweat plasters against his moist shiny forehead. Three half-burned candles in a cluster on the desk provide Isaac with enough light to write.

Camp at Valley Forge in Pennsylvania, December 23, 1777

To my Dear WIfe Elizabeth and sons, I am safe and unharmed. My love and affection to you and each of the boys. Please give the same to your father and sisters and Brother Richard. It seems mor and mor I am to pass the season here in Pennsylvania. I pray our new son is warm and well.

The men in my company also are well, tho some suffer for lack of shoes stockings and coats. Our Circumstances in leaving Fort Ti in July haunts us still.

I deeply regret the business of the Army has kept me from writing for these passed weeks. Only a few days after encamping at Whitemarsh Gen'l Howe obligated us to send our tents and baggage north for safekeep. Our Army and his stared across a small valley at each other for several days. Sum scurmishes, of which I was not involved, proved no advantage for either side and General Howe quit the field in favor of wintering in Philadelphia. We moved our camp once and then again to the spot we now occupy. Our brigade caught a bit of luck and got our tents before removing from Whitemarsh. Much of the army did not and had to make do as they could in violent snowstorms.

We spent the last two days felling trees, building hutts and fortifications for our winter quarters. NevertheLess our regiment will be obliged to stay in our tents for some days to come as many regiments had none until yesterday. We must shift for ourselves to gain provisions. The inhabitants near us are of a greedy spirit and will not share unless forced.Daily we see General Howe has sent men to strip those same inhabitants of there possessions against us making use of them. Yet, our spirits are high in spite of such disagreeable circumstances - many of us suspect we will be able to bring an end to this war in the next campain.

Your Most Loving and Obedient Husband -

Isaac Frye

Isaac yawns, causing Goodale to begin a yawn. A raw barking cough cuts it short. "Zeke, you ought to go to the hospital tomorrow. Your ague has got worse."

Goodale's voice light and raspy, "I hate the idea of doing so, but you may be right."

"I checked with the colonel. He says General Washington started building hospitals in this quarter in April. Each hospital is for just one type of sickness, so there's less chance of getting something else. The surgeons are saying the men are healing faster."

Goodale gives a slight series of nods. "Alright, I'll go tomorrow."

"I bet they've got some decent stoves to keep everyone warm too. Staying in this tent on these freezing nights certainly isn't helping you."

"It's not. I am worse every night and a different worse every morning."

Isaac rises and gets his boots. "I'll go get you some warm rum."

"Get whiskey if they've got it. It kills the phlegm better. There're a few shillings in my chest. Get a pint if you can."

"Aye, I'll see what I can do."

Honor and Valor

11 WINTER QUARTERS

> "... The soldiers in cutting their firewood, are to save such parts of each tree, as will do for building, reserving sixteen or eighteen feet of the trunk, for logs to rear their huts ..."
>
> From the General Orders
> Headquarters at Valley Forge, December 20, 1777

The thunks of axes on trees and thocks of hatchets and adzes shaping logs defy any sense of rhythm. Thousands of men work through the dreary gray afternoon toward the common goal of shelter. The enormous volume of activity serves to raise everyone's spirits a little. The clearing around camp grows as the men take the trees at the edges to feed the Army's efforts to construct over a thousand huts for their winter quarters.

In his tent, damp from the previous day's rain, Isaac sits writing in a new orderly book. Earlier, he stretched one side of the canvas wide open with the hopes of drying the whole tent faster. The rain had brought some welcome warmer air during the day, yet preceded a miserable freezing night. Inside the tent, the ground is finally dry and hard, giving a sense of comfort that had gone missing in the cold and difficulty of the past weeks.

Isaac organizes the new book into sections. One for muster rolls and another for the accounts of each of his men. Each account has two parts--one for pay, and another for credit to buy items from the public stores such as shirts, coats, and shoes. The orderly books had come with the news the Army had secured their back pay. However, to receive it, Mr. Weeks, the regiment's paymaster, required new rolls detailing the time each man was present. Isaac finishes the muster roll then cleans his quill and firmly sets the cork atop his ink bottle. Feeling stiff and cramped from two hours of writing, he moves to stand in front of his tent. After stretching his arms and swinging them in circles to get his blood flowing, he sees Livermore coming from behind the tent.

Livermore joins him. "Got your rolls completed?"

"Just now. You?"

"Yup, handed them to Gilman a few minutes ago."

"How's he liking all this extra work?"

"Not at all."

A light cold rain begins to fall. Isaac points inside his tent. "I feel like I just got dry, you want to sit inside? It doesn't look like this will last long."

Livermore looks west where the sky is lightening, "Sure. I'm sick of being soaked and cold."

Once inside, Isaac looks at his chest with his mouth turned down in regret. I'd offer you some rum, but I gave the last of mine to Zeke when he left for the hospital."

"I understand. I was about to ask what you thought of Gray and McClary objecting to sending our men out to forage?"

"We can't eat our principles or good intentions. We've been low on provisions since we got to White Marsh, and the commissary's been worse than useless. None of us like it, though Gray took his protestations too far, I think. He had nothing but principles to offer as an alternative to eating."

"He's been the conscience for the whole regiment since the spring." Livermore looks down and laughs under his breath. "I do give Dearborn credit for standing his ground. I can't believe he told Gray he was welcome to take his complaints to his Excellency and

Congress."

"Dearborn's not one to turn the other cheek. I wouldn't want to cross him."

"Nor me. He's as determined a man as I've met."

"Right." Isaac purses his lips and shakes his head. "It took me aback when he said he'd recommend hanging for any man who steals from or tries to injure any of the inhabitants when we're out foraging."

"I would doubt our men would do such, though it makes me wonder what sort of men are in the rest of the army."

"Hard to know, though the orders to muster them twice a day should keep most from straying."

Livermore looks up, noticing the raindrops had stopped their gentle pelting of the tent. "We should get ourselves about checking on the progress of the huts."

Late that afternoon, the Third Regiment's officers assemble inside Scammell's tent. Scammell and Dearborn wait in the middle between the two center poles. The others, twenty-seven in all, stand in silence around the periphery.

Scammell, with his hands clasped behind his back, walks a small circle. He takes in the faces of the assembled men as he collects his thoughts. He stops and straightens his shoulders and inhales and exhales a deep breath. "Gentlemen, I ... I see before me twenty-eight brave and steadfast officers. Six months ago, there were forty of us. Granted, two are sick, and Hawkins is in Albany. I am of a mind that we take a few moments to remember those gallant men who were with us not so long ago."

After half a minute, Scammell collects himself. "That wasn't how I intended to begin this meeting. I have good news. Well, good news for ten of you. General Poor has granted ten furloughs for our regiment. In a moment, we'll draw straws to see which of you will be travel home in a week or so. I'll be staying. General Washington has requested that I occupy the office of Adjutant for the Army."

Isaac sees Scammell's internal conflict play across his face with a glad smile on his lips, but only weariness in his eyes. Stone calls out, "Hip Hi-",

Scammell whirls toward him, raising his palm to silence him. "That's not," Scammell softens his expression and smiles with appreciation at Stone, "public knowledge, though your sentiment warms me. His Excellency granted Colonel Dearborn a furlough, which is in addition to the ten from General Poor. Thus, Henry, will you verify there are ten long straws here." He passes a handful of straws to Dearborn.

A moment later, Dearborn holds up one, showing it to everyone. "Any longer than this one will indicate a furlough." He hands the straws back to Scammell, who moves around the tent, offering the straws to each man.

Of the six captains, Isaac and Livermore fail to draw a long straw. After Scammell passes out the last straw, he returns to the middle of the tent. "Should we not conclude this war by this time next year, I will see to it that all of you who will remain here this winter shall have furloughs next winter."

The next morning, Isaac and Sergeant Wilkins walk around the walls of the company's first hut, which still lacks a roof. They inspect the work, particularly the chimney. "I think it looks good, though a few spots on the walls need more chinking."

Wilkins nods, acknowledging Isaac's assessment. "Aye, sir." Wilkins lifts his eyes in the direction of the camp's center. "Colonel Scammell's coming our way."

After thanking Wilkins, Isaac walks to meet Scammell. "Good morning sir," Isaac offers as he salutes.

"Good morning to you, Captain Frye. Have you been introduced to His Excellency?"

"No, sir."

"Well you're about to be, you and Private Carlton. So get him and yourself looking as sharp as you can and come to my tent. I've recommended Carlton for service in His Excellency's Life Guard. I told him of Carleton's bravery during the battles up north. He wishes to meet Carleton and interview you regarding his character and service."

For a moment, Isaac is speechless. "Yessir. We will be at your tent shortly."

Half an hour later, Isaac, his coat and trousers brushed as clean as they could be, given almost a year of service, accompanies Carleton. He wears an old coat, but a new shirt beneath. His trousers, being his only pair, carry stains of blood, mud, and sweat and patches and tears in a dozen places. Scammell waits outside his tent. He makes a show of looking them up and down, appraising the quality of their appearance.

"It's better than you were looking a few minutes ago. It's of no moment. His Excellency will not be expecting anything more." To Isaac, "Have you told Carlton what we're about?"

"Yes."

"Good. Let's be on our way. You're both to address General Washington as Your Excellency when I make the introductions. Understood?"

Both give affirmatives as they walk. They approach the stone house serving as Washington's headquarters, and Scammell steps ahead of them. "I'll enter first and see if His Excellency can meet with you. If so, I'll summon you in and make the introductions.

A few seconds after Scammell shuts the door, it opens again, and he nods, "Come in."

The main room, to the right of the door, contains several tables covered in papers with ten chairs scattered around the tables. Washington and another man in a uniform, similar to Washington's sit at the table nearest the large fireplace where a cheery, warm fire burns.

Scammell steps a bit to the side, "Your Excellency and Captain Gibbs, I present to you Captain Frye and Private Carleton of my regiment. Both are from Wilton in New Hampshire." Isaac and Carleton offer smart salutes.

Washington's demeanor is serious as he meets both men's gaze before returning their salute. "Please have a seat." He motions to a trio of chairs on the opposite side of the table. "Captain Gibbs is the commander of my Life Guard."

Ten minutes later, Isaac and Carleton walk back toward the third regiment's part of the camp. "Congratulations, Carleton, tis a great and well-deserved honor."

"I hope I serve well, though I am near speechless for having met General Washington in person."

"You'll do well. Tell the men and gather your things. Captain Gibbs expects you within the hour."

•••

Isaac sits on the warm earth a few feet back from the fireplace and leans against the lower bunk on the right. His legs stretch across the middle of the hut. In his lap rests a smooth board serving as a writing desk. He uncorks the inkwell and sets it on the ground beside him. Eight bunks line the sides of the fourteen by sixteen foot windowless hut. The fireplace and its shallow firebox lined with caked and hardened clay dominate the end opposite the small door.

Livermore and his company's first lieutenant, David McGregore, sleep in the bunk opposite Isaac. Penniman and Jonathan Cass, his company's ensign, have the bunk nearest the door on the opposite side. Benjamin Ellis, the first lieutenant of his cousin's company, has the bunk opposite Penniman and Cass. With the door shut, the space near nearby is tolerable, while near the fireplace, it is warm.

The imperfections in the door and frame allow air to draft in and keep the chimney drawing the smoke outside. A hard gust of wind pushes the smoke back down, and it mingles with smells of McGregore's whiskey and the peach brandy Livermore likes. All these improve on the underlying odor of the moldering straw they had received for bedding.

Isaac shakes off a yawn and begins writing.

Winter Quarters, Jan 10, 1777

Dear Brother, I've just rec'd your lins. Hearty warm congratulations to you and Hannah. A second set of Twin boys. I've always said you were blessed and your five sons and five dotters further prove I am correct. Please convey my love and affection to Uncle Joseph and Aunt Bell. I wish I were home now and able to visit in person. Insted I and the rest who drew short straws are to spend winter with General Washington in our camp west of Philadelphia. Your idea of naming

Charles E. Frye

the new twins George Washington and John Hancock is a fine one in the spirit of our new country.

We have at last settled into camp and the past few days we have got a chance to rest. We were two weeks hutting. I sit in one tonight. It is good to have a warm place to sleep. Tis much better than a tent, tho I would prefer my own barn as it is cleaner and the straw is likely fresh. Our commander was appointed as Adjutant of the Army so that leaves Captain Livermore in charge and yours truly as his second.

The local inhabitants and now others from farther away have begun selling the men provisions beer spirits and anything else we can pay for. We last month rec'd our pay for most of 1777 so the men can buy the cloths they sorly needed. Many spent the rest on wisky and such. I sent the balance of mine to Elizabeth and pray she has got it by now.

We muster and Drill each day and some time goes to halling clean water from the creeks when melting ice from our roof is not enough. We spend time chinking our huts and out on Foraging parties.

Keep sending news of family and friends as it lifts our spirits.

Humbly and with Love your Brother

Captain Isaac Frye

Isaac waves the paper in front of the fireplace and checks to be sure the ink is dry before folding it. He yawns long and hard then adds two pieces of wood the fire. He sets the ink and board on the desk next to his bunk before turning in for the night.

•••

Honor and Valor

Isaac leaves the hut to stretch his legs and find some fresh air. Now mid-February, clouds sag thick and somber above the trees on the horizon. Gray sky meets darker gray trees. Behind him, tufts of light brown grass and hundreds of huts break up a sea of mud. A few days earlier, the heaviest rain of the year had washed away any snow and flooded the roads.

Isaac wanders out of General Poor's cluster of huts. His stomach growls as he crosses the main road leading into and out of camp. Ahead, another man wearing a bright blue coat, marking him as part of the Virginia Line, walks his way. He carries a spontoon; the half-spear General Washington had ordered all officers carry.

As the man draws near, Isaac sees a buff cockade on his hat, like his own, marking him as a captain. Isaac nods in greeting. "Good afternoon, Captain."

"Good afternoon, sir. I'm afraid I'm at a disadvantage with your not wearing a uniform."

"I'm Captain Isaac Frye of the Third New Hampshire Regiment. There as yet have been no uniforms in the public stores for our regiment. Though, I s'pose it's proven valuable to look like militia until we don't."

"Well met sir, and I believe you." A broad grin breaks through the man's weathered features as he offers his hand. "I am Captain John Steed of the Eighth Virginia." He points to his right. "These huts here are ours."

Isaac shakes hands with Steed and notes the Virginian's brown eyes and the way they turn down a little, giving him a kindly appearance. Isaac's stomach growls, demanding food. "I beg your pardon, our brigade received no provisions Thursday, and I ate the last of my food two days ago. I fear my belly is confused."

"It's the same for us. The commissary's not had any provisions since running short on Monday."

"Aye. We may go to Colonel Scammell tonight and make an inquiry. He is also our regiment's commander, and we believe he will positively tell us when provisions will arrive."

"I'd like to hear what he says." Steed sighs. "I'm out walking to take my mind and belly off of these circumstances. A bit of conversation might help, as well."

"It might; I was doing the same. We've become rather tired of our hut's four walls."

Steed smiles in commiseration, "Where in New Hampshire are you from?"

Isaac tells of his farm and family before asking Steed for his story.

"I'm from New Jersey and lived for some time about two days walk north of here, where father and brother still have their homes. Now my home is in Virginia. In the northern part though well west of here. General Gates' is my neighbor to the north, and General Lee, Charles Lee, that is, lives to my south. It's good land, and I've got easy access to the Potomac."

Isaac inclines his head with appreciation. "I knew, though, I cannot recall how, that Gates was from Virginia. He seems a capable general."

"You think he deserves the credit for the victory against Burgoyne?"

"Somewhat. I mean, in hindsight, Schuyler's preparations made it possible, though we won two battles and a siege with Gates in command and to his credit we did."

"So, the old man had some fight in him, eh?"

"The men did. Gates did the job of a commanding general. Arnold and Poor were the only generals I knew of who were close to the fighting."

"Ah, that makes sense."

"What about Lee? I ask as he is, in name, my division commander, yet so far as we know, he is still a prisoner held in New York."

"Yes, that's right. As for the man, he loves his dogs. I think he prefers their company to most men."

"If they're loyal, I expect he may have good reason."

"Well said." Steed chuckles.

"You have trouble with Indians in Virginia?"

"No, not usually. But in the last months, they've broken the Treaty of Pittsburgh. There've been problems well west of here, but they've stayed north of the Potomac and out of Virginia. My father and brother have moved everyone out of Pennsylvania to my farm for safety. They were too close to where the Shawnee and Delaware raided." Looking weary, Steed rubs his forehead. "It's a part of living so far west."

How about you? Indians much trouble in New Hampshire?"

"Not for a generation in the south. The Abenaki keep to themselves, mostly in Canada or the northern parts of Massachusetts Bay."

"Your men get in either of those battles against Burgoyne?"

"Aye, we did." Isaac goes on for several minutes, describing the battles and the eventual surrender of Burgoyne. "How about you? Your men see any fighting?"

"We did at Brandywine. We were in the reserves, but word came early in the afternoon that another column under Cornwallis with Howe himself was moving to flank us from the north. We high-tailed it for five or six miles and started forming battle lines at Birmingham Meetinghouse. Tis a Quaker district. We were on the far right. I forgot to explain that everyone calls our regiment the German regiment for having so many of them in the ranks. So what happens? We had to fight the Bavarian mercenaries in Howe's division. It's the daftest thing, Germans paid by an English king to fight Germans in America fighting for their country. As for the battle, their Jaegers pushed us hard, and for not being too well organized, we could only hold for a bit. Cornwallis's hit our center hard too. No real choice but to retreat. We lost one killed and four wounded. I don't think it compares to what you described in that first battle, but it was the most firing I've ever seen, and I've seen a few battles."

"When we fought Burgoyne, he had no place to go, so they fought hard. We all knew the land too. Both sides had been over it twice. It sounds like your men did very well despite the outcome."

"They did. We hauled several cannon with us, and that's the fastest I think those have ever moved."

The two captains pause to look out over the valley to the south of camp. In the east, the sky shows the first signs of growing dark, and the light wind turns cold.

Turning back toward camp, Steed casts his gaze about the breadth of the camp. "No cookfires."

"Aye, and somehow it seems the wisest course is to pretend nothing is amiss."

Steed chuckles then buttons the top button of his coat. "What's winter like in New Hampshire?"

"More snow. Colder. I don't remember so many days with rain and mud like here."

"Snow is an event here, but mud is a way of life."

The two begin walking back toward the huts. Steed asks, as if he is wondering aloud, "You said you're with Poor's Brigade. So you were the ones they said had a mutiny up at Fishkill?"

"Aye," his tone glum, "we did." Isaac tells the story as they return.

A few hours later, in their hut, Isaac sits at his field desk with Livermore. Their field desks pushed together several feet in front of the fire to make a single larger surface. Two lanterns illuminate stacks of the regiment's muster rolls. The three lieutenants and Ensign Cass use another field desk between their bunks to play cards.

Isaac sighs in frustration. "A roll for the extra month's pay. I thought we did this once already, right after twas announced."

"We did, and now that Congress and General Washington have agreed upon the date, we must do so again. The twenty-ninth of December is the date. Any man in camp or any but for their duty who would have been gets the pay. They are to be listed with their rank on the twenty-ninth."

"What about men who have lost rank or been promoted? Two of my corporals are now privates for misdoings that happened after that date."

"I s'pose, to be fair, tis got to be the rank they held on the twenty-ninth."

"Aye." Isaac pauses as he looks down his company's roll. "I had three whose enlistments were up, and they've left."

"Include them. Congress agreed to pay them when they were here."

"Aye, and no for those we left up in Albany and Fishkill. I think that covers everyone?"

"Sounds like it. Nobody left for furloughs until the fourth of January, so we'll include all the officers."

Isaac chuckles to himself. "You'll make a fine colonel one day."

"I hope not. Winning the war next season while I'm a captain would be my wish. Then I'd be back home building and living in a proper house and maybe courting a fine woman."

They continue writing the roll for the paymaster in silence for several minutes. Livermore stops and looks to Isaac. "I know its no easy thing for you to be here instead of home with your wife and sons, especially the new baby. Most of us here don't have families of our own."

"I'm like you, and everyone else, I gave my oath. War takes men from their families. My father and brothers were gone for many months in the last war. I've gone and done worse now to my wife and sons. None of us expected we'd be planning a fourth year of fighting in a war or that gaining our liberties would become gaining independence."

"Tis true, none of us knew it would go like this."

The following morning half an hour before noon, all of Poor's Brigade assembles on the parade ground down the hill below their huts. On Washington's orders, they had done so twice a day at random times since early January. Dozens of the men appear disheveled, and others tilt and lean, delirious and incoherent, in the ranks. Livermore has command of the regiment, and Isaac is beside him is second in command.

Isaac turns to Livermore. "One of us should report to General Poor that our men are no longer fit. It's been five days since they last had a meal. They look drunk, except its from hunger."

Livermore nods, acknowledging the logic and imperative in Isaac's voice. "I'll send Paymaster Weeks to General Poor's headquarters to report. He's as genial and optimistic as they come." He turns about and approaches Weeks, who is positioned a dozen paces to their rear.

Twenty minutes later, they make their way back to their huts, Isaac and Livermore walk behind the men who march ahead of them. Isaac asks, "Do you think Weeks will prevail?"

"Insofar as reporting accurately to General Poor? Yes, certainly. He's got such a pleasant manner. One often fails to notice he has argued and won until after he's left and gone."

As they approach their hut, Isaac sees Weeks walking back from the middle of the camp. "Let's see what came of his reporting."

Weeks, a tallish man in his early twenties, with an unassuming and gentle demeanor, waves as he catches sight of them and hurries his step to meet them. "It seems our timing was fortuitous. General Poor took me with him to bear witness of or men's plight directly to General Washington."

Livermore's eyebrows raise with respect and surprise. "Good. What came of that?"

"Colonel Scammell perceived General Poor's mood upon our arrival and took us directly to His Excellency. General Washington seemed genuinely taken aback as I described our men."

Isaac exhales in relief. "What then?"

"He dismissed me and was calling for the Commissary-General. Though I think that was more about starting the proper sort of rumor. There must have been other complaints today since there were no provisions given out Thursday."

Livermore's shoulders sag a bit in disappointment. "At least we've been heard. I hope something comes of it. Thank you, Mister Weeks."

Isaac, his expression grim, nods. "Our need has been known for days. Something has to be in the works."

Weeks strokes the whiskers on his chin thoughtfully. "I think you're both right and there's reason to-"

Back in the direction of the parade ground, shouts and whoops of excitement interrupt Weeks. The ruckus draws the men out of their huts, and Isaac, Livermore, and Weeks make their way to the forefront. Below on the road, five to six dozen cattle move toward camp driven by a trio of men on horseback.

The men give the cattle as boisterous a welcome as they can manage as the herd ambles toward the middle of the camp. Livermore puts his hands on his hips. "Only a few look scrawny. The rest look fit and healthy. It's Providential."

Isaac grins. "Aye. No arguments from me."

•••

Isaac walks, a month later, with Goodale toward the camp, still several miles away. The late morning sky is sunny with only a few high clouds, though the air is chilly. The hospital Goodale spent the past months in is now out of sight. Isaac carries his spontoon with his right hand and Goodale's satchel, filled with papers on his left shoulder. Goodale, a shadow of his former self, is gaunt and moves with stiffness in his joints.

Behind them, Peter Chandler, who recently arrived from Albany, carries the rest of Goodale's possessions in a pair of knapsacks on each shoulder and a blanket under his left arm. Chandler, a quiet wiry man, is seven years younger and an inch shorter than Isaac. He hums to himself as he walks.

Goodale holds up a hand, indicating he needs a rest, and they all stop. Isaac offers Goodale some whiskey he had brought for the occasion. Goodale takes a tentative sip, and Isaac hides all outward signs of relief that Goodale doesn't cough. "Take your time. We've got all day if we need it."

"Hope not. Tell me the news. I've not heard any for a week now."

"It seems we are to have a new drill manual. It comes from this Prussian baron. Von Steuben is his name. He's been training General Washington's Life Guard for several days now. They are to learn it first and then teach it to the rest of the army. Von Steuben knows no useful English, so he's resorted to all manner of gestures to get his point across. It's been entertaining to watch. Colonel Scammell says he's got one of the best military minds in the world. I expect we will be drilling with the new manual any day now."

"Prussian? Didn't we fight them?"

"Aye. Just those our former king employed."

Goodale begins walking again, and Isaac falls in beside him and motions Chandler to stay back out of earshot.

Goodale nods toward Isaac's spontoon. "What's with that?"

"There's one waiting for you in our hut. All officers are to carry them now instead of muskets. Washington's orders. He intends us to command without distraction. I s'pose it's for the best. I've got my pistols if all else fails."

Goodale snorts with derision. "We'll see about no muskets."

"It's been adopted in every regiment. Lighter than a musket and perfectly capable of fending off a bayonet and skewering your foe before he can recover."

They walk several minutes in silence before Goodale asks, "How's Chandler as your waiter?"

"He's done well. Discrete and reliable. Having him take care of things has been a relief."

"Good. Any news from home?"

"Not for two weeks. Elizabeth, Sarah, and the boys have hunkered down with plenty of food packed away in the root cellar. So far, they've not had any hardship. You get any lines?"

"Several, though not so good. Elly says they're in a bad way. They've got wood enough to keep warm, but the garden was poor, and she's of a mind that I need to come home and put things right. My sister says the same. With Eben a prisoner, she's got nowhere to turn."

"We'll talk to Colonel Scammell. It'll take General Washington's approval."

"Have we got paid?"

"Yes, through January. Mr. Weeks has yours. We'll see him first when we get back."

"How long does mail take to reach home?"

"Two, sometimes three weeks."

"We'll see if my pay fixes things. If not I hope the Colonel can help. Will you make sure he knows?"

"I will. Livermore and I are to meet him tomorrow to observe the Prussian and his training methods."

"As they lean into the rise leading into the camp, the smell of dead carcasses greets them. Oh, I almost forgot, take care not to drink any water unless you know where it came from. All the streams have got fouled. Carcasses not properly burned and for the usual laziness of men not willing to walk a few extra steps to the vaults to relieve themselves."

"I'll get some rum or cider we get back."

"Cider's cheaper by far. The sutlers keep raising their prices. Their greed flies in the face of all we're doing."

"Well, some of the locals are helping in the hospitals. They were decent to me, so I guess I don't blame them as I've heard we've taken a good bit from them, and that was after General Howe helped himself."

"Aye, though for not knowing them, tis difficult to have sympathy."

The windy gusts of a late March day escalate as the sun drops into the trees on the horizon to usher in a chilly night. Several brigades are on the parade grounds implementing General Von Steuben's methods for the first time. The new manual of arms dictates maneuvering begins with the way the men stand at attention with their heels two inches apart, toes pointed outward, and their heads turned a little, so each man's left eye aligns with his buttons. One of the members of Washington's Life Guard walks through the ranks of Isaac's company with the sergeants following behind. The guard inspects each man for the height and angle he holds his musket, where each hand grasps the musket, the level of his eyes, the tilt of his head, and the repairs needed to his clothes.

The new manual of arms changes the arrangement for how the regiment parades. Now the companies form two ranks instead of four. As ranking officers, Isaac and Livermore each wait at the front of one half of the regiment. The lieutenants and second lieutenants do the jobs of the captains in the absence of the officers on furlough."

Livermore glances toward the northwest, then calls out to Isaac. "We've got about half an hour of daylight. What do they need to work on most?"

"Priming and loading." Isaac shrugs his shoulders and approaches Livermore. "Every marching maneuver as well. But if they can get the loading down, twill build some confidence."

"Good thinking. The uniformity and precision of all this is a great deal to absorb in a few hours."

"Sounds like we will be at this every day, twice a day, until we've got it perfected."

"At the very least. We'll need the sergeants to work with their men every night until they can all recite the whole of it from memory.

"Good thinking."

"Captain Frye"

Isaac turns to see Ensign Cass approaching with a letter in hand. The ensign's typical thin-lipped serious demeanor is in place, but his eyes hold a happy look, indicating the potential for good news. "Ensign Cass, what is it?"

"We received this from Lieutenant Hawkins in today's dispatches from Albany."

Isaac takes the letter, unfolds it, and scans the dozen lines, then returns it to Cass. "Thank you. That is good news."

As Cass departs, Livermore raises a curious eyebrow.

"After he wrote, Hawkins went home for a few weeks of furlough. He confirmed Elijah Mansfield and Ezra Fuller of my company recovered enough to be sent home with him. They'll muster on the first of April in Wilton and march here with any others who have recovered. The best news was Eben Drury was released and has also recovered."

"Glad to hear that. I figure about half of my wounded have been sent home as well. Gives me some hope that we'll be better than half strength when we leave here."

•••

Isaac, with Goodale and Hawkins, stand in the center of their hut, raising cups of rum. The wet din of a late April rain shower patters on the hut's roof. Four lamps cast light and shadows on the faces of thirty-one men. The entire company fits inside, given the officer's hut has two fewer bunks. They gather to toast the return of Hawkins, and several men now recovered from their wounds.

Goodale leads the first toast. "Twas taken in our first meeting with Burgoyne and today returns to us, to Eben Drury."

The men raise their cups to the farmer from Temple, "To Eben Drury." Drury nods in appreciation. His features are hollow despite spending a few weeks at home.

Hawkins leads the next. "Wounded in our first meeting with Burgoyne and today returns to us, to Elijah Mansfield." Cups raise again, this time to the short fiery farmer from Amherst, whose

Honor and Valor

wolfish grin dominates his features as he takes in the recognition.

Isaac raises his cup high. "Wounded in our second meeting with Burgoyne, he stood with us even though he had only joined our ranks a few days earlier, and today he rejoins us. To Ezra Fuller."

Cups raise toward the young black man from Mason. He looks uncertain for not knowing the men well; he joined the company late for being sick. Hearing the toast echoed by every man present brings a small smile to his lips.

Isaac addresses the men, "We'll toast the others once they get here. In the meantime, help Drury and Fuller learn the new drill. Don't let them keep us from perfect marks from the inspectors. You've done well these past few days. I expect the same tomorrow and each day after." Isaac raises his cup again. "We'll soon, I expect, have orders to do our duty and woe to General Howe should he meet us on the battlefield. Drink up, gentlemen."

A few hours later, Isaac examines Hawkins's coat. Hawkins turns toward the lantern on the desk to illuminate the ink lines on the side. "I'm standing as straight as I did at your home. Your wife had John with his back to me so she could draw this line." He points out the lowest of the lines, wide and a little washed out, halfway up his thigh. "He was right scared of me. It took putting out a bit of maple sugar on the table where he could see it with a promise he could have it if he'd got close enough to have her mark his height. Otherwise, he's a happy giggling little boy. Having a stranger with a military coat in the house put him ill at ease."

Isaac steps back. "Of them all, he has the happiest disposition. Tis good hear he's kept that quality."

"This one here is where I marked Abiel." Hawkins points out a line at his hip, then another, several inches higher, below his ribs. "That's one's for Isaac Junior."

Isaac moves his hand up and down along his own side, comparing where he last remembered his son's heights to the marks on Hawkins' coat. I've missed half a foot of him growing. Thank you. That was a good use of your coat."

Isaac moves to sit on the floor, leaning against the lower bunk, rereading the letter from Elizabeth. Hawkins sits opposite reading

Isaac's notes on General Von Steuben's manual of arms.

Isaac looks up. "Thank you for carrying what Elizabeth sent me. I'm grateful you looked in on her while you were home."

"You're welcome, though I know you'd have done the same for me, especially if it involved some maple sugar and a mug of hot buttered rum."

"How'd she look? Healthy?"

"On the whole, yes. Though our wives carry a heavy burden. It's been three years with no end in sight. Everyone's spirits have turned somewhat grim. They're living one day to the next."

"I expect that's why she said Isaac Junior's spending time living with her father, and Abiel with Hannah and Richard. It's been almost a year since I've seen them. Did you see much of them?"

"I did. Elizabeth's father got a deer, so John Stevens and I helped him butcher it and smoke the meat. Isaac Junior was there for that. The smokehouse Timothy made during the summer has seen a lot of use in a short time, so I know they've been eating well. Timothy and old Jon Greele had time to hunt and a good deal of luck. Richard was out with the militia til December, and John Stevens did what he could to help everyone. It's put the whole town behindhand on everything with so many men gone for so long."

"I'm relieved to hear there was enough to eat. Elizabeth wrote they've eaten one of the ganders. They should be getting a few goose eggs soon."

"That reminded me, I forgot to mention Ruth Greele died a few days before we left to come here."

"That's terrible. How's Jon doing?"

"Like you'd imagine. He needs help. Seven daughters still at home, the oldest being sixteen and the youngest two."

"I thought he's got a boy, Abiel's age."

"He does. Hannah Whitney and Phebe Parker took the children in for a few days."

"How's Phebe? Elizabeth hasn't mentioned her since I left."

"The selectmen said she could say in Josiah's house and use his land until the war's over."

"Good. Josiah dying the way he did still puts a knot in my

stomach."

"Mine too."

Hawkins thumbs through the sheaf of notes on the new drills. "You have all this committed to memory?"

"Aye, though I've had four weeks of practice."

Hawkins gives a dubious huff. "It works?"

"It does. Seeing it, then doing it makes a difference. We'll not be out-maneuvered by the redcoats or their paid Hessian dogs, I'm sure of it."

Several evenings later, Isaac sits at his desk, preparing the next day's roll. A stick keeps the door open a crack to draw in fresh air. Cass, McGregor, Ellis, and Penniman sit around the other desk in their waistcoats playing their usual game of Whist while Hawkins and Livermore rest on their bunks.

Cass grins at Ellis. "That's two more for us."

A moment later, the door opens, and two crisp knocks on the frame precede a head poking in.

Ellis turns to the door. "C'mon in Captain Fish."

The New Yorker steps in and looks to Ellis then Isaac. "You two coming tonight?"

Ellis gets up, "Just in the nick of time to save these two. Cass and I are up over twenty tonight."

Isaac dries his quill. "Aye, trying to get ahead with my rolls. I'll get my hat and coat."

Hawkins asks, "What's this about?"

Isaac rises. "Colonel Scammell decided we ought to maintain the light companies. A few of us meet a couple nights a week to learn the tactics and such. We've gone out with Captain Parr from Morgan's regiment twice on their patrols."

Fish, tall, large-boned, with thick dark hair, takes over. "There's a knack to passing a body of men through terrain without being seen. We've been learning to set up attacks where a few do the deed, and the rest cover the retreat—doing so at intervals on differing routes to force pursuit to choose between at least two paths. It slows them and makes it easy to get away. Last time we covered how to coordinate two or three independent groups in a way each wouldn't know about the other."

Isaac retrieves his hat from the peg by his bunk as Goodale enters the hut. "Did you get your discharge?"

"I did. Colonel Scammell was good to his word. General Washington approved it after dinner. Approved Nathan Gilman's too."

The others put their cards down and congratulate Goodale. Cass asks, "When will you be leaving?"

"Tomorrow morning. Gilman and I will go together as far as Concord."

Livermore rises and shakes Goodale's hand. "I'm glad for you and your family. You have everything you need?"

"I do. Being sick kept me from spending my pay, though I hear it's not worth much beyond the paper these days."

Isaac hands him a sealed packet. "Won't stop me from sending mine with you to give to my wife."

Goodale takes it with a little mock bow. "Gladly, Sir. I'll tell her you're well in spite of putting up with me."

"You'd best get your things packed. I expect you'll want to get an early start." Isaac turns to Captain Fish, "We should get going. I've slowed us down enough."

With a nod to Goodale, Fish moves to the door. "Sounds like the Colonel's been busy. Doubt he'll notice we're a bit late."

Honor and Valor

12 THE MARQUIS

"... General Washington had entrusted me to conduct a detachment of two thousand four hundred chosen men to the vicinity of Philadelphia. It would be too long to explain to you the cause, but it will suffice to tell you, that, in spite of all my precautions, I could not prevent the hostile army from making a nocturnal march, and I found myself the next morning with part of the army in front, and seven thousand men in my rear...."

Letter to Madame de LaFayette from Marquis de LaFayette
Valley Forge Camp, June 16, 1778

Ruben Hosmer sits, leaning against the door frame. Will Burton props his head on his elbow to listen. Sick for the past week, His eyes hollow and pallor wan. The sick hut. They had begun calling it so a week ago when there were six taking half the bunks, and now only two are empty. In the bunk below Will, Martin stirs. Across from them, Sergeant Hall pushes his head up on a blanket to better hear.

Hosmer moves his knees to let James Hutchinson through, carrying rum for the men inside. A few clouds do little to interrupt the early afternoon sun. A steady breeze blows much of the constant unpleasant odor, usually in the camp, to the east. Hosmer rests his cup, already half-empty on one knee. "We got the orders yesterday to get ourselves cleaned up on account of the news the King of France threw in with us. I admit to being pleased the orders also said there'd be no exercising this morning."

Martin lifts his head and coughs before he can cut in, "Get on with it, Ruben. What was the cannon fire for?"

Hosmer holds up his hand and motions for Martin to back down. "The first cannon was mid-morning to call us to parade for inspection. All the brigades formed up. I can't recall seein' even half so many men paraded at the same time."

Ebenezer Abbott, the large sixteen-year-old, with a confused and fevered look, pokes his head down from the upper bunk behind Hosmer. "Even the guards? Who's guarding the camp?"

"The regular guards paraded. All with their regiments. I heard General Washington sent Colonel Morgan's men out to guard-."

"How many men was it?" Sergeant Hall cuts in, his voice at least an octave lower and crackling with phlegm.

"Gray and Sergeant Wilkins said at least eight thousand. Cap'n Livermore had command. We stood there for the better part of an hour. Major Fish-eye come through the ranks with the captains, inspecting us. They wrote down every little thing. I think we did well. All the drills and such sunk deep into our heads, so we looked our best."

Hosmer takes a drink and licks his lips before looking to Hutchinson, waving his cup "Hutch, you got any extra?"

"Nope. Keep talking."

"Fine. Once the inspectin' was done, we each got three blank cartridges. Reverend Evans read a proclamation to the brigade about the King of France. That man can make any words sound good, and he turned these straight to milk and honey. Then they fired the second cannon. It was the signal for us to march out of regiment formation and into a set of grand ranks. Not even a second after we halted, the thirteen cannons fired. Boomin' one at a time faster than I could say the names of the states. Then from the far right, the men in the front started firin' quick one right after the other. It took two full minutes to reach us, and when it got to the far end of the first rank, the second rank on the left took up the firing. Once we got done, we all gave a huzzah and a long live the King of France."

Hosmer takes a drink and clears his throat. "They fired the thirteen cannon again, and we all fired our second blank, same way as the first. The sound of the muskets was like a livin' thing, traveling up and down the ranks. I don't recall even one misfire, though I think there had to be a few. We huzzah'd the friendly European powers. Then we fired the last round, and huzzah'd the American states. That one was the loudest. We marched off smartly on account of knowin' we'd be getting an extra gill today." He raises his cup to the men inside. "The officers are to dine with General Washington in the middle of camp up by his headquarters, where it's nicer. They've got it all laid out on boards as well as they can make it. I say we're better off here with our rum and afternoon and evening to rest."

Hosmer grunts and pushes himself upright. "You good gentlemen get your rest, and we'll be seein' you back in the ranks soon."

Isaac bites into the last carrot from his plate. He sits near the end of a long makeshift table, wide boards laid on the backs of chairs. A dozen officers crowd around each of the sixty such tables, and a hundred more gather in groups drinking and conversing. The sun, an hour from the horizon, blankets the scene in a warm light.

Isaac holds the finger-sized stub of the carrot up. "As good as these taste, I can't help feeling guilty for not letting them grow. We may need them if this war lasts into another winter."

Livermore, seated across from Isaac, slices into a hunk of veal. Holding it on his fork, he tips it toward Isaac. "Let's hope not. The only thing I want to feel tonight is full." He pops the veal into his mouth and chews with contentment.

Hawkins sitting to Isaac's right, reaches for his cup. "Amen to that. Best meal Congress's provided us, by far."

Isaac begins slicing into his second veal steak. "Aye, a lot's changed in a few months."

Penniman, next to Livermore, turns to regard Isaac. "What'd General Washington take so long to say to you when we arrived? He seemed to know you."

"I met him once back in January when I vouched for Eb Carlton to move into his Life Guard. He said Carlton's been an exemplary

Honor and Valor

member. Then he surprised me. He said his wife Martha told him that Carlton's got excellent manners, and had him assigned to her personal guard."

"That's it? I mean that's good and all, but it seemed he spoke a bit longer?"

"He went on a bit about how disciplined our men have looked this past week. I figured he said that to most of us."

Penniman snorts. "All I got and gave was a bit of pleasantry. I mean, at least he shook my hand."

Livermore laughs and gives Penniman a companionable slap on the back. "Much the same for me."

"Right, but he's given you an earful during drills more than once."

"Exactly, so I'm quite happy with pleasantries."

A few hours later, Isaac and Livermore, cups in hand, relax a dozen paces back from one of the bonfires lit for the celebration. "General Washington only bid you a pleasant good evening?"

"No, he went on a bit about how well we've learned the new manual and that he's got a mind to put us to more of a test, possibly soon."

Isaac sighs with a note of frustration. "Colonel Dearborn's not returned. None of the other captains either. They'll know nothing of the new manual."

"I know, yet General Washington seemed impatient, so I expect we'll have to do for ourselves."

"I s'pose. But, we've done well thus far."

Livermore raises his cup for a toast. "Here's to doing well a bit further."

"Aye, a bit further."

The following morning an hour after breakfast, Isaac moves between the ranks of his company with Sergeant Wilkins following. He stops in front of James Hutchinson. "His shirt collar button's missing."

Wilkins makes a note in a small leather-bound inspection book. As they move on to Jacob Blanchard, Ensign Cass strides up to the company. "Captain Frye, sir."

Isaac turns. "What is it?"

228

"General Poor's ordered all officers to attend him at his headquarters immediately. He says it won't take long and to have your sergeants continue the inspection."

"I'll be on my way."

Isaac and Hawkins are among the last of the officers under General Poor to arrive. Poor addresses the officers, who crowd around him. "Gentlemen, please, if you would, form five ranks, one for each regiment by rank and date.

Isaac moves to the middle rank with Livermore on his right, and Mr. Weeks on his left. Then come Jacob Blanchard, the quartermaster, and Edmund Chadwick, the regiment's new surgeon.

General Poor, a short man whose shrewdness and knack for being present when decisions of importance get made, steps up on a stump. It gives him the advantage of seeing all the men before him. "Gentlemen, this morning, his Excellency General Washington's orders included that all officers of this army must swear a new oath of allegiance. You have already sworn a similar oath at one point or another since the start of this war. However, General Washington wishes this newest oath to be sworn by every officer for the sake of its completeness and consistency."

Poor scans the faces of the assembled officers. He pauses on several, adding sternness to the air. "Ensigns Cass and Chase, as well as myself, have already sworn. The ensigns will bear witness to your oaths. I will read it once so you can hear it, then I'll administer it, and before you leave, you'll sign a roll certifying you have given your oath."

Poor takes a sheet of paper from inside his coat, then clears his throat with his tone taking on power as he reads. "I, you'll state your name, do acknowledge The United States of America to be free, independent and sovereign states and declare that the people thereof owe no allegiance or obedience to George the Third, King of Great-Britain, and I renounce, refuse, and abjure any allegiance or obedience to him, and I do swear, or affirm, that I will to the utmost of my power to support, maintain, and defend the said United States against the said King George the third, his heirs and successors, and his and their abettors, assistants and adherents and will serve the said

Honor and Valor

United States in the office of, you'll state your rank, which I now hold with fidelity according to the best of my skill and understanding."

Poor's intensity brings silence to the immediate vicinity, and he pauses, letting it sink in. "Do any of you have a reason not to swear this oath?" Seeing no one so much as shift their weight from one foot to another, he nods once. "Then let's be about it."

•••

The regiment rests on the parade grounds four afternoons later, taking a water break. Isaac and Hawkins review a sequence of instructions for splitting the ranks to bypass obstacles with Sergeant Wilkins. Sweat glistens and drips from their brows in the heat of the sunny afternoon, the warmest of the season. The sun intensifies the radiance of the bright spring-green leaves on the trees behind them. The parade grounds packed hard by two months of thousands of men marching, play host to several felled trees serving as the obstacles.

"Restart the drill if anyone fails to keep the spacing once they're moving in a file." Isaac turns and begins walking to a point where he can observe. As he reaches that point, he catches sight of a pair of officers striding in his direction.

After a moment, he recognizes Dearborn and Captain Ellis, and waves them over, then turns and calls to Livermore at the rear of the regiment.

After welcoming them back, Livermore and Isaac take turns briefing them on the new manual of arms, the Baron, now General Von Steuben, spontoons, and even confirm the news of the alliance with France.

Dearborn turns his attention back to the men and their drill. "Is this all the men?"

Livermore frowns, uncertain of Dearborn's expectations. "There are several dozen sick. The camp is much cleaner now than it was a few weeks ago."

Dearborn furrows his eyebrows skeptically. "You mean it was even worse?"

Livermore does not grin though he manages to look a little

sheepish as he wipes his brow on his coat sleeve. "Much. Poor discipline. It's long since been addressed."

"I'll take your word for it. Have the other officers returned?"

Livermore shakes his head. "Only Hawkins. Lieutenants Goodale and Gilman resigned two weeks ago."

Dearborn's narrows eyes, betraying a bit of disgust. "Well, the others should be arriving soon. Are there tents available? I think I'd rather not move into these huts."

"I believe the quartermaster has begun issuing them recently." Isaac looks to Livermore, who confirms with a small nod. "I'll send some men to get them."

Dearborn frowns, lips pursed in frustration as he considers the circumstances of his return. Then his expression softens. "Quite a lot has changed here. Let's get into the details tonight. I want to dine with you captains and the staff officers." He looks to Livermore. "Will you arrange it?".

"I will, sir."

...

Will enters his regular hut several days later, looking alert, though thin. He pauses a moment allowing his eyes to adjust before turning to his bunk just right of the door.

Further in, Sergeant Asa Wilkins looks up from the button he is replacing on his waistcoat. "Aren't you sick?"

"No, Mister Chadwick says I'm fit and can go back to all my normal duties tomorrow."

"Good. What about Corporal Martin?"

"Still sick. No sooner than I had my bunk cleared out, Mister Chadwick told Hutchinson to take it. He spent too much time caring for us and caught what we had."

"How about Sergeant Hall?"

Hall steps into the doorway, his large frame blocks much of the light. "I'm fine. Thank you for asking."

Wilkins, now unable to see his button looks up. "Good, the men have needed your fearsomeness to keep them in step. Now get in here, you're blocking my light."

Hall moves by Will to the bunk opposite Wilkins. "What this? Sewing?"

"Aye, yesterday's general orders. We now have Friday afternoons for the upkeep of our clothing, and I'll be damned if I'm going to be worse off than the privates."

"How many needles we got?"

"One." Wilkins grins.

"Where's your brother and Hughes?"

"The took a detail to clean, inspect, and repair tents. They've got three needles."

Hall laughs. "I could use some food. I'm of a mind to find our sutler and see if he's got any jerky. Either of you fancy anything?"

Wilkins shakes his head. Will looks up. "I'll come. Not sure what I want, but I am hungry now, and the evening meal is not for a while yet."

Before Will makes it out the door, Wilkins adds, "Burton, you'll be on tent detail tomorrow. They'll be carrying our tents for the season back here, and we're to patch and sew up any tears and cut new poles if need be."

"Yes, Sergeant Asa."

Will waits ready to fix the next problem as Hawkins and Sergeant Wilkins inspect each tent. Jacob Blanchard and Peter Chandler stand with Will. For two days, they stitched and patched a dozen tents, including several for the officers. Hawkins instructed them on how best to repair all the small holes using tiny stitches and a patch on both sides.

Hawkins finishes inspecting the last of the tents and turns to the privates. "Well done." He stops, something catching his eye.

Behind them, Will hears Isaac call out for Uriah to beat assembly.

"Get these last two rolled up tight and fall in. Don't be late." Hawkins sets off at a quick pace with Wilkins following.

Will and Uriah stand at the end of the first and second ranks, respectively, of the right half of the regiment behind Livermore. The officers gather around Livermore, who presumably gives the reason for the entire brigade parading.

Hawkins returns to the company. "General Poor's and Varnum's Brigades are as of now assigned under General Lafayette. We're to march as soon as we load our tents. Before that, we'll draw provisions for three days."

Will and Uriah, an hour later, pull the ends of a tent side folded long ways between them. Uriah begins rolling his end toward Will. "Why would we get assigned under that French general? He came back into camp only a week ago. What's his name?"

"Lafayette. I heard he's a general in our army now, and he's a Marquis in France."

With the tent rolled into a compact log, Uriah sets it atop a small stack of other tent sides, and he and Will lift the next side to be folded and rolled. "Well, he must be something extra special. My Ma used to call her best apple tarts that."

Will laughs.

"I know what you mean. I've heard it more than once that General Washington treats him like a long lost son. I heard he's naught but a year older than you."

Uriah deposits the rolled tent log on the pile, and they pick up the last one. "I don't know much about French nobility. I s'pose they fancy themselves the same as ours-, I mean the English." Irritated, Uriah shakes his head. "Can't get used to being a different country."

"Me neither. Tis no different to my mind, other than us in an army, and we still haven't got our liberties."

Sergeant Wilkins walks from around the side of the nearest hut. "Cut the gabbing, you two. Finish that. We're mustering out front of the huts, and you better be there before I am."

Uriah doubles his speed, and within a few seconds, dumps the rolled tent on the pile as they dash for the far side of the hut.

A minute later, Wilkins returns, walking with Hawkins and Isaac. Wilkins's eyes narrow as he gives Will and Uriah a stern look before winking with satisfaction that they had obeyed.

Isaac addresses the company. "We're to march late tonight and gain the north side of the Schuylkill by way of Swede's Ford. Poor's and Varnum's brigades along with Potter's militia will march. We've got half a dozen cannon, an escort of dragoons, a company of Colonel

Morgan's men, and some Oneida scouts. Once we set up our camp, we'll send out patrols into the countryside to observe, and if possible, disrupt the enemy. Get our wagon loaded, then get some rest as you'll not likely get any until this time tomorrow or later." He turns to Hawkins, who shakes his head, indicating he has nothing to add. Then to the men, "Fall out."

The half-moon's light provides enough for Will to see the Schuylkill River at the ford. They left at midnight and marched for what seemed like two hours to get to this point. The company waits a hundred yards upstream, watching the ford and the woods on the far side. Varnum's Brigade had crossed first with a few men wading over and securing four ropes to sturdy posts. The Oneidas followed and now guard the way ahead to ensure no surprises. The wagons with the five cannons and their carriages followed. With each wagon, the men and horses pulled hard to get past the midpoint, where the water was higher than the wagon wheels.

The First New Hampshire Regiment begins to cross with General Poor leading, astride a glossy dark horse. Once he reaches the far bank, he uses his spontoon, sending each company in a new direction to aid Varnum's men.

Will moves next to Joseph Gray. "What do they call this ford again?"

"Swedes. We crossed here when we first came into camp. The bridge of wagons is gone. The water's a foot higher. Last of the spring melt, I expect."

"Cold then?"

"Sure, but better than icy."

The sound of a horse approaching from behind causes both to turn and hear Wilkins relay that it's their turn to form up and cross.

They cross, holding their muskets and possessions high while hooking an elbow round one of the four ropes. Will trudges up the bank, soaked from the bottom of his ribs down. To Uriah, who had his hands full carrying his drum high, Will returns his knapsack of provisions. "A shame you can't carry things inside your drum."

Uriah shrugs his nose wrinkling as his eyes narrow with a bit of confusion. "Little things are just fine. Just can't risk damaging the skin."

"I know. Twas wishful thinking."

After two hours of marching, the predawn light begins replacing the moonlight. Despite so many men moving through the gentle hills north of the river, the songs of orioles and chickadees waft in through the trees. They arrive, still damp from the fording, at a crossroads by a church near the top of a hill. The church has a low stone wall surrounding it and a graveyard. A small cluster of homes lies along on the road approaching the church. Varnum's men busy themselves setting up their part of the camp on the north side of the church.

General Poor meets in front of the church with several officers, including two in French uniforms. Will stares at them, particularly younger of the two foreigners. He is the center of attention as he motions to the north, and then the east while giving orders.

After a few moments, Wilkins gives Will a nudge in the back. "Leave off the staring."

Will turns away. "Is that General Lafayette?"

"It is. Don't call attention to yourself."

Within thirty minutes Will, Uriah, and John Drury work to set up the tents for the sergeants and corporals. Drury, recovered from his shoulder wound, has grown taller and more muscular than Uriah for the commissary being well-stocked with provisions for two months. The two hold the ridge pole aloft as Will scoots inside with the support poles. He pokes the spike on atop each pole through the corresponding holes in the ridge pole. "Okay, poles are in."

From outside the tent, Wilkins fills in everyone nearby. "Once the tents are up, eat a cold meal, get some rest until noon when we are to assemble and move out to our post for the night."

Poor's Brigade occupies the area downhill and southeast of the church. Once they finish, Will eats and then moves off to the southwest below the crown of a large hill to get a view of the river. Afterward, he turns to return and hears the pewl pewl of an oriole. After a moment of thought, Will tries the call on his fife, matching it on his second effort. Crouching down, he tries again, hoping the oriole will return the call. It must have moved on as the lower-pitched dee-daw dee-daw of a chickadee responds. He mimics this one

Honor and Valor

on the first try. The chickadee returns his call. Will turns at the sound of approaching footsteps and sees Wilkins.

"Was that you making all those calls?"

"Most of them."

"Well done. Now get back to your tent and rest. We'll be out on picquet duty all night."

Early in the afternoon, Sergeants Wilkins and Hall lead Will and the twenty men assigned to their detachment north. They march back the way they had come in the early morning. Twenty minutes later, they take a sharp turn to their right and march another twenty minutes to the north. Wilkins calls them to a halt two hundred yards past a crossroads.

Wilkins turns to Will. "Burton, play those bird calls you were doing this morning."

Will blinks in surprise as he draws out his fife and plays the oriole and chickadee calls.

Wilkins turns back to the men. "You'll be in groups of three. That first call will signal to send one from each group back to this large chestnut tree to take your evening meal. You'll take turns eating. The second is to call you all back, but use care not to be detected. If you hear him play retreat, run, and we'll meet back where we first turned to come this direction."

Wilkins has Will play each call again and reiterates their meanings. "Gray and John Drury will be runners and stay here with Burton and me." Wilkins and Hall divide the others into groups of three. They send them out at a spacing of forty paces to either side of the road in a "V" shape, with the point being the tree where Wilkins posts his group.

The afternoon and evening pass with them seeing only a pair of Colonel Morgan's men passing through their line, heading to the east. The still air of the clear night makes their work easy.

Well after midnight, Will hears what sounds like Sergeant Hall's voice up ahead. "Tadmore." Another deeper voice responds. "Tufton."

Wilkins nudges Gray. "Get ready, someone's coming in."

A few seconds later, Will sees the shape of a man running in a low crouch along the side of the road. Wilkins's voice is calm. "Over here."

One of Morgan's men, by dint of carrying a long rifle, carefully steps into view. "We've got trouble coming, a big column of redcoats. They marched out of Philadelphia around to the north of here. They'll be here in an hour or so. They've got double maybe triple our numbers. Get word back to camp."

The rifleman looks about, gaging the terrain in the moonlight. "Don't be here when they arrive. I expect they've got more scouts than you've got men."

Wilkins thanks the rifleman, who departs, silently retracing his steps. "Gray, you got that?"

Gray nods. "Yes, Sergeant."

"Go to General Poor and tell him exactly what you heard. We'll wait here another quarter-hour in case more information comes in."

Gray makes his way to the road and takes off; his long strides carry him out of sight in seconds.

Wilkins turns to Drury. "You heard it all too?"

"Yes Sergeant, I did."

"Wait half a minute, so you'll not be caught together. If there are no problems, take the message to Captains Livermore and Frye, then to Lieutenant Hawkins. Understand?"

Drury nods and waits a dozen seconds, then looks to Wilkins, who nods, sending Drury on his way.

"Keep your ears open, Burton. If you hear any rifle or musket fire in the distance, give that second bird call."

The woods and road stay quiet for ten minutes before Will hears Sergeant Hall challenging someone who gives the countersign.

Half a minute later, a low voice calls, "Sergeant Wilkins?"

"Over here."

The same rifleman steps off the road to find them. "Get your men back to camp as fast as possible. The enemy is less than two miles away. They moved faster than we figured."

Wilkins looks to Will. "Call them in."

Will puts fife to lips and gives the dee-daw dee-daw call several times. Within a minute, the men all arrive.

Wilkins counts the men. "Form up on the road. We're to double-time it back to camp. The enemy has got a large body of troops coming this way."

They turn east, towards camp, as the first light of day pushes into the horizon. The sight of it gives Will a second wind. Most of the next ten minutes are uphill, and they arrive in camp winded. The encampment is full of activity. Wilkins directs them toward their tents and calls them to a halt as they cross paths with Hawkins.

"Gather your belongings. We're to move the cannon down that way." Hawkins motions west toward the gap below the hill they had learned as being called Barren Hill for its lack of trees and broad top.

As Hawkins speaks, the camp grows quiet, and the sound of sporadic musket and rifle fire drifts in from the east. Within seconds, the shouts of officers and sergeants infuse new urgency into the camp.

"You've got to the count of fifty to be back here with your belongings. Go!" Wilkins starts counting in a measured, steady way. Will dashes for the tent before "three, get mine Burton!" and returns at "forty-five with his and Sergeant Wilkins' knapsacks."

Hawkins addresses them. "You're assigned to move that cannon over there. It's the last one." He points to a cannon in its carriage with a team of two horses. "Don't let it stop, or it'll sink. There's two ropes to help pull. There's two planks over here to lay over any muddy spots, carry those ahead. You'll see the ruts from the others. The First and Second Regiments have gone ahead to provide cover for the fording. The New Yorkers'll follow. Varnum's men will be along in a quarter-hour, they're out delaying the enemy. Get going."

Wilkins assigns Will to the rope on the right between Jacob Blanchard and Humphrey Cram. They move downhill on the narrow road cut into the lower slope of the hill. Sergeants Hall and Wilkins lead the horses, keeping their pace steady. Ten minutes pass before they reach the river, and the little road turns upriver along the bank. Blanchard looks ahead then mutters, "Now the work begins."

To the west, in the distance, they hear three warning cannon fire. Hall realizes what it signifies. "Those are warnings from the camp at Valley Forge. Put your backs into it. Don't stop. We need to get to the ford as fast as we can."

For almost two miles, they pull the carriage and cannon along the little road. It veers around a tree-covered hillock before turning back to the river. A hundred yards later, they arrive at the ford. The thick spring grass on the bank now lies trampled by the cannon, their crews, and a thousand soldiers. The other cannon, already crewed and positioned, fan out to offer a hearty welcome to any redcoats coming toward the ford.

Livermore meets them and points to one last space. "Bring it around so you can turn it to face back this way." He points back the way they came. "Then get yourselves across. General Varnum's men will be along at any moment."

Exhausted and sweating from the past two hours of exertion, Will pushes into the flow of the river. The cold waist-high water feels welcome. As he reaches the far side, the chilly air quickly causes him to shiver.

Ahead Hall wrings his coattails and turns back to the others with Will. "Cold enough for ye boys?"

Hawkins strides toward them. "Form your ranks, Gentlemen. We're to take up a position over there." He points to up a small hill to the east.

In two minutes, they quick-march to the far side of the hill and take in the scene across the river. The first company of General Varnum's Connecticut regiments begin crossing the ford. Will catches glimpses through the trees of the Rhode Island regiments, making their way down the same route they had come with the cannon.

Above and back in the direction of the churchyard, the sounds of musket and irregular cracks of rifles sound closer with each passing minute. After the Rhode Island Regiments cross, small groups of riflemen and Oneida warriors reach the ford. Captain Allan McClane's company of horsemen gallop down the road with McClane and General Lafayette bringing up the rear. Above them, now sounding very close, musket- and rifle-fire continues as the remaining riflemen and Oneidas give proof of the enemy being within range of the rear guard. Less than a minute later, Will sees those guards firing and then moving from tree to tree in a skillful retreat. Looking to the left, the artillerymen have come across leaving the cannon.

Lafayette and McClane wait by the cannon for the last of Morgan's men and the Oneidas to race down the road and cross the river. Lafayette crosses last.

Will turns to Uriah. "Do you think the redcoats will try to cross?"

"They're in easy range. They'd be fools to attempt it."

Joseph Gray laughs. "Worse than fools. They can't get within fifty paces of those cannons for worry a rifleman will put an extra hole in their head. They thought us trapped. It's downright suspicious they show up on all sides of us at almost the same time."

...

Isaac and Livermore sit in their hut with Dearborn and Ellis. The interior is clean as the officers had moved their possessions to their tents during the past week. The warm weather and general stuffiness of the huts, even after they had cut windows into each side, made the tents preferable. A half-empty bottle of Madeira, courtesy of Dearborn, rests between them on the only remaining desk.

"They left almost immediately?" Dearborn's voice is incredulous.

Livermore nods. "There was nothing to be gained—no way to get the cannon, no way to approach the river. We could have marched back to camp by way of Gulph Road if they had forded and come at us from downstream. Once they left, we brought the cannon over to our side."

Ellis pours a little more Madeira for himself. "They could have burned your entire camp. Instead, they just left?"

Isaac turns his head and sneezes. The others murmur blessings. "Enough of Captain Parr's riflemen were still in the woods on the north side to cause their staying to be hazardous. We sent men to watch the tents that night, and the next morning we forded back over and took up residence in the original camp."

Livermore finishes his Madeira. "Marched back here this morning. Though I swear, we're all weary of fording that river and marching about in wet trousers."

"A shame one spy brought so much havoc." Dearborn sips his Madeira. "I did see Wilkinson earlier today. He swears the spy was a former lieutenant from Proctor's artillery. Hercules Courtenay was the name. Did any of you know the man?"

Isaac and Livermore shake their heads in denial.

"Wilkinson had accounts of him being in and out of camp for knowing Proctor's officers. It was possible he learned of the orders and had time to confirm where you camped. McLane's men saw him meet with some of the enemy between there and Philadelphia. Then Colonel Harrison, who overhead, and took offense to Wilkinson's claim. He said Courtenay has long been a leader in Baltimore's Sons of Liberty and more likely, if it was him, he was giving misinformation to Clinton's soldiers."

Isaac finishes his Madeira. "Wilkinson has a penchant for leaving an opening for discord in his wake. Been doing so since I first crossed paths with him in New York more than two years ago."

Dearborn pours a bit more into Isaac's cup and then some for Ellis and Livermore. "He's young and not overly careful. Besides which, I doubt there was only one spy. Things in this camp have grown too cozy. We need to move out and take the fight to Clinton."

Livermore raises his cup. "Here here." The others follow suit. "Take the fight to Clinton."

Dearborn sets his empty cup on the table and nods to Isaac and Livermore. "Thank you, that was quite remarkable." He re-corks the bottle and frowns. "We've had six men die these past two weeks, and it seems more are getting sick by the day. Have any of you lost men?"

All three nod.

"Who?"

Isaac waits for a second. "Elisha Mansfield."

Ellis adds, "Levi Butler."

Livermore finishes, "John Garland in mine. Dennet's lost two, and McGaffey one."

Dearborn sets his jaw and lowers his eyes for a moment. "Have the men empty everything from those huts we keep for the sick. New straw and air them out for few hours before letting the sick back in. I'll see Mister Chadwick tonight."

Dearborn rises. "I need to get back to learning this new manual. I'll be taking command tomorrow." He looks to Ellis. "Are you ready to do the same?"

"Aye."

"Good. I'll see you all tomorrow at morning exercises."

They all thank Dearborn for bringing the Madeira as he departs.

A few seconds later, Dearborn pokes his head back in. "I quite nearly forgot. Our division's commander General Lee arrived yesterday. The recent exchanges secured his freedom. Be on the lookout for him."

13 FEVER

"Officers are to see that the mud plaistering about the hutts be removed and every other method taken to render them as airy as possible; they will also have the Powder of a Musquet Cartridge burnt in each hutt daily to purify the Air or a little Tar if it can be procured—The Commissary of Military Stores will provide blank Cartridges for this Purpose.

General Orders
Valley Forge, May 27, 1778

Isaac lays with his arms folded over his eyes and two pages from the manual of arms rest on his chest. From outside, footsteps approach, and Isaac raises his arms. The single candle on his desk barely illuminates the face peering in through the open flap. "Ensign Cass, What is it?"

"Two letters for you. I'll put them at the end of your cot. You feeling well?"

"Not especially. I worry that I might be coming down with the same ague as Colonel Dearborn and Captain Ellis."

"I hope not. You'll forgive me for not tarrying."

"No, don't, and thank you for bringing the letters."

Isaac sits up and lights two more candles, then leans to the foot of his cot and retrieves the letters. The smaller of the two from Major Abbot and the other from Elizabeth. Isaac sighs and opens Major Abbot's first.

Wilton, May 10, 1778

Captain Frye,

It pains me to pen this unfortunate news on account of my being in Temple yesterday. I was found by Madam Abigail Oliver. She had news of her Husband, Aaron who inlisted last year in your Company. He was a prisoner on one of the ships in Wallabout Bay and was released early last month. He traveled to his home in two weeks, but arrived quite sickly and took to his bed. She said he did not leave it again and Perished on the last day of April. She and three sons are quite Destitute and She asked me for his Pay up through the Time of his death. I told her I could not as Congress Pays the Continentals and the first item toward those ends would be to report his death to you and then the matter is to be in your hands. She awaits Your Advisement on what should happen given such unfortunate Situation.

Your most Humble and Obed Servant

Abiel Abbot, Major.

Isaac sighs then pinches out two of the candles. Taking Major Abbot's letter, he leaves his tent and moves to the one immediately behind his but sees no light from within. "William Adrian? You here?"

"I am. Just resting. Come inside."

Isaac tells Hawkins of the letter's contents. "I'm not feeling well, would you mind taking this to Mr. Weeks. I don't know what's involved in getting Oliver's widow his back pay. I am of a mind to get a full night's sleep so I can fight off this ague."

"Aye. I'll see what can be done. A shame."

A minute later, Isaac re-lights the extra candles on his desk and breaks the seal on Elizabeth's letter. It is thicker than usual. As he unfolds the paper five small locks of hair bound by bright red ribbons fall into his hand. The letters "I", "A", "J", "T" and "E" inked, one letter on each ribbon. Isaac Jr's is a darker brown than Isaac remembers. Timothy's is bright and blond. Isaac rolls Elizabeth's between his thumb and fingers for the space of several breaths sensing the familiar texture.

Wilton, May 10, 1778
To my Dearest Husband, Yesterday I rec'd yours of the 15th last. We are all well and I hope you have gotten to see the marks I put on Lieutenant Hawkins coat We all miss you and hope you are well and pray for a swift victory this season so we can be done with this war. Father sends his love and affection to you. He made small barow for Isaac Jr. to carry manuer up to spread round the apple trees. It took three trips for the boys to lose their interest. I kept after them and we got all the trees in good shape for the season. Mr. Stephens and Father plowed the field and planted rye seed two weeks ago. Luckily no heavy rain and the shoots have come up well.

We go to the meetinghouse most Sundays, today included. Some good news from there. The story as Phebe Parker told is John Greele come over to her place with his hat in his hands. She said she never had seen a more desperate and willing to please look on a man's face. He's got six daughters & one son in that small house. Phebe insisted he add on to it and he already placed to large stones at the corners.

Sarah also sends her love and affection & it seems she is taking note of mister William Pierce. She does not admit so, but her look says otherwise.

That is all the news I have for now. I hope to have more lines from you soon.

Your loving Wife,

Elizabeth

Isaac gently sweeps the locks of hair onto the page and re-folds the letter, then slips it into the pocket of his waistcoat.

•••

Isaac walks with Hawkins, Livermore, and Lieutenant Andrew McGaffey, crossing through the field in the middle of the camp. Clouds hang low, and the air feels thick with the promise of rain within the hour.

McGaffey clears his throat. "Did yesterday's orders a cause you gentlemen unexpected concern? Particularly the details for assembly and marching give the impression we're to be leaving camp. Half of our brigade is sick. Six of our regiment's officers remain furloughed."

Livermore snorts and shakes his head. "For the sick, no. Even Colonel Dearborn is sick, though he has ignored it for the past three days."

Hawkins offers, "Dearborn does look a bit better today."

"He does," Livermore continues, "and such makes my point. Let us say the enemy was to march out of Philadelphia this very minute. I say quite a few of those who are sick would find a way to shoulder their firelocks and march to meet them."

McGaffey's tone shifts to careful neutrality, "What of our officers? Dearborn and Ellis returned as arranged. I've heard nothing from Captain McClary."

Again, Livermore shakes his head. "As far as I know, the same arrangement applied to McClary as to Gray, Stone, and the rest."

Isaac starts to speak, but his voice cracks and he coughs several times before the words come out. "Even asking Dearborn if any of them had contacted him would be fooling. Seems to me such is for General Poor to ask."

"It is." Livermore stops, causing the others to halt. "Tis a bad idea to have this conversation within hearing of our men. We don't know their reasons for not returning, and until we do, we would do well to presume their honor is intact. To do otherwise is to dishonor ourselves."

The others nod with appreciation.

As they continue back toward the huts now ringed with the tents of the officers, Livermore turns to Isaac. "You sound terrible. Take the afternoon and rest. You need something to get you over this ague."

"Aye." He coughs once. "I will."

•••

Isaac sits before Colonel Philip Van Cortlandt, who commands the Invalids Corps at Valley Forge. Finally, fit for duty after seven fever-ridden weeks, Isaac looks to the stack of rolls before the colonel. "Sir, do you have orders for me?"

Cortlandt sits behind a smaller writing desk than what General Washington had in the room. "I've got nearly two hundred men for you to march to White Plains in New York. General Washington established his headquarters there. Are you well enough to leave tomorrow?"

Isaac dips his head in acceptance as Cortlandt finishes. "I am Sir."

The weary eyes of the Second New York Regiment's commander inspect Isaac's new brown coat from above his sharp aquiline nose. "Good. I see you received one of the new coats. All the men going with you should also have one."

"Sir, will we have wagons or horses?"

"Three wagons is all we can spare—no extra horses. You'll assemble the men this afternoon. Have them draw provisions for a week. Retake the roll tomorrow before you march" The colonel hands him a strip of paper with the orders for the commissary to supply the provisions. "All that clear? You know where to take this?"

"Yes, Sir."

"Good. Please give my regards to General Poor. Tell him I expect it shall be at least another month before I can rejoin my regiment."

"I will, Sir."

"Your company was one of those hit hardest by this fever, was it not?"

"Aye, Sir, it was. Five of my men died of it. Seven, I believe, are marching tomorrow. Yet, half my men will remain here."

"We'll do our best to see they recover quickly."

Honor and Valor

"Thank you, sir."

An hour later, Isaac moves among the tents where his men who are still sick lay recovering. Most of the tents have one side staked up to let the late July breeze in—Isaac ducks into the tent Will Burton shares with Sergeant Wilkins. Burton's face is bright red, flushed with fever.

He mumbles, "Cap'n Frye, sir. You're well now."

"I am. I'm taking letters for home when I march tomorrow. Have you got one written?"

"It's in my knapsack at the end by my feet. It's on top."

Isaac unfastens Burton's knapsack and finds the letter.

"Sir, what's the date today?" Burton's tone is woozy with fever.

"July twenty-second."

"Good. The letter's only a day old."

Isaac turns to Wilkins. "How about you, Sergeant Wilkins? Anything to send home?"

"Aye, the same. In my knapsack."

Wilkins looks exhausted and hot, though sweating, rather than fevered. "You're looking better this afternoon. Have they brought you any water?"

"Yes, sir. Twice since noon."

Isaac steps back outside the tent. "Good. You both do as the surgeons tell you, and I will see you in a week or two."

Only Wilkins responds. "I hope so, sir."

Isaac looks to Burton.

"I will, sir."

•••

Sarah wipes her forehead with the back of her hand. A basket lined with sackcloth hangs half-filled with raspberries on her other wrist. Above, the sun heats the muggy late morning air making even light work a sweaty affair. "I cannot believe this has been my fourth summer with you and the boys. I barely remember the times before the war."

On the other side of the berry patch growing over half a dozen rails of the fence separating the house yard and the hayfield to the west, Elizabeth straightens. She steps out from the lush lucerne growing at the edge of the field so she can see Sarah. "Let's have a drink of water in the shade."

After pumping enough water, Sarah carries the bucket and ladles to the simple maple bench beneath the shade of the trees on the north side of the house. "I remember when the war started. I was so excited to prove I could be of benefit to you instead of a burdensome child."

Elizabeth sets her ladle on the rim of the bucket. "I've never thought you a burden. I don't know what I would have done without you. What began as an alarm to prove our resolve became a war, and it has gone on far longer than any of us could have predicted. What's got you thinking so?"

"Tis nothing about me, and I don't mean that it should be. It's… it's this war. It's put so much of the life I expected beyond of reach. I guess it was the militia marching yesterday. Tis the third summer they've gone off. Before that, William's brother Asa left this spring to serve with Isaac. Now William and Richard have gone with Captain Mann for Rhode Island. Last year it was to keep General Burgoyne's men from marching on us. But Rhode Island? What's there that's worth any of our men's lives?"

"I don't know. Major Abbot says some of the Franch navy is there, and there's a chance to defeat King George's ships and troops. Though, if another threat came from Canada, I am certain we'd ask for help from all the nearby states. Though I agree, not knowing and not getting on with our lives is like a slow poison." Elizabeth rolls her eyes and shakes her head, sighing with disgust. "We only hear what happened, well after it happened, so there's no sense in trying to guess at what we cannot know."

"You're right. Tis infuriating how there's no talk of how or even if the war will end. If I wasn't here helping you, knowing that I'm needed, I'd have no escape from despair."

"You would be doing something useful, of that I have no doubt. You, Mary Gray, and Phebe Cram have spent a good deal of time on Sundays in the company of Mister William Pierce."

"Not just William. There's Zeb Cram, John Greele, and Dan Kenney. Every one of them marched."

"I know. I'm only teasing a little. Tis difficult for any of you to imagine your futures while this war goes on and on. But, the war will not stop our wants and wishes. We have to go on. Two weeks ago Jon Greele married Phebe Parker- I guess it's Greele now. I am so happy for Phebe. She has had it the worst of any of us."

"I know. We all enjoyed ourselves after the ceremony. Yet, so much has happened since."

Elizabeth drinks another ladle-full, then rises. "We have to carry on. We must make better habits and do what we can to find some happiness, and if need be, make some for ourselves. Let's finish picking the berries. We can start by having some after dinner with the last of the cream."

14 NORTHWARD

> *"The Tents of the whole Army are to be struck three times a week on Mondays, Wednesdays & Fridays from ten in the morning 'till two in the afternoon when the weather will permit; The Officers will be careful to have the ground between and where the tents stood well cleansed."*
>
> General Orders
> Head-Quarters W. Plains, Aug 20, 1778

Joseph Gray jogs back toward Isaac along the road leading north from White Plains. Isaac and the forty men remaining under his command make their way between the grassy sides of the narrow hard-packed road. Their shadows, in the late afternoon sun, stretch off into the pasture on their right. The fields they pass each contain tents enough for a regiment or two. The road runs along the left side of a half-mile-wide valley. It serves as one of several arterials linking the brigades of the Continental Army to Washington's Headquarters back in the village. At the head of their column, Gray tells Sergeant Asa Wilkins that the Third Regiment's encampment is three campsites ahead.

As they come into their encampment, the smells of evening meals cooking mix with the unpleasant odors of an encampment that has stayed too long on the same ground. A pleasant breeze blows from the southwest and helps disperse the worst of the camp's air.

Within five minutes, Isaac's command erodes to the seven men of his own company. Wilkins marches alongside the file led by Corporal Godfrey with Gray, Chandler, Foster, Amos Holt, and Hosmer. They come to the row of officer's tents for the Third Regiment. Each of the officers has a larger cavalryman's tent, and in neat rows beyond are the tents of each company's men. The next to last row has just one officer's tent, and only two tents for the men, while the other rows have six to ten smaller tents. Hawkins stands outside this tent in conversation with his neighbor Benjamin Ellis.

Isaac calls out to Hawkins, "Looks like the size of our company just doubled," then grins as Hawkins turns with a startled look.

"Good evening sir, welcome back." Hawkins takes Isaac's offered hand and gives it a hearty shake. "I was beginning to think you'd grown fond of our old camp and decided to stay there."

Ellis chuckles and offers his hand. "He was just sayin' so."

"Aye, that's as false as false can be. Thought the march here was proof that I'd forgotten the scent of fresh air, and I'll not be giving that up again anytime soon."

The men cooking their meals at the fires past the end of the farthest tent, begin striding toward their recently arrived compatriots. Isaac dismisses his command to go about setting up their tents and cooking their meals.

After his tent is up, Isaac and Hawkins sit with the Ellis cousins amid their tents on folding stools. The sun dips behind the ridge to the southwest as they talk. Hawkins rubs his chin with both hands, with his eyes downcast.

Isaac clears his throat. "What's eating at you?"

"Got some bad news to give you."

"About?"

"When we fought Cornwallis by Monmouth Courthouse, John Drury was killed."

Isaac exhales and doesn't take in a new breath for several seconds. He closes his eyes and shakes his head before inhaling. "How?"

"About a week after we left you behind, Colonel Dearborn got leave to pick a regiment of light troops to add to what General Scott already had. Myself, Hall, Martin, and Drury went with him. On the day of the fighting, we picked a smaller group. The heat of that day had got to some of the men, so only those who handled it went. The four of us included. There was a hot engagement in an orchard for half an hour. It was a vicious, angry fight, and both sides lost men. A ball took him through the eye. Quick as that he was gone. A fine lad who was turning into a fine man."

"You write to his mother?"

"Aye. Didn't think it right to wait."

Isaac nods and pounds his hand on his knee a few times in frustration. "Thank you, though I've got some bad news as well. Goodman, Abbott, and Fuller all died while I was sick. I wrote and carried the letters to their kin with me.

"My God. Was it that bad there?"

"Aye, though I wasn't in a state to know the details."

"What of our other men?"

I saw Robert Wilkins, Cram, and Burton before I left. Burton looked the worst off that day, so I told him I'd promote him when he joined us. The new arrangement pays musicians better. He's not one to pass up that sort of opportunity."

Hawkins, nodding while he listens, swallows hard. "I hope he pulls through."

William Ellis adds his wishes for the same. "Glad you got well and brought the last couple of my men with you. I can't recall hearing of so virulent a fever. It killed more than one healthy man in less than two weeks. Thankfully, there's been nothing like that here. The phlegm from standing piquet on a rainy night is the worst of it."

Isaac rises. "I could use some rum. Any other news before I go and get some?"

The others get up as well, and William Ellis responds. "A little over a week ago, the New York regiments got moved out from under General Poor. Gave us Moses Hazen's Canadians in their stead."

"Hazen huh?"

"He's a rascal for certain, but just like General Stark, we're damned glad he's our rascal."

"Aye, true enough. Good to know that sooner than later."

∙∙∙

On a muggy afternoon two weeks later, the rain and winds which had drenched and muddied the previous three days finally roll off to the northeast. Thin clouds of mosquitoes drift everywhere, but especially near the soldiers and their tents. Isaac marches with his company as they and the regiment emerge from the wooded hillside east of their camp. The exercise of crossing the creek at the edge of the woods while maintaining their formations finally resembles a professional maneuver.

The sight of the regiment, to Isaac, continues to hold a strange unfamiliarity. The men all wearing the same brown coats with red facings and bright pewter buttons embossed with the number three. No longer are they the gritty militia-look-alike counting on the enemy to underestimate them.

Dearborn dismisses the regiment for the day with an admonishment that alarms to march may come at any hour.

Isaac walks with Hawkins alongside the fifteen men currently comprising their company. Ahead, by the officer's tents, a squad of nine men waits in a single rank, standing at rest. Robert Wilkins is in command.

Hawkins chuckles. "Looks like we'll have to learn it all again tomorrow with three squads."

"Aye, true, though, that's good news."

Wilkins calls the men to attention as Isaac and Hawkins arrive. After exchanging salutes, Isaac orders Wilkins to dismiss the men to set up their tents at the end of the short row. Isaac also notes Wilkins' serious demeanor is not changing.

Wilkins gives the orders but immediately turns to Isaac. "Sir, I've got some news. Not of a good sort."

"What is it?"

Wilkins reaches into his knapsack and takes out a fife. "Burton-," he starts and stops his voice heavy. "Burton died a few days before we left."

Isaac's eyes widen in shock, then he accepts the fife. "Were you with him?"

"I was. Cram, Blanchard, and Pierce were too. They all knew him from home. He had a couple of better days right after you left, but then the fever set on him again, and he wasn't strong enough."

Isaac tucks the fife into his coat. "Go tell Ballard and Martin before they hear it from the others."

"Ballard! Martin!" Hawkins barks towards the tents. "You're wanted over here."

Isaac nods, acknowledging Hawkins's quick thinking. To Wilkins, "Better they hear it from you since you were there. I'll join you before you tell them. Anyone else?"

"No. The Perrys and the Youngmans are still there. I didn't get to the hospitals or hear anything about Ezra Fuller or Lewis."

Wilkins hands Isaac a small packet. "These were Burton's. His letters and pay."

Hawkins keeps his voice low. "Not supposed to happen. That's three boys who didn't see their eighteenth-year thanks to this war."

Isaac swears under his breath. "I know."

"I sent Hutchinson's and Mansfield's letters to Major Abbot. I thought it better he deliver them to their families with more respect than a mail carrier should have to muster."

"Twas wise."

"I should be the one to look his father in the eye. Not that he'll want to hear anything I have to say." Isaac nods in the direction of Martin and Ballard approaching. "We should gather the men tonight and say some words to remember the ones who died."

•••

A few bright yellow and dark red trees, harbingers of autumn, stand out near the tops of the high ridges and hills to the south of Danbury, Connecticut. Yet, the warm afternoon and clear sky argue in favor of continuing summer. South of the hills, a few buildings comprise a supply depot. Next to the depot is the encampment of General Poor's four regiments. Beside them, a brigade of Massachusetts soldiers set up their tents.

Isaac walks with Livermore, Ellis, and Stone toward Lieutenant

Honor and Valor

Colonel Dearborn's tent. The shouts of sergeants ordering the men through their drills and the pounding of stakes for tents on the other side of the road drown out the ordinary and pleasant sounds of the valley.

"I expect," Livermore begins, as he responds to Stone's question. "Since he has only sent for the captains, this may be about the empty positions. Maybe the Congress approved some commissions."

"Hope so." Stone's voice too gruff. "I'm doing far too much of my own desk work." He grins as he finishes.

Ellis gives Stone a hard look with one eye squinting. "Damn, have I been doing this all wrong for the past year and writing all those rolls myself?"

"Yup. Lieutenants and ensigns do the writing. Captains do the signing. That's it. I thought you knew." Stone laughs harshly.

Ellis jabs a good-natured feint with his elbow at Stone, who catches it with his forearm. "Do you think I would trust my cousin to do my rolls? I heard about that Pennsylvania adjutant who got cashiered on account of his rolls being wrong. I've got more honor than to have Ben get me sent home to my wife and farm for the rest of the war."

Isaac chuckles. "So it's Ben that's kept your honor intact by not letting you trust him."

They all laugh at that as they enter Dearborn's tent.

As the de-facto commander of the regiment, Dearborn claimed Scammell's marquee for his use when the army moved out of Valley Forge in June. Two large rugs line the interior, with a cot and chest to the left and a desk set between the center poles. Dearborn and Captain Norris from the Second Regiment wait to the right of the desk, as the four captains file into the empty side of the tent.

Dearborn wastes no time. "Back in May, Congress decided the organization of infantry battalions would be somewhat different than we've done. Before the year ends, we'll reorganize our companies and officer them to reflect the new arrangement. We will have nine companies instead of eight, though only six captains. The first three companies are under Colonel Scammell, myself, and I am pleased to present to you, Major Norris. I expect you heard was exchanged not long ago."

Norris steps forward and receives congratulations on his promotion and warm welcomes to the Third Regiment. He offers to host them in the evening to make the best possible use of two bottles of Madeira provided by Colonel Scammell.

Dearborn holds up a finger to indicate having more business. "General Poor approved the reorganization of the regiment based on promoting all the ensigns to lieutenant. The officers for each company are as follows. First is Livermore's with Lieutenant Dennet. Second is Frye's with Lieutenant Ellis. Third is Stone's with Lieutenant Penniman. Fourth is Ellis's with Lieutenant Chase. McGregore will be promoted to captain and take the Fifth with Lieutenant Boynton, who will also serve as our Adjutant. Our current Adjutant Gilman is promoted to captain and has the Sixth with Lieutenant Cass. Lieutenant McGaffey is to be promoted to Captain Lieutenant. He will command the Colonel's company with Lieutenant Hoit, who will be our quartermaster. Hawkins and Simpson are promoted to the rank of Lieutenant Commandant, and they will command mine and Major Norris' companies with Lieutenants Leavitt and Blanchard. We expect more recruits soon and will assign the men within the next months. Today and this evening, I will meet with those who will be promoted or assigned to new companies. Thus, please keep this news about the companies to yourselves until tomorrow. Do any of you have anything to say?"

Stone clears his throat. "Surprised Penniman isn't a captain. He's been doing the job for a year now."

"Frankly, I don't know why either. Colonel Scammell may know something we don't."

Stone's eyebrows rise in surprise as he nods. "Thank you, sir."

Dearborn smiles. "That's all for now. Go ahead and get a start on Major Norris' offer. I'll join you after I've seen the others."

In his tent with the Third Regiment's captains, Norris pours the third round of Madeira. Stone leans forward and touches the index finger of his free hand to his temple. "You know, I've been meaning ask one of you who was there last summer. Did Colonel Hale surrender half your regiment to a dozen men hiding in the trees?"

Ellis nods with one eyebrow cocked to show his curiosity in

Honor and Valor

whatever answer Norris provides.

Norris sets the bottle down on the desk. "Might as well have been only a dozen. It was more than twenty." He nods once to Isaac. "You know Colonel Hale. He's prickly about his honor and won't go back on his word once he's given it. I will say, in his favor, we had no idea it wasn't two hundred men surrounding us on three sides. It was too quiet, and we had nothing to charge at as we weren't formed up in the first place. I s'pose if there's a fault to lay at his feet, it's that we weren't in a posture to fight or even defend ourselves."

"So," begins Livermore, his jaw set and brows knit in accusation. "Where is he now? He ought to be here leading his regiment."

Norris blows out a heavy sigh. "Home. He gave his word that he'd abide by the terms of his parole."

Stone keeps his tone soft. "Just like that. Quit the cause." Then he slips into a snarl. "Quit on us?"

"Don't shoot the messenger." Norris holds up a hand in supplication. "Especially the messenger with a second bottle."

"Fair point. Fair point." Stone holds out his empty cup.

Norris pours the next round. "I'll take the major's prerogative and change the subject. Do you prefer Whist or Brag?"

"I'll drink to anyone who says Whist." Stone leads the others in raising their cups.

•••

Jonathan Burton, Will's uncle, leans back against the wall next to the front door, his arms folded with one hand gripping Will's fife. Beside him, Major Abbot sits on a bench, gazing around the room. The warm light of three oil lamps and half a dozen candles on Isaac's kitchen table does little to add cheer. Isaac, Richard Whitney, and his wife Hannah sit at the table with William Pierce. Elizabeth and Sarah dole butter rum into warm cups from the pot on the stove. Timothy Holt rocks his fifteen-month-old grandson, Timothy, to keep him comfortable and asleep.

Having recounted much of what he could about the summer, Isaac begins covering the fall. "We spent much of the time moving our camp as we got word of the enemy coming from New York or Rhode Island or up the Connecticut River. The one happy event was a large and very military celebration on the anniversary of our victory over Burgoyne. A few days after that, we marched to Hartford. On our way, Colonel Dearborn got word his wife, Mary, was very ill. He left us to go to her and made it home only a few days before she died."

Sarah gasps. "How horrible. Did they have any children?"

"Aye, two young daughters. He had to arrange for their care. He didn't return for a month. During that time, we camped a bit north of Hartford, where we built a hospital, which took us into November. Too many men have taken sick in spite of General Washington's orders to keep the camps clear of filth. We were much better off when on the march. Even so, it was far better than what went on at Valley Forge last winter. We went back to Danbury for the second time just before Colonel Dearborn returned. Less than a week after, we got the orders to set up huts for the winter. Of course, the next day, an alarm came, and we got ordered out to Fishkill when the enemy came up the Hudson. They rather underestimated us and left as quick as they came. Those of us who had furloughs due, on account of not getting one last winter, departed a few days later. It was the day after the last snowstorm."

Burton asks, "How many of your men died from the fever?"

Isaac sighs, the energy leaving his face as he looks to the ceiling for a just answer. "Eight. Our regiment and my company had the worst of it last summer. Half of our officers were sick for a week or more. Even Colonel Dearborn. I've never been so thoroughly afflicted in my life."

Isaac waits to see Burton's slight nod, then looks to Richard and William. "You went to Rhode Island?"

Richard nods and set his cup down. "We did. Twas a well-intended and well-executed mess. The French couldn't seem to commit to a fight. When it seemed we had our best chance, they loaded their men onto their ships and sailed for Boston. That left General Sullivan without enough men. Even though we'd taken some of their redoubts, they only served to help cover our retreat. There were a fair number of skirmishes, but our regiment saw no fighting.

William snorts. "King Louis' men seemed to think rather little of doing any fighting. The talk was they lacked superior numbers, and for that alone decided Rhode Island wasn't worth their effort."

Isaac sips from his cup. "We'd heard the French officers were none too keen on taking orders from any American, even General Washington. It's a shame. Many of us think if the French had taken an aggressive posture, we'd have cleared the enemy out of every state north of the Carolinas."

Elizabeth's father, keeps his voice smooth and low to avoid waking his namesake, "Then what do you expect next season? Will the French come into the fold?"

"I don't know. We need the French and their navy. Somehow they must join with us to remove the enemy from Rhode Island while keeping the King's navy from concentrating its strength in any one place. I fear a stalemate if the French don't find a way to act on our behalf. We'll have to take New York sooner or later, and for now, the King's navy makes that a most difficult task. Add to that, the massacres out in the Mohawk Valley. The towns have gone to Congress asking for a response. If Congress grants it, twill take half the army to cover the ground, and I don't see the Iroquois just walking away from their lands."

Isaac sighs and puts his cup down. "Tomorrow's Sunday. Tis my first Sunday back." He looks to Major Abbot and Elizabeth before continuing. "I don't know what to expect. A quarter of the men we signed and mustered aren't coming back, and that's fresh news to some of their families."

Elizabeth takes Major Abbot's cup and refills it. Before she returns it, she turns to Isaac. "Tis not your fault. Being sick wasn't in your control. You told me more than a hundred must've died."

Major Abbot accepts the cup from Elizabeth. "She's right, but you're still going to have the opportunity to talk to them. At least to those that are willing. I'll be there early and make sure the word is out that you're willing to do so."

Elizabeth fixes the Major with a gaze, her eyes narrowed and lips pursed. "Make sure they know he almost died too. We're all sorry and stricken to the bottoms of our souls for what's happened."

"They'll know."

"They weren't there. They didn't- Nothing I know of could've helped." Isaac closes his eyes, his brow knit in frustration and strain. "I'll look anyone who needs it in the eye and tell them their sons, brothers, or husbands were good solid men who did all that was asked of them and more. They still got sick. Damn near all of us got sick. We were there because we chose to do our duty. We all chose to fight for our liberties and independence."

Richard clasps Isaac's shoulder. "Like the Major said, we'll go early and make sure that's well known. Some may not like hearing it, but I don't think they'll say anything lest Meshech Weare hears of it in Exeter. He's lost his son, yet I hear he's as ardent as ever for the cause of independence."

"Here, here." Major Abbot stands and raises his cup. "To the cause of independence!"

The others raise their cups and repeat the toast.

Elizabeth raises her cup toward Isaac. "To Captain Frye."

The others raise their cups and in unison, "To Captain Frye."

Jonathan Burton raises his cup. "To those who aren't coming home. Though we wish it were otherwise."

Everyone rises and quietly moves to toast Burton's cup. "To those who aren't coming home."

Honor and Valor

SOURCES

Chapter 1: Goodbyes

Davis, Gilbert A. 1903. "History of Reading, Windsor County Vermont" Vol. II Revised and improved. Windsor, VT.

- P 170-72: Biography of William Adrian Hawkins. Describes the Irish/English heritage of William Adrian Hawkins, his birth in Bordeaux, France, how he came to America as child, and that he was a tailor. He was also from Northboro, and likely knew Jonathan Livermore at that time.

Massachusetts Vital Records Project 2005 - 2015. "Vital Records of Andover, MA to the end of the year 1849" Accessed August 2017 at http://ma-vitalrecords.org/MA/Essex/Andover/.

- Uriah Ballard's birth shown as Oct 7, 1758.

Bouton, Nathaniel D.D. 1874. "State Papers. Documents and Records Relating to the State of New Hampshire During the Period of the American Revolution, from 1776 to 1783; Including the Constitution of New-Hampshire, 1776; New-Hampshire Declaration for Independence; the "Association Test," with names of Signers, &c.; Declaration of American Independence, Jul 4, 1776; the Articles of Confederation, 1778." Published by the Authority of the Legislature of New-Hampshire. Volume VIII. Edward A. Jenks, State Printer, Concord, NH.

- p. 409: On Friday, Dec 6, 1776 in the Provincial Congress it was represented "That Rev'd Mr. Jonathan Livermore of Wilton has in Sundry instances been Enimical to the Liberties of America—Therefore Voted, That the said Mr. Jonathan Livermore be cited to appear before the general Assembly of this State on the Second Wednesday of the sitting of said Assembly after the twentieth day of Dec instant to answer what may be objected against him in that behalf..."
- p. 449: On Jan 1, 1777, "Rev'd Jonathan Livermore of Wilton appeared before the Provincial Congress and defended himself against the charges of being Enimical to the Liberties of America, and the Congress voted that the complaint be dismissed."
- P 454 Jan 7, 1777, New Hampshire House of Representatives heard an account of how Ezekiel Goodale captured runaway New York prisoners (Torys and Regulars who were taken prisoner and marched to Exeter).
- Pp 458-59: Shows that Meshech. Weare, Esqr Col. Nicholas Gilman; Col. Josiah Bartlett, Ebenezer Thompson, Benjamin Barker, Mr. Thomas Odiorne, John Dudley, Capt. Josiah Moulton, Maj George Gains, John Wentworth Jr., Col. Peabody & Dr. Levi Dearborn were voted as members of the state's Committee of Safety on Jan 10, 1777.
- P 464: Jan 14, 1777, New Hampshire House of Representatives votes to give 20 pound signing bonus to enlist for three years.
- P. 466: Jan 15, 1777, William Hawkins gets orders, assigned under Captain Scott. Captains Wear and Gregg also appointed.
- P 467: Jan 16, 1777, Captain Richard Beal appointed to 3rd Regiment.
- P 482: Letter dated Feb 6, 1777, confirms that Colonel Scammell's new regiment did not at that time have uniforms.
- P 488 William Breeden of Temple resigns commission—his name was beneath William Hawkins on p 466.
- Pp 490-92: Feb 13, 1777 letter from Maj. General Sullivan to Committee regarding the recruiting money for the 3rd Regiment, which explains that captains Gilman, Robinson and Scott took their money, but Captain House was not present and had not yet received his. Because Capt. Scott had decided to take a position in the first regiment, once he reached Exeter (about Feb 20, 1777) he declined the commission in Scammell's regiment, and gave that money to the committee, who signed it over to Isaac on March 4.
- P 502 A transcription of Isaac Frye's captain's commission is provided. It was signed by John Jay, President of Congress June 16, 1779. The footnote tells that it was given in lieu of Captain Scott "who declines". The footnote also shows that the committee of safety appointed Isaac as a captain in Scammell's regiment on February 26, 1777, and so presume Abiel Abbot, as muster master took the news to Isaac along with orders to appear to receive his

orders and sign for his recruiting money. The footnote shows Isaac received orders on March 4, 1777 from the Committee of Safety to recruit a company, and he received 300£ to pay bounties, for which he must account.

Livermore, Abiel Abbot and Putnam, Sewall 1888. "History of the Town of Wilton, Hillsborough County, New Hampshire with a Genealogical Register" Marden & Rowell, Printers, Lowell, MA.

- Pp 252-253: Biographical sketch of Jonathan Livermore. Includes that he was dismissed in February and was no longer paster or teacher.
- Pp 90: Shows Abiel Abbot as with the rank of major and the role of muster master for Wilton.

The Society 1911 Paper read by Smith, Jonathan, "Two William Scotts Of Peterborough, N. H." Proceedings of the Massachusetts Historical Society, Volume 44. Pp 495-499.

- Shows that of the two Captain William Scotts. They were first cousins and both from Peterborough. One was taken prisoner twice and given orders by General Washington to recruit a company of rangers. The other was part of Cilley's First NH Regiment. There are several records in the state papers around this time that refer to the first, but not the latter. Isaac replaced the latter, who was mentioned in Sullivan's letter of Feb 13, 1777.

State of New Hampshire, April 1, 1777. Muster roll taken at Wilton, NH by Abiel Abbot showing that the men who signed received 20£ in the form of one 10£ and two 5£ treasury notes.

Thwing, Walter Aliot 1902. "The Livermore Family of America". W.B. Clarke Company, Boston, MA.

#75 Daniel and #89 Jonathan as great grandsons of Samuel Livermore.

Chapter 2: Recruiting

Evans, Charles. 1921 "Oaths of Allegiance in Colonial New England" Proceedings of the American Antiquarian Society. October 1921, Volume 31, Part 2

- P. 415: "Regarding the manner of taking the Oath; the New England custom was by holding up the right hand, as opposed to the custom in England of holding, or laying the hand on the Bible, or kissing it."

Frye, Isaac 1778 "Muster Roll of Captain Isaac Frye's Company in the third New Hampshire Battalion now in the service of the United States Commanded by Colonel Alexander Scammell for November 1778." Signed on 21 Dec 1778.

- Has final notes for Aaron Oliver, with a death date of 30 Apr, 1778. As written: "Taken Prisoner July 7, 1777 released from captivity on and died April 30, 1778.

Griffin, S.G. 1904 "History of Keene, from 1732, when the Township was Granted by Massachusetts, to 1784, when it Became a City." Sentinel Printing Company, Keene, NH.

- Pp. 217-218: Describes situation of Captain Gregg's illness and resignation, and Colonel Scammell in Keene onMay 9, 1777 to aid with recruiting.

Grundset, Eric G. (Ed.) Diaz, Briana L., Gentry, Hollis L., and Strahan, Jean D. 2008 "Forgotten Patriots, African American and American Indian Patriots in the Revolutionary War, A Guide to Service Sources, and Studies". National Society Daughters of the American Revolution. Accessed online at: https://www.dar.org/library/research-guides/forgotten-patriots, September 2017.

- Pp 51-56: Alphabetical List is of African American patriots, including Ezra Fuller of New Ipswich and Aaron Oliver of Temple.

Hammond, Isaac, W. 1885. "Rolls of the Soldiers in the Revolutionary War 1775, to May, 1777 with an appendix, embracing diaries of Lieut. Jonathan Burton" Volume I of War Rolls. Volume XIV of the Series. Parsons B. Cogswell, State Printer, Concord, NH.

- Pp. 572-574: Lists the men in Moses Nichols 6th NH Regiment of militia who signed for Continental Service in 1777. Note that Major Abiel Abbot was in this regiment and as muster master knew when and where to send Isaac and Hawkins for their recruiting.

Hammond, Isaac, W. 1887. "Rolls of the Soldiers in the Revolutionary War 1775, to May, 1777 with an appendix, embracing some Indian and French War Rolls." Volume III of War Rolls. Volume XVI of the Series. John B. Clarke, Public Printer. Manchester, NH.

- Pp. 856-858: Shows the men from Temple receiving bounties in April 1777, showing Josiah Stone, whose name is likely covered up on the National Archives scan.

Kent, Josiah C. 1921 "Northborough, History" Garden City Press, Inc. Printers, Newton, MA.

- P. 88: Shows William Hawkins living in different district in 1770 than Deacon Jonathan Livermore.

Knoblock, Glenn A. 2016 "African American Historical Burial Grounds and Gravesites of New England" McFarland & Company, Inc., Publishers, Jefferson, North Carolina.

- P. 54: Describes Aaron Oliver as being a free black man who was born in Malden, MA, and lived in temple, NH. Additionaly, Knoblock includes, ... December of 1778 must have been viewed as heaping more misery on a family already in crisis. This warning came just seven months after Abigail's husband Aaron Oliver had died. ... while serving in the 3rd New Hampshire Regiment, was taken prisoner at the Battle of Hubbardton ... Held as a prisoner in the British prison ships at Wallabout Bay in New York, Oliver was released from captivity and returned home to Temple in April 1778, but died less than a month later." The warning refers to the practice towns used to "warn out" poor black families.

Livermore, Abiel Abbot and Putnam, Sewall 1888. "History of the Town of Wilton, Hillsborough County, New Hampshire with a Genealogical Register" Marden & Rowell, Printers, Lowell, MA.

- Genealogy section used to determine backgrounds of Wilton men.
- Pp 246-248: Joseph Gray's narrative. This was written well after the war, and Gray states the company rendezvoused at Charlestown #4 on May 1, 1777, then marched to Fort Ticonderoga where Capt. Frye was stationed. The latter implying Isaac was already there.

National Archives, June 15, 1777. "A Muster Roll of Captain Isaac Frye's Company in the Third New Hampshire Battalion of Forces in the Service of the United States Commanded by Colonel Alexander Scammell".

- Shows enlistment dates of all men in Isaac's Company, starting March 13 for privates Stone and Drury of Temple. Used this to determine which men had not yet arrived at Fort Ticonderoga in June.

Honor and Valor

National Archives, September 5, 1777. "A Muster Roll of Captain Isaac Frye's Company in the Third New Hampshire Battalion of Forces in the Service of the United States Commanded by Colonel Alexander Scammell".

- Shows enlistment dates of all men in Isaac's Company with their terms of service.

Spaulding, R.C. 1892 "The Leeman Family - Pioneers of West Dunstable" Granite State Monthly v14. H.H. Metcalf and A.H. Robinson, Concord, NH. Pp 375-377.

- P 377: Gives Samuel Leeman's birth date, location, and enlistment date, however, the circumstances of his death are incorrect—he died at Hubbardton, not Saratoga.

State of New Hampshire, April 1, 1777. "Muster roll taken at Wilton, NH by Abiel Abbot showing that the men who signed received 20£ in the form of one 10£ and two 5£ treasury notes", Manuscript.

- Shows which men were part of the first groups to march to Fort Ticonderoga. The handwriting looks to be William Adrian Hawkins'. The sequence of signatures suggests other men showed up this morning and committed to service, but their enlistment dates on subsequent rolls show they did not begin service until April and May, making it also likely that Major Abbot and Lieutenant Hawkins accumulated some of the names at later dates.

Chapter 3: Preparing for the Enemy

Baldwin, Thomas W. 1906. "The Revolutionary War Journal of Col. Jeduthan Baldwin 1775-1778" The De Burians, Bangor, ME.

- Various entries for April and May of 1777: These provide weather reports and some of the reports of skirmishing with enemy scouts.
- Includes the planning and construction of the redoubts at the French Lines.
- General Poor arrives on May 20.
- July 5 Journal entry.

Bouton, Nathaniel D.D. 1874. "State Papers. Documents and Records Relating to the State of New Hampshire During the Period of the American Revolution, from 1776 to 1783; Including the Constitution of New-Hampshire, 1776; New-Hampshire Declaration for Independence; the "Association Test," with names of Signers, &c.; Declaration of American

Independence, Jul 4, 1776; the Articles of Confederation, 1778." Published by the Authority of the Legislature of New-Hampshire. Volume VIII. Edward A. Jenks, State Printer, Concord, NH.

- P 467: Shows that men passing through Charlestown on their way to Ticonderoga were to be provided with a quarter pound of powder, a half pound of lead or bullets, and two flints.
- Pp 514-515: Noah Emery's letter of March 14, 1777 describing the condition of the route from Charlestown to Ticonderoga. The time for sleds is ending and wheels may not be possible until mid-summer.
- Pp. 528- 529: The committee on "Wednesday, April 2, 1777, Voted, That orders immediately Issue to Brigadier General Poor to march off what Companies & parts of Companies are equipped belonging to the three Continental Battalion s in this State, under proper officers immediately to Ticonderoga and that when any party shall be marched off there be a proper return made to this house or Committee of Safety immediately, of such officers & soldiers so marched." Hence Isaac marching earlier to Fort Ticonderoga.

Brown, Lloyd A. and Peckham, Howard H. 1939. "Revolutionary War Journals of Henry Dearborn 1775-1783" The Caxton Club, Chicago, IL.

- P. 98. States Dearborn was exchanged on March 24, and appointed a Major in Scammell's regiment on that day. He arrives at Ticonderoga on the 20th to find Burgoyne's fleet already close to Fort Ti.

Gray, James, 1939 "Epsom Revolutionary War Soldiers" Online at http://www.epsomhistory.com/epsom/soldiers/revwar.html, last accessed Jan 2018.

- May 18, 1777 Letter to his wife shows he and Capt. McClary are at Charlestown #4, and will depart on Tuesday, two days later for Ticonderoga. McClary is sick. This means they will not arrive until May 20, and it sounds like neither has been to Ticonderoga yet. He says it has been rainy and muddy.
- June 26, 1777 Letter to his Father-in-law says he arrived at Fort Ti on the 28th of May. He says the whole camp was alarmed on the 17th of June for small arms fire a half mile north of the Lines (presuming the old French Lines adjacent Fort Ticonderoga). He indicates there are about 4,000 men at Camp, and one in four is unfit for duty. On the 18th of June, his company was ordered to be the garrison company for Fort Ticonderoga.

Griffin, S.G. 1904 "A History of the Town of Keene From 1732, when the Township was Granted by Massachusetts, to 1874, when it Became a City. With Events of Interest in the History of the City from 1874 to 1904, by Frank H. Whitcomb." Sentinel Printing Company, Keene, NH.

- P. 218: Letter of May 9th, 1777 from Alexander Scammell to Keene's Committee of Safety. Describes Scammell as having come to Keene, probably on this date, from Exeter, which fits with Scammell arriving at Fort Ticonderoga on May 20.

Hammond, Isaac W. 1887 "Rolls and Documents Relating to Soldiers in the Revolutionary War with an Appendix Embracing some French and Indian War Rolls" Volumne XVI of the Series. John B. Clarke, Public Printer, Manchester, NH.

- P. 9: Shows Thomas Powell as a Drum Major in the 3rd Regiment until May 28, 1779 when he was demoted to a common drummer.
- P. 16. Lists Moss, Lucas, and Ross as deserters on April 29, June 5, and May 3 of 1777.

Hurd, D Hamilton. 1885. "History of Hillsborough County, New Hampshire" J.W. Lewis Company. Philadelpha, PA.

- P. 440: Two paragraphs telling about Samuel Leeman's family history and his service.

Livermore, Abiel Abbot and Putnam, Sewall 1888. "History of the Town of Wilton, Hillsborough County, New Hampshire with a Genealogical Register" Marden & Rowell, Printers, Lowell, MA.

- Genealogy section used supply information for Elizabeth's April 18 Letter.

Scammell, Alexander 1777 "June 8, 1777 Letter to Naby Bishop" Manuscript. Accessed online at: https://www.fortticonderoga.org/blog/of-love-duty-and-affection/ Jan 2018.

- States that he arrived on May 20, 1777, and the 3rd Regiment is stationed at the old french lines.

Scammell, Alexander 1777 June 25, 1777 Muster Roll of the Officers of the 3rd Regiment.

- Shows one captain, two first lieutenants, five second lieutenants and five ensigns absent which corresponds to the number recruiting on the June 15th rolls. Thus, the recruiting lasted beyond June 25, 1777.

Smith, Albert 1876 "History of the Town of Peterborough, Hillsborough County, New Hampshire, Report of the Proceedings at the Centennial Celebration in 1839; An appendix containing the records of the original proprietors; and a genealogical and historical register." The Press of George H. Ellis, Boston, MA.

- P. 292: States that Randall McAlister was "severely shot through the neck" during the Battle of Breed's Hill.
- P. 140 in the genealogical register: "RANDALL MCALISTER lived in the east part of the town, on land north and embracing part of the William Field farm. We have no means of determining when he came to town, only that it was before the Revolution. He came from Scotland as a soldier in the British army, and deserted at Boston a short time before the battle of Bunker Hill. He was among the Americans in this memorable battle, and was badly wounded in the mouth and side of the neck, the ball having entered the mouth and come out, one half in the back of the neck, the other in the mouth. A comrade, who knew the circumstances of his desertion, and the danger of his falling into the hands of the enemy, took him on his back and carried him over Charlestown Neck to a place of safety."
- P. 18 in the genealogical register: Describes the Blair property being near to Cunningham Pond on the eastern side of Peterborough. Blair's daughter, Mary, married Randall McAlister.
- P. 81 in the genealogical register: Describes William Field who married the daughter of Randall McAlister, and lived near the "old Blair place".
- P. 140 in the genealogical register: Describes Randall McAlister living on the east side of Peterborough adjacent to William Field's farm. Cunningham Pond. This is just through the notch between Pack Monadnock and Temple Mountains on the north side of the Wilton/Peterborough road.

Spaulding, Charles S. 1915 "An Account of Some of the Early Settlers of West Dunstable, Monson, and Hollis, N.H." Telegraph Press, Nashua, NH.

- P. 19. Provides a short biography of Ensign Samuel Leeman, including about his fiance dying suddenly in 1773, and of selling his farm in January of 1775.

St. Clair, Arthur 1777 "American Force at Ticonderoga, June 28, 1777" Manuscript, U.S. National Archives.

Honor and Valor

- Shows which regiments and that of just over 3,600 men, almost 2,100 were fit for duty.

Wright, Robert K. Jr. 1989. "The Continental Army" Center of Military History United States Army, Washington, DC.

- P. 198: shows the 2d New Hampshire regiment as being reassigned to the New Hampshire Brigade in the Northern Department on April 28, 1777. This would not have happened until Poor had marched the 1st and 2nd, along with the New York Regiments north.

Chapter 4: Flight

Baldwin, Thomas W. 1906. "The Revolutionary War Journal of Col. Jeduthan Baldwin 1775-1778" The De Burians, Bangor, ME.

- Pp 109 - 110: July 5, 6, and 7 Journal entries provide the time of 10:00pm for the evacuation order on July 5th, that the main body of the Army made it to Castleton on the 6th, Rutland on the 7th. Tells of capturing 8 prisoners from the raiding party and taking about forty cattle.
- P 110: Rainy on the afternoon and night of July 8th, while marching through the mountains to "Arthington" on the 9th, and ultimately to Fort Eward on the 12th.It shows staying the day before arriving at Fort Edward in a place called "Bro" and was shown as if the name was partial. Given he states marching 20 miles from Arlington, this was very likely Hebron, NY.

Baxter, James P. 1887. "The British Invasion from the North, the Campaigns of Generals Carleton and Burgoyne from Canada, 1776-1777 with the Journal of Lieutenant William Digby of the 53rd, or Shropshire, Regiment of Foot" Joel Munsell's Sons, Albany, NY.

- P 235: Describes the colors taken from the battle at Fort Anne (led by James Gray and where Capt Richard Weare was wounded) as a handsome flag of thirteen stripes of alternating red and white with thirteen white stars on a blue field.

Brown, Lloyd A. and Peckham, Howard H. 1939. "Revolutionary War Journals of Henry Dearborn 1775-1783" The Caxton Club, Chicago, IL.

- P. 99: Describes the order to evacuate Fort Ticonderoga, and marching before the break of day on July 6, and the events that befell the baggage train and rear guard that day, and the following

- day. This includes that Captain Richard Weare was wounded at Fort Anne, as part of two severe skirmishes that involved the main baggage train.
- P. 100: Describes the sequence of arriving on the Hudson River opposite Saratoga, that some when north to Fort Edwards for a few days, then they retreated south due to the advances of the enemy, to Moses Kill (about a mile north of Fort Miller), and then to Saratoga on August 1st and to Stillwater (about two miles south of Bemis Heights) on August 3rd, after Tory and Indican skirmishes increase. Dearborn begins new Journal entries on August 3,1777 at Stillwater, indicating that paper is now available to the officers for personal use (letters and journals).

Fitzpatrick, John C. "The Writings of George Washington from the Original Manuscript Sources, 1745-1799" in "The George Washington Papers at the Library of Congress, 1741-1799" accessed throughout 2015 and 2016 at https://memory.loc.gov/ammem/mgwquery.html

- Jul 13, 1777 Letter from General Washington to Major General Phillip Schuyler informing him of 40 barrels of powder and a supply of lead being sent to Peekskill. This is to replace what was lost to the enemy during the flight from Fort Ticonderoga. Tells that as of the 9th Schuyler had not heard from St. Clair or the army since the evacuation.
- Jul 18, 1777 Letter from General Washington to Major General Phillip Schuyler confirms that as of the 10th, Schuyler has not yet made contact with St. Clair. Washington also confirms that ten pieces of artillery were sent to Peekskill.
- Jul 24, 1777 Letter from General Washington to Major General Phillip Schuyler reports the enemy has a great number of horses, but no wagons, and are moving slowly enough to allow time to prepare defenses.
- July 27, 1777 Letter from General Washington to Major General Phillip Schuyler that informs Schuyler that the British Army on York (Manhattan) island is no larger than what is necessary to hold the place, implying no threat to Schuyler's army.

Gray, James, 1939 "Epsom Revolutionary War Soldiers" Online at http://www.epsomhistory.com/epsom/soldiers/revwar.html, last accessed Jan 2018.

- July 7, 1777 Entry describes himself as being at Fort Anne, making it his and Richard Weare's companies that were assigned to the main baggage train.

Honor and Valor

Hadden, James M. 1884. "Hadden's Journal and Orderly Books. A Journal kept in Canada and upon Burgoyne's Campaign in 1776 and 1777 by Lieutenant James M. Hadden, Roy. Art." Joel Munsell's sons, Albany, NY.

- Pp 483-504: Appendix 15 discussion of Col. Nathan Hale's capture and its circumstances.

Smith, William H, 1882 "The St. Clair Papers. The Life and Public Services of Arthur St. Clair, Soldier of the Revolutionary War; President of the Continental Congress; and Governor of the North-Western Territory with his Correspondence and Other Papers." Vol. 1 Robert Clarke & Co, Cincinnati, OH.

- P. 54: Indicates St. Clair wrote to B.G. Enoch Poor that he had the "...strongest assurances from Congress that the King's troops were all ordered round to New York," and that such had been corroborated by a spy.
- P. 62: Tells of a large force of the enemy approaching the American works on the west side (Isaac) on June 30. As the enemy drew close, Major Wilkinson ordered a sergeant to fire upon one particularly daring enemy light infantryman who got within 40 yards. The sergeant did so, and apparently hit the enemy soldier who fell. Then every American on the "banquette" behind the parapets rose and fired a volley. No command to do so had been given. Two more rounds were fired before discipline returned. The result was a lot of smoke and the enemy retreating helter skelter.
- P 422: In a letter dated July 7, at Otter Creek (Just to southeast of Rutland), St. Clair write to the President of the Vermont Convention. He tells that while in route to Castleton they met a small force of the enemy,out rounding up cattle and dispersed them while taking a few prisoners.
- Pp 423-424: Letter to Phillip Schuyler indicating plans to go directly to Fort Edward by way of Manchester if supplies are available there, or to divert further south to Bennington to get supplies. They must have found some supplies in Manchester.
- P 425: St. Clair writes a letter to Governor Bowdoin dated 9 July from Manchester, VT.
- P. 68: Tells of the dismissal of the two Massachusetts militia regiments who had become unruly. Also tells, in the footnote, of the poltroon flight of Colonel Hale and his regiment who fled at the first firings of Hubbardton.
- P. 69: Tells of reaching Fort Edward on July 12

St. Clair, Arthur 1778 : Proceedings of a general court martial, held at White Plains, in the state of New-York by order of His Excellency General

Washington, for the trial of Major General St. Clair, August 25, 1778" Printed by Hall and Sellers, Philadelphia. Accessed online at: https://archive.org/details/proceedingsofgen00stcl

- P. 16: Tells the eastern militia regiments leaving the picketed fort on the evening when the column reached Castleton, and being stopped by General Poor, who threatened to turn out a party of men to fire upon them.
- P. 26: Tells the order of march as being Poor's brigade followed by Patterson's brigade, then the militia.

Wickman, Donald H., Ed. 1997 "Breakfast on Chocolate: The Diary of Moses Greenleaf, 1777." The Bulletin of the Fort Ticonderoga Museum 15, no 6, pp 482-506.

- P. 497: Indicates that St. Clair and therefore his element learned, sometime on the evening of July 7 of the action at Skenesboro and the loss of their baggage.

Chapter 5: Trials

Baldwin, Thomas W. 1906. "The Revolutionary War Journal of Col. Jeduthan Baldwin 1775-1778" The De Burians, Bangor, ME.

- Pp 111 - 114: July 27 through Aug 5 provides dates for the army's movements to Stillwater and Half Moon; these match Dearborn's. He makes particular note of the artillery moving to Saratoga on July 22.

Brown, Lloyd A. and Peckham, Howard H. 1939. "Revolutionary War Journals of Henry Dearborn 1775-1783" The Caxton Club, Chicago, IL.

- P 100: Describes initially sending a substantial force to Fort Edward, but upon learning the enemy was moving south, they moved south to Moses Creek (which is just north of Fort Miller). Then he provides August 3 as the date they move to Stillwater, which is just two days after moving to Saratoga. On August 5, he provides that he was on the advanced picquet that day.

Hammond, Isaac, W. 1885. "Rolls of the Soldiers in the Revolutionary War 1775, to May, 1777 with an appendix, embracing diaries of Lieut. Jonathan Burton" Volume I of War Rolls. Volume XIV of the Series. Parsons B. Cogswell, State Printer, Concord, NH

- P 52: Lists the men in Elisha Woodbury's company of Stark's

Regiment who fought at Bunker Hill; this list includes David Hall as a private.

Kelly, Christina 2011. "Schaghticoke in the American Revolution, Major Van Veghten scalped" on History of the Town of Schaghticoke Blog. Access June 2018 at: https://schaghticokehistory.wordpress.com/2011/08/

- Presents what seems to be a story from the point of view of Mr. Acker about the death of Major Van Veghten. There are curious gaps, for instance that Gray does not include that the major was scalped. Neither account includes a date, and Gray's was given much later in life. I chose to combine them as the parallels seemed obvious.

Ketchum, Richard M. 1999. "Saratoga Turning Point of America's Revolutionary War" Owl Books, United States of America.

- Pp 273-278: discussion of various incursions of the Indians employed by Gen. Burgoyne. All but one of these accounts are corroborated by both Ketchum's sources, and others. The lieutenant and nine privates killed at a breastworks a mile from Fort Edward was not substantiated by any source.

Livermore, Abiel Abbot and Putnam, Sewall 1888. "History of the Town of Wilton, Hillsborough County, New Hampshire with a Genealogical Register" Marden & Rowell, Printers, Lowell, MA.

- Pp 246-247: The part of Joseph Gray's narrative encompassing the guarding of the inhabitants of Schaghticoke. This includes corroborating Dearborn for crossing at Loundon's Ferry on the Mohawk River.

National Archives, Rolls of Brigadier General Enoch Poor's brigade (1st, 2nd, and 3rd NH and 2nd and 4th NY regiments) dated Sept 4-6, 1777. Accessed from 2014-2018 on www.Fold3.com.

- Shows a great number of men of the 2nd and 4th New York Regiments deserted, particularly on August 2, 1777.

Rensselaer County 1876. "Schaghticoke, Boyntonville, Schaghticoke Hill" Map in County Atlas published by F. W. Beers & Co., New York.

- Shows location of Dutch Reformed Meetinghouse in what is now called "Old Schaghticoke", the road from the ferry to the meetinghouse, and then a little further southeast, the road down which Major Van Veghten and Mr. Acker went (down hill into a forested area, before coming out into a cleared area where Major Van Veghton's farm is located).

Sylvester, Nathaniel Bartlett 1880. "History of Rensselaer Co. New York with Illustrations and Biographical Sketches of its Prominent Men and Pioneers."Everts and Peck, Philadelphia, PA

- Pp 455-456: Account of the attack upon and scalping of Major Derrick Van Veghten.

Vermont Historical Society 1870. "Collections of the Vermont Historical Society"Vol. Montpelier VT.

- Pp 188-189: July 19 letter from the NH committee (Meshech Weare) to Brigadier General John Stark ordering him to Charlestown #4 to await and command troops being sent there, and to coordinate with a counterpart (Seth Warner) in Vermont.
- P 190: July 24 letter to Brigadier General John Stark confirming that he has heard from the NH Committee and that three regiments are being sent to his aid.
- P 194: Aug 5 letter from Meshech Weare to the New York Committee of Safety confirming New Hampshire had, ten days prior, called up three of the remaining 12 (of 18 total) regiments and sent them to Number four under General Stark, and that Stark had already sent 700 men on to Seth Warner, with a total of 1500 men anticipated.

Chapter 6: 40 Man Scout

American Antiquarian Society. 1901 "Collections and Transactions of the American Antiquarian Society: Vol.VIII p. 119

- P 119: Describes Daniel Day as a marksman and carrying a Pennsylvania rifle.

Anburey, Thomas 1784. "Travels Through the Interior Parts of America in a Series of Letters by an Officer" William Lane, Leadenhall Street, London, England.

- Pp 391-398: Describes the Fort Hunter Mohawks arriving in Burgoyne's camp and Anburey's observations of them in their camp on Batten Kill. This confirms the composition of the "body of Indians" as being a minority of warriors.

Brown, Lloyd A. and Peckham, Howard H. 1939. "Revolutionary War Journals of Henry Dearborn 1775-1783" The Caxton Club, Chicago, IL.

- Pp 101-103: On August 15 the army retreats further south to Fort Abraham, which is near Half Moon, and they were able to draw tents from the Army's stores for the first time since leaving Fort Ticonderoga. Three days later they moved to a camp on the south side of the Mohawk River by Louden's Ferry. News of Stark's victory at Bennington reached them on the 20th, four days after the battle. On August 25, they learned of the battle at Fort Stanwix.
- P 104: September 4: "a Scout of 40 men under Command of Capt. Fry of Colo. Scammels Regt. was Surpris;d By a Body of Indians & others Consisting in the whole of about 300. We Lost out [of] our scout 9 men kild & taken—".

Montrésor, J., Andrews, P. & Dury, A. 1777 "A map of the Province of New York, with part of Pensilvania, and New England." A. Dury, London, Downloaded from the Library of Congress, https://www.loc.gov/item/74692645/.

- Used an excerpt of this map as Map 5 and the basis for General Poor's directions for Isaac's 40-man Scout.

National Archives, Rolls of Brigadier General Enoch Poor's brigade (1st, 2nd, and 3rd NH and 2nd and 4th NY regiments) dated Sept 4-6, 1777 and 1-2 Jan, 1778. Accessed from 2014-2018 on www.Fold3.com.

- Shows the men who were either "On Scout", "Duty" or "Missing" with the date of September 3, which corresponded to those on Isaac's Scout. Subsequent Rolls taken on January 1 and February 1, 1778 resolve the whether the missing men turned up or were presumed captured or killed. See Appendix A for the complete list of men on the scout.
- Shows the men who were on command or with Colonel Scammell on September 5, in Albany. Scammell clearly had three companies of what were likely the light infantry. For about a month preceding Gate's order to place Major Dearborn in command of a light infantry regiment, each regiment was required to furnish one light infantry company. 157 men, including officers were listed in Scammell's detachment at Albany.

Poor, Enoch. 1777 "Enoch Poor's Brigade orderly book, 1777 November 23-December 6" New-York Historical Society, Mss Collection (Campbell Mumford papers (Box 23, Folder 8 - Obtained PDF from Reference Desk, Feb 28, 2019.

- Shows that scouting parties and such groups were organized using men and officers from all five of Poor's regiments. Composition of these groups cycled requiring each regiment to furnish varying ranks of men to each party, such that no regiment bore these tasks to a greater extent than any other.

Thacher, James, 1827. "Military Journal during the American Revolutionary War, From 1775 to 1783; Describing Interesting Events and Transactions of this Period; with Numerous Historical Facts and Anecdotes from the Original Manuscript." Second Edition, Revised and Corrected. John Cotton, Printer, Boston, MA.

- P. 96: Quote at start of chapter.

Watt, Gavin K. 2002. "Rebellion in the Mohawk Valley - The St. Leger Expedition of 1777" The Dundurn Group, Toronto, Canada.

- P 274: Describes the encounter between the Fort Mohawks and Isaac's scouting party.

Chapter 7: On the Edge

Bemis, Charles A. 1881. "History of the Town of Marlborough, Cheshire County, N.H., with the Report of its Centennial Celebration in 1876; also Embracing Genealogies and Sketches of Families from 1764 to 1780" George H. Ellis, Boston. MA.

- P 56: Describes Andrew Colburn's headache on the morning of September 19, 1777 and that he was mortally wounded in the early part of the battle.

Brown, Lloyd A. and Peckham, Howard H. 1939. "Revolutionary War Journals of Henry Dearborn 1775-1783" The Caxton Club, Chicago, IL.

- Pp 103 - 104: Tells of encamping at Stillwater on Sep 9, and then Bemis Heights on Sep 13, 1777.

Byrd, Martha 1973. "Saratoga Turning Point in the American Revolution" Auerback Publishers, Philadelphia, New York, and London.

- Pp 77 - 89: General background on the lead up to and during the Battle of Freeman's Farm.

Dawson, Henry B. 1858 "Battles of the United States by Sea and Land: Embracing those of the Revolutionary and Indian Wars; the War of 1812 and the Mexican War; with important documents" Johnson, Fry, & Company, New York, NY.

- Pp 285 - 289: Tells of sequence of battle, particularly the Arnold's counter march to the center occurred in the woods, and of Colburn's reconnoitering party of light infantry on the east side of the Hudson on Sept 18. This must have been the light infantry arrangement from the New Hampshire regiments that was shown in the NH rolls of September 5th which showed three full companies drawn from the ranks of all three New Hampshire Regiments being on command with Colonel Scammell in Albany.
- P 290: Describes Gates removal of Arnold from command as occuring on 25 September, 1777.
- P 301: Wilkinson reports that one regiment responded, initially to Dearborn and Morgan's engagement with Forbes; that was Cilley.
- P 306: Burgoyne's report to Lord George Germain describes Arnold's foray to turn the British center under Burgoyne to the right, and that Frazer checked it.

Furneaux, Rupert. 1971. "The Battle of Saratoga" Stein and Day Publishers, New York.

- Pp 164 - 190: General background on the lead up to and during the Battle of Freeman's Farm.
- P 191: Describes shortage of ammunition, including that the left division (Arnold's) had failed to draw new ammunition on the 20th.

Griswold, William A. And Linebaugh, Donald W. Eds. 2016 "The Saratoga Campaign" University Press of New England.

- Pp 45-57: Describes the orders of battle with sequence and timing of both American and British units. In particular that Cilley's regiment was out first, got hit hard, and retreated, then found Scammell and returned to the field.
- General background on the battles and fortifications in Chapters 2 and 3.

Hoyt, Edward 2007 "The Pawlet Expedition, September 1777" Vermont History. Summer/Fall2007, Vol. 75 Issue 2, p69-100

- Describes Benjamin Lincoln's command, which released the American prisoners on September 18, 1777.

Charles E. Frye

Ketchum, Richard M. 1999. "Saratoga Turning Point of America's Revolutionary War" Owl Books, United States of America.

- Pp 350-374: General background on the lead up to and during the Battle of Freeman's Farm.

Lamb, Roger 1809. "An Original and Authentic Journal of Occurrences during the Late American War from its Commencement to the Year 1783", Wilkinson and Courtney, Dublin, Ireland

- Pp 158-159: Describes the early action of the battle at Freeman's farm. In particular that the grenadiers and light companies were on the American left under Acland and Balcarres. These units initially fought off the 1st NH who were forced to retire. Soon afterward the 3rd NH arrived, joined with the first to come again, but then were ordered to countermarch into the gap between Frazer's and Hamilton's elements to attempt to turn the smaller center element of Burgoyne's army.

Moore, Frank 1860 "Diary of the American Revolution from Newspapers and Original Documents" Vol 1. Charles Scribner, New York.

- Pp 497-498: Sep 20, 1777 Letter from Enoch Poor. States Scammell did not leave his post until taken off the field, wounded.

National Archives, Jan 1 and 2, 1777. Muster rolls of all companies in the Third New Hampshire Battalion of Forces in the Service of the United States Commanded by Colonel Alexander Scammell. Accessed from 2014-2018 on www.Fold3.com.

- Shows the which men were killed or wounded in the battles of Saratoga. In particular Beal, McClary, Stone, and Gray's companies suffered roughly half the casualties as a percentage that Wedgewood, Livermore, Frye and Ellis's did.
- Shows Jonas Perry was not at Saratoga, probably very sick during the spring of 1777, and did not join the regiment until the next spring at Valley Forge, when his name first appears on Isaac's company rolls.
- Shows Ezra Fuller as joining the regiment between 24 Sep 1777 and 2 Jan 1778. Specifically the 5 September roll shows 30 privates, and the 23 Sep roll has 29, which accounts for Josiah Stone having been killed at Freeman's Farm (also noted on 2 Jan Roll). Fuller was listed as on furlough already on 2 Jan 1778. See next comment.
- On the 2 Jan 1778 roll, ,six men: Ezra Fuller, Peter Chandler, Elijah Mansfield, David Heseltine, Jonathan Drury, and Amos Fuller were

listed as on Furlough. My theory is that they were wounded during the battles of Saratoga. Other reasons for absence, such as "Sick in Camp" or "Taken Prisoner Sep 19" were provided. Supporting this is General Poor's practice of granting furlough to men who had been wounded in battle—Captain James Gray is an early example after the battle at Fort Anne in July 1777. This roll also lists Ezra Fuller as having joined since the last roll implying he likely joined the regiment around the time of Freeman's farm.

- The January 1778 rolls varied by company, with some listing which battles their men were killed or wounded at, an others not doing so. Uniformly, they listed a number of men on furlough that logically corresponded with a plausible number of wounded men. Otherwise some companies had no wounded men.
- Shows that Captain Elijah Clayes was in command of the 2nd Regiment after Colonel Winborn Adams was killed on Sept. 19, 1777.

National Park Service. Transcription of Letter, Lt. Col. Alexander Scammell to his brother, September 21, 1777, Saratoga National Historical Park Library, The Hoyt Collection. Accessed Aug 2018: https://www.nps.gov/nr/twhp/wwwlps/lessons/93saratoga/93facts3.htm

Neilson, Charles 1844. "An Original, Compiled, and Corrected Account of Burgoyne's Campaign: And the Memorable Battles of Bemis's Heights, Sept. 19, and October 7, 1777" J. Munsell, Albany, NY.

- Pp 130-146: General background with details to compare to Dawson, Ward, Lamb, and Griswold, et. al.

Rhode Island Historical Society 1899. "Publications of the Rhode Island Historical Society New Series" Vol VII. Stoddard Printing Company, Providence RI

- P 148: Diary of Enos Hitchcock - describes battle of Freemans farm. Gives time of 3:40 that described the latter part of the battle being taken up and fought for next three hours.
- P 149: Describes the mornings of the 20th and 21st where they were turned out at 3:00am and 4:00am respectively, ready to march.

Scammell, Alexander 1777. September 21, 1777 Letter to Samuel Scammell.

- Tells of Adino Goodenough being shot through both hamstrings with one ball, and a ball striking the breach of his gun.
- Indicates he had command of one regiment of militia and that it was in the earlier part of the battle.

- Does not include the forty-five minute lull others describe before the start of the mid and late afternoon part of the battle.

Scammell, Alexander 1777. Letter to Phebe Colburn. Accessed Online, Sept 2018 at: https://m.facebook.com/saratoganhp/photos/the-battle-of-freemans-farm-september-19-1777about-700pmhundreds-of-men-and-boys/1512496522110196/

- Tells that Colburn was killed three hours into the fighting.
- Tells that Colburn's watch and shoebuckles were plundered by an enemy burial party and that they were made to pay dearly.

Scammell, Alexander 1777 September 26, 1777 Letter to Jonathan Chadbourne from Camp Now or Never. Schoff Revolutionary War Collection, 1766-1896, Manuscripts Division, William L. Clements Library, University of Michigan.

- Tells of the horses from the British Artillery lying dead on the field during the battle.
- Tells of the timing of the New York troops arrival being about the same time as Learned's Brigade arriving. Prior to this, Morgan's men were on their left, then went to the right of Cilley with Hull.
- Tells of Cook's regiment in conjunction with an adjustment by Cilley allowing for the 3rd Regiment to retreat.

Squier, Ephraim 1878. "Diary of Ephraim Squier, Sergeant in the Connecticut Line of the Continental Army," in The Magazine of American History with Notes and Queries. Vol 2.

- Pp 692-694: General information about the events surrounding the Battles of Saratoga and the surrender of Burgonye.

Stearns, Ezra. 1906 "History of Plymouth, New Hampshire" Vol. 1 The University Press, Cambridge, Massachusetts.

- Pp 154-155: Affidavit of Joshua Thornton, who was the fifer for Captain Gray's company. Says Gray never commanded again after Fort Anne. Penniman, who Thornton lived with prior to the war, commanded at Saratoga. Says Scammell was wounded. Must have been at Bemis Heights because Scammell does not mention in his earlier letters, but Poor does. Thus, my supposition is this was likely a minor wound that was bound and Scammell returned.

Ward, Christopher. 1952. "The War of the Revolution" vol. 1 Macmillan, New York, NY.

- Pp 504-511: Initially puts Cilley's regiment on the left of Morgan facing Fraser's column. When Scammell joined them, they evidently returned here, strong firing until Arnold counter-marched them to attack the center where he saw the greatest opportunity.

Chapter 8: Victory

Armstrong, Samuel 1997 "From Saratoga to Valley Forge: The Diary of Lt. Samuel Armstrong" The Pennsylvania Magazone of History and Biography. Vol. CXXI, No. 3 July 1997.

- Pp 249 - 250: Describes the various actions taken by the American army from Oct 8 though the 17th.

Arnold, Isaac N. 1880. "The Life of Benedict Arnold: His Patriotism and His Treason" Jansen, McClurg & Co., Chicago.

- P 197: Describes Poor's early afternoon orders to not fire until after the enemy fires their first volley.
- P. 202. Describes the initial assault on Balcarres' redoubt by Paterson's and Glover's brigades, including

Brown, Lloyd A. and Peckham, Howard H. 1939. "Revolutionary War Journals of Henry Dearborn 1775-1783" The Caxton Club, Chicago, IL.

- Pp 108 - 109: Tells that the NH Regiments formed their line at about 3:30 and joined in general battle. They pursued the retreating forces under Burgoyne, who unsuccessfully tried to make stands for three quarters of a mile until they reached Breyman's redoubt. Poor's men would have only been part of the first quarter mile, then Learned's and Ten Broeck's men continued the push, while Poor's men went to Balcarres' redoubt.
- Pp 109 - 111: Tells of the actions from Oct 8-17. Includes that on the 11th Poor's brigade arrived with some field pieces, and that they encamped on Burgoyne's right, meaning to the north and west.

Bacheller, Nathaniel. 1777. October 9th, 1777 letter to his wife. Transcript provided by Eric Schnitzer, Saratoga NHP.

- Implies Scammell's regiment was on the right of Poor's line in the early stages of the Battle. Gates had sent Scammell's men north and west, possibly in the line of fire of Morgan's men. Tells of Gates sending Arnold to tell Morgan not to fire on them.
- Puts Gates and Arnold in the field, and at least one of Arnold's aide

de camps (Varick or Franks).
- Describes Arnold asking for men to attack Bacarres Redoubt. These were Paterson's and Glover's men.

Dawson, Henry B. 1858 "Battles of the United States by Sea and Land: Embracing those of the Revolutionary and Indian Wars; the War of 1812 and the Mexican War; with important documents" Johnson, Fry, & Company, New York, NY.

- Pp 291- 294: General Background for Battle of Bemis Heights.
- P 293: Describes Arnold sending Patterson's men, against Balcarres' Redoubt. This occurred just before Poor's troops arrived.

Griswold, William A. And Linebaugh, Donald W. Eds. 2016 "The Saratoga Campaign" University Press of New England.

- General background on the battles and fortifications in Chapters 2 and 3.

Hillsborough County, New Hampshire Probate Court, Probate Records of Isaac Frye.

- The record contains a list of Isaac's household possessions at the time of his death. The list included two pairs of matched pistols. While the significance is not known, it seems likely one pair would have been obtained at Burgoyne's surrender given the prominent role Scammell's regiment played during both battles.

National Association of Wheat Growers. 2018 "Wheat Facts" Accessed online on 26 November, 2018 at https://www.wheatworld.org/wheat-101/wheat-facts/

- Wheat was first planted in the United States in 1777 as a hobby crop. Thank you to my wife, Amanda Frye, for pointing this out and that the proverbial "Barber wheat field" was mostly likely planted with rye.

Neilson, Charles 1844. "An Original, Compiled, and Corrected Account of Burgoyne's Campaign: And the Memorable Battles of Bemis's Heights, Sept. 19, and October 7, 1777" J. Munsell, Albany, NY.

- Pp 167: Describes Poor's order not to fire first as they approached the Grenadiers.

Scammell, Alexander 1777 October 26, 1777 Letter to General Horatio Gates from Livingston's Manor. Horatio Gates Papers. Obtained at the University of California Irvine Science Library.

- Tells of the pay chest being lost at Skenesborough. It contained "Two Hundred & Ninety Two Pounds, Nineteen Shillings, & Six Pence." This was about one month's pay for the officers of the regiment.

Stearns, Ezra. 1906 "History of Plymouth, New Hampshire" Vol. 1 The University Press, Cambridge, Massachusetts.

- Pp 154-155: Affidavit of Joshua Thornton, who was the fifer for Captain Gray's company. Says Gray never commanded again after Fort Anne. Pennyman, who Thornton lived with prior to the war, commanded at Saratoga. Says Scammell was wounded. Must have been at Bemis Heights because Scammell does not mention in his earlier letters. He also mentions Sanderson of his company, of Moultonborough's altercation with Beal. Everything rings true.

Stone, William L. 1895. "Visits to the Saratoga Battle-Grounds 1780-1880" Joel Munsell's Sons, Albany, NY.

- P 145: Tells of Cilley's men leading the charge up the hill to start the battle on Oct. 7. Cilley had been indignantly responding to hearing the British commander's orders to fix bayonets and charge the damned rebels.

Wilkinson, James. 1816 "Memoirs of My Own Times" Vol. 1 Abraham Small, Philadelphia.

- Pp 267-268: Describes the daily alarms being curtailed and the beginning of the battle on Oct 7, 1777.
- P. 271: Tells of assisting the wounded commander of the Grenadiers, Major Acland.
- P 278: Tells of circumstances of Oct 8, 1777 and General Lincoln's wounding.
- Pp 300-325: Describes Oct 14 - 19, 1777 and includes the details of where the men were on the 17th, including their rising at 3:00 AM.

Chapter 9: Breaking Point

Bingham, Hiram, Jr. 1901 "Five Straws Gathered from Revolutionary Fields" Cambridge, MA

- Pp 20-22: Letter from Fishkill of November 3rd, indicating they arrived a day earlier, and knew they were bound for Philadelphia. Tells of confusion and want of money. This suggests the march was miserable as it should have been accomplished in half the time in good weather.

Boyle, Joseph L. 1997 "From Saratoga to Valley Forge: The Diary of Lt. Samuel Armstrong" The Pennsylvania Magazine of History and Biography vol 121 no. 3.

- P 252: Weather from late October through November.

Brown, Lloyd A. and Peckham, Howard H. 1939. "Revolutionary War Journals of Henry Dearborn 1775-1783" The Caxton Club, Chicago, IL.

- P 112: Tells of being ordered to Albany and arriving at midnight after marching 38 miles. This makes sense as Dearborn's men were camped two miles further north of Poor's on the 17th.

Hamilton, Alexander 1777. "From Alexander Hamilton to Major General Israel Putnam, 9 November 1777," Founders Online, National Archives, version of January 18, 2019, https://founders.archives.gov/documents/Hamilton/01-01-02-0338. [Original source: The Papers of Alexander Hamilton, vol. 1, 1768–1778, ed. Harold C. Syrett. New York: Columbia University Press, 1961, pp. 356–357.]

- Shows through his implied timeline that the troops who mutinied like knew of Howe taking Philadelphia and they still balked at orders to join Washington.

Hamilton, Alexander 1777. "From Alexander Hamilton to George Washington, 10 November [1777]," Founders Online, National Archives, version of January 18, 2019, https://founders.archives.gov/documents/Hamilton/01-01-02-0339. [Original source: The Papers of Alexander Hamilton, vol. 1, 1768–1778, ed. Harold C. Syrett. New York: Columbia University Press, 1961, pp. 357–360.]

- Tells of Hamilton setting his next task to get Poor's men to march, and that he would be meeting with Poor himself.

Hamilton, Alexander 1777. George Washington Papers, Series 4, General Correspondence: Alexander Hamilton to George Washington 15 Nov 1777. Retrieved from the Library of Congress, https://www.loc.gov/item/mgw448814/.

- Indicates Poor's Brigade crossed the Hudson on the Nov 13.

Livermore, Abiel Abbot and Putnam, Sewall 1888. "History of the Town of Wilton, Hillsborough County, New Hampshire with a Genealogical Register" Marden & Rowell, Printers, Lowell, MA.

- Pp 248: The part of Joseph Gray's narrative. Tells of being ordered on a force-march 36 miles to Albany on Oct 18, 1777. Also describes the events that occurred at Fishkill in early November, 1777, where Gray describes a corporal being the leader of the mutiny and who was slain.

National Archives, Jan 1, 1778 through Dec 21, 1778. Muster rolls of Isaac Frye's company in the Third New Hampshire Battalion of Forces in the Service of the United States Commanded by Colonel Alexander Scammell. Accessed from 2014-2018 on www.Fold3.com.

- Shows how long each of the eight wounded men (Blood, Chandler, Drury, Fish, Fuller, Fuller, Hesselton, and Mansfield) was on furlough, and when they rejoined the company. Fish did not rejoin and last appeared on the Sep 1, 1778 roll.

National Archives, Jan 2, 1778 Rolls of all companies in Poor's Brigade. Accessed Feb, 2019 on www.Fold3.com.

- Shows all men who deserted since the September 5, 1777 roll, and the date of their desertion. Twenty five men deserted, who were not caught from Nov 1 through Nov 13 from Fishkill. Most were from the 2nd NH regiment, particularly Robinson's Company.
- Shows Private Jonathan Sanderson from Captain Norris's company, 2nd NH regiment as died on Nov 5, 1777. Shown as a private. Other Captain Beal, no other man died on Nov 5 or 6. Thus, Sanderson is the presumed leader of the mutiny. Note that Sanderson was a Private on earlier rolls as well—thus not a corporal as Gray and Thornton claimed much later. It is likely the deserters elected Sanderson as their corporal, rather than him holding this rank in the Continental Army.

Putnam, Israel, 1777. George Washington Papers, Series 4, General Correspondence: Israel Putnam to George Washington on Nov 7, 1777.

Retrieved from the Library of Congress, https://www.loc.gov/item/mgw448806/.

- Confirms Poor's men were supposed to march south to Washington on Nov 5, 1777. Interesting notes about the 4th and 2nd NY Getting some Cloths and money, and now are better off than most continental regiments. Then in providing Washington some perspective about the NY regiments under Poor, he describes the deserters in August (about 100) as having gone over to the Enemy.
- Cursory telling of Captain Beal's death.
- Washington responds on the 11th and approves all of Putnam's measures, including directing Congress to send money to Putnam's department.

Scammell, Alexander 1777 October 26, 1777 Letter to General Horatio Gates from Livingston's Manor. Horatio Gates Papers. Obtained at the University of California Irvine Science Library.

- Excerpt at the beginning of the chapter.

Scammell, Alexander 1777 Nov 6, 1777 Letter to General Horatio Gates from Fish Kill. Horatio Gates Papers. Obtained at the University of California Irvine Science Library.

- Tells of the 3rd Regiment's Quartermaster being "put off" by the commissary when trying to settle accounts. Complains again about the pay and justifies that his men richly deserve their pay.

Snow, Dean R. 2016 "American Orderly Books, Saratoga, September 15 to October 17, 1777"

- P 14: Tells of Scammell's regiment receiving 46 pairs of shoes on Oct 7, 1777, which is the last time there is any note of shoes being received - and by the the time they reach Washington a quarter of the men are without shoes.

Stearns, Ezra. 1906 "History of Plymouth, New Hampshire" Vol. 1 The University Press, Cambridge, Massachusetts.

- Pp 154-155: Affidavit of Joshua Thornton states that "Capt. Beal was killed by a soldier of our company, one Sanderson, who went from Moultonborough, N. H." However, the rolls of Gray's company, of which Thornton was the fifer, show no one named Sanderson. There is a Jonathan Sanderson in Norris's company in the 2nd regiment and that man is listed as dead on Nov 5, 1777.

Washington, George, 1777. George Washington Papers, Series 4, General Correspondence: Israel Putnam to George Washington, November 7, .1777. Retrieved from the Library of Congress, https://www.loc.gov/item/mgw448723/.

- Describes the mutiny, confirms they were to and did cross the Hudson at the level of Fishkill (King's Ferry (from Hamilton's of 9 Nov.

Washington, George. 1777 "Letter from George Washington to Israel Putnam dated 11 November 1777"

- Acknowledges with amazement the fact that the New Hampshire troops have not been paid in ten months, and generally approves of Putnam's handling of the situation.

Wolf, Judy 2019 "Mutiny at Fishkill Ends Tragically: The Zachariah Beal Story" accessed online at: http://www.fishkillsupplydepot.org/tribute/beal.html in January and February, 2019.

- Describes several perspectives on the mutiny in which Captain Beal was killed. Includes excerpt of Israel Putnam's Letter of November 7, to Washington appraising him of the situation.

Chapter 10: White Marsh

12th Grade Honors History Class of Philadelphia-Montgomery Christian Academy. 2017 "The Battle of Whitemarsh: Driving Tour" Accessed in April 2019 at https://battleofwhitemarsh.weebly.com/maps.html

- Includes a series of maps showing the disposition of troops and action during the Battle of Whitemarsh from December 5 through 8, 1777. These maps were redrawn from the original manuscript maps produced by John L. Mangan and R. T. Sadleir. The original maps are owned by the Fort Washington Historical Society. These maps show the area where Washington's army was encamped, the terrain, and the movements of American and British troops.

Brown, Lloyd A. and Peckham, Howard H. 1939. "Revolutionary War Journals of Henry Dearborn 1775-1783" The Caxton Club, Chicago, IL.

- Pp 114 - 117: Tells of arriving at Whitemarsh and the role the regiment played during the stand off and skirmishes that comprised the Battle of Whitemarsh. In particular that he led the regiment out late on Dec 7 with the intent of baiting the British horse troops.

Egle, William H. 1893."Journals And Diaries of the War of the Revolution With Lists of Officers And Soldiers, 1775-1783". Harrisburg, PA.

- P 215: Diary of Lieut. James McMichael stating the militia were sent out at 8:00 am on December 5 to skirmish, which corresponds with Dearborn's journal stating firing was heard at 9:00 am.

Gray, James. 1777 Letter dated 23 December, 1777 to his wife, Susan Gray.

- Gray noted the unfriendly inhabitants, a summary of events leading to the Continental Army moving into winter quarters.

Poor, Enoch. 1777 "Enoch Poor's Brigade orderly book, 1777 November 23-December 6" New-York Historical Society, Mss Collection (Campbell Mumford papers (Box 23, Folder 8 - Obtained PDF from Reference Desk, Feb 28, 2019.

- Contains Washington's orders and assignments at the level of the Continental Army, and then General Poor's additional orders for duties within the brigade. These provide insight into daily organization and administration of the encampment, but do not include special orders or exceptional events such as skirmishes or battles.

Simcoe, John Graves. "A Journal of the Operations of the Queen's Rangers from the End of the Year 1777, to the Conclusion of the Late American War (1789)" Originally published in 1789. Kindle Edition.

- Describes the events of the night of December 7, 1777:"On the 7th, at night, Major Simcoe with the Queen's Rangers, and a part of dragoons under Captain Lord Cathcart, took up the position of some of the troops who had retired; this post was sometime afterward quitted in great silence, and he joined the column that was marching unde General Gray." These are possibly the dragoons mentioned by Henry Dearborn.

Vance, Sheilah. 2012. "Six Days in December: General George Washington's and the Continental Army's Encampment on Rebel Hill, December 13 - 19, 1777" Kindle edition, The Elevator Group.

- For background relating to moving from White Marsh to Valley

Honor and Valor

Forge. Noting Vance indicates they have no tents - this is not true for all.

Washington, George. 1777 "Orders from George Washington to the Officers Commanding the Brigades of Generals Enoch Poor and John Paterson, 19 November 1777"

- Directs them to march via Trenton, NJ in order to join forces.

Washington, George 1777 "Order of Battle, 4–5 December 1777," Founders Online, National Archives, version of January 18, 2019, https://founders.archives.gov/documents/Washington/03-12-02-0494.
[Original source: The Papers of George Washington, Revolutionary War Series, vol. 12, 26 October 1777–25 December 1777, ed. Frank E. Grizzard, Jr. and David R. Hoth. Charlottesville: University Press of Virginia, 2002, pp. 534–535.]

- Shows Poor's brigade on the left side of the American right - placing them in the center of the first line.
- This is also part of the basis for using the northeast part of Camp Hill as the site for Poor's encampment.

Washington, George 177 "George Washington to Continental Congress, November 23, 1777" George Washington Papers, Series 3, Varick Transcripts, 1775 to 1785, Subseries 3A, Continental Congress, 1775 to 1783, Letterbook 3: Sept. 1, 1777. [Manuscript/Mixed Material] Retrieved from the Library of Congress, https://www.loc.gov/item/mgw448898/.

- On the fourth page, Washington indicates Poor's brigade arrived in the White Marsh camp on November 22, 1777, and implies Larned's men were a day ahead.
- Washington tells they are deficient in shoes, stockings, breeches, and blankets.

Chapter 11: Winter Quarters

1928 Valley Forge encampment to June 18, 1778. [Map] Retrieved from the Library of Congress, https://www.loc.gov/item/gm71000868/.

Bingham, Hiram, Jr. 1901 "Five Straws Gathered from Revolutionary Fields" Cambridge, MA

- Pp 23-24: The 3rd Regiment's Paymaster, William Weeks' Feb 16, 1778 letter to an anonymous recipient from Valley Forge tells of.five days of men not receiving even a tenth of their rations and he blames Washington. He notes Washington was made aware of the circumstance that day and beef arrived shortly afterward on that same day.

Brier, Marc A. 2004. "Tolerably Comfortable: A Field Trial of a Recreated Soldier Cabin at Valley Forge" National Park Service, U.S. Department of the Interior, Valley Forge National Historical Park. 27 Pages.

- Describes the construction and conditions of the log huts Washington's army built at Valley forge. This showed the interior temperatures in the center of the hut ranged from the low forties if the fire went out to the upper seventies when the day was warm. There was about a twelve to fifteeen degree difference between the bunks near the fireplace versus the door.

Brown, Lloyd A. and Peckham, Howard H. 1939. "Revolutionary War Journals of Henry Dearborn 1775-1783" The Caxton Club, Chicago, IL.

- P 117: Dearborn notes their tents were ordered into camp on the 9th and on the 11th notes they struck their tents, to imply they recieved them.
- Pp 118-120: Hutting begins on Dec 23. Entry for December 31, 1777 tells that they are still living in tents and that he knows he is going on furlough on the following Sunday. He leaves for home on January 4, after noting the weather from the first through the fourth as pleasant.

Donovan, D., Rev, and Woodward, Jacob A. 1906. "History of Lyndeborough New Hampshire 1735 - 1905" First Published by the Lyndeborough Historical Committee and then Tufts College Press, H.W. Whittemore & Co.

- P 177: Biography of Ebenezer Carleton stating that he was transferred into his Excellency General Washington's Guard on Jan 1, 1779. However, the rolls show him to already be there as of 1 Jan 1778, likely the year is a typo.

Hammond, Isaac W. 1884. "Town Papers Documents Relating to Towns in New Hampshire, New London to Wolfesborough, with an appendix, Embracing some documents, interesting and valuable, not heretofore published, including the Census of New Hampshire in 1790 in detail." Volume XIII. Concord, New Hampshire. Carson B. Cogswell, State Printer.

- Pp 557-558: Shows that in 1780 Ezekiel Goodale petitioned for lost and un-depreciated wages. "... and then marched to Penselvana: &

Continued there til Apr 30 1778 when by reason of Continued applycations from my Family of their Distressed Circumstances I procuered a Discharge & Come home..." The committee allowed him the depreciation of his pay.

National Archives, August 1777 through July 1778 Pay Abstracts for Colonel Cilley's 1st New Hampshire Regiment. Accessed from July 2019 on www.Fold3.com.

- Shows that pay for Aug, Sep, and Oct, was likely process and paid in late December or Early January, then Pay for Nov and Dec was likely processed and paid in early February. This would have been done for all regiments.

National Archives, Jan 1778 through Nov 1778 Rolls for the companies of the 3rd New Hampshire Regiment. Accessed from July 2019 on www.Fold3.com.

- Shows which officers were on furlough and those who remained, living in the huts, for the entire winter.
- Shows when Hawkins arrives with Fuller and Mansfield between April 4 and May 1.
- Shows Goodale discharged on May 1. After being on the roll as present on April 4. Same for Lieutenant Nathaniel Gilman.
- Shows that in late March, Isaac with Dan Livermore are the ranking officers. Captain Stone's company has no officers, and First Lieutenant David McGregor from Livermore's company was likely commanding that company into May.
- Indicates Hawkins was on furlough in March of 1778. The roll at Valley Forge reflects this prior to Hawkins's arrival sometime prior to May 2, 1778.

Poor, Enoch. 1778. "Orderly book of the 3rd New Hampshire regiment, 1781, Jan. 13 - Feb. 4, Valley Forge, Pa."
https://hdl.huntington.org/digital/collection/p15150coll7/id/23709/.
Manuscripts, Huntington Digital Library. Accessed Sep 27, 2019.

- Indicates the job of brigade adjutant was on a rotation, with an officer from each regiment on a five-day rotation. Ensign Jonathan Cass was listed multiple times as being the third regiment's officer serving in this capacity.
- Listed various events such as the availability of clothing and pay, details for guard duty or to gather firewood, etc.

Strong, Nathan 1778. "Orderly book with accounts of Capt. Nathan Strong's company the 4th New York Regiment, 1777, Mar. 19 - 1778, June 12,

Peekskill, N.Y., Valley Forge, Pa." 171 pages. Manuscripts, Huntington Digital Library. https://hdl.huntington.org/digital/collection/p15150coll7/id/23076 Accessed July 2019.

- Strong is a captain in the 4th NY regiment, part of Poor's Brigade and this orderly book, which contains records back into 1777 until nearly the end of 1778 shows the dates that pay, supplies, and provisions arrived at Valley Forge

Unknown Artist. Early 1800s. Portrait of Jonathan Cass. Obtained online at https://www.geni.com/photo/view/356769491270001214?album_type=photos_of_me&end=&photo_id=6000000031092344053&project_id=&start=&tagged_profiles= Accessed on 9/28/2019.

Washington, George, 1777. "General Orders, 18 December 1777," Founders Online, National Archives, accessed April 11, 2019, https://founders.archives.gov/documents/Washington/03-12-02-0573.
[Original source: The Papers of George Washington, Revolutionary War Series, vol. 12, 26 October 1777–25 December 1777, ed. Frank E. Grizzard, Jr. and David R. Hoth. Charlottesville: University Press of Virginia, 2002, pp. 626–628.]

- Washington proscribed a standard size for the hutts and how many men by rank should be housed in each: twelve enlisted and two company's officers, which would have been eight under normal circumstances.

Washington, George, 1777 "General Orders, 26 December 1777," Founders Online, National Archives, accessed April 11, 2019, https://founders.archives.gov/documents/Washington/03-13-02-0001.
[Original source: The Papers of George Washington, Revolutionary War Series, vol. 13, 26 December 1777–28 February 1778, ed. Edward G. Lengel. Charlottesville: University of Virginia Press, 2003, pp. 1–2.].

- Washington's orders restrict passes out of camp and order regiments to take more frequent rolls in order to curtail incursions into the countryside that resulted in "cruel outrages and robberies." and plundering that was mentioned in the previous day's general orders.

Washington, George, 1778. "General Orders, 24 January 1778," Founders Online, National Archives, accessed April 11, 2019, https://founders.archives.gov/documents/Washington/03-13-02-0287.
[Original source: The Papers of George Washington, Revolutionary War Series, vol. 13, 26 December 1777–28 February 1778, ed. Edward G. Lengel. Charlottesville: University of Virginia Press, 2003, p. 328.]

- "Three days provision to be issued to the troops on Mondays & four days provision on Thirsdays 'till further orders." Establish the days the food (provisions) was provided by the commissary to the men

Washington, George, 1778. "General Orders, 15 February 1778," Founders Online, National Archives, accessed April 11, 2019, https://founders.archives.gov/documents/Washington/03-13-02-0456.
[Original source: The Papers of George Washington, Revolutionary War Series, vol. 13, 26 December 1777–28 February 1778, ed. Edward G. Lengel. Charlottesville: University of Virginia Press, 2003, pp. 542–544.]

- Included order to submit rolls for all men who were present on December 29, 1777 as they were to receive an extra month of pay.

Washington, George. 1778. "General Orders, 24 March 1778," Founders Online, National Archives, accessed Sep 27, 2019, https://founders.archives.gov/documents/Washington/03-14-02-0258.
[Original source: The Papers of George Washington, Revolutionary War Series, vol. 14, 1 March 1778–30 April 1778, ed. David R. Hoth. Charlottesville: University of Virginia Press, 2004, pp. 285–287.]

- Orders all brigades to begin exercising at 9:00 AM the next morning. Exercise in this case meant the new manual of arms from Von Steuben.

Washington, George. 1778. "General Orders, 28 March 1778," Founders Online, National Archives, accessed Sept 27, 2019, https://founders.archives.gov/documents/Washington/03-14-02-0304.
[Original source: The Papers of George Washington, Revolutionary War Series, vol. 14, 1 March 1778–30 April 1778, ed. David R. Hoth. Charlottesville: University of Virginia Press, 2004, pp. 331–332.]

- General officers reset the prices for liquors sold by brigade sutlers. "At a board of the Brigadiers and officers commanding Brigades the prices of sundry liquors were fixed as follows and now ratified by the Commander in Chief (viz.) West-India rum or Spirit at 15/ Continental rum 10/ Gen 9/ French brandy 19/ & Cyder royal 2/ pr quart and in larger or smaller quantities at the same rates."
- Brigade inspectors appointed to ensure the conformity in "...establishing a Uniform System of useful Manœuvres and regularity of discipline must be obvious, the Deficiency of our Army in these Respects must be equally so; the time we shall probably have to introduce the necessary Reformation is short, without the most active Exertions therefore of Officers of every Class it will be

Charles E. Frye

impossible to derive the Advantages proposed from this Institution …"

Wright, Robert K. Jr. 1989. "The Continental Army" Center of Military History United States Army, Washington, DC.

- P. 143: A diagram showing the new arrangement of troops by rank in an infantry regiment.

Chapter 12: The Marquis

Brown, Lloyd A. and Peckham, Howard H. 1939. "Revolutionary War Journals of Henry Dearborn 1775-1783" The Caxton Club, Chicago, IL.

- Pp 120-121: Tells of the detachment under Lafayette marching from camp. He is apparently in camp the next day for the alarm being given for the detachment having been surrounded, and the rest of the camp at Valley Forge was "turned out".

Historical Society of Montgomery County. 1900. "Historical Sketches: A Collection of Papers, Volume 2". Norristown, PA Herald Printing and Binding Rooms.

- Pp 292-305: Contains a synthesis of the events at Barren Hill from May 18-21, 1778. Several earlier sources such as Lossing and Steadman were used and compared as well as the account of one of Lafayette's aids.

Lafayette. 1837. "Memoirs Correspondence and Manuscripts of General Lafayette" Accessed online at https://www.gutenberg.org/files/8376/8376-h/8376-h.htm on 6 Oct, 2019.

Linn, John B. and Egle, William H. Eds. 1896 "Pennsylvania Archives. Second Series. Reprinted under direction of the Secretary of the Commonwealth." Vol. III Clarence M. Busch, State Printer of Pennsylvania. Harrisburg, PA.

- Pp 130-131: Letter from Lieutenant Captain Hercules Courtenay to the Council of Safety expressing his dissatisfaction with being left out of the new arrangement for Proctor's artillery.

National Archives, Jan 1778 through Nov 1778 Rolls for the companies of the 3rd New Hampshire Regiment. Accessed from July 2019 on www.Fold3.com.

- May 2 roll shows Will Burton, Christopher Martin, David Hall, and seven other privates as being sick from Isaac's company. Will and Hall had recovered by June 2.

Sparks, Jared, 1834. "Retreat of the Marquis de Lafayette from Barren Hill, May 20th 1778" Scanned Map. Accessed online Oct 25, 2019. https://digitalcollections.nypl.org/items/510d47da-f138-a3d9-e040-e00a18064a99

- Shows layout of encampment and route of retreat.

Strong, Nathan 1778. "Orderly book with accounts of Capt. Nathan Strong's company the 4th New York Regiment, 1777, Mar. 19 - 1778, June 12, Peekskill, N.Y., Valley Forge, Pa." 171 pages. Manuscripts, Huntington Digital Library. https://hdl.huntington.org/digital/collection/p15150coll7/id/23076 Accessed July 2019.

- Strong notes on May 16 the receipt of tents for his company's use.

Washington, George. 1778 "General Orders, 5 May 1778," Founders Online, National Archives, accessed September 29, 2019, https://founders.archives.gov/documents/Washington/03-15-02-0039.
[Original source: The Papers of George Washington, Revolutionary War Series, vol. 15, May–June 1778, ed. Edward G. Lengel. Charlottesville: University of Virginia Press, 2006, pp. 38–41.]

- Includes the plan for events on May 6 relating to the news of the alliance with France.

Washington, George, 1778. "General Orders, 14 May 1778," Founders Online, National Archives, accessed September 29, 2019, https://founders.archives.gov/documents/Washington/03-15-02-0114.
[Original source: The Papers of George Washington, Revolutionary War Series, vol. 15, May–June 1778, ed. Edward G. Lengel. Charlottesville: University of Virginia Press, 2006, pp. 121–122.]

- Washington sets aside Friday afternoons for the soldiers to work on their clothing.

Washington, George, 1778. "From George Washington to Major General Lafayette, 18 May 1778," Founders Online, National Archives, accessed September 29, 2019, https://founders.archives.gov/documents/Washington/03-15-02-0152.
[Original source: The Papers of George Washington, Revolutionary War Series, vol. 15, May–June 1778, ed. Edward G. Lengel. Charlottesville: University of Virginia Press, 2006, pp. 151–154.]

- Lafayette's orders concerning his detachment of 2200 men with the purpose of providing security for the Valley Forge camp and to perform reconnaissance missions.

Wilkinson, James. 1816 "Memoirs of My Own Times" Vol. 1 Abraham Small, Philadelphia.

- P 829: Describes the unit assigned to Lafayette as "... to approximate an elite corps to the enemy, General Washington selected about 2400 of his best troops and detached them ... under the command of the Marquis de la Fayette ...".
- P. 830: mentions that a Lieutenant C* who was left out of the arrangement in 1777 for Proctor's Artillery Regiment was disgruntled and entered into a correspondence with British General Howe and became his spy. This same person frequented the camp at Valley Forge as he was friendly with members of his former regiment. Wilkinson suspects this was the source that tipped of the British in Philadelphia. John Marshall's 1832 "Life of Washington confirms as much."
- Pp 831-833 describes the sequence of events of the 20th. Wilkinson was present.
- Pp 833-834 contains a transcript of a 20 May, 1778 letter from Alexander Scammell to Captain McClane who commanded a company of scouts for Lafayette's detachment. Scammell wrote this from the camp at Valley Forge, indicated he was not commanding the 3rd Regiment. Given that Dearborn was not either, command must have fallen to Captain Livermore, the ranking officer present also trained in Von Steuben's manual.

Chapter 13: Fever

Brown, Lloyd A. and Peckham, Howard H. 1939. "Revolutionary War Journals of Henry Dearborn 1775-1783" The Caxton Club, Chicago, IL.

- P 122: Dearborn notes being sick with an ague from May 28 through 30, and then on June 5th admits to finally being completely over it. Sounds like influenza, and others such as Isaac had it and then a secondary issue that kept them ill for over a month.

Grundset, Eric G. (Ed.) Diaz, Briana L., Gentry, Hollis L., and Strahan, Jean D. 2008 "Forgotten Patriots, African American and American Indian Patriots in the Revolutionary War, A Guide to Service Sources, and Studies". National Society Daughters of the American Revolution. Accessed online at:

Honor and Valor

https://www.dar.org/library/research-guides/forgotten-patriots, September 2017.

- P 55: Lists Aaron Oliver as a Mulatto.

Knoblock, Glenn A. 2016 "African American Historical Burial Grounds and Gravesite s of New England" McFarland & Company, Inc., Publishers, Jefferson, North Carolina.

- P. 54: Describes the circumstances of Aaron Oliver's imprisonment, release, and death.

Livermore, Abiel Abbot and Putnam, Sewall 1888. "History of the Town of Wilton, Hillsborough County, New Hampshire with a Genealogical Register" Marden & Rowell, Printers, Lowell, MA.

- P 248: Gray notes the he and his captain (Isaac) were left behind, sick, at Valley Forge when the Army moved on to White Plains.

National Archives, Jun 1778 through Nov 1778 Rolls for the companies of the 3rd New Hampshire Regiment. Accessed from July 2019 on www.Fold3.com.

- June and July Rolls for Isaac's company list him and many of his men as sick.
- Each roll lists the date of death for the men who died of the sickness.

Washington, George, 1778. "General Orders, 27 May 1778," Founders Online, National Archives, accessed September 29, 2019, https://founders.archives.gov/documents/Washington/03-15-02-0237.
[Original source: The Papers of George Washington, Revolutionary War Series, vol. 15, May–June 1778, ed. Edward G. Lengel. Charlottesville: University of Virginia Press, 2006, pp. 234–235.]

- As more men became sick such measures as removing the mud plastering and burning of powder cartridges to cleans the air were enacted.

Chapter14: Northward

Brown, Lloyd A. and Peckham, Howard H. 1939. "Revolutionary War Journals of Henry Dearborn 1775-1783" The Caxton Club, Chicago, IL.

- Pp 132- 42: Dearborn's entries describing the encampments and travels of the Third Regiment from August through December of 1778.

Hadden, James M. 1884. "Hadden's Journal and Orderly Books. A Journal kept in Canada and upon Burgoyne's Campaign in 1776 and 1777 by Lieutenant James M. Hadden, Roy. Art." Joel Munsell's sons, Albany, NY.

- Pp 483-504: Appendix 15 discussion of Col. Nathan Hale's capture and its circumstances.

National Archives, May 1778 through Aug 1778 Rolls for the companies of the 3rd New Hampshire Regiment. Accessed in October 2019 on www.Fold3.com.

- Shows Isaac's company was by far hit by the sickness the hardest. Seventy One percent of Isaac's company was sick in July versus the regimental average of forty percent. Dennet's and Livermore's companies were the only others with just over fifty percent sick.
- The July roll for Isaac's company is not in Isaac's handwriting, likely Hawkins. This sets up the discussion regarding Drury and those who died at Valley Forge after the army marched.
- Showed Captain Stone has having no officers under him from the end of July in 1778. His last lieutenant, Eaton, had been granted a discharge by George Washington.

Washington, George, 1778. "General Orders, 7 June 1778," Founders Online, National Archives, accessed September 29, 2019, https://founders.archives.gov/documents/Washington/03-15-02-0356.
[Original source: The Papers of George Washington, Revolutionary War Series, vol. 15, May–June 1778, ed. Edward G. Lengel. Charlottesville: University of Virginia Press, 2006, pp. 338–344.]

- Describes the new arrangement of the infantry battalions containing nine companies, six captains, and a captain lieutenant.

Honor and Valor

Charles E. Frye

APPENDIX A

MEN ON THE 40-MAN SCOUT

I first learned of this scout about twelve years before writing this book. Henry Dearborn's journal contained the following entry for September 4, 1777:

> "4th a Scout of 40 men under Command of Capt. Fry of Colo. Scammels [sic] Regt. was Surprised By a Body of Indians & others Consisting in the whole of about 300. We Lost out [of] our scout 9 men kild & taken —"

Not long after, I contacted Eric Schnitzer, a historian and Interpretive Ranger at Saratoga National Historical Park. He provided a reference to Thomas Anburey's account of the Fort Hunter Mohawks arriving in Burgoyne's camp. They carried news of ambushing an American party while in route. As I was writing Chapter Six, I contacted Schnitzer again and our discussions led me to analyze the rolls of Poor's brigade. I had also located an orderly book from Poor's brigade for 1778. Orderly books contain the general orders from the division or army commander, and that of the brigade commander. The latter provided insight into the organization of such a scouting party. Poor rotated the burden of providing officers, non-commissioned officers, and privates from the five regiments of his command. The officers of the later scouts or duties would be from successive regiments. Thus, Poor assigned men from each of the five regiments to such duties.

Honor and Valor

From rolls of Poor's Brigade (1st, 2nd, and 3rd NH and 2nd and 4th NY regiments) dated Sept 4-6, 1777 I learned the names of the men on the scout. From the rolls of January 1-2, 1778, which were the next available, I learned their dispositions, which I give in Chapter Six.

Here is a roll of the forty men:

Rank	Name	Company	Regiment
Cpt	Frye, Isaac	Self	3d NH
1Lt	McCally, Nathaniel	Morrill	1st NH
Sgt	Burges, Archibald	Pells	2nd NY
Sgt	Kemp, William	Morrill	1st NH
Sgt	McEvers, John	Smith	4th NY
Cpl	Griffiths, Samuel	Hallet	2nd NY
Cpl	Lovekin, Steven	Blodget	2nd NH
Cpl	Roome, Benjamin	Walker	4th NY
Pvt	Bartley, Andrew	Strong	4th NY
Pvt	Bennet, John	Hallet	2nd NY
Pvt	Boutwell, Asa	Emerson	1st NH
Pvt	Collins, Edward	Walker	4th NY
Pvt	Cook, Daniel	Rowell	2nd NH
Pvt	Day, Daniel	Ellis	3d NH
Pvt	Hazard, James	Hallet	2nd NY
Pvt	Hilton, John	Robinson	2nd NH
Pvt	Hoff, William	Pearsee	4th NY
Pvt	Holmes, Thomas	Walker	4th NY
Pvt	Hopper, John	Pells	2nd NY
Pvt	Jackson, Thomas	Smith	4th NY
Pvt	Jenness, Jo	bBeal	3d NH
Pvt	Jupiter, Silas	Pells	2nd NH
Pvt	Kieff, Arthur	Walker	4th NY
Pvt	Ketchum, Joseph	Hallet	2nd NY
Pvt	Leeland, Isaac	Blodgett	2nd NH
Pvt	Newell, Andrew	Stone	3d NH
Pvt	Page, Samuel	Gilman	1st NH
Pvt	Post, Samuel	Pearsee	4th NY
Pvt	Richey, Alex	Walker	4th NY
Pvt	Russell, Noah	Emerson	1st NH
Pvt	Seeds, George	Walker	4th NY
Pvt	St.Lawrence, George	Walker	4th NY
Pvt	Taylor, Benjamin	Emerson	1st NH

Charles E. Frye

Pvt	Terry, Samuel	Sackett	4th NY
Pvt	Thompson, James	Frye, E.	1st NH
Pvt	Thornton, Nathaniel	Strong	4thNY
Pvt	Vandevour, John	Sackett	4th NY
Pvt	Walsh, Joseph	Walker	4th NY
Pvt	Warden, Darius	Smith	4th NY
Pvt	Wooster, James	Beal	3d NH

Honor and Valor

APPENDIX B

PATRIOT ANCESTORS IN *HONOR AND VALOR*

The following list is for any who are members of or interested in joining lineage societies. These include: Sons and Daughters of the American Revolution and Founders and Patriots. The list consists of characters who have a part in Honor and Valor. A "?" follows the birth location when I was unable to confirm this individual is the same as the person portrayed herein.

Main Characters

Will Burton (b. 1764, Wilton, NH)
Isaac Frye (b. Feb 6, 1748, Andover, MA)
Elizabeth (Holt) Frye (b. Nov 25, 1749, Andover, MA)
Ezekiel Goodale (b. Sep 8, 1743, Shrewsbury, MA)
William Adrian Hawkins (b Jan 18, 1742, Bordeaux, France)

Minor Characters

Abiel Abbot (b. Apr 19, 1741, Andover, MA)
Solomon Acker (b. Mar 27, 1753, Rhinebeck, NY)
Zachariah Beal (b. 23 Aug 1741, Newbury, MA)
Jacob Blanchard (b. Jun 22, 1758, Andover, MA)
Uriah Ballard Jr. (b. Oct 7, 1758, Andover, MA)
Asa Boutwell (b. 17 Feb, 1761, Lyndeborough, NH)
Ebenezer Carlton (b. 1754, Litchfield, NH)
Jonathon Cass (b. 29 Oct, 1753, Salisbury, MA)
Peter Chandler (b. 25 Mar, 1775, Andover, MA)
Andrew Colburn (b. 1 Mar, 1735, Dudley, MA)

Honor and Valor

Henry Dearborn (b. 23 Feb, 1751, North Hampton, NH)
Dan Cook (Unknown)
Ebenezer Drury (b. Aug 4, 1743, Hollis, NH)
John Drury (b. 28 Feb, 1761, Hollis, NH)
Benjamin Ellis (b. 13 Apr, 1755, Keene, NH)
William Ellis (b. 28 Apr, 1738, Dedham, MA)
Amos Emerson (b. 12 Dec, 1738, Haverhill, MA)
Nathan Fish (b. Oct 20, 1749, Groton, MA)
Amos Fuller (Unknown, likely born in Wilton, NH)
Caleb Gibbs (b. 28 Feb, 1748, Newport, RI)
Nicholas Gilman Sr. (b. Oct 21, 1731, Exeter, NH)
Nicholas Gilman Jr. (b. Aug 3, 1755, Exeter, NH)
Richard Goodman (b. Abt 1744?, Unknown)
Joseph Gray (b. Mar 19, 1761, Wilton, NH?)
John Godfrey (b. 1760, Hollis, NH?)
Elisha Grout (b. 1735, Worcester, MA?)
David Hall (b. Jan 24, 1754, Mason, NH)
John Hilton (Unknown)
Amos Holt (b. Feb 16, 1760, Andover, MA)
Nehemiah Holt (b. 1756?, Andover, MA?)
Timothy Holt Sr (b.Jan 17, 1721, Andover, MA)
Reuben Hosmer (b. Dec 5, 1739, Concord, MA)
Richard Hughes (Unknown, possibly from Sanbornton, NH)
James Hutchinson (b. Abt 1759, Milford, NH?)
Job Jenness (Unknown)
William Kemp (Unknown, possibly 1752, in England)
Joseph Lewis (Unknown, town of enlistment was Wilton, NH)
Samuel Leeman (b. Aug 7, 1749, Monson, NH)
Daniel Livermore(b. 7 Apr, 1749, Watertown, MA)
Elijah Mansfield (b Jun 26, 1747, Lynn, MA)
Christopher Martin (b May 31, 1757, Andover, MA)
Randall McAlister (b. Sep 21, 1744, Scotland)
Nathaniel McCalley (11 Nov, 1748, Unknown)
John McEvers(b. 1750, Bergen, NY?)
Hercules Mooney (b. 1710, Ballaghmoor, Ireland)
Andrew Newell (Unknown)
Aaron Oliver (b. Aug 25, 1749, Malden, MA)
Adna Penniman (b. 5 Oct 1752, Uxbridge, MA)
Ichabod Perry (Sep 20, 1761, No. 2, Westmoreland, NH)
Jonas Perry (b. 18 Jan 1747, Lexington, MA)
Asa Pierce(b. 21 Sep, 1760, Wilton, NH)
Enoch Poor (b. 21 Jun, 1736, Andover, MA

Charles E. Frye

Thomas Powell (b. 1760, Chester, NH?)
Stephen Richardson (b. Mar 3, 1747, Attleborough, MA)
William Rowell (b. Abt 1749, Haverhill, MA)
Noah Russell (Unknown)
Alexander Scammell (b. 16 May 1742, Mendon, MA)
Benjamin Smith (Unknown - many by this name, Temple, NH?)
Nathaniel Smith (b. 8 Apr 1758, Epping, NH?)
John Steed (b. 1746, NJ)
Benjamin Stone (b. 14 Jul 1743, Atkinson, NH?)
Josiah Stone (b. Nov 10, 1729, Watertown, MA)
Ben Taylor (b. 8 Mar, 1759, Dunstable, NH?)
James Thompson (b. 1757, NH?)
Philip Van Cortlandt (b. 1 Sep, 1749, New York, NY)
Derrick Van Veghton (b. 9 Jun, 1739, Albany, NY)
George Washington (b. 22 Feb, 1732, Westmoreland County, VA)
Meshech Weare (b. 16 Jun, 1713, the Third Parish, NH)
Richard Weare (b. 17 Aug 1752, Hampton Falls, NH)
James Wedgewood (b. 30 Mar, 1746, North Hampton, NH)
William Weeks (b. 28 Apr 1755, Greenland, NH)
Asa Wilkins (b. 5 Aug, 1757, Amherst, NH)
Robert B. Wilkins (b 20 Sep, 1755, Amherst, NH)
James Wilkinson (b. 24 Mar, 1757, Charles County, MD)

Honor and Valor

APPENDIX C

CORRECTION REGARDING JAMES OTIS

While writing the last chapter of this book, I considered the possibility of Isaac visiting James Otis's farm in Westfield, MA, on his way home in 1778. I decided to research whether James had served further in the militia, particularly in the Rhode Island campaign in the late summer of 1778. Newly available information convinced me that I portrayed the wrong James Otis in The War has Begun.

There were at least two James Otis's with fathers named Joseph. Newly available genealogical research shows the James Otis I used was born in 1751 in New London, CT. I also found information on a second James Otis, who was born September 20, 1755, in Barnstable MA, and this proved to be a far better match. It coincided with George Washington's orders, which affirm the new adjutant for the Third Regiment as the son Colonel Joseph Otis, commander of the Barnstable, MA militia.

With regard to the correct James Otis, he was likely not married. The New England Historical and Genealogical Registers show he graduated from Harvard College in 1775. He was "lost at sea" in 1790. Based on this, I also found after his service with the Third New Hampshire Regiment; he became an ensign in Col. Henry Jackson's Additional Continental Regiment in May 1777. He resigned this commission in April 1779.

His name does not appear in either New Hampshire's or Massachusetts' rolls of the Revolutionary War. Only the records in the Peter Force Collection provide definitive proof of his service.

Honor and Valor

Charles E. Frye

ABOUT THE BOOK COVERS

The musket, or firelock, called such with equal frequency during the American Revolution, used in the cover art for this series dates to colonial times in America. It is a Dutch-made firelock, and its manufacture dates to the 1740s or 1750s. These were still common in New England in the 1770s.

A historical society from one of the towns in southern New Hampshire owns this weapon. For many years a family with a surname common to that region owned it. Their family history includes the story of one of their ancestors carrying it during one of the Saratoga battles.

I did some research and learned there were at least seven men of that surname who could have carried it. Two men were with the New Hampshire Continental regiments, and I eliminated them, as they carried the French-made Charleville firelocks. Of the remaining five, only one was in a militia unit that served on the west side of the Hudson during the Saratoga campaign. The unit was Captain Gershom Drury's company of Colonel Daniel Moore's Battalion of NH Militia. This unit is not one known to have taken part in any of the battles.

After doing the research, it is clear there is at least some truth to the original story. It is plausible the words battle and campaign got confused. I provided the identity of the man who best fit the musket's story to the historical society as the likely owner.

Thank you to Eric Schnitzer, Interpretive Ranger at Saratoga National Historical Park, who helped with narrowing the militia units down to the one regiment and confirmation of the New Hampshire Continental units carrying the French muskets.

Honor and Valor

ABOUT THE AUTHOR

Charles E. Frye is a geographer, cartographer, information scientist, and U.S. Army veteran. His interests include genealogy, history of the American Revolutionary War, and major league baseball. As he learned of Isaac Frye's story, he applied his skills to design an approach to use geographic information systems to organize and document historical research projects. Applying this approach to Isaac Frye's story yielded a wealth of information that could be organized many ways. This supplied the skeleton for *The War has Begun*, the first of four books in the *Duty in the Call of Liberty* series. Today he lives and works in southern California.

More books by Randy Hain

Essential Wisdom for Leaders of Every Generation

A practical collection of helpful insights and actionable ideas to equip leaders and aspiring leaders to thrive in all areas of their lives.

Essential Wisdom for Leaders of Every Generation, Randy Hain's eighth book, offers today's leaders and aspiring leaders a practical collection of helpful advice and actionable ideas drawn from his thirty-plus years of senior leadership, coaching, and consulting experience to successfully navigate all areas of their lives.

Essential Wisdom is a must-have guidebook filled with insights, ideas, and best practices that all professionals should think about and do well in order to be more effective in their roles. Leaders and aspiring leaders of every age and any stage of their career journey will find practical nuggets of wisdom they can use to accelerate their success.

Upon Reflection

Helpful insights and timeless lessons for the busy professional.

Randy Hain's ninth book offers timeless lessons and practical ideas on a myriad of topics drawn from his 30+ years of senior leadership, executive coaching, and consulting experience to help fuel the career success and personal growth of busy professionals from every generation.

Written through the author's own practice of intentional reflection, **Upon Reflection** is a thoughtful book that will benefit everyone. Experienced professionals will gain helpful new perspectives and be reminded of what they hopefully know and believe but sometimes forget to practice. Younger professionals discover valuable insights into the timeless values, virtues, and best practices that make for a richer life and a successful career. All readers will find great value in the various relevant topics and encouragement the book offers to slow down, savor the moments, and be more reflective.

All books available on Amazon

More books by Randy Hain

Being Fully Present

Being Fully Present: True Stories of Epiphanies and Powerful Lessons from Everyday Life, Randy Hain's tenth book, contains true and personal stories drawn from his life as a husband, father, person of faith, and business leader. The book will inspire and challenge readers to more thoughtfully examine how they see the world, engage differently with the people they encounter, and seek to learn helpful lessons from situations and challenges they face in daily life.

Being Fully Present is an eclectic collection of thought-provoking stories. They illustrate the importance of eliminating distractions, listening actively, developing self-awareness, and being open to the lessons gleaned from every meeting and situation. Through Hain's authentic style, decades of intentional practice, and hard-fought wisdom, readers will understand the critical importance of journaling, frequent reflection, and cultivating a mindset of continuously "mining for gold" from current life and favorite memories.

Becoming a More Thoughtful Leader

Inspired by countless executive coaching conversations with leaders around the world and the author's own 30+ year business career, *Becoming a More Thoughtful Leader* taps into his unique reflective style to offer actionable best practices and insights on a host of leadership topics. This book, his 11th, shares genuine experiences, candid observations and hard-fought wisdom in each thought-provoking chapter. The eclectic topics range from vulnerability to accountability to patience to addressing workplace disconnectedness...and much, much more. The key to understanding and fully utilizing the book is recognizing the subtle challenge to look in the mirror and be more thoughtful about your own growth as a leader, but to also be more thoughtful about investing in your work colleagues and everyone you encounter throughout the day.

All books available on Amazon